John Wilcox was born in Birmingham and was an award-winning journalist for some years before being lured into industry. In the mid-nineties he sold his company in order to devote himself to his first love, writing. His previous Simon Fonthill novels, THE HORNS OF THE BUFFALO, THE ROAD TO KANDAHAR, THE DIAMOND FRONTIER, LAST STAND AT MAJUBA HILL and THE GUNS OF EL KEBIR, were highly acclaimed. He has also published two works of non-fiction, PLAYING ON THE GREEN and MASTERS OF BATTLE.

Praise for John Wilcox's Simon Fonthill novels:

'As good as it gets for fans of soldiering in Queen Victoria's Day' *Bolton Evening News*

'Wilcox writes with an intimate knowledge of the African continent, an encyclopaedic knowledge of the Victorian era when the British Empire was at its peak, and all the dash of a great adventurer' *Nottingham Evening Post*

'The story rattles along at a tremendous pace and once started, it was difficult to put down' *Eastern Daily Press*

'Vivid descriptions of the battle scenes and perceptive analyses of the strategies behind them' *Yorkshire Evening Post*

'A glorious adventure story that beautifully captures a sense of the wild North Western frontier' *Western Daily Press*

'A rollicking account of a turbulent period in Britain's imperial past' *Good Book Guide*

By John Wilcox

The Horns of the Buffalo
The Road to Kandahar
The Diamond Frontier
Last Stand at Majuba Hill
The Guns of El Kebir
Siege of Khartoum

Masters of Battle
Playing on the Green
(*Non-fiction*)

SIEGE OF KHARTOUM

JOHN WILCOX

headline

First published in 2009 by
HEADLINE PUBLISHING GROUP

First published in paperback in 2009 by
HEADLINE PUBLISHING GROUP

3

Cataloguing in Publication Data is available from the British Library

ISBN 978 0 7553 4560 1

Typeset in Sabon by Avon DataSet Ltd, Bidford on Avon, Warwickshire

Printed in the UK by CPI Mackays, Chatham, ME5 8TD

Headline's policy is to use papers that are natural, renewable and recyclable
products and made from wood grown in sustainable forests. The logging and
manufacturing processes are expected to conform to the environmental
regulations of the country of origin.

HEADLINE PUBLISHING GROUP
An Hachette UK Company
338 Euston Road
London NW1 3BH

www.headline.co.uk
www.hachette.co.uk

For three splendid old friends and followers
of the fortunes of Simon Fonthill:
Nigel Cole, Peter Jackson and Jim Farrand

Acknowledgements

As always, I readily acknowledge the debt I owe to my agent, Jane Conway-Gordon, for her constant encouragement, and to my editor at Headline, Sherise Hobbs, whose suggestions and gentle criticism so improved the original manuscript. Before his untimely death, my good friend Lieutenant Colonel Chris Stuart Nash, late of the Royal Artillery, proved invaluable in describing exactly how Fonthill would have directed the fire of the two penny steamers in halting the attack on Omdurman, and I would equally have been lost without the help of the staff of the London Library, who never fail to find that lost forgotten book that sheds contemporary light on the period I inhabit during the creation of my novels. Lastly, my thanks, as always, go to my wife Betty, loving proofreader, research assistant and critic extraordinaire.

There have been few events in Victorian England that have been written about so extensively as the expedition to relieve Gordon in Khartoum. I read widely in researching this novel, but the books I found particularly helpful I list below.

England's Pride by Julian Symons, Hamish Hamilton, London, 1965

War on the Nile by Michael Barthorp, Blandford Press, Poole, Dorset, 1984

In Relief of Gordon, Lord Wolseley's Campaign Journal, edited by Adrian Preston, Hutchinson, London, 1967

Gordon. The Man Behind the Legend by John Pollock, Constable, London, 1993

The War in Egypt and the Soudan by Thomas Archer, Blackie & Son, London, 1888

The Stolen Woman by Pat Shipman, Bantam Press, London, 2004

Fuzzy Wuzzy by Brian Robson, Spellmount Ltd, Tunbridge Wells, 1993

Prisoners of the Mahdi by Byron Farwell, Longmans, Green & Co., London, 1967

The Colonial Wars Source Book by Philip J. Haythornthwaite, Arms and Armour Press, London, 1995

Ponsonby by Henry Ponsonby, Macmillan & Co., London, 1942

Henry and Mary Ponsonby by William M. Kuhn, George Duckworth, London, 2002

Queen Victoria in Her Letters and Journals, selected by Christopher Hibbert, Penguin Books, Harmondsworth, 1985

Many of the above, I am afraid, are out of print now, but copies can almost certainly be found in the London Library and the British Library.

The Nile from Cairo to Khartoum in 1884

Chapter 1

The Syrian trader shielded his eyes against the sun and squinted along the banks of the Nile, where the great brown river bent as it wound to the south, ever more deeply into the heart of the Sudan. The fertile flood plains bordering the Nile in northern Egypt had long since given way to the barren nothingness of yellow sand and rock that now ushered the river on its way through to its source a thousand miles away. The dangers posed by the bouncing white waters of the three cataracts that lay behind them had almost been a welcome diversion to the Syrian and his small party, although their boat had been overturned twice, forcing them to clutch at rocks and then lose three precious days in salvaging what they could of their belongings from debris-strewn beaches on inlets downriver.

Balancing himself against the gentle list of the *filuka* as it made steady progress upriver under its triangular sail, the man concentrated his gaze ahead, on the left bank of the river.

Slim but broad shouldered, and of medium height, he was dressed in the ubiquitous long, shirt-like *jibba* of the desert, caught in the middle by an embroidered belt through which was thrust a sheathed dagger. His feet were tucked into open sandals, showing dirty toes and feet and ankles the colour of dark chocolate. His face, what little of it could be seen between the folds of his loosely wound *esharp* or headscarf,

1

seemed even darker, with high cheekbones and a black beard. The eyes, though, were of a light brown, betraying that his origins were not from this Nubian part of Africa and hinting at something within – a gentleness, or was it uncertainty? – that sat ill with his general appearance. For it was clear that, whatever the eyes might suggest, the Syrian carried himself warily, with an air of militant readiness for whatever violence the river and its people might present. This trace of aggression was reinforced by a nose that had been broken at some time and now appeared hooked and predatory. In fact, if the eyes had been black instead of a gentle brown, the man would have looked more like a marauding Pathan from the cruel hills of India's North-West Frontier than a peaceful trader of the Nile.

He spoke at last, at first as though he was murmuring to himself, so that the boatman at the stern could not hear. 'I've had just about enough of this bloody river and its cataracts.' Then he turned. 'There's a village up ahead, Ahmed,' he said, still quietly. 'Do you think that if we paid off the boatman there we could buy camels?'

The accent was that of an upper-class Englishman and the words came incongruously from the Arab. They had been addressed to the smaller of his two companions, a slim man with the light-coloured skin of an Egyptian, similarly bearded but with the delicate features of a skilled clerk and looking, perhaps, more at home in a Cairo counting house than here, in the Sudan of the Mahdi. Ahmed Muhurram, proprietor of the excellent Metropolitan Hotel in Cairo, rose unsteadily and joined Simon Fonthill, formerly lieutenant in the 24th Regiment of Foot and captain in the Queen's Own Corps of Guides, Indian Army, in the prow of their *filuka*.

The two men stood in silence for a moment as, slowly, the village came more clearly into view.

'I think we get camels there,' said Ahmed eventually. 'But I am not sure. You think all bloody Egyptians know about camels and the desert. But I keep telling you I don't know the bloody desert. I don't like it, nor the bloody sand, you know. It gets into ears, underpants, testicles, et cetera, et cetera, et cetera . . .'

Fonthill gave a theatrical sigh. 'Yes, I confess I have noticed that, but you're the only bloody Arab we have and you've just been promoted to Honorary Camel Master on this trip – unpaid, of course.'

The two men grinned. 'I tell boatman to pull into village,' said Ahmed and wobbled his way to the stern, where the white-clothed boatman was sitting, half dozing, his skullcap pushed to the back of his head and his arm slung over the long tiller.

Simon Fonthill climbed forward over their packs on the crowded deck to where 352 Jenkins, his former batman and now his servant, boon companion and fellow adventurer in the service of General Lord Wolseley, commander-in-chief of the British Expeditionary Force to the Sudan, was lying asleep on a sack, a happy dribble of saliva trickling down his chin. Jenkins – his Christian name long forgotten since he had formed part of a holding company of the 24th at Brecon barracks, where the presence of many Jenkinses in this definitively Welsh regiment had forced each to be known by the last three digits of his army number – lay curled like a cat. He too was dressed as an Arab, a pose given verisimilitude in his case by his naturally dark countenance and coal-black eyes and hair. Unlike Fonthill, there had been no need for Jenkins to dye his hair, moustache and beard, which now lay stiffly upon his chest, spread like a child's bib. Even in repose, the Welshman displayed the strength of a pithead collier. At five foot four, some five inches shorter than Simon, he seemed almost as broad as he was tall, and within the folds of his *jibba*, it was clear that he was strongly muscled. Five years of campaigning with Fonthill as a scout to British forces in Zululand, Afghanistan, the Transvaal and Egypt had hardened Jenkins's already formidable physique.

Simon grinned at the familiar figure and gently prodded the sleeping man's bottom with his toe. Immediately he found himself staring into the barrel of a long-barrelled silver Colt revolver, which appeared as if by magic from the folds of Jenkins's garment.

'Ooh, sorry, bach sir,' grunted the Welshman, sitting up. 'I never did like to be woken, specially not with a toe up me balls, like, see.'

'Yes, well, put that damned revolver away before the boatman sees it. It's not the sort of weapon that people would carry in the Sudan – not unless you're an officer in the US cavalry, that is.'

'Right.' The Colt disappeared back into Jenkins's midriff and he wiped his beard with the edge of the *esharp* that, predictably, had slipped down the back of his neck. 'What's 'appenin'? We repellin' boarders, is it, then?'

'No.' Simon sat down cross-legged next to his friend and produced a crumpled map. 'Take a look at this. Here we are, just upstream of the Third Cataract and Dongola, the big town we passed last night, you remember?'

Jenkins nodded. 'Yes, I would 'ave appreciated the chance for a run ashore and a drop of somethin' refreshin', like, instead of scurryin' past in the dark like rats swimmin' up the Conwy.'

'Don't talk rot. You know we are vulnerable in towns. And anyway, this is Mosselman country. You won't find alcohol outside Cairo. Now listen.' He pointed at the map. 'You see where we left the train at Sarras, just over the border in Sudan

– although there's no real border, of course. We took to the Nile there and we've sailed about, oh, some two hundred miles, but it's taken bloody ages, not to mention the difficulties of the cataracts. If we stay on the Nile, which, in theory anyway is the safest way, in that trade follows the river and we are supposed to be traders, then we will be forced to go back up to the north on this great loop before coming back south again towards Berber.' He eased his buttocks on the cross-planking. 'Not only will we have to fight our way through another two cataracts . . .'

Jenkins rolled his eyes. 'God forbid.'

'Quite. Not only that, but we will also go about three hundred miles out of our way, costing us precious time. From what I understand, Gordon is now completely surrounded and besieged in Khartoum; no one is sure how long he can hold out, and my orders are to get through to him as soon as possible.'

'So?'

'So, there's a village up ahead. If Ahmed can buy us some camels there, I propose that we ride south-east across the desert, here and here, cutting out these two big loops of the Nile. We could save ourselves two weeks or even three and come out at Berber, the last big town before Khartoum.'

'What about water?'

'Good point. But this map shows that there is a track across both pieces of desert, and that track wouldn't exist unless there were wells along the way. And, of course, we will fill our water bags before we start.'

Jenkins sniffed and then looked about him in some alarm as the *filuka* listed in response to the tiller. 'Oh bloody 'ell,' he exclaimed, pointing to where long grey shapes lay on the rocks that came down to the water's edge on the port side. 'Look, crocs!'

'Oh for goodness' sake! We've seen dozens so far in this part of the Upper Nile. They are not going to bother us if we don't bother them. You know that.'

'Yes, well. I 'ope this village place 'as a proper landin' stage. I don't like crocodiles, I 'ave to acknowledge. 'Orrible things.'

Fonthill sighed. 'Crocodiles don't worry me, but,' and he jabbed his finger on to the map again, 'I must confess that the Mahdi's army does. In this first part of the desert we are not too deep into his territory. In fact, we are in the area ruled by the Mudir of Dongala, who, according to Wolseley, is supporting the British. But this *is* well and truly the Sudan now, and the Mahdi is winning fanatical support all over this huge country. And once we cross the Nile again, here, at about this place called Abu Dom, we will be well and truly in the land of the Dervish. What's more, Berber, here, fell to the Mahdi's hordes in May, and we shall have to change our tune there.'

'What d'you mean?'

Fonthill scratched his beard. 'Being Syrian traders has got us so far, but we really don't have any artefacts to trade now – we left most of 'em being carried down the Nile at the Second Cataract – and I don't see my knowledge of Persian Pushtu helping us if we get into trouble with tribesmen out in the desert or in Berber.'

'But we've got old Amen and 'is Arabic.'

'True. But we won't be able to sustain our role as traders. We shall have to be true Mosselmen, though still Syrians, mind you, from the north, coming to join the Mahdi in his great crusade.'

'Blimey. You'd better tell me again about this Mahdi bloke. Where did 'e come from then? Oh, lor!'

Jenkins grabbed a gunwale as a large crocodile, disturbed

by their approach, slipped off a rock and slid underneath them, causing the boat to rock gently. Over the years, the Welshman had proved himself to be a completely fearless warrior, a fine horseman, a crack shot and a loyal and shrewd comrade. Simon, however, had found that his rock of a servant was undoubtedly fissured. In addition to an immoderate and uncontrollable love of alcohol, he lacked any sense of direction and hated heights and water. Now, it seemed, a fear of crocodiles must be added to the list.

Fonthill looked ahead and saw that they were approaching a rickety wooden landing stage. He tucked the map away. 'Don't worry about the crocs. I'll tell you about the Mahdi later. Pick up that rope and throw it to Ahmed when he jumps ashore.'

The boat was swiftly tied up to a post on the landing stage, and Fonthill stepped ashore and looked about him carefully. He knew that the Mahdi's militant followers wore a rough kind of uniform: a shirt-like garment with wide sleeves, patched with squares of black, white, red and yellow cloth, not unlike harlequins. He had seen none so far, and indeed, now only the usual scattering of peasant *fellaheen*, sitting in the shade occasionally waving away the flies, or idling down the filthy main street, met his gaze. Yet the place exuded a threat he could not place. An intangible air of evil emanated from the sloppily whitewashed mud boxes of houses. They might be in the Mudir of Dongola's territory, but the whole country was now in the grip of the Mahdi. One slip and their mission could be over before it had even begun. Yet his body ached from sitting for so long on the hard cross-thwarts of the boat. It was time he looked around. He waved to Ahmed and Jenkins to join him and moved away so that they could not be heard.

'Right,' he said. 'Ahmed, tell the boatman that you are

going to find food and then see what you can do about camels. We shall need three good riding beasts and two pack animals for what we have left of our baggage. We should not tell the boatman that we are leaving him here until we can be sure we have transport. Three five two, you stay on board and keep an eye on our things. But don't feed the crocodiles.'

'What are you goin' to do, then, bach sir?'

'I feel the need to stretch my legs and make a reconnaissance. I'll be back in about half an hour. I don't think there's much to see.'

Nor was there. The village was nothing more than a collection of mud huts, baked hard by the sun and populated by several million flies and a handful of Sudanese, their eyes as black as their faces. The flies hardly seemed to worry the people, even though the insects crawled into and around the eyes, only occasionally prompting a languid wave of the hand to disperse them for a second or two before they were back. Fonthill realised that the physical characteristics of the Arabs he had observed on the Lower Nile had now virtually disappeared, and that people here were more purely African. Those not muffled in the pervasive *esharp* headdresses revealed hair treated with oil or mud and twisted into elaborate braids. Despite the fierce sun, little girls and boys ran around wearing nothing more than a light fringe of black string about six inches long around their waists.

On their way up the Nile, Fonthill had worked hard to imitate the unhurried lope of the Arab, and dressed as he was in dusty and anonymous clothing, he seemed to attract little attention as he made his way slowly down what appeared to be the main avenue of the hamlet. He was half hoping that some distinct trail would lead out into the desert to the southeast, showing that the main route across the wasteland to the loop of the Nile started from there, but the street petered out merely into a beaten patch. And then the flat, gravel-strewn desert stretched out before him, featureless except for a little scrub and the occasional tree of the desert, a large-leafed shrub that was useless to thirsty travellers in that, when cut, it oozed a milk-like substance that was poisonous to drink.

Fonthill sighed. The horizon far away was indistinct, perhaps a purple smudge of hills, but more likely to be the edge of a heat haze filled with dust. He knew that the country was vast, the biggest in Africa, larger than France, the new Germany, Austria, Italy, Spain, Portugal, Switzerland, Greece, Great Britain, Holland and Belgium combined; and yet only some three million people lived out there. He was aware that they were plagued by sleeping sickness, guinea worm, malaria, yellow fever and leprosy and that their life expectancy was no more than twenty-five or thirty years. No wonder they flocked to the Mahdi's green and white banners! He offered them escape, however intangible, from their misery. Fonthill waved away the flies from his eyes and recalled something that General Gordon, who had previously served time here as governor general on behalf of the Egyptian government, had written about the country: 'No one who has ever lived in the Sudan can escape the reflection what a useless possession is this land. Few men can stand its fearful monotony and dreadful climate . . .'

He turned to make his way back, selecting this time a different but still quite similar street. His nostrils twitched as they were assailed by a familiar smell, and at a turning to the right in a small square, he saw dozens of camels tethered, with white-robed men of the desert milling around between them. He caught a glimpse of Ahmed in earnest conversation with a man. Ah, good. A camel market. They were in luck! This little village was not as dead as it seemed. He hurried away, for he had no wish to interfere with Ahmed's bargaining. Despite

Ahmed's protested hatred of the desert, the little man was a born negotiator; an Egyptian *fellaheen* of the river, who had escaped the whips of the Turkish tax collectors to set up his small hotel in the native quarter of Cairo, from which he had emerged two years before to accompany Fonthill and Jenkins as scouts for General Wolseley's successful campaign against the revolt of the Egyptian Colonel Arabi. No, Ahmed would do better without him – and anyway, Simon did not want to draw attention to himself. They had been lucky up till now. Best not to press that luck too far.

He walked on, back towards the river, and followed the street as it veered away to the right, so that he realised he would emerge away from the village a little, further downriver. Indeed, the Nile's influence immediately manifested itself in the form of a few scattered cultivated patches emerging from the now muddy sand: peas and a little corn and sorghum, which he knew the natives ground into a flour to become the principal ingredient of an unleavened bread called *durra*. It was refreshing to see a flash of colour enlivening the pervading ochre. Nevertheless, Fonthill realised that he was becoming increasingly uneasy as he walked. The heat and flies? No, he was used to both now. He swivelled his head. No one was following and the street was empty, except for the inevitable mongrel dogs sniffing at the accumulated filth piled against the mud walls of the houses. Whatever it was, it seemed intangible and yet quite persistent; again that sense of evil – a sourness, like a taste in the mouth. No, more a smell. Yes, a smell.

Yet he had no time to discover its source, for ahead of him, as though by magic, had appeared two men, walking towards him with a sense of purpose not displayed by the few children and adult loungers he had encountered so far. Had they doubled up a side street to get ahead of him and cut him off?

They were dressed in the loose folds of Sudan, but, thank God, their dress showed no obvious signs of allegiance to the Mahdi, although their eyes glowed black and they paused, waiting for him. Ah! It was to be an encounter.

Fonthill forced himself to maintain his steady, leisurely pace and approached the pair, his left hand resting lightly on the curved dagger at his waist. His mind raced. The men seemed to be villagers, unshod and with mud-caked beards, yet they too had daggers tucked into their waistbands. Despite his efforts to appear nondescript, Simon was clearly not of the region. He had dressed, of course, as a trader and must appear to be a man of more substance than was to be found in this fly-infested village on most days. Rich pickings in this seemingly deserted back street. Casually, he looked behind him. No one. If he shouted now, his companions on the *filuka* would not hear him, for he had wandered too far. If this was to be a fight, there would be no Jenkins to help him this time. He cursed inwardly his stupidity in walking alone in this baking heat, but he maintained his steady pace and the two men moved slightly apart so that he would be forced to walk between them.

Abreast of them at last, he nodded his head and gave the conventional Arab greeting, '*As-salaam alaykum*,' but received no response. Instead, one of the two men addressed him in quick Arabic. Fonthill shook his head and replied in his Pushtu, 'Alas, I am from Syria and do not speak your tongue.' This produced only a frown. The other man now stepped forward, fingered Simon's *jibba* and put out his other hand, rubbing his thumb and forefinger together in the universal request for money. His breath was heavy and carried the smell of food highly seasoned.

Fonthill thought quickly. He had a little money in his purse, but to present it meekly would be no guarantee that his throat would not be cut afterwards. Even if he was spared, so servile a capitulation could encourage an attack on the whole party, perhaps tonight, while they slept on the *filuka*. There could be further loot to be plundered from the boat. No. He had to resist. But how? Both men were tall and armed with the ubiquitous dagger, but they were also slim and, by the look of it, undernourished. At least Simon was stronger.

As the *baksheesh* gesture was repeated, Fonthill's mind raced. He had to attack while he had the advantage of surprise, for these two would think that they had the Syrian at their mercy. But how? Unlike the redoubtable Jenkins, he had no skill with a knife, and there were two of them. Then, from years ago, he recalled the tactics of Osbert Wilkinson. Wilkinson, the sixth-form bully at Shrewsbury school, when Simon was a first-former, a humble fag or servant to the prefects. Osbert, the great Osbert, had a technique with small boys whom he thought were being cheeky. Could it possibly work here?

Simon allowed his face to light up in recognition at the request for money. He nodded, and gently dislodged the man's hand from his garment, as though to thrust his own inside to find his purse. Then, in one swift movement, in a recall of Osbert's technique, he placed both of his hands on the other's wrist and twisted it fiercely, whirling the man around as though quickly winding a wheel, so spinning his arm behind his back. He then pulled the man's little finger out and backwards so that it broke. Osbert, of course, had never gone that far, but here it was clearly necessary, and the Arab howled in pain. The other assailant had advanced hesitantly, but Simon pushed the first man fiercely towards him, so that the two fell backwards into the dust in a welter of arms and legs. The second man was the first to recover, and as he scrambled to his feet, Simon spun around and kicked the heel of his sandal into the man's groin; then, as he doubled up in pain, kneed him in the face.

The action took only a matter of a few seconds, and Simon suddenly found himself the master of the situation, standing wide legged, looking down on the two men at his feet. Slowly he withdrew the dagger from its scabbard and reached down to the throat of the man who lay still clutching his broken finger and whimpering. The man's jaw dropped as, wide eyed, he shook his head in terrified denial. But Simon merely cut a few inches off his beard and blew it into his face. Then he withdrew the Arab's dagger from its sheath and threw it far over his shoulder.

The other would-be assailant had regained his feet but showed no sign of fight. He backed away, one hand clutching at his bleeding nose, and then turned and fled. Simon gestured after him to the man with the broken finger in an unmistakable gesture, and he too shuffled to his feet and ran.

Sweat pouring down his face and breathing heavily, as much from the narrowness of his escape as his exertions, Simon watched them go. Would they return with reinforcements? He was still far from the *filuka* and had no clear idea of the way back. He would have to risk that, for to repeat his steps through the village would be asking for trouble and might indeed prejudice Ahmed's negotiations with the camel dealers. No, better to find the Nile and walk back to the boat along the river bank, hoping that news of his obvious ability to defend himself would spread and deter other robbers. He blew out his cheeks as he tried to regain his breath and discovered that he was trembling. He was glad that he had not had to use the dagger in earnest. God bless dear old Osbert, the Bully of the Sixth! At least no one had been killed, and he doubted, on reflection, if retribution would fall on the boat party. Would the two men admit that they had been beaten in unarmed combat by one seemingly effete Syrian? Unlikely. Even so, this village was no place to linger. The warnings he had received in Cairo about the dangers that stalked this primitive land had already been demonstrated.

He lengthened his stride, and as the street ended abruptly and he emerged on to the Nile river bank, the source of the persistent smell was revealed. Crocodiles! At least a dozen of them, lying on the sand below the rocks and exuding a smell that Fonthill could only equate with rotten fish. He wrinkled his nose and took an involuntary pace backwards. His brain told him that he was in no danger, for he was far enough away – twenty-five, thirty feet? – to edge past the reptiles without prompting an attack. Yet he had read that crocodiles could charge at up to twelve miles an hour over short distances, faster than he could run, and at least two of the larger animals nearest to him had now turned their great heads to regard him with yellow, malevolent eyes. Below them were smaller reptiles, lying somnolently – females nurturing their buried eggs, with the bigger males protecting them? A jumble of further half-forgotten statistics suddenly thrust their way into his brain: the jaws of a crocodile contained up to sixty teeth and could exert a pressure of – what was it? – three thousand pounds per square inch, or something like that. And in Egypt alone they were said to cause about two hundred human deaths a year. God knows what depredations they were responsible for in this desert land, where they were more plentiful and no statistics were kept. Simon had boasted to Jenkins that crocodiles didn't bother him. But that was then and this was now. He must be careful, very careful.

Taking deep breaths, he edged away to his left, back towards the main part of the village, keeping his eyes firmly on the great beasts nearest to him, who followed him with their heads. They must be used to humans, he reasoned, living so close to the village, and therefore would be unlikely to attack unprovoked. Or did they live close to the village because it was a good food source? He lengthened his sideways step, keeping his eyes locked on to those of the male crocodiles.

At last he had made enough ground to be out of danger, and he turned to make his way back to the boat, which he could see some quarter of a mile away. Then a movement to his right and a little ahead caught his eye. Down by the river, a young boy was walking slowly back from the water's edge, carrying a long line at the end of which wriggled a small fish. The look of immense joy on the face of the urchin brought an answering smile from Simon, for it immediately triggered the memory of the sense of triumph that had surged through him when he landed his own first trout on the banks of the River Wye, near his home, many years ago.

The boy, perhaps eight years of age, was dressed – or half dressed – in a makeshift garment of old sacking that trailed to the ground behind him from one shoulder, leaving the other bare. His hair was black and curly and he looked thin and undernourished, although his eyes were bright as he concentrated near the water's edge on unhooking the fish from his line. His back was to the river and he was completely absorbed in his task and unaware of the strange swirl of water that moved just behind him.

Fonthill just had time to scream a word of warning before the crocodile struck, flashing from the water in a grey, gleaming mass of watery scales. The shout startled the boy so that he jumped forward, causing the crocodile's jaws to miss his leg by a couple of inches. Instead, its teeth caught in the rough weave of the sacking, tearing it from the boy's body and then waving it in the air, in an attempt to free it from its jaws.

'Run!' screamed Fonthill to the boy. And he ran towards

him, waving an arm in a pathetic attempt to distract the crocodile while fumbling under his *jibba* with his other hand to extract his Colt. Then he remembered that he had left the revolver in his pack on the *filuka*, anxious that it should not protrude from his gown and attract attention. He only had his dagger.

The boy, however, did not run. He had retrieved one end of his sacking and, pathetically, was pulling at it, for what reason Fonthill, still some twenty feet away, could not perceive. Still running, Simon recalled a little of what he had read about crocodile attacks.

'The tail!' he screamed, forgetting that the boy would not understand a word. 'The bloody tail,' he shouted again.

As if prompted, the monster – it seemed all of twenty feet long – suddenly swung its great tail from the water in a glittering arc, intending to knock the lad into the river and probably breaking his legs or back in the process. But the boy jumped nimbly over the tail and then jumped again as it swung back, as though he was playing skipping in a school playground. With immense courage, the lad flipped his end of the sack across the crocodile's eyes and then darted to his right, his hand going to the ground.

Fonthill suddenly realised what the boy was doing. He was trying to rescue his fish, which now lay by the side of the great reptile!

It was at this point that the crocodile became aware of Simon, who stood panting a few feet away, his knife pathetically in hand. Simon became aware of an intense stare from the reptilian eyes and that awful, musky smell. From the corner of his own eye he saw the boy retrieve the fish, almost from under the belly of the crocodile, pull again at the cloth, so tearing it free, and jump away. At least *he* would be safe now, if he ran. But how would the croc attack his new enemy?

A quick heave of those stubby forelegs and the frightening charge, or the swing of that deadly tail again? Fonthill realised that perspiration was pouring down into his eyes and blurring his vision, but that his mouth was completely dry. Running meant turning his back on the monster, who could outpace him over the short distance to the rocks anyway. He had to face it and be ready. Whatever the first attack, he had to evade it. After that . . . he was probably finished. Once again there was no resourceful Jenkins to come to his aid here, as so often in the past.

It was the tail, in fact. But the giant reptile was still half in the river, and the water was just deep enough to retard slightly the great sweep of the tail as it sent up a high plume of spray. This gave Fonthill a split-second warning, and somehow he was able to jump over the scales, as the boy had done. But he knew as he did so that he would not be able to evade the second, reverse sweep, for he lacked the agility of the urchin and the sweat was half blinding him.

The boy, however, had not fled the scene. Clutching his fish in one hand and his rag in the other, and now completely naked, he danced back towards the reptile on twinkling feet, waving the cloth to distract the great head. For a second the crocodile was bewildered, not knowing at which target to strike. Then the tail, half coiled now on the sand, flicked out at the urchin. He jumped again, but this time just a little too slowly, and the end caught his ankle, spinning him over in mid-air and landing him a few feet higher up the beach. Immediately, the crocodile lurched forward.

But Fonthill was even quicker. He ran up behind and beside the body of the beast and, aware that he had no choice, flung himself astride it, his knife poised. He knew it would be useless to try to penetrate the armour-like scales, and so he plunged the blade into the eye of the crocodile, sinking it as deeply as he could to reach the brain and then twisting to retrieve it, as the Zulus did with their assegais.

The animal flung up its head and a great primeval roar came from its throat. Simon was immediately thrown away, half into the water, as the crocodile writhed, its head tossing from side to side and blood pouring from its eye. It seemed unaware of its tormentors as it swung in pain, the tail thrashing the water and the huge jaws gnashing abortively. Then, slowly, as man and boy watched in awe, the head sank to the ground and the tail began to move, perhaps reflexively, sliding the body gradually back into the water until it disappeared, leaving a thin trail of blood rising to the surface.

Fonthill lay gasping for a second and then, realising the danger, splashed to his feet and ran up the beach. Gathering the boy, fish and all, under his arm, he ran to the safety of the path above the sand and the rocks. There the two lay for perhaps half a minute, trembling and sucking air back into their lungs.

Sitting up, Simon looked down at the urchin and summoned up a grin. 'Bloody close shave I'd say, wouldn't you?' he gasped, feeling the need to communicate, although realising he could not be understood. 'Just as well old 352 wasn't here, eh? He would have wet his breeches.' His grin widened at the thought. 'My word, lad, you're a plucky young devil. I'm not sure whether I saved your life or you saved mine. Bit of both, I think.'

The boy stayed looking up unsmilingly at Simon with wide brown eyes. Then, in one swift movement, he picked up the fish and began gnawing at it savagely, spitting out skin and bones but gulping down the flesh.

For the first time, Fonthill realised how emaciated the boy was. The upper part of his body was corrugated by protruding ribs, and his stomach bulged unnaturally. Despite the strength of those leaps, his legs were as thin as matchsticks. As the lad bent over the fish, Simon observed that his back bore the signs of what appeared to be many beatings. Some of the scars were old, but others were quite new, for there had hardly been time for scabs to form along the weals.

Simon's lip curled in disgust. 'What swine would whip a little boy like that?' he said, half to himself. 'And you're starving, you poor little bastard. But that raw fish isn't going to do you much good, you know.'

He leaned over and gently began to remove the fish from the boy's hands. Immediately the lad swung away, hunched his back and continued to gnaw at his catch. Simon sat back and let him be, instead looking around. The beach, thank goodness, was untenanted by crocodiles, and only a swathe of blood and disturbed sand showed where they had so nearly met their deaths. There was not a soul to be seen along the river path in either direction, and he could only presume that no one had witnessed the encounter down below.

Simon left the boy and, with great caution, descended the rocks to the sand, where he retrieved his dagger and, on quick afterthought, the scrap of cloth that lay near the water's edge. It had probably saved both their lives, and the lad deserved to keep what was left of it.

Somewhat to his surprise, the boy still sat where he had left him, his wide brown eyes fixed on Fonthill and the skeleton of the little fish, minus the head, at his feet. Simon squatted beside him and gave him the fragment of cloth. With a solemn air of decorum, the boy accepted it and wrapped it round his tiny waist, as best he could, to cover his genitals. Then he looked up and gave an almighty belch, followed by a slow, wide smile.

Grinning back, Simon extended his hand, and was surprised when, after a second or two, the boy put his own hand in it, tightened his grip and solemnly shook hands, European style.

'Well done, lad. Now,' he pointed to his own chest and said, 'Simon.' Immediately the grin came back and the boy pointed a finger at his small body and said something Fonthill could not catch.

'What on earth are we going to do with you, my boy, eh?' Simon pulled at his beard as he examined the wasted frame before him. 'Whoever your parents are, they seem to favour whipping you before feeding you. So I suppose the first thing to do is to take you back to the boat and give you a good meal. Come on then, oh mighty crocodile hunter, let's find you something to eat that's better than raw fish.'

The two stood and, hand in hand, began walking slowly back towards the jetty. Simon was surprised to find himself feeling self-conscious and was aware of the strange figures they cut, merchant and semi-naked urchin, both of them leaving little puddles of water behind them as they walked side by side along the river bank. Part of Fonthill's discomfort – he had almost forgotten now the affray in the street – lay in the fact that he expected that at any moment the boy's parents would appear and demand his return. What would he do then? He shrugged. He would cross that bridge when he came to it. As it was, he tightened his grip on the boy and walked on.

They reached the boat without being accosted and found the boatman in the stern stirring a large pan of *durra* and meat of some description, flavoured with dates. It smelt delicious. The boy's eyes widened and his grip tightened on Simon's hand as they stepped over the gunwale and met the astonished gazes of Ahmed and Jenkins.

'Who the bloody 'ell is this, then?' demanded the Welshman. 'An' where 'ave you bin, all dripping wet, look you?'

'Oh, just a bit of fishing,' said Simon, sitting down, drawing his knife from its scabbard and wiping the blood from its blade on the side of a sack. 'Ahmed, see if you can talk to the boy and find out his name and where he is from – particularly if his parents live in the village.'

'I can tell you now,' replied the Egyptian, his eyes fixed on the urchin. 'His parents are almost certainly dead. He is slave boy, and if his master comes looking for him we can be in trouble. You do not take slave from the Sudanese, Simon. Oh no.'

'Oh lord,' said Fonthill and ruffled the boy's hair.

'Poor little bleeder.' Jenkins took the boy's hand. 'You 'ungry, lad? Course you are. Stay an' 'ave a bit of supper with us, then. Eh? What d'yer think? Eh?'

It was clear that the boy did not understand, but Jenkins had travelled the world refusing to speak a word of anyone else's language, and somehow, the mellifluence of his Welsh sing-song had always broken through any language barrier it confronted. It did so now, and the boy gave Jenkins his big, slow grin, revealing white, even teeth.

The Welshman kneeled down before the boy and, taking out his grimy handkerchief, moistened the end and began cleaning the mud from the narrow cheeks. The grin disappeared and was replaced by a fretful frown, and the urchin turned his face from side to side in the universal action of a small boy who hated having his face washed.

Jenkins winked at Ahmed, who shook his head in puzzlement. 'What do you want us to do with him, Simon?' he asked.

'Can you find out his name and where he comes from? And tell the boatman that we've got a very important guest for dinner.' He gestured towards Jenkins's filthy handkerchief. 'I don't think you're making much progress there, 352. Fetch a bowl of water and do the job properly. He ought to be cleaned up for dinner.'

As Jenkins sponged down the boy, who stood quite still in what seemed to be amazement at the attention being devoted to him, Ahmed interrogated him. The conversation went on for some time, with the boy becoming more voluble as it continued and the Egyptian's face becoming more concerned.

'All right, Ahmed,' said Fonthill. 'I don't want his life story. Just enough to know where we can take him so that we can leave him safely.'

'Ah. That will not be easy. You see,' Ahmed wrinkled his brow as he tried to find the right words, 'boy says he does not remember father or mother but was brought up by Catholic nuns in Khartoum. When he was old enough to work, perhaps four years, he was put out to merchant in the town. That merchant put him in slave market right away – a bastard, I think, eh? – and boy then bought by Mahdi follower, who keeps him since. The man beat him regularly and give him very little food. Boy escapes and ends up here, et cetera, et cetera, et cetera . . .'

Fonthill and Jenkins exchanged glances. 'These et cetera bits are important, Ahmed,' said Fonthill. 'How long ago did he escape and how did he find his way here?'

The Egyptian had a further exchange in Arabic with the boy. 'He say he escape about week ago, further up Nile, and hide. Then he walks to here and lives by begging – he don't get much – and fishing. His name is Mustapha, by the way, and he don't know second name. He is eight, I think.'

'No. Ten.'

The words came from the boy, who turned his head from one to the other and grinned proudly.

'Good lord,' exclaimed Simon. 'You speak English!'

'Yes, but no very good no more. I was taught by Irish nuns

in Khartoum, bejabbers.' The grin widened even further, if that was possible, but then faded and he turned to Simon. 'I thank you for saving me from . . .' His voice faltered as he sought for the English word. 'From *timsah*.'

'That is crocodile,' explained Ahmed.

' 'Ere. What's this about a crocodile, then?' Jenkins's head turned to look across the brown water in some consternation.

Simon then related his tale – including his clash with the two Arabs – finishing just as the boatman called them to the stern to eat. Fonthill delved into a pack and pulled out a clean shirt that he slipped over Mustapha's head, tying it at the waist with cord and rolling up the sleeves. It was so voluminous on the boy that it looked like a *jibba*, and he seemed in no way out of place as they all sat on the cross-thwarts at the stern, eating with their fingers – no one more eagerly than Mustapha. Simon, however, ordered that a keen watch be kept on the shore and Jenkins's Colt kept close to hand.

'We should talk,' said Ahmed at the end of the meal. The three men walked to the prow, leaving the boy and the boatman to wash the utensils.

Ahmed looked anxiously down the main street and then up and down the river path as he spoke. 'Apart from danger from robbers, we cannot keep escaped slave,' he hissed. 'To Sudanese that is robbery and they don't like it. He said his master was follower of Mahdi, and we get into big trouble if he finds the boy with us.'

'So . . . what do we do with 'im?' asked Jenkins. 'We can't exactly go lookin' for this bloke to give 'im back, now can we?'

Ahmed shook his head. 'No. But this whole village will know now that we have him and word will go across desert, et cetera, et cetera, et cetera. We let him keep shirt and just leave him here.'

'Oh, blimey,' said Jenkins. 'Not that shirt, bach sir, if you don't mind. That's yer best. There's an old one of mine 'e can 'ave. But,' he cast an eye back to where the boy was chatting happily to the boatman, 'it don't seem right to leave 'im 'ere. 'E was starvin' when we found 'im, and if this bloke that bought 'im finds 'im again, there'll be 'ell to pay, see, judgin' by the state of the lad's back.'

'Quite.' Fonthill spoke meditatively. 'I agree that we can't leave him here.' He frowned. 'I am beginning to feel that he should come with us to Khartoum. It's dangerous but it could be the lesser of the two evils for him. And he could be useful to us.'

Now Jenkins and Ahmed exchanged worried glances. 'Is this wise, Simon?' asked the Egyptian. 'There will be trouble if we meet his master, and if we have to fight he will be very much in the way, I think.'

Fonthill smiled, but there was little humour in it. 'If we do meet the bastard who flogged him, I might just restrain myself from killing him long enough to offer to buy the boy from him. Look here,' he bent forward, 'slavery is endemic in the Sudan. It's the biggest trade in this blasted country and it would be perfectly normal for us to be travelling with a slave boy. It is an absolute boon that he speaks English and that he grew up in Khartoum. I'll wager he will know a way into the city, even beleaguered as it is. As for being in the way in a fight – God, you should have seen him with that crocodile. If I saved his life, he certainly saved mine. No. I think he comes with us. Now, Ahmed. What about camels?'

Ahmed shrugged his shoulders, but his face lightened. 'That is good news. I get three good riding camels and two pack camels in the square in morning. Your camel, Simon, is very pretty.' They all grinned at the old joke. 'I give low price for them. What is more, I am told that trail across desert to

Abu Dom starts about one mile downriver. We cannot miss it. Does the boy walk?'

'Ah, 'e's as light as a Welsh collie,' said Jenkins. ' 'E can sit on the baggage.'

So it was that the little cavalcade set off early the next morning, leaving the Nile behind them, with Mustapha walking proudly in the lead in his new shirt but with the old scrap of sacking tied round his head. Simon, riding at the head on a camel certainly as ugly as the others, wrinkled his eyes at the blood-red sun as it rose slightly to his left, and wondered if Alice his fiancée had forgiven him yet.

Chapter 2

Far from the heat and dust of the Sudan, Major General Sir Henry Ponsonby, Private Secretary to Her Majesty Queen Victoria, walked to the window in his office at Osborne House and contemplated the view. It was pleasing enough: long, well-tended lawns stretching to the gravelled driveway and then, beyond, to the rows of coniferous trees giving the Queen's summer palace on the Isle of Wight the privacy that she craved. On the other side of the great house, where the Queen had her bedroom, drawing and sitting rooms, the view led of course to a sparkling sea, the Solent, where the crisp white sails of passing yachts gave a Mediterranean aspect to indulge Her Majesty.

Not that Ponsonby craved a better view. He was content that his office was functional and comfortable enough in its overfurnished way. He smiled at the thought. His wife had shuddered on her first visit to Osborne: 'Quite the oddest combination of upholstery,' she had confided to him. 'All those hideous presents they have received, and as ill-arranged rooms as I ever saw . . .'

'If you think these rooms are ugly,' he had replied, 'you should see Balmoral!'

Ponsonby's smile turned melancholic as he conjured up his wife's face. He missed Mary so much. For fourteen years, since, as a young colonel in 1870, he had been rather controversially appointed as Private Secretary, he had followed the Queen on her rigidly set perambulations between her palaces and country houses around the country and on the Continent: Osborne for Christmas and the first two months of the New Year; Italy or Germany (to visit her many relations) in March; Windsor in the spring; Balmoral, Scotland, in May; Windsor for at least part of June; Osborne in July and August; back to Scotland for early autumn; and then Windsor before returning to the Isle of Wight again. Buckingham Palace was now comparatively untenanted. The Queen hated London. But for a monarch in semi-retirement, she travelled with a determination that bordered on obsession. The trouble, however, was that Mary Ponsonby was only occasionally allowed to travel with the royal party. Sometimes she stayed with her husband in the small cottage in the Osborne grounds they had recently been granted, but rarely did she accompany the royal party to Scotland or abroad. The Ponsonbys' grace-and-favour apartment in a tower at Windsor Castle was their family home, and Sir Henry devoutly wished that the Queen would spend more time in her Berkshire castle, so allowing him to be with his beloved wife and their five children. But it was not to be – and where the peripatetic Queen of Great Britain and Empress of India went, so must he go too.

A tall, erect man – a bearing instilled by years of service in the Grenadier Guards, Britain's premier regiment – Ponsonby's natural elegance was only slightly marred by the rather scruffy tail coat he wore and the elastic-sided boots that certainly could benefit from a touch of polish. His long nose, hooded eyes and slightly unkempt beard gave him a lugubrious air, but those who knew him – and the Queen, her ministers and all her many courtiers and household staff members now knew him very well – were aware that underneath the air of melancholy lay a strong and even satirical sense of humour. It was an unusual attribute for a professional courtier in this formal and rigid environment. He had begun life at court as an equerry to the Queen's husband, Prince Albert, the Prince Consort. Ponsonby grew to admire the man, but found him completely humourless, a serious failing in his view. In fact, he and Mary joked that the sombre Prince reminded them of the Snark in Lewis Carroll's poem, noted for:

> . . . its slowness in taking a jest.
> Should you happen to venture on one,
> It will sigh like a thing that is deeply distressed
> And it always looks grave at a pun.

Henry's sense of humour, however, also concealed a determination that, as usual, was leading him now into conflict with his Queen.

Ponsonby sniffed at the view, then walked back to his desk and picked up a newspaper from the pile that lay there. The headline caused him to wince. 'GORDON BESIEGED!' it shrieked. The second in the stack gave him no respite: 'NET TIGHTENS AROUND GENERAL GORDON'. The second deck of the headline asked, in smaller type: 'Can Relief Expedition Arrive in Time?' The third broadsheet followed the same theme: 'GORDON SURROUNDED'.

'Damn the man,' murmured Ponsonby, sitting down at his desk and leaning back in his chair. 'Damn the half-crazed Christian lunatic. Is there no other story to catch the public's imagination?'

He knew, of course, that there was not. General Gordon, 'Chinese' Gordon, was England's hero. The news that the man was trapped on the banks of the Nile in a walled town, surrounded by thousands of black followers of the so-called prophet Mahdi, all baying for his blood, was stirring stuff for a populace brought up on Britain's success in colonial warfare – yet one that had become increasingly dissatisfied recently at being fed an unaccustomed diet of defeat at Isandlwana in Zululand and Majuba in the Transvaal.

Yet it was not Gordon's plight in itself that sat so heavily on Ponsonby's shoulders. It was the fact that the Queen herself shared every ounce of her people's indignation at what was perceived to be the government's vacillation in sending Gordon out to the Sudan in the first place, and then its tardiness in attempting to rescue him now that the man was in trouble. Despite her virtual withdrawal from public life since the death of her beloved husband twenty-three years ago – a retirement that she was gradually beginning to put behind her now, with gentle encouragement from Ponsonby and her government – Victoria had always taken the keenest interest in army and naval affairs. She was, as she liked to remind everyone, a soldier's daughter after all. It was anathema to her, then, to see her country humbled, as she put it, by 'wild Arabs who do not stand against regular good troops at all'. A blow, she demanded, 'must be struck'. The Queen undoubtedly was a jingoist – and, equally undoubtedly, her prime minister was not.

Once again, Ponsonby stood between the two. This, of course, was his task in life. The Queen often wrote directly to her ministers and even to her generals, at least to those who were her favourites, such as Sir Evelyn Wood, Commander-in-Chief of the Egyptian Army. But the practice, which had been encouraged by Disraeli, her last prime minister, did not exactly meet with the approval of the present incumbent, William Ewart Gladstone, 'the People's William'. It was Ponsonby's responsibility, therefore, to be the interface between the Queen and the outside world and to put the monarch's often injudicially vehement words into more restrained language. It was also his duty to advise the Queen personally on political matters. And here was the rub: Victoria was a convinced right-wing Tory, still yearning for the flattery, the dynamism and the forceful imperialism of Disraeli. Ponsonby, on the other hand, was a Liberal and recognised as a supporter of Gladstone and his anti-imperialist foreign policy.

Yet again, then, Sir Henry was wondering how to restrain his royal mistress and to persuade her that her prime minister had a mandate from the people to carry out his policies in the way he thought fit, without constant criticism from the monarch.

He threw down the newspapers with a sigh. Then he opened a drawer, adjusted his pince-nez and took out a bundle of royal crested notepaper, each sheet carrying messages written in ink in the Queen's fine, strongly sloping hand. They dated from the previous few months and had all been 'interpreted' by him and then conveyed in his own upright hand to their recipients, usually the Prime Minister or members of his Cabinet.

He selected one, laid it on his desk and read:

To Mr Gladstone
The Queen feels very strongly about Sudan and Egypt and must say she thinks a blow must be struck or we shall never be able to convince the Muhammedians that they have not beaten us. We must make a demon-stration of strength and show determination and we must not let this fine and fruitful country . . .

Ponsonby raised his eyes to the ceiling at this. Everything he had read about the Sudan had convinced him that it was a huge, barren wilderness that offered little except drought, disease and slavery. It was formally ruled from Cairo as part of the Ottoman Empire, as was Egypt, yet Britain, with the approval of Turkey, had taken over the handling of both countries' fiscal affairs to protect her own interests there, including the Suez Canal. Sorting out Egypt's books, however, was one thing. Putting down a seething rebellion in the baking deserts of the Sudan was quite another. He fully shared Gladstone's view that Britain could not afford to send troops to crush a rebellion that had probably been caused by Turkish and Egyptian cruelty. And Gordon, of course, had been sent not to fight, but to withdraw the Egyptian garrisons in the Sudan. Sighing, Ponsonby read on:

> ... *with its peaceable inhabitants, be left a prey to murder and rapine and utter confusion. It would be a disgrace to the British name and the country will not stand it. The Queen trembles for General Gordon's safety. If anything befalls him the result will be awful.*

Sir Henry knew when to let the Queen's anxiety and anger have its head, and he had done little to mitigate the tone of this draft. Gladstone's reply, as usual, had been courteous, seemingly conciliatory, and above all verbose, so that it was difficult to detect whether he was agreeing with the Queen or not. It was the length of his letters and the orotund syntax and style of them that so infuriated Victoria, prompting a remark that would live on down the decades: 'He talks to me as though he was addressing a public meeting.'

Selecting a second draft, this time to Lord Hartington, Secretary of State for War, Ponsonby read:

Gordon is in danger: you are bound to try and save him. Surely Indian troops might go from Aden? They could bear the climate. You have incurred fearful responsibility.

The third was written a week later and was a direct instruction to Ponsonby:

The Queen wishes to cipher to Mr Gladstone: Am greatly distressed at the news about Gordon. You told me when you last saw me, Gordon must be trusted and supported and yet what he asked for repeatedly nearly five weeks ago has been refused. If not only for humanity's sake, for the honour of the Government and the nation, he must not be abandoned.

Ponsonby grinned. The old lady certainly did not pull her punches, and, surprisingly for a head of state who rarely read newspapers, disliked meeting her ministers and had had little contact with the outside world, she had a knack of understanding public opinion. And, of course, both she and it had a point. The government *had* dithered about Gordon and had taken an unacceptably long time to make up its mind to fund an expeditionary force to rescue him. This was because Gladstone himself, obsessed with the problems of Ireland, could not bring himself to take an interest in a junior general who had got himself into trouble in a faraway land. Gordon's supporters had not exactly been helped by the conflicting messages that had arrived from him before the telegraph had been cut. In this context Ponsonby had heard that General Wolseley had sent out two highly experienced scouts to ascertain Gordon's exact position. He shrugged and put the drafts back into the drawer. The Queen had eventually had her way and the expedition had been sent. But the controversy had not gone away. Now the question was: would its ponderous movement up the Nile prove too late to rescue the nation's hero?

Pulling a sheet of his own notepaper towards him, Ponsonby dipped his pen into the ink and began writing:

> *General Sir Henry Ponsonby presents his humble duty to Your Majesty and begs to . . .*

It was the usual way he addressed the Queen; indeed, letter-writing was the conventional mode of communicating with her. Although he quite often met her for dinner with other members of the royal family and household, they transacted normal business in the form of letters to each other, delivered to and fro in red-leather-covered dispatch boxes, carried by liveried footmen, even though they lived and worked under the same roof. Only rarely did he meet the Queen face to face to discuss business.

It was a surprise, then, when a footman entered after a discreet tap at the door. 'Her Majesty would like to see you at your earliest convenience, sir.'

Ponsonby put down his pen. 'Very well,' he said, and followed the man down the long corridor. He was ushered into a large drawing room, where the Queen was sitting at one of the two identical desks, placed side by side, where years ago she would sit in happy working communion with Prince Albert. Miniatures and photographs of her husband and many children cluttered the desk, and tall marble pillars broke up the length of the chamber.

He bowed. 'Good morning, Your Majesty.'

The Queen inclined her head and smiled, revealing two

rather rabbit-like front teeth. But the smile lit up her slightly podgy countenance, giving evidence of what must have been great vivacity in her youth. 'Good morning, dear Sir Henry,' she replied. Despite their differences she was always impeccably courteous to him, although he remained standing and she remained sitting, as usual.

She waved a copy of the Conservative magazine, the *St James's Gazette*, which represented the extent of her recreational reading these days. Sir Henry, of course, preferred its Liberal competitor, the *Pall Mall Gazette*. 'We have been referred to as being "a jingo",' she said. 'What pray is that exactly?'

'I believe it means someone who holds rather conservative views, ma'am.'

'Oh. And what is its provenance, then?'

'Ah, I think the word was used as a, er, strong affirmation in some sort of music-hall verse that became the vogue six years or so back, when you will remember, ma'am, your government of the day was considering whether we should intervene in the Russian war with Turkey.'

'Really. Do you remember the words of the verse?'

'I think so, ma'am.' He cleared his throat. 'It went something like this:

> *We don't want to fight*
> *But by jingo if we do*
> *We've got the ships*
> *We've got the men*
> *We've got the money, too.*'

The Queen lifted her eyebrows. 'Quite apt, in its way, I suppose. But rather vulgar, don't you think?'

'Indeed. I quite agree.'

'Well, enough of that. What I wanted to talk about, Sir Henry, was poor General Gordon . . .'

Ponsonby gave an inward groan. Did the bloody man have to dominate *everything*? He inclined his head. 'Ma'am?'

Chapter 3

Fonthill and his three companions rode to the south-south-east, following a trail that was not exactly well beaten but was defined enough for the compass to need consulting only rarely. As the desert and the heat demanded, their pace was slow – their camels hardly put three miles into the hour – and Simon found the soporific gait of the beasts congenial, once he had become used again to the nodding motion and the gentle roll that the saddle allowed. He pondered the task that lay ahead of them and then found his mind turning back to the interview with General Wolseley in Cairo, five weeks before.

Wolseley had been genuinely grateful for Fonthill's prompt response to his cable. 'After all,' the General said, pumping Simon's hand as though trying to extract water, 'it's not every man who would postpone his wedding to risk his neck in the armpit of the world that is the Sudan.'

'Quite so, sir,' said Simon. 'I fear that neither you nor I are popular at what is to be my new home in Norfolk.'

'Yes, well. I do hope that your fiancée will forgive us both. Country must come first, I am afraid, and you are just about the only man I can trust to do this job. Now, sit down.'

As always with Wolseley, the briefing had been detailed and to the point. Simon, Jenkins and 'that marvellous little hotelier of yours to speak the lingo' were to travel by train and boat up the Nile and then into the Sudan. Disguised as traders, they were to make their way through the country to where the Mahdi's army was encamped, besieging Khartoum, and then, somehow, enter the city, stay only long enough to form an appreciation of how long General Gordon could hold out, and make their way back to where, by that time, Wolseley would be well advanced up the Nile.

'There. Not much to ask, eh, my boy?'

'A mere trifle, sir. Just a stroll, by the sound of it.'

Then the familiar joshing had stopped. 'It's damned dangerous, Fonthill. If you are captured, it could mean mutilation before decapitation, or worse – incarceration in one of the Mahdi's camps. Do you still feel you can do it?'

'Of course, sir. But surely you must have heard directly from the General giving you this information before the telegraph was cut?'

It was at this point that Wolseley had become embarrassed – far more so than when he apologised for aborting Fonthill's wedding. As the question was answered, Simon realised that the General's embarrassment was on behalf of his old friend, General Gordon, the man whom he had been responsible for sending out to the Sudan.

'Y'see, Fonthill, he's a wonderful man. One of the best soldiers I have ever known. But it's as if the sun, or the damned situation in that arid land, has got to his head. In five days alone, he sent thirty telegrams back to Cairo, and in a month five lengthy papers, offering completely different proposals for resolving the situation. He was supposed to come out to organise the evacuation of Egyptian troops in the country. Then he telegraphs saying that he planned to "smash" the Mahdi. He blows hot and cold, and now that the line is cut we don't know how long he can hold out.'

Wolseley tapped his cigar. 'He's got about eight thousand men in the city – it's more of a town, really, horrible place. I probably won't be able to reach Khartoum until the end of January. Can he hold out until then? In theory he should be able to, because we know he has plenty of ammunition, food and water. But I must know for certain, because it will affect my strategy on the advance with the relieving column. I want you to find out, Fonthill; assess for yourself the defences of the town and the state of mind of my old friend, and tell him he has to hang on until the end of January. But . . . don't stay with him. Get back to me as soon as you possibly can.'

'Yes, sir. I understand the need. But why me? I believe you have a proper intelligence department set up here, with men already out in the field. Why me?'

'Because, my dear Fonthill, the army officers whose opinion on Gordon's state of mind and ability to defend the town I would respect, would never get through the Mahdi's hordes. And those who could wouldn't have the skill to make the assessment. You can do both. You've done this sort of thing before for me – and for Roberts in Afghanistan. You can do it, me boy. You'll have to black up, of course, but I know you can get through. Pay of major again, with whatever you want for your Welshman and Egyptian.'

Fonthill kicked his heels into the flanks of his camel, more in reaction at the memory of the conversation than in hope that the beast would quicken its robotic plod. It did not, of course. Yet they had so little time! It was mid-October now. They should reach Khartoum in about a month's time, if they were unhindered. And there lay the rub. The Dervishes were massed in the desert from Berber to Khartoum. Could the little party get through without being discovered? It was, he had to admit, a long shot.

He looked up ahead, where, despite the white heat of the sun, Mustapha was running towards a rocky hill that rose from the plain and obscured the trail ahead. He grinned. The boy's energy was amazing considering how badly he had been treated. It was remarkable what a couple of good meals had done for him. And he would be useful in Khartoum, there was no doubt about that. Then the grin disappeared. Was he endangering the boy's life by taking him with them? He shrugged. The life of an escaped slave was short, whatever his age. At least he would be well looked after with them . . .

His reverie was interrupted as Mustapha reached the top of the slight hill ahead, paused there and then turned and came running back as fast as those matchstick legs could carry him. He ran to Simon and pointed behind him.

'Men coming,' he said. 'Mahdi. Mahdi.'

'Damn.' Simon called back to Ahmed: 'Dervishes ahead. Remember, we two are from Syria, coming to join the Mahdi to follow the true faith. You are tired of the lax religious ways of the Egyptians and are doing the same. Tell the boy. If you have to speak to me, speak very quickly in sing-song English and let's hope they think it's Syrian Arabic. Three five two: if we have to fight, only the Colts. No time for rifles.'

Jenkins nodded. After much thought, they had decided to bring three British Army-issue Martini-Henry rifles, instead of the Remingtons that the Dervishes were using. The Martinis were more accurate but their British origin could betray them, so the guns were carefully swathed in anonymous cotton and packed away.

As Ahmed was briefing the boy, three men crested the rise ahead of them at a fast pace and came riding towards them, the stocks of their rifles resting on their thighs, their fingers on the triggers. Their faces were swathed, so that only their eyes could be seen between the folds of their *esharps*, but they wore the multicoloured patches of the Mahdi on their long gowns, and wide cross-handled swords hung from their belts. Their attitude was unmistakably hostile, and a gasp came from Mustapha, who immediately took shelter behind Simon's mount.

As their leader approached, the boy hissed up at Simon, 'He my master. Bad man.'

'Oh blast!' breathed Fonthill. In a country covering nearly a million square miles and with a population of only just over two million, they had blundered into Mustapha's previous master. It was damned bad luck – or had the man followed them from the village?

Ahmed had ridden slightly ahead, raised his hand and given the customary greeting. But the Dervish gave no answering 'We-alaykum e-salaam waramet allah wabarakatahl.' Instead, he brushed ahead of Ahmed, pointed to Mustapha and broke into forceful Arabic.

Quickly Ahmed intervened, and replied with many gestures towards Fonthill and Jenkins. It was clear that the Dervish was having none of it. Ahmed turned and murmured to Simon: 'He says the boy is his and that he wants him back, pretty damn quick, you might say. I have explained how we found him, but he accuses us of stealing. Better give him the boy.'

Simon slowly moved his hand beneath his *glabya* until he felt the reassuring curve of the Colt. 'Tell him I will buy the boy off him,' he murmured.

Ahmed translated, but the response was clearly in the negative and the Dervish reached behind his saddle and produced a long, coiled whip. At this, Mustapha shrank further behind Fonthill's camel, his brown eyes now wide with fear.

Simon raised his hand to the Arab and, fixing his eyes on those glaring at him from the slit between the folds of the *esharp*, spoke again to Ahmed, but this time very quickly and firmly. 'Tell him that I have grown fond of the boy and that he can name his price.'

The response came with a snarl and an uplifted middle finger. With a quick movement, the Arab uncoiled the whip and swung it so that it caught Mustapha across the shoulders. The end also flicked Fonthill's camel across the haunches, so that the animal started, almost unseating Simon. Not sufficiently, however, to prevent him drawing the Colt and firing. At such close quarters the bullet could not miss, and it took the Arab in the chest, blasting him on to the sand. In one fluid movement, Fonthill fanned the hammer of the revolver with his left hand and delivered two more shots, hitting the second Arab in the shoulder but missing the third, whose camel had reared in alarm. It did not matter, however, because Jenkins's shot shattered the man's brain. Coolly Fonthill took aim at the second Dervish, who, mouth agape, was clutching his shoulder, and shot him also in the breast. Within seconds, all three Dervishes were sprawled on the sand, their blood colouring it, and the desert became quiet again as the echo of the shots died away.

Ahmed struggled to control his camel, which had shied at the gunshots, and looked at Fonthill with shocked wide eyes.

Jenkins's jaw had dropped. 'Bloody 'ell, bach sir,' he said. 'I know you've grown a bit 'arder like, since the old days. But did we 'ave to kill 'em all?'

Simon did not reply, but slowly tucked his Colt back under the folds of his dress and then reached a hand down to Mustapha. The boy, his eyes as wide as Ahmed's, gripped the hand and was hauled up on to Fonthill's saddle, perching before him.

Then Simon looked across at his companions and spoke slowly. 'Three points. Firstly, anyone who beats a boy like that deserves to die. Secondly, I do not wish to lose Mustapha, for all kinds of reasons . . .' His voice faltered for a moment and then went on strongly. 'Particularly because he will be very useful to us in Khartoum. Thirdly, we could not afford to let any of these Dervishes escape to tell the story. This is a cruel country and we are on a very dangerous journey. We can take no prisoners.' He ran his hand through Mustapha's curls and spoke to him, more softly. 'Now, you go on ahead to that rise again and make sure that we are alone in this bloody desert. Stay there and keep watch while we see if we can get rid of these bad men. Off you go.' And he handed the boy down.

Mustapha scampered away and the three men descended. Jenkins reached into their packs and retrieved a small collapsible spade, while Ahmed gathered in the Dervishes' camels and Simon, his eyes cold, bent over the Arabs and confirmed that all three were dead. Luckily the desert here had lost the hard, gravelly texture found at the beginning of their trek and the sand was looser, enabling them to shovel depressions deep enough to take the three bodies and their rifles.

Fonthill looked up. A solitary vulture was wheeling high overhead. 'It won't be long before that fellow attracts more of his kind, and they will probably dig up the bodies,' he said, in the flat monotone that he had used since the killings. 'But we can't help that. And the skeletons won't tell any stories in this godforsaken place anyway. Come on, we have no time to waste.'

'What do we do with camels, Simon?' asked Ahmed.

'Ah yes. We'd better strip them down a bit and bury whatever will show them to be mounts from the Mahdi's army. We will bury two of the saddles and let Mustapha use the third on the best of the three camels. We can spread our loads across the other two and add them to the pack animals. They could be useful currency anyway. Let's do it quickly.'

They all set to, and within fifteen minutes the loads had

been redistributed and this small patch of desert sand had returned to its virgin state. If it wasn't for the extra camels linked behind Jenkins's mount on lead reins, the three Dervishes might never have existed.

Mustapha was recalled from his guard post and hoisted on to the fourth camel, to his great delight. Then he was sent some hundred yards to the front to scout ahead. Fonthill looked up and saw that the solitary vulture had now been joined by three others, all of them wheeling overhead in seeming disinterest, but clearly marking the spot where violence had erupted – for those, that is, who had the desert skills to understand the signs.

'Damn,' said Simon. Then he shrugged his shoulders. 'Can't be helped,' and he tapped the rump of his camel. The beast arched its long neck and broke into a clumsy trot for a few moments before dropping back into its somnolent, head-nodding walk, the wide pads on its feet sending up sprays of sand grains as it flicked them behind with each stride.

Jenkins eased his camel alongside Simon. 'You all right, bach sir?' he asked.

Fonthill remained looking ahead. 'Of course. Why?'

The Welshman wrinkled his nose. 'Well, see, I just wondered, like . . .' His voice tailed away. 'It's just that, well . . . I never seen you kill anyone like that, see. It was all a bit strange, like. You know . . .' Although Jenkins was from North Wales, his voice always lapsed back into the lilts and intonations of the valleys when he was embarrassed or concerned – which was not often. It rose at the end of every sentence, as though he was asking a question.

'No, I don't know.' Fonthill spoke sharply. 'I didn't exactly enjoy it, if you must know, but it had to be done, that was all. God, I've seen you kill enough men.'

'Yes, well, that's me, look you. I was more or less brought

up to it, I suppose. But you weren't, and it was . . . well . . . a bit strange and not like you, that's all.'

'It's over and done with, and that's all there is to it.' Simon turned his head to look up at the sky behind him. 'I only hope that the sound of those shots hasn't carried too far and that those blasted birds aren't going to act like a signpost.' He frowned. 'I can't think what those Dervishes were doing so far north; this is supposed to be the territory of the Mudir of Dongola, who has thrown in his lot with the British. I didn't expect that we would meet the Mahdi's Dervishes until we crossed the Nile again at Abu Dom and were on our way to Berber. I suppose it shows that they are growing in confidence and ranging further from Khartoum. Ah well.'

He lifted himself awkwardly in the saddle to look ahead. 'Damn, I can't see Mustapha.' He raised his voice and shouted forward. 'Ahmed. Go on a little and make sure the boy's all right, there's a good fellow.'

The little Egyptian raised his hand and urged his camel forward.

Jenkins fell silent but continued riding at Fonthill's side. Eventually he coughed and nodded ahead. ' 'E's a nice little lad, isn't 'e?'

'Who? Ahmed or Mustapha?'

'Oh, come on, bach sir. You know who I mean. The little lad.'

Fonthill frowned again. 'Yes. He's got spirit.' The silence, unusually awkward between the two, fell again. Then, after some twenty seconds, Simon spoke. 'You know he will be . . . er . . . very useful to us when we get to Khartoum,' he said, staring straight ahead.

'Oh, o' course, o' course. Very useful. Good thing, though, that you got rid of his previous owner, so to speak. I just 'ope that none of these other Dervish blokes got to know 'im when 'e was knockin' about the town, like.'

Fonthill turned his head sharply. 'Why?'

'Well . . . I mean. It might be a bit awkward us explainin' why 'e's with us, particularly if 'is owner 'asn't shown up to collect 'is pay and rations, like.'

'Well, we'll handle that when we come to it.'

Once more they rode in silence. Then: 'We shan't be able to keep 'im, though, o' course.' Jenkins spoke as though to himself. 'I mean, what would we do with 'im? Couldn't exactly take him back to Miss Alice, now, could we, sayin' we've brought this little chap back to live with us, as a sort of mascot to 'ave about the 'ouse. That is, of course, if there's to be a weddin' after this little lot is over.'

Fonthill swung round in the saddle. 'Of course there's going to be a wedding. Don't talk such rot.'

'No offence intended, bach sir. It's just that you 'aven't spoken about Miss Alice for ages, and I just wondered . . .'

'There's nothing to wonder about, for God's sake. Nothing at all.'

'O' course, o' course. I just wondered, that's all.'

Chastened, Jenkins let his camel and its two attendants fall back, to leave Fonthill to ride alone once more. Immediately, Simon felt guilty. Why had he been so testy with Jenkins? For eight years the two had shared an equable relationship, more that of comrades and friends than master and servant. It was a bond unusual in this Victorian age, where the line between classes was rarely crossed, but it was one forged in war and danger. Each had saved the other's life on several occasions, and gentle banter had always been the basic form of intercourse between them. They were at ease with each other and rarely had they exchanged words in anger. Why then had he snapped at Jenkins now?

Fonthill sighed. It was true that his killing of the wounded man had been uncharacteristic, and now that the necessary orders for the disposal of the evidence had been given and the adrenaline had stopped surging, he was still shaking a little. But it had had to be done, for they could not let the man return to his fellow tribesmen and give the alarm about this strange, warlike little group about to enter their domain. Jenkins, a born soldier and a ruthless killer himself when he had to be, would know that. Yet there was more to it than that, of course. Three five two had discreetly but carefully warned him that his taking the boy along could risk the success of their mission – and chided him for seeming to have dismissed Alice from his life.

Fonthill shook his head. True again. He looked ahead to where he could now see the boy's brown curls gently nodding to his camel's gait. There was no doubt that Mustapha's arrival – his courage, his cheerfulness and the undoubted affection he showed to his new master – had added a new, lighter dimension to their dangerous mission. Perhaps – and he frowned at the thought – it had reminded him for a moment of how great was the sacrifice he had made in eschewing the warmth, love and promise of domestic life with Alice Covington in favour of answering Wolseley's call to serve his Queen and country. But oh, the great soldier knew how to pluck the patriotic strings all right! What was it his cable had said? 'Desperate times for us here stop Must save Gordon stop Only you can help me stop Can you come Cairo immediately stop Bring your Welshman stop.' Or something like that. It was a call that could not be resisted, Alice knew that. But she had taken it hard, for their wedding was only two months away. Of course, he had had to reject firmly her pleas to come with them. Her experience and reputation as a more than able war correspondent, earned in the man's world of the campaigns in Zululand, Afghanistan, Sekukuniland and the Transvaal, had given her a confidence and – yes – headstrongness that had taken her into great danger in all of those places. Of course he could not be burdened on this expedition with the responsibility of her presence, and anyway, there could not possibly be a role for her out here in this harsh, merciless land, where women were condemned by the Muslim creed to be little more than domestic servants and breeding machines. She would stick out like a sore thumb in the desert. Yet she *had* taken it badly, and of course, he could not allow her to risk her life by resuming her role as war correspondent . . . He shook his head again. Had he lost the love of his life, the woman for whom he had yearned all through her betrothal and then marriage to another and who now was to be his at last? Would she ever forgive him?

His miserable reverie was interrupted by Jenkins, once more at his side, but this time displaying a sense of urgency.

'We're bein' followed. I thought you ought to know.'

Fonthill stirred in the saddle. 'Who? Where?'

'I caught a glimpse of an Arab bloke – just the top of 'is head behind these dunes that 'ave started to appear. Back there on the left. 'E's some way away, p'raps a quarter of a mile, see, but 'e's there all right.'

Simon turned and scanned the soft dunes that had now materialised as they plodded deeper into the desert away from the Nile. He could see nothing.

'Right. I don't see why anyone should follow us unless they have some ulterior motive.' He whistled softly and waved his arm to call back Ahmed and Mustapha. 'If there are many of them, then our Colts probably won't get us out of trouble. Unwrap the rifles; give one to Ahmed, you take one and I'll have the third. Put rounds up the spouts of each one, but we should keep them under wraps as best we can across the saddles, ready if we have to use them but not showing that they are British issue. Do it now.'

Fonthill explained the situation to the others when they joined him, and then, when the rifles were distributed, he ordered Ahmed to ride in the rear. 'Same as before, old chap,' he said. 'Explain that we're Syrians off to see the Mahdi. If there's trouble, no one shoots before I do. And you, Mustapha, ride off and make your escape if there *is* trouble. Is that understood?'

The boy nodded, but his eyes were wide and sparkling in the hot sun.

'Now let us ride on,' said Simon, 'as though we haven't a care in the world.'

It was at least a quarter of an hour before the men following caught up with them. There were about twenty of them, all dressed anonymously in native, desert fashion but none of them, he noticed with relief, wearing Mahdian patches. Yet to Simon's eye there was something strange about them. Their camels were well groomed, and what could be seen of their saddles under the riders showed leather well oiled and almost polished. The skins of the riders were also lighter than those of the local *fellaheen*. And the stocks of their rifles protruded from smart leather holsters. If it was not for their dress, they could have been a cavalry unit out on patrol.

The leader was a small man with a large moustache that protruded well either side of the gap in his face scarf. He gestured one of his men to come forward, spoke to him quietly so that only the two of them could hear, and the man then addressed Ahmed in Arabic. The two conversed and the man addressed his leader again, once more in low tones so that Fonthill could not hear. But the leader's response this time was loud and perfectly clear.

'Syrians,' he said, his voice high and clipped. 'Don't believe a bloody word of it. Sergeant, have the troop surround 'em and then relieve them of their weapons.'

Fonthill urged his camel forward. 'That won't be necessary,' he said. He unwound his *esharp* so that his face could be seen. 'Fonthill,' he said, 'late of the 24th Regiment of Foot and Queen's Own Corps of Guides. This is Sergeant Major Jenkins and our two Egyptian friends who are helping us on our mission.'

'Good lord!' The man unwound his own *esharp* to reveal a red face down which perspiration trickled into his great walrus moustache. 'Mission!' he spluttered. 'What mission? I'm Captain Hicks-Johnson, serving on Lord Wolseley's intelligence staff, and if you are English and on a mission then I would damned well know about it. Now, tell me who you really are and what you are doing out here in land that is under the Mudir of Dongola's jurisdiction.'

'Ah,' said Simon in conversational tones, 'that explains it. You are with the Mudir in Dongola, I presume, and these men are Egyptian troops. Is that so?'

The aggression did not leave the captain's face, but he spoke more quietly now, drawling his words again in the manner of an upper-class Englishman. 'It's none of your damned business who these men are or where we are based. Answer my questions: who are you, what are you doing here and what were those shots I heard back there? Come on now, I want the truth.'

Fonthill sighed. 'I understand your curiosity about us, Captain,' he said, 'but I cannot afford to be delayed. We are working directly for Lord Wolseley on assignment to his column. We are on our way to Khartoum to take messages from the General to General Gordon . . .'

'Wolseley employs natives to do that.'

'I know. We have to do something a little more . . . ah . . .

interpretive than merely handing over a letter. Then we must return to Lord Wolseley as quickly as we can. Those are my orders. As you can appreciate,' Fonthill gave a polite smile, desperately controlling the frustration that was welling up inside him, 'we are in a race against time, so I would be grateful if you would allow us to continue.'

'Not so fast. What about those shots we heard?'

'Ah yes. We had a little trouble with three Dervishes – Mahdists according to their clothing . . .'

'What?'

'Yes, it seems they are penetrating further north now. I am afraid we had to kill them.'

Hicks-Johnson's jaw dropped for a second. 'Rubbish,' he said. 'We have followed you for about two miles. We've seen no bodies or signs of a fight and I doubt if there are Dervishes for miles. The villages around here are friendly, and it's my job to see they stay that way. Dervishes wouldn't come near Dongola.'

'Well they did. We buried the bodies.' Simon gestured behind him to where six specks in the sky were now circling very low. 'Those vultures know that, even if you don't.'

The officer turned and ran his eye again over the three men and the boy. Then he fixed his gaze firmly on Mustapha, who was grinning happily at the exchanges. The expression on the boy's face seemed to antagonise Hicks-Johnson further.

'What about the boy?' he demanded. 'I suppose he is on special secondment to the General personally as well, eh?' His languid tone had now become a sneer.

Fonthill restrained himself and then exchanged glances with Jenkins, giving the smallest of nods to the shrouded rifle that lay across the Welshman's saddle and then to the Egyptian sergeant. 'No,' he said patiently. 'He is a slave boy whom we picked up back by the Nile. He knows Khartoum well and will be invaluable to us when we get there. And speaking of special secondment, I should tell you, Captain, that I have the temporary rank of major and Mr Jenkins here that of company sergeant major. If you delay us further, I must report you to the commander-in-chief. Now, please stand aside. That is an order.'

Conflicting emotions now ran across Hicks-Johnson's face. It was clear that he could not bring himself to believe that, as an intelligence officer with responsibility for tribal affairs in the Mudir of Dongola's territory, he would not have been informed of this party's presence in the area. Long periods of control over Egyptian troops, with no interference from senior officers, had given him complete confidence in his own superiority. Yet Fonthill's crisp, public-school English and air of command made him pause. Then his basic instincts took control.

'Dammit,' he said. 'I'm not having it. Don't believe a word of it. No Englishman could ever penetrate into the heart of the Sudan and get through the Mahdi's army into Khartoum. I don't know what your game is, but you're coming back to Dongola with me to present your credentials to Major Herbert Kitchener, my commanding officer. We'll see what he thinks of your cock-and-bull story. Sergeant . . .'

But he got no further. Fonthill had produced his Colt as if by magic, and Hicks-Johnson found himself looking down its barrel as it was presented a few inches from his face.

'Sarn't Major.'

'Sir,' Jenkins responded in his best parade-ground voice.

'Take this officer's revolver. It's just beneath his *glabya* here. Yes, that's it. Good.' Fonthill allowed himself a quick look at the Egyptian sergeant. The man was looking on with consternation – and indecision. Simon had taken a gamble. He knew that the troops of the Egyptian army were of poor quality. Since the Mahdi had set up his standard, he had defeated force after force sent against him from the Khedive in Cairo. Egyptian troops were badly paid, had poor morale and were the despair of the British officers who occasionally led them. That was why the British had been forced to send Wolseley out with his army composed mainly of British soldiers. Was this Egyptian sergeant made of sterner stuff?

'Sergeant.' Fonthill addressed him directly. The man's jaw dropped, as did the muzzle of his rifle. 'If you or your men make any effort to disarm us or stop us, this officer will be shot. The responsibility for his death will be yours. I am a British Army major engaged on a special mission and I am not to be impeded. Do you understand?'

The sergeant shot a quick glance at Hicks-Johnson, but the captain, against whose temple Fonthill's Colt muzzle was now pressing, was staring straight ahead, his eyes bulbous. The Egyptian's head slowly nodded. 'Yes, *effendi*,' he said.

'Good. Now, order your men to put their rifles back in their holsters. Do it NOW!' The order, issued in that familiar parade-ground bark by an Englishman, jerked the Egyptian, and he issued an order in Arabic. The troop slowly replaced their rifles in their holsters. They were all clearly bewildered by the turn of events and by these seeming *fellaheen* who behaved like English officers.

'Splendid. Now listen to me. Your officer will come to no harm unless you attempt to stop us. You will now return to your barracks and you will NOT follow us. Do you understand?'

'Yes, *effendi*.'

'We will borrow the captain for perhaps an hour to ensure our safe conduct, and he will then be released, but if you follow us or try to interfere with us in any way, he will be shot. Again, do you understand?'

'Yes, *effendi*.'

'Very well. Now. Dismiss.'

With one last questioning look to Hicks-Johnson, which went unanswered, the sergeant wheeled his camel away and led his men back the way they had come. The last man looked back and allowed himself a great white-toothed grin at the sight of the captain, still staring fixedly ahead, the revolver at his forehead.

'Ahmed,' called Fonthill, 'make sure that they are well on their way and then rejoin us.'

The Egyptian gave a smile and a nod and moved away.

It was not until he had gone well out of sight that Simon lowered his Colt. 'Right,' he said, tucking the revolver back under his *jibba*. 'I am not going to apologise to you for the rough stuff because you brought it upon yourself. We can let nothing – *nothing*, d'you hear me? – stop us in the important work we have to do.'

Hicks-Johnson did not reply, and refused to engage in eye contact with Fonthill. Face set, he sat in his saddle staring ahead.

'Now,' resumed Simon, 'we will take you with us for a mile or two and then hobble your camel and leave it behind. We will tie it to a bush if we can find one. We will take you a little further and then return your revolver to you and drop you off. You must walk back to your camel. I appreciate that we are putting you in some danger, but that is your own fault. I hope you are right in thinking that those Dervishes we met are the exception in these parts. Let me warn you once more that if you try any stupid heroics or attempt to escape before we release you, I shall have no hesitation in shooting you.'

As before, the captain made no reply but directed his gaze ahead, as though refusing to accept Fonthill's presence.

Simon shrugged his shoulders. 'Right, Jenkins,' he called.

'Take the captain's rein and lead him and let's be off. Mustapha, you scout ahead but keep us in sight.'

The little party resumed its progress to the south-east, following what remained a reasonably well-marked but not well-beaten trail. When Ahmed rejoined them, Fonthill gestured for Hicks-Johnson to dismount and his camel was haltered and tied loosely to a stunted mimosa bush. He was then mounted on Mustapha's camel, while the boy walked, leading the beast, until after about another half-mile Simon gestured to the Englishman to dismount.

'This is where our ways part,' he said. 'Sarn't Major, give the captain his revolver but cover him with your rifle and shoot him if it looks as though he is going to fire his weapon.'

The little transaction was carried out in silence. 'If it makes you feel any better,' said Fonthill, looking down at the small but erect figure below him, who was silently replacing his revolver in its holster, 'you should know that every word I have told you is true and that we are working directly for Wolseley. Your Major Kitchener may know about us but I doubt it. The General likes to keep his and our cards close to his chest. I hope that if and when we meet again, you will have understood why we had to do what we did. Now, safe journey home.'

Hicks-Johnson at last broke his silence. 'Do you really think that you can reach Khartoum?' His lip curled under his moustache. 'You are a child in this desert.' He gestured. 'Those *girbas*, the goatskin bags holding your water, for instance. You have them sewn with leather thongs. Pah! They will dry out and break in this heat and you will lose all your water. Everyone knows you should have them sewn with thread. You will never reach Khartoum, for if the Mahdi doesn't kill you, the desert will. However,' his voice now dropped in pitch, 'I want you to know that, whoever you are, you have made a lifelong enemy of me. You have broken every rule in the book by threatening me, by preventing me from doing my duty and, worst of all, by humiliating me in front of my men. Damn you, Fonthill. If by some chance you do survive and return, I will see you in hell, I promise you.'

Fonthill gave him a mock salute. 'I will look forward to it. Have a nice walk. Good day, Captain.'

With that, the little caravan continued on its way, leaving Captain Hicks-Johnson staring after them for a long while, until, at last, he turned on his way and began the long journey back to Dongola.

Within three minutes, both Ahmed and Jenkins formed up alongside Simon and for a while they rode in companionable silence – a silence that was, inevitably, finally broken by Jenkins.

'Well,' he said, 'it's been a nice day so far, look you. We've killed three Sudanese gentlemen, just like that,' and he snapped his fingers, 'then we meet the only English officer for miles and we stick our bayonets up his arse, so to speak. Quite a day, isn't it?'

Fonthill forced a reluctant smile. 'Well,' he said, 'I am not proud of any of it but it is what we had to do. If that little bounder had forced us to go back with him to Dongola it might have been days, even weeks, before Wolseley could be found to clear us. Our chances of getting through to Gordon in time would have been considerably reduced. And what would the General have felt about us getting in that sort of a mess? I hate to think of it. One thing, though: probably without realising it, the little twit gave us a tip about the water bags. We must get rid of these ones with leather thongs and replace them with bags sewn with thread as soon as we can. Ahmed, can you do that?'

The Egyptian nodded. 'As soon as we reach Nile again.'

But Jenkins was preoccupied. 'I 'ope you don't mind me askin', but would you really 'ave pulled the trigger if 'e'd gone on and tried to get 'is men to arrest us?'

Simon thought for a moment and then, looking fixedly ahead, he nodded. 'Oh yes.'

'Blimey,' said Jenkins loudly. He half smiled but stayed silent.

They rode for a little longer before Ahmed spoke. 'Simon,' he asked, 'why did that officer not believe you? Why do he behave like that?'

Fonthill blew out his cheeks. 'I have a little sympathy with him in that we must have looked the most unlikely messengers for Wolseley. But, dammit, the man was supposed to be an intelligence officer and should have been able to engage in some thinking outside the normal frame of things. I am afraid, Ahmed, that the British officer class can be downright stupid at times. And vain, too. You notice that he said my greatest sin was humiliating him in front of his men.'

'Amen to all that,' said Jenkins. 'But, bach sir, I would watch your back a bit when we return to the army lines – if we ever do, that is.'

'Oh, we'll return all right. But we've got to get in to Khartoum first, and that is not going to be easy, although,' and he turned to smile at Mustapha, who had joined them, 'we will do it with the aid of General Mustapha here, head of our own special intelligence service.'

The boy did not quite understand, but he realised that he had been brought into the brotherhood, and his broad grin brought smiles from them all.

That night they camped off the track, and slept coldly under the clearest of star-strewn skies. Three days later, without further incident, they met the Nile again, just above Abu

Dom, and crossed it during the hours of darkness. Once ashore on the eastern bank, Simon instituted a watch rota as they slept. Now they were truly in the Mahdi's territory, where his banners flew as far as the Abyssinian border, more than eight hundred miles to the south. If their journey had been dangerous before, now the threats facing them had multiplied a hundredfold. Before them, nearly two hundred miles away, lay the Nile again and the town of Berber, so recently captured by the Dervishes. Should they take to the river there once more, or trust to the vastness of the desert to see them through to Khartoum? Simon shrugged his shoulders. He would take that decision when he had to.

Chapter 4

Alice Covington was furious. She stood, the letter in her hand, gazing unseeingly across the lawns of the house, out over the flat fields of Norfolk, to where a wood rose in the distance, wreathed in early-morning mist as though in a mantle of smoke. She crushed the letter into a ball, then smoothed it flat to read again.

'How dare he!' she muttered. 'How dare he!' It was bad enough that Simon had gone off to the Sudan with Jenkins, forcing the cancellation of the wedding, but to have interfered with her own life like this was infuriating. It was so *typical* of a man and yet so *untypical* of Simon, who she had always considered to take a modern, liberal view of a woman's role. For God's sake, it *was* 1884, not 1834! Women, at least intelligent women, were emancipated now and not subjugated to the rule of their husbands – and certainly not their fiancés. How could he!

She strode to the drawing-room table, pulled up a chair, sat down and read the letter again. It was on the familiar *Morning Post* notepaper and headed 'From the Editor'.

My dear Alice,
Thank you for your letter, which, since the dispatch of Lord Wolseley to the Sudan, I must confess I had half expected. What I had not expected, however, was to

receive a visit from your fiancé, Mr Fonthill, en route himself to Cairo, a little over a week ago.

May I say, in passing, what a delight it was to meet him for the first time. Of course I remember your stirring account in our columns of his adventures in Alexandria two years ago during the shelling of that port. Although you could not name him then, I was able – with the help of certain friends at the Horse Guards – to put two and two together when you announced your engagement, a little over eighteen months after the tragic death of your husband. You will recall that I wrote and congratulated you then.

But I digress. Mr Fonthill was not able to tell me the nature of his assignment in the Sudan, although it is clearly involved with the expedition to relieve General Gordon in Khartoum. I only wish that I could have commissioned him to send back reports for us! However, he did make a special request to me, and this was the reason for his visit.

He said that, on his departure, he had asked you not to write to me requesting me to reinstate you as a war correspondent with Lord Wolseley's column now preparing in Egypt, and that you had replied that you could not promise but would carefully consider his request. Now, of course, you have written to make that request. Mr Fonthill delineated in some detail why he was particularly anxious that I should not employ you again in this way, pointing out that the Sudan expedition would be a far more dangerous undertaking than any campaign you have covered before and that the particularly arduous nature of the journey up the Nile and then the advance to Khartoum would be singularly unpleasant and hazardous for a woman. I *will not go into the detail of the specific points he made about dangers from disease in that arid country, the ferocity of the Mahdi's followers and their complete lack of respect for women.*

Perhaps his most telling point, however, was his final one. He explained that he knew his task would place him in extreme peril and that he would find it hard to focus on the work and to carry it to a successful conclusion if he knew that you were in any kind of danger. I may say that he was touchingly explicit in describing how much he was yearning to rejoin you and spend the rest of his life with you, and that he could not face the thought that you might not be there waiting for him on his return Clearly, he loves you very much.

At this point, Alice threw back her head and stifled a sob.

I have to confess, my dear Alice, that much as I would welcome receiving once again your graphic – and so often exclusive! – dispatches from this latest war, the husband and father in me could not but respond to his plea. Therefore I must decline your offer to cover the expedition for us.

I trust that you will understand my reasons and that you will compose yourself to waiting for the successful and I know most welcome return of Mr Fonthill, once the campaign is over.

Yours most affectionately,
Charles Cornford, Editor

'Madam.'
Alice stood, moved to the window and furtively wiped

away the tears before turning back to face Mary, the housekeeper, who had entered quietly. 'Yes, Mary?'

'Here are the three menus Cook is offering for you to choose from for tonight.' She advanced and put them on the table, averting her eyes from Alice's obviously tear-stained cheeks. 'It will only be three sittings, won't it, madam? I have prepared the best guest room.'

Damn! For a brief moment, in the fury prompted by Cornford's letter, Alice had forgotten that, today of all days, Simon's mother and father were due to arrive in the late afternoon to stay for a couple of days. Charlotte Fonthill, Alice's formidable mother-in-law-to-be, had more or less invited herself with her husband after receiving Simon's hurried letter announcing the postponement of the wedding and his departure to the Sudan. Hosting them was a chore that Alice could do without at this stage. Oh, Major Fonthill was a gentle, self-effacing delight, but Mrs Fonthill was a shrewd, strongly opinionated woman whose task in Norfolk would be to find out the exact nature of Simon's mission and also to sniff out any scent of discord in the couple's relationship. Alice was not sure that she could face that at this point. It would be a difficult couple of days.

She sighed. 'Yes, just the three of us. Now, let me see. Yes, I think the vegetable soup, the turbot, the sorbet, the lamb, and . . . oh, I don't mind. Let Cook choose the dessert. Tell Mr Jeffries that I will happily leave to him the matter of wines. And Mary . . .'

'Yes, madam.'

'Remind Beales that he is to take the brougham to meet Major and Mrs Fonthill off the London train arriving at five twenty-five. Now, that will be all.'

Alone again, Alice read Cornford's letter once more, and as she did so, the germ of an idea began to form in her mind.

She hurried to the panelled library and, in a pigeonhole in her work bureau, found the letter she was seeking. Putting it to one side, she penned a formal and courteous reply to Cornford; then, taking more care and frowning in concentration, she wrote a second letter, read it through with a mixture of apprehension and satisfaction, sealed it, applied a stamp and rang for the maid.

'Please have Beales take this to the village for posting immediately,' she ordered. 'It is quite urgent and important and if he goes now he will catch the second post of the day.'

Immediately Alice felt much better, and her anger towards Simon abated as she conjured up his diffident smile, his beautiful broken nose, and the feel of his strong arms about her. She smiled sadly as she recalled his sensitivity, an attribute that had really not suited him for life in one of Queen Victoria's regiments of the line and yet had not prevented him from earning a reputation, within certain circles in the higher echelons of the army, for bravery and resourcefulness as a highly unorthodox scout and spy. Oh, how she hoped that those qualities would sustain him in this terrible task that had been put upon him now, on the virtual eve of their wedding!

Alice, like Simon, had grown up near Brecon in the Welsh borders and their fathers had served together in the Welsh regiment, the 24th of Foot, becoming stout friends. The children had seen each other intermittently in their young years but had drifted apart when each had been sent away to boarding school. Later, Alice had been sent abroad to be 'finished' and Simon had entered his father's old regiment after attending the new officers' training establishment at Sandhurst. A ball for her coming out had sparked a juvenile love for her in Simon, but she, facing the excitement of freedom and a possible career, had gently rejected him.

That career had eventually burgeoned when, after

receiving and gratefully publishing a series of anonymous articles from Alice in the *Morning Post*, Cornford had reluctantly agreed to post her to the then journalistic backwater of South Africa as a foreign correspondent. The breaking out of the Zulu War had given her the chance to shine as a war reporter, and despite her gender (although there had been precedents of women reporting wars for British newspapers), she had won a reputation for her further coverage of wars in Afghanistan, the Transvaal and Egypt. Her path had crossed with Simon's on all of those campaigns, and she had been instrumental in helping him successfully to defend a court-martial charge of cowardice in Zululand.

That charge had been brought by Simon's old commanding officer, Colonel Ralph Covington, who had fallen in love with Alice. In a temporary reaction to the violence of war, she had agreed to marry him and retire from journalism, but before doing so she had covered one more campaign, that of General Wolseley's successful fight with the Sekukuni tribe in the eastern Transvaal. There, she had realised her mistake, and had acknowledged to Simon her underlying and strong love for him. She decided to tell Covington after the defining and brutal battle against Chief Sekukuni. Alas, in that battle the Colonel had sustained disfigurement and the loss of an eye and an arm, with the result that Alice felt she had to honour her commitment and had married him. In Egypt two years ago, however, Covington had been killed at the Battle of Tel el Kebir, and she and Simon were reunited at last.

Alice smiled at the memory of the passion and joy with which she had accepted Simon's characteristically diffident proposal of marriage after the battle. That diffidence came not only from Simon's habitual self-doubt about his worth, but also because Covington's death had left Alice a rich woman, with a large estate in Norfolk, and it had taken him a little time to overcome the worry that he might seem to Alice to be an opportunist. What nonsense! For the sake of Covington's memory, however – and not from a sense of dutiful propriety, for Alice cared nothing for society's opinion – they had decided to wait fourteen months before announcing their engagement. It had been an awkward period of some strain, with Simon living at his parents' home in Brecon with the magnificent and loyal 352 Jenkins, and unsure of how to employ his time.

The wedding would have solved all that, of course, for the estate in Norfolk needed a man's controlling hand and it had been agreed that, despite Simon's reluctance to step too completely into Covington's shoes, he would move into the great house and run the estate, with the help of Jenkins as estate manager. Then had come Wolseley's cable . . . Damn the man!

It seemed more like early autumn than late summer as Alice stood at the door to welcome the Fonthills' carriage when it rolled up. She had always had great affection for the couple, although rather more for the Major than his formidable wife, and the news of the engagement had brought together again the two families. She could not resist a happy smile, then, as the pair stepped down and opened their arms to her.

Mrs Fonthill, her hair completely white now under her bonnet, and distinctly matronly in figure, was still a handsome woman, with her son's strong jaw but nothing of his hesitation in her eyes. The Major, unusually clean-shaven for the time, wore his greying hair long, curling to his collar. He resembled Simon in his regular features and gentle brown eyes, but his military background was evident in his soldierly, erect bearing. Together they were a fine-looking couple, and Alice embraced them with genuine affection. Then everything was hustle and bustle as bags were unloaded and the brougham was taken back to the stables.

'Now,' said Alice, 'would you care for tea before you bathe, or something stronger? We dine at seven thirty.'

'Tea, bath, something stronger and then dinner, in that order,' boomed Mrs Fonthill. She stood in the hall and gazed around approvingly. 'I had forgotten how splendid your house is, my dear. Will you be able to run it with Simon away?'

'Of course she will,' the Major cut in quickly. 'She's been doing it well enough on her own for nearly two years.'

Alice shot him a grateful glance. 'Mary will show you to your room and will bring you hot water for you to spruce up a little – not that you look as though you need it. My word, no! We will have tea in the drawing room in, shall we say, fifteen minutes?'

'Yes,' said Mrs Fonthill. 'Then we must talk.' And Alice's heart sank.

In fact, when they were finally esconced in the comfortable drawing room, the interrogation proved comparatively painless. 'All I can say, my dear Alice,' said Charlotte Fonthill, replacing her cup with great care in its saucer, 'is that I am so glad the invitations had not gone out.'

Alice smiled wryly. 'Yes, but I am afraid they were printed, virtually ready to go. They are dated, of course, so will all have to be done again.'

A quick glance was exchanged between the Fonthills, although Alice was a little surprised and greatly relieved that Mrs Fonthill was able to restrain herself from saying, 'Oh, so there *will* be a wedding, then?' Instead, she nodded in sympathy. But she did demand to see Wolseley's cable, which Alice duly produced.

'But what does it mean, for goodness' sake?' Charlotte demanded. ' "Only you can help me." How extreme! Did

Simon know what he meant, and have you heard from him yet?'

'Good lord, no. He will only have been in Cairo for a couple of days, if that. But of course he will write when he can, although I doubt if he will tell me what he is up to.'

'Mmmm.' The Major's eyes were half closed in concentration. 'I met Wolseley, just after he had lost an eye in the Crimea. A brilliant chap, even then. Clearly marked out for the top. Hugely brave, of course, but even as a young feller he was shrewd and careful. Believed in getting the best possible intelligence about the enemy before attacking him. That's why he's called on Simon.' He looked up at the two women. 'Our intelligence in the army has never been up to much, don't you know. But Simon has proved that he's good at it. I bet he's sending him up the Nile into the Sudan to see . . .'

He stopped, realising that Alice's eyes had widened in consternation. 'Sorry, my dear. Didn't mean to alarm you. Simon knows how to look after himself, particularly with dear old 352 to back him up.'

'What I can't understand,' broke in Charlotte Fonthill, 'is why the boy came out of the army in the first place. He could have had a first-class career, like his father, as a regimental officer. All this hole-and-corner nonsense is not seemly. He should be in uniform.'

George Fonthill coughed. 'I think that miserable business of the court martial upset him, you know. He felt that Covington had brought the charge unfairly, and anyway, he was disillusioned with him and his class of senior officers. And, I must confess, he had grounds. At Isandlwana, where his old battalion was butchered, he lost many friends, mainly the fault of General Chelmsford and his staff, who treated the Zulus with contempt and failed to erect proper defences at the camp. Then, at Majuba, the Boers were completely underrated by General Pommeroy-Colley with similar results. In Simon's experience, so many of the senior officers who, of course, purchased their commissions were incompetent. More intent on hunting, pig-sticking and shooting than on learning their trade.'

Fonthill shrugged. 'But somehow he seems to have found a niche in this rather unorthodox role he follows now, being close to the army but not part of it. Wolseley obviously rates him, anyway.' He smiled at his wife. 'And you know, my dear, I didn't do all that well as a regimental officer. Major isn't a particularly high rank.'

'Nonsense! You were happy to retire to run the estate, and anyway, you won the Victoria Cross in the Mutiny. Very few have done that.'

Major Fonthill smiled his diffident smile and fell silent.

'Alice,' continued Mrs Fonthill, 'at least you won't be gallivanting off again anyway. I always enjoyed your writing in the *Post*, you know, if not the radical political views that crept into it. I do hope you are not still influenced by this awful man Gladstone. It's his fault that that fine Christian General Gordon is holed up in Khartoum, of course. If only he had had the courage of dear Lord Beaconsfield and not shillied and shallied about for so long. If only . . .'

Major Fonthill put his hand on his wife's arm. 'Please, dear,' he murmured, 'perhaps we can leave politics alone for today, don't you think.'

'Do have another cup, dear Charlotte,' said Alice sweetly.

The evening and following day passed equably enough, but Alice was glad to wave goodbye to them at last, for on the morning of their departure she had received the telegram for which she had been waiting. It said simply: '*No promises but delighted see you here 11.30 on 19th if convenient to you. Regards Bonard.'*

She immediately called her coachman. 'I am going to London tomorrow, Beales. Be ready to take me to catch the eight thirty.'

Her arrival at Liverpool Street station the next day was, as ever, something of a shock. Alice had danced with death in the face of diverse enemies in the North-West Frontier of India, on the borders of Mozambique and in the desert of Egypt, but she still felt intimidated by the hiss of escaping steam, the clatter of baggage carts and the mass of people in these glass and steel temples that were the London terminal stations. It was the country bumpkin coming out in her, she presumed – the shock of the abrupt change from the tranquillity of the country to the bustle of the capital. She summoned a hansom cab and settled into it with relief.

Secure in the buttoned cushions inside, she pulled out a small powder compact and studied her face. It was not beautiful – the perhaps too strong line of the jaw, something she shared with Charlotte Fonthill, prevented that – but she had to concede that it was feminine enough to be pretty, with the soft fair hair peeping from under her hat, the high cheekbones, and her best feature, the large grey eyes that bespoke determination but a slight promise of sensuality. Alice dabbed a little powder on her cheeks. She must, she really must, make a good impression.

She looked again at the telegram. 'No promises.' What did that mean? Was it Bonard merely laying out a fallback position if she failed to please, or was he reneging on what could only be interpreted as at least a half-promise? Alice fumbled in her small handbag and produced the letter that Henri Bonard, the managing editor of Reuters, had written to her following her return to England after reporting Wolseley's successful conquest of Egypt two years ago. The letter was short but to the point.

> *My dear Miss Griffith,*
> *I have read with admiration your reports from Egypt and, earlier, from the Cape and Afghanistan. If ever you should consider forsaking the* Morning Post *for pastures new, please ensure that you let me know. I may be able to offer you something equally if not even more interesting.*

That was definitely promising enough and made her feel better. Then she looked again at the heading on the notepaper and a small thrill of apprehension ran through her. Reuters. Reuters! The very name spoke of urgency, reliability and, in a word, news. She had done what little research on the company she had had time for before setting out. It had been founded only thirty-three years ago in London by a German, Paul Julius Reuter. The establishment of the telegraph had put the fledgling company on its feet, and Reuter had shrewdly established the agency's base by reporting swiftly on economic affairs from around the world, so that bourses in every capital city had come to rely on it. His reporters' dispatches from the wars of Austro-Prussia and Franco-Prussia had extended its scope and reputation so that it was now the biggest news agency in the world.

And that was the rub: the word *news*. Alice had won her reputation as a war correspondent who wrote vivid, considered pieces of some length from the front line for a daily newspaper. It's true that she had, as Cornford granted, occasionally provided exclusive stories, what the Americans called 'scoops', but her main forte was giving her readers colour and a sense of actually being at the great events she was recording. A news agency, she knew, wanted facts presented accurately and, above all, quickly. Could she hurry and scurry to catch deadlines by the hour in that way?

Alice sighed and shrugged. At twenty-nine she was by no means too old a dog to learn new tricks. *And she was determined to get out to the Sudan!*

The Reuters office at the lower end of Fleet Street was a complete contrast to the *Morning Post*. Firstly, it was smaller, for it did not house the great printing presses needed to turn out the editions of a daily newspaper. Reuters relied completely on the telegraph to disseminate its messages. The main difference, however, lay in the atmosphere of the place. Whereas the *Post* exuded an air of stately dignity, as befitted one of the great national organs, the agency reception area was rather scruffy and it breathed business and pace, with young men – they were all men, of course – bustling through the entrance office as though the existence of faraway institutions such as the *New York Herald* and *Corriere della Sera* depended upon the length of their stride. As perhaps it did!

She was ushered very quickly into the small office of Mr Bonard, who turned out to be dainty, rather plump, quite young – perhaps thirty-four or -five? – sporting a neatly trimmed Vandyke beard and speaking with a French accent. Behind him glowed a coal fire in a small grate, and on his desk stood one of the new telephone apparatuses. All very appropriate, thought Alice, for the head of the world's greatest international news agency.

'My dear Miss Griffith,' he said, indicating a rather threadbare chair opposite his desk, 'or should I call you Mrs Covington?'

'Thank you, Monsieur Bonard. I prefer to use Griffith as my professional name.'

'Very well. Tea, or something stronger?'

'Tea, thank you.'

'Very well.' He pressed an electric buzzer, which sounded in an outer office – again, all very modern and in keeping – and gave the order to a young lady. 'Now.' He settled back in his chair. 'You have left the *Post*, it seems?'

'Yes.' This was the part Alice had dreaded. How to explain Simon's humiliating action? She had long ago decided to tell the truth. 'You may have heard that I lost my husband at Tel el Kebir?'

'I did indeed. Please accept my commiserations.'

Alice nodded gravely. 'Thank you. It was two years ago, and he died as he would have wished, facing the enemy.'

'Quite so. You must have been proud of him.'

'Indeed. However, I became engaged to be married again just two months ago, to a very old friend whom I knew long before I met Colonel Convington.' Even now, Alice felt a little uneasy that the comparative speed of her exit from widowhood seemed slightly disrespectful to Covington's memory; the reference to the longevity of her relationship with Simon somehow eased that.

'I see. Now please accept my congratulations.'

'Thank you. Unfortunately, my fiancé dislikes the thought of me going to the Sudan to continue my work for the *Post* and made a request to Charles Cornford, the editor, asking him not to employ me as a war correspondent on General Wolseley's expedition. Mr Cornford felt impelled to acquiesce to his wishes, although I believe that without this ... er ... complication he would have been happy to have used my services again.'

'Ah, I see.' Bonard's expression had subtly changed, and

Alice realised that, in this ridiculously male-dominated world, he too felt uneasy about defying the wishes of her soon-to-be husband. How infuriatingly unfair! But she must not lose her composure. She hurried on.

'However, I am, of course, a free person well past the age of majority, and I have no children and no other formal ties. Monsieur Bonard, you have never met my fiancé and have made no promises to him.' She sat very erect in her chair. 'I am now one of the most experienced war correspondents in Fleet Street. I have covered the British Army's campaigns in Zululand, Afghanistan, the Transvaal and Egypt, and I must tell you, I have no intention of sitting at home while Wolseley's attempt to rescue General Gordon, one of the greatest news stories of the century, is unfolding in Egypt and the Sudan. One way or the other, I will go to the Middle East to report on this campaign, but you were kind enough to suggest an interest in me, and that is why I came to you first.'

Bonard smiled. Dammit! Was he going to patronise her? 'What you say does you credit, Mrs . . . ah . . . Miss Griffith, and I yield to no one in my admiration for your talents as a journalist. Nevertheless . . .' He let his voice tail away for a moment, and then: 'May I ask what your relationship now is with your fiancé?'

Alice forced a smile. 'Not exactly cordial at this moment, but of course I appreciate his concern for my safety.' She then played her ace. 'We will, of course, be married on his return.'

'His return?'

'Yes, he himself left for the Sudan a little over a week ago. He is undertaking important intelligence work, answering directly to General Wolseley.'

'Ah, I see.' Bonard looked down at his desk and rearranged a small pile of telegraph forms there. When he looked up, his manner and expression seemed unchanged, but Alice knew she had won. The slight cloud that had entered the room at the mention of Simon's intervention had disappeared, and Bonard's smile now seemed less strained. She had gambled that no editor could resist employing a seasoned journalist who – weak and feeble woman though she might be – had a direct line through to the commander-in-chief of the army in the field.

Bonard cleared his throat. 'As I said, your attitude does you credit, madam, and in this modern age, I certainly would not approve of the placing of . . . what shall I call it . . . any artificial restraints on a person's legitimate ambition to further her career. I shall therefore be delighted to offer you a position as an accredited representative of Reuters with General Wolseley's column – if, that is, you feel that your husband will not intervene with the General and persuade him to reject you?'

Alice had thought this through. It was another gamble but one on which she felt she could wager with confidence. Although Simon had told her nothing of his mission, she felt convinced that he would stay in Cairo only long enough to be briefed before setting out up the Nile and then into the forbidding wastes of the Sudan, out of contact with Wolseley. He would therefore not know of her appointment until his return – too late to intervene. 'Oh no,' she said. 'He would never consider doing such a thing once you have appointed me. He would, you see,' she smiled sweetly, 'have played his hand and lost, and he would accept that.'

Bonard roared with laughter and slapped his thigh. It was clear that he was amused by this strange marital battle. 'You remind me of Joan of Arc,' he chuckled. 'Though as a Frenchman, perhaps I should not say that to an English lady.'

Alice inclined her head. 'I consider it a compliment, sir.' She smiled.

'There is one more thing I must put to you, dear lady.' Bonard's face was now quite serious. 'I appreciate that you have faced danger in the many campaigns that you have covered for the *Post*. Indeed,' a ghost of a smile flickered across his features and then was gone, 'it is one of the reasons why I was attracted to you working for us. In news agency work, courage is often as important as the ability to write and to gather information. You will understand, of course?'

Alice nodded, a little puzzled at the way the conversation was going.

'Good. Well, it has become very clear that the Sudan is an unusually dangerous part of the world. The Dervishes, as well as being fanatically brave – they believe that being killed by unbelievers automatically gives them a place in Paradise, and they therefore almost throw themselves on to British bayonets – are also incredibly cruel. They usually kill the enemy they wound in battle, and they pay no regard to the niceties of gender differentiation.' The Frenchman's face was now a study in disgust. 'If a woman in their society commits adultery, she is stoned to death.'

'So I have heard,' said Alice, trying to sound non-committal.

'Yes, well, this cruelty extends to non-combatants, such as journalists. You will know, of course, that Edmund O'Donovan of the *Daily News* was killed back in '81 when General Hicks and his force was massacred by the Mahdists?'

'Yes.'

'You will also know that *The Times* had a man installed with Gordon in Khartoum?'

Alice nodded. 'Of course. Frank Power, I knew him. I have been reading with admiration the few pieces he has been able to smuggle out of the city.'

'Well, I am sorry to tell you that we have just heard that he and Gordon's second-in-command, Colonel Stewart, together with the French consul in Khartoum, have all lost their lives. It seems that Gordon decided that they must leave Khartoum as the Dervishes closed in. They escaped on one of the small steamers that Gordon still retains.' Bonard gave a Gallic shrug. 'After successfully running the gauntlet of the Dervish fire, they got some way downriver and then ran aground. A local sheik offered them food and shelter and then had them all murdered. Their heads were cut off and sent to the Mahdi.'

Closing her eyes, Alice shook her head in disgust. 'I am so sorry. Power was a good man and a fine journalist.'

'Indeed. But you see how dangerous this awful place is.' Bonard's face was now quite grave. 'Admittedly, you will be with Lord Wolseley's column and therefore under the army's protection. But Wolseley's force will be vastly outnumbered by the Dervishes, and unlike in other campaigns, these savages are well armed. Everyone in the General's little army – soldiers and civilians alike – will be in danger. Are you quite sure that you are prepared for not only great discomfort, but also great danger?'

Alice's heart seemed almost to stop as Bonard spoke. She thought of Simon out there in that brutal land and appreciated anew the perils facing him. Then, realising that any hesitation might be misconstrued, she nodded her head slowly. 'I am quite prepared, Monsieur Bonard, to face the dangers you describe.' She forced a smile. 'It is, after all, part of the job, is it not?'

Her smile was returned. 'Very well,' said Bonard. 'I felt it only . . .'

He was interrupted by the arrival of tea. As they drank, and nibbled biscuits, Alice's last apprehension about the work she would have to undertake was removed when Bonard confirmed that Reuters already had a man out in Egypt who would be joining the expedition to report the hard news. She, however, would be free to express herself, as with the *Morning Post*, by writing more discursive feature pieces on the back of hard news developments. It was exactly what she would have wished, although she resolved she would work damned hard to scoop her colleague whenever she could. It was, after all, a man's world, and she had always used male tactics to survive in it. To hell with them all!

On the train returning to Norfolk later that day, with rail tickets for Brindisi and steamship tickets for Alexandria safely in her bag, she thought again of Simon. In the corner of her compartment she clasped her hands together and silently prayed for his safety.

Chapter 5

The strip of land some hundred and eighty miles wide that separated the two stretches of the Nile in its great loop to the north was a wilderness of rocks and ravines and gullies. It lacked the soft sand and dunes of the west and north-west, but it was even more inhospitable in that the fresh-water wells were fewer and the distances between them greater.

In the three days they had been travelling since the river crossing, Fonthill and his companions had seen no one in this inhospitable land, where rock and hard gravel lay under their feet and the sun beat down on them with an intensity even greater than before. Simon estimated that the temperature must be in the hundred and twenties. In the distance, shimmering in the furnace-like heat, they could make out a purple smudge on the horizon – the hills, he hoped, where they would find water at Jakdul Wells, the only source for ninety miles. He had decided not to take the well-established trail that led directly to Berber, for he wished to defer further confrontation with parties of Dervish warriors as long as possible, and he also felt that the town, now a hotbed of Mahdism, would be a dangerous place for them. Instead, he had set a course for the small township of Metemmeh, on the Nile yet some hundred miles further south. The journey across the desert would take longer in distance as well as precious time, but Fonthill felt it would be safer and they should be able to reach Jakdul well before their water ran out.

Yet as they trudged along, the hills seemed to grow smaller, more distant. Even the camels began to feel the heat, and their pace slowed. Simon estimated that they were now making progress at a rate of less than twenty-five miles in their twelve-hour travelling day, far slower than he wanted, for Gordon was surrounded!

Night brought blessed relief, when the temperature dropped to what seemed like a pleasant seventy degrees and they were able to lie on their backs and stare up at a sky that was bejewelled with diamond stars. Now, although the North Star was still well in sight, the Southern Cross had appeared above the horizon, as though to lure them onwards. The desert's brief moments of dusk conjured up memories of the beautiful grey eyes Simon had left far behind him. Thinking of the problems they might face on reaching Khartoum, he decided to discover a little more about Mustapha and his knowledge of the city. On the third night, he invited the boy to bring his bed roll near to him.

'Who were your parents, Mustapha?' he asked.

The boy's ever-present grin disappeared. 'I don't know properly,' he said, in that sing-song voice incongruously inflected by the brogue of the Irish nuns. 'I think my father was slave, captured in the south and brought to Khartoum. He dark, I think. People dark in the south. You know that Arabic name for this country is Bilad-es-Sudan, means Land of the Blacks. This means those people. My mother, they say, was woman from the north, lighter skin, you know.'

'Was she a slave too?'

'Oh yes. Everybody slave in Khartoum. Big market there for slaves. They come downriver to be sold.'

Simon recalled that the Sudanese had only three trading commodities: ivory, gum and slaves. And of the three, slaves were by far the largest. He knew that Gordon, in his previous roles as governor general of Equatoria in the south and then of the Sudan, had worked untiringly to put down slavery but with only little success. Yet six months ago, on arriving in Berber, Gordon had issued a proclamation declaring that slavery was legal again – presumably to win popularity and ease the way for the withdrawal of all the Egyptian outposts in the Sudan. Fonthill sighed.

'Don't you remember your parents?'

'No, master. Remember only nuns. Irish ladies, famous in Khartoum.'

'Did the nuns bring you up, then?'

Mustapha gave his great wraparound grin, lightening the darkness. 'Yes, until they gave me to merchant man to give me work there. Man was bad, so he was, and sold me as slave to make money. But man you killed was worse. He beat me all day.'

Fonthill groaned inwardly. The memory of killing two men in cold blood – the second already wounded – had weighed heavily with him since the encounter. What an example to set to a young boy! He tried to make amends. 'Killing another human being is never a good thing to do, you know, Mustapha,' he said, blinking up at the three belt stars of Orion. 'It should only be done in the last extreme.'

'What you mean?'

'Well . . . er . . . if the man you kill will kill you if you don't kill him first.'

'Ah. Was my master going to kill you, then?'

'What? Oh, well . . . perhaps he was, I am not sure. But he was certainly going to whip you, and shooting him seemed, at the time, the only way of stopping him. It was . . . um . . . rather extreme, I grant you.' He turned to face the boy. 'I acted in haste and I am not sure I did right, however.'

'Why not? He whipping me, wasn't he?'

'Yes, well. Never mind.' Simon gave up. 'Tell me how well you know Khartoum.'

'What you mean, master?'

Fonthill realised that the boy had a directness and honesty that was unusual and rather endearing. 'Well, you know that the army of the Mahdi is camped all around the city and is trying to get Gordon Pasha to surrender?'

'Yes. Other master say that Gordon Pasha was ...' he hesitated as he sought the right words, 'bad man. He not believe in the Expected One nor in Allah. He not ... er ... darlin' boy at all.'

Simon grinned at the Irish colloquialism. 'Yes, he certainly does not think that the Mahdi is the Expected One, the new prophet. Nor do we. We believe that he is just a political holy man who wants power. But Gordon Pasha certainly believes in Allah – Allah, his own God. But that is by the way. Listen, Mustapha, we want to get in to Khartoum without the Mahdi's soldiers stopping us. Do you know a way into the city that we can use without being seen?'

'Of course.'

'What?'

'Oh yes.' The boy was grinning again, pleased that he had knowledge not possessed by his new master. 'People – ordinary people, not soldiers – come and go through little gate all the time. Sometimes they caught but not often. I can do it.'

'That is splendid, Mustapha. Just what I wanted to hear. But more of this later; now get some sleep.' He regarded the boy with affection. 'We have some hard riding to do tomorrow in the sun. We must start well before dawn.'

'Yes, master.'

*

Fonthill had decided that, given the conditions, it was best to start their journey each day at three a.m. and ride as far as possible in the cool of darkness and daybreak before the sun came up. Then they would rest as best they could at midday before continuing in the late afternoon. The little camp, then, stirred very early the next morning, and Simon was pulling on his sandals when Jenkins strode up to him, his face severe in the semi-darkness.

'We've got an 'ell of a problem, bach sir.'

'What?'

The Welshman held out his goatskin water sack. 'Bloody thing's virtually empty.'

'Well, did you finish it last night? That was stupid.'

'No. It's this sack, see. These thread things used to sew it together 'ave allowed the water to seep through in the night an' nicely wet the bleedin' sand, look you.'

Fonthill gripped the sack. There was only a little pool of precious liquid at the bottom. As he looked up in consternation, a cry came from Ahmed. 'My water sack has emptied, Simon.'

'Oh God!' Fonthill rolled over and reached for his own sack. The thing had virtually collapsed and he too had only a spoonful left at the bottom of the goatskin.

'But the damned things have worked well enough over the last few days . . .' They had decided to carry their water in goatskin sacks on the advice of experienced desert travellers in Cairo. These *girbas* had the pleasant property of allowing a small amount of evaporation, keeping the liquid almost cool. The sacks had served them well until the second crossing of the Nile.

Ahmed joined them. He held up the thread from his own goatskin sack. 'It has rotted.' He shook his head. 'That is why people at the river wondered why we changed bags with leather thongs. Leather thongs swell when wetted and make bag watertight, they say, but I thought captain *effendi*, as white man, would know better, et cetera, et cetera. I am sorry, Simon.' He hung his head.

Fonthill's eyes narrowed. 'It's not your fault, Ahmed. It's mine for being taken in by that bastard Hicks-Johnson.' He shook his head. 'Ha, a word of advice indeed! He was trying to kill us. No doubt about it. What a swine!' He rose to his feet. 'Let's see exactly how much water we have left.'

But Mustapha's bag was also empty, and the little water they had left between them hardly filled the small tin mug that Simon carried. Fonthill beckoned to the others and they all squatted in the sand in a semicircle.

'Right,' he said, 'I reckon we have come about ninety miles – perhaps rather less – and that we have the same distance to go. That's about three days with just this amount of water between us.' He held up the mug. 'If we meet someone, perhaps we can beg a little water, but we have been alone so far and clearly this is a track that is hardly used. Consequently, gentlemen,' he gave a grim smile, 'it looks as though we are in for a very hard time. If necessary, we can kill a camel and drink its blood, but I am not sure that that would be a good thing for us.'

He frowned and desperately tried to recall the little he had ever been told about survival. It had not been exactly a prime curriculum subject at Sandhurst. 'I will carry the water we do have in this cup wrapped in the goatskins. We must ration it and only take a sip each at morning, midday and night. This means that we shall have probably nothing left for our last day, but we should reach the wells at Jakdul by that evening.' He smiled. 'At least the camels will be all right; I only wish we could regurgitate liquid the way they do. I read somewhere that a man can last three days in the desert without water. I estimate that we do have three days, but we also have a little water, so we should get through if we are disciplined and if we don't have to fight a pitched battle.'

Ahmed wrinkled his brow. 'What kind of battle is pitched, Simon, please?'

Jenkins cleared his throat. 'Oh, it's one where you put your 'ands in buckets of black pitch and throw the stuff at each other,' he explained.

'Ah, I see.'

Fonthill sighed. 'Thank you for that, 352. It was most helpful. Now listen. There are some things we can do to reduce the thirst.' He reached to the ground and picked up a round pebble. 'Pick a couple of these before the sun gets on them, and while they are cool, put them in your mouth. It should help to produce saliva. Breathe through your nose to prevent water vapour escaping through your mouth and – 352, listen – cut down on the talking. By the same token we must ride passively to conserve energy, and above all try to reduce the amount we perspire. Sweat is precious water leaving our bodies. And I am afraid that we must cut down on what we eat, because our bodies use water to digest food.

'From now on, we ride only at night and try and sleep during the day, but we must make a start now while we are quite strong. Ah, one more thing. If you have to pass water – and the need to do so will obviously recede the further we go – pee on your handkerchief and use it to moisten your lips and the inside of your mouth. It won't kill us. All right? Any questions?'

There were none. Jenkins and Ahmed nodded glumly. Mustapha grinned, as though it was a great game.

Fonthill handed round the cup. They each took a sip, carefully licking their lips to ensure that no drops had escaped, and then they all mounted and set off.

*

The first few hours, of course, were quite bearable, and it was true that the stones helped to moisten the mouth, until they became hot and had to be tossed aside. Then, as the sun began to climb towards its zenith, each one became aware of his thirst. For his part, Simon concentrated on following his compass bearing towards those distant mauve hills that never seemed to get any nearer. He also tried to conjure up the face of Alice: softly waved fair hair, even white teeth, small, slightly retroussé nose and those wonderful grey eyes . . . It diverted him for a few minutes, but no more.

Then, as his mouth grew increasingly dry and his tongue seemingly larger, Fonthill's thoughts inevitably turned to Hicks-Johnson. He could not conceive that an Englishman, a fellow officer, could deliberately have caused them to change their water bags, knowing that they were about to enter one of the most arid parts of the world, where the efficient carrying of water often presented the difference between life and death. He doubted if even the Dervishes would break such a fundamental rule of the desert: kill your enemy by all means, but don't let him die of thirst. He ran his tongue over cracked lips. Why should the man have done that? Being captured in front of his men, as they stood impotently by, was surely an insufficient reason to condemn fellow nationals to a slow death? And why the fuss in the first place? Presumably because his sense of *amour propre* as an intelligence officer was offended by not being told of their presence in his area. What tosh!

Simon shook his head slowly. He knew that Queen Victoria's army had faults at the top. The army's commander-in-chief at the Horse Guards, the Duke of Cambridge, was the Queen's cousin and one of the most reactionary elements in Her Majesty's armed services, whose basic view was that the great Duke of Wellington had got most things right sixty years before and therefore there was no need to change the way the army was structured. Yet for every Cambridge there were Wolseleys and Robertses, bright and able young generals pushing for reform and, gradually, achieving it. Most of the officer class were first rate: able and, above all, brave. A minority, however, were fundamentally stupid men who risked the lives of the courageous soldiers under them by their lack of professionalism. The Empire had thrived despite such men. Now one of them had done his best to hand down a death sentence on Fonthill and his companions. Simon looked at them now, drooping on their saddles, their heads down and all of them trying desperately not to think of water. Well, damn Hicks-Johnson! He wouldn't win!

At midday they halted, tethered their camels and rigged makeshift shelters under which to hide from the sun. They all moved slowly now, not only because of Fonthill's strictures to avoid creating excessive perspiration – they were sweating enough anyway – but also because their thirst was making them listless.

Simon unravelled the scraps of goatskin and produced the precious tin cup. As he had feared, evaporation had reduced the contents somewhat. On a thought, he rummaged in the pack on one of the camels and produced two small bottles from his modest medical bundle: quinine and iodine. He poured a little from each bottle into the cup. Well, it was liquid, at least, and would help their water go just a little further, and the chemical properties would do them no harm.

The four of them sipped with care, wrinkling their noses at the taste. The liquid, however, did give them some solace, and with Fonthill squatting rifle in hand and taking first watch, the others composed themselves to sleep as best they could under their shelters.

As Simon sat, he looked around him, mouth open at the desolation that surrounded them. Rocks were now breaking through the surface of the plain – a development that he took as a welcome sign that they were nearing, however imperceptibly, the hills that housed the wells. Nothing stirred, however, except the occasional scorpion scuttling in the sand or a lizard slowly moving its tail as it lay happily in the blazing sun on the side of a boulder. White ants went about their strenuous business. Did they not need water? Nothing was growing in the yellow-brown earth. Overhead, there were no birds to present the hope that a lucky shot might provide a trickle of blood for them to eke out their remaining water just a little further. Simon took out his knife with the thought that a snake might obligingly offer another source of liquid. But nothing of substance seemed to be alive in this awful place. Everything was quiet, except the four of them, stirring occasionally.

With the sun moving down towards the west, they set off again, saying nothing, mounting their camels and moving towards the distant line of hills, which, at last, seemed to be palpably nearer, although still smudged in the heat haze. Mustapha's life-affirming grin had long since disappeared, and Fonthill's concern lay more with him than the others, for the boy was thin and must surely have less resistance to hardship, despite his tough upbringing. But there was little he could do for him except occasionally give him a cracked, warm – oh yes, warm all right! – smile.

They plodded on through much of the night, heads nodding with the pendulum movement of the camels, Simon refusing to stop while the comparative cool of the darkness nurtured them and reduced somewhat the pangs of thirst. They had all employed the handkerchief trick, but now their urine was a yellowish brown and, despite their need, no one could bring himself to apply the filthy cloth to his mouth. What saliva anyone had left was thick and foul-tasting.

Just before dawn, Fonthill called a halt and they drank what was left of their water. The liquid, of course, was almost hot now, but it was still savoured by each man. Simon only pretended to drink, merely wetting his lips and gesturing to Mustapha to take his share and finish the cup. Then they lay to rest, still, however, taking it in turns to stand guard, for Fonthill reasoned that the nearer they got to Jakdul Wells, the more chance they would have of meeting Dervishes.

The next day was a nightmare for them all. The last drop of the water, taken only a few hours before, seemed a distant memory, and none of them could sleep. Fonthill decided therefore that they would reduce their midday halt, for they had to gamble that they would reach the wells before they all expired.

So it was that, with the sun almost directly overhead, they walked on, even the camels now seeming to falter in their stride. At this point, Simon fingered his Colt and wondered whether the time had come to shoot one of the pack animals and drink its blood. But he dredged up from his memory the half-forgotten warning that consuming the blood of an animal such as this would transmit life-threatening bacteria to the drinker. He put away the revolver.

He seemed to have acquired a lump in his throat, and both neck and head were throbbing with pain, prompted by what seemed to be a great tightening of the skin across the face, neck and scalp. His tongue had hardened into a senseless weight that clung to the roof of his mouth, and he found difficulty in swallowing.

Occasionally, bouts of dizziness would descend on him, forcing him to clutch at the saddle to stop himself falling.

At one point, a strange, leafless bush materialised from out of the harsh floor of the desert, and Jenkins half fell from his mount, knife in hand. Simon tried to mouth a warning that the shrub might be the poisonous tree of the desert, but he could not speak and the Welshman hacked at the trunk, split it open and held it up. Nothing came from it. It was as devoid of liquid as anything else within their range of vision. Jenkins gave a wry, lipless smile and threw it away. They rode on.

Through the night they travelled, by the light of a moon whose merry brightness seemed to mock their misery. Between bouts of dizziness and moments of nodding sleep, Fonthill, in the lead, forced himself to consult his luminous compass so that the little cavalcade, now strung out over a distance of some two hundred yards, remained on course.

At some point in the half-darkness, he became aware that the last camel – that of Mustapha – was riderless. He hauled round the head of his beast and held up a hand to halt the others, who watched him with lacklustre eyes as he rode by them. About a quarter of a mile to the rear he found the boy, trying to crawl on his hands and knees to keep up with the convoy. Slowly, Simon dismounted and picked up the little body, threw it over his shoulder and mounted again, lowering Mustapha on to the hump of the beast, virtually on his lap. With one arm around the boy, they plodded on to rejoin the others.

A little before dawn, Fonthill realised that the track was beginning to climb and that their camels' pads were starting to slide a little on bare rock. It was difficult to see their surroundings clearly in the poor light, but it was clear that they were moving upwards between rocks that rose high on either side of them. Simon tried to recall the little he had been told of Jakdul. The wells, he remembered, were on a kind of small plateau, surrounded by jagged hills that erupted with hardly any warning out of the plain. He realised that his camel had lifted its head, as though sniffing the air, and had begun to increase its pace. It smelt water!

Weary, dizzy and half-conscious as he was, Simon, however, also smelled danger. He held up his arm until the others drew alongside. He tried to speak, but the lump of iron that was his tongue hardly moved. Eventually he was able to croak.

'Nearly there,' he whispered. 'Might meet Dervish at the wells. If questioned, Ahmed say we lost water bags in accident. We're Syrians, remember. Have guns ready but covered. Ahmed lead.'

Cautiously they crept upwards. But within the hour, it was impossible to restrain the camels. Scenting water, they broke into a lumbering gallop, and it was all their riders could do to hang on. Fonthill was aware that they were charging through a scattering of tents on either side, but there was no stopping the beasts, who careered between a screen of boulders. Just ahead, he caught a glimpse of starlight reflecting upon . . . yes . . . water!

Disregarding their riders, the camels shouldered their way forward and sank their snouts in a low pool. Ahmed flung himself down and plunged his face into the water, but Jenkins, rifle in hand, slid down from his beast and held up his hand to Simon. 'Give me the boy,' he croaked. Simon did so and followed him down to the ground. 'You drink with the boy,' said Jenkins. 'I'll keep watch.'

Nodding gratefully, Fonthill carried a semi-conscious Mustapha to the edge of the pool and laid him down. He cupped water in his hand and poured it gently on to the boy's face and then into his half-open mouth. The lad coughed and his eyes widened. Immediately, he twisted in Simon's grasp and plunged his face into the pool. Simon summoned up a grin to Jenkins, gulped down two handfuls of the brackish but nectar-like water, stood, took the Welshman's gun and gestured to him to drink also. He then stayed on guard for a moment, but realising that somehow their mad dash to the water had gone undetected by whoever was sharing the wells with them, he laid down the rifle and began drinking again.

Eventually they had had their fill and they all lay back gasping, although the camels stayed methodically gulping down the water. Fonthill stood – and then immediately collapsed, his head swirling. Shaking it, he was able to push himself slowly on to all fours and looked around. The camp remained silent, but he could make out five low-lying Bedawi-like tents pitched either side of the track they had followed. As far as he could see, there were no other occupants at the wells.

They were in no condition to move yet, however. They had all drunk too much and too quickly, particularly Mustapha, who now lay doubled up with pain in his stomach.

Jenkins nodded to him. ' 'E'll be all right,' he gasped. 'What 'e wants are a few good belches and lots of farts.' He rumbled and then burped himself. 'There you are,' he said. 'Feel much better now.'

Fonthill picked up the boy and made him sit upright. Then he pushed his head into his knees, irrelevantly recalling touchline treatment while winded during a schooldays rugby match. 'Take deep breaths, now, lad,' he urged. 'Then you'll feel better.'

He looked around carefully again. All seemed quiet in the tents, some one hundred and fifty yards away. The camels had now ceased drinking and instead stood issuing great malodorous belches of their own. Simon nodded to where a small circle of rocks could be seen, away from the other dwellers on the plateau. 'Let's move over there and set up camp,' he said. 'Come on. We can't stay here all night and we must not draw attention to ourselves. Move the animals.'

They found that the presence of water had created ground growth and they were able to stake the camels so that they could graze. Then they set up their bivouac-type shelters within the rock enclosure, and once more taking it in turns to stand guard, with Fonthill claiming first watch, they slept exhaustedly.

They all woke late the next day, feeling weak and dispirited but with a ravening hunger. As Jenkins prepared food, Simon took a long look at their fellow tenants of the wells. To his relief, they were not wearing the patched, multicoloured *jibbas* of the Mahdi, and they seemed to be completely uninterested in the activities of the newcomers, washing clothes and cooking over languidly smoking fires. He called Ahmed.

'Who are they?'

Ahmed shaded his eyes. 'I don't know, Simon. Just because I am Egyptian, I don't know everything. I don't know nothing about this bloody desert. Perhaps the boy . . .?'

Simon waved Mustapha over to them and pointed. 'Who do you think they are, lad?'

The boy's great grin had quickly returned. 'Oh, they black men from the south. Not Mahdi soldiers, but I think . . .' his eyes narrowed in concentration, 'they traders, come this way so not to meet slavers. Look, they have pots and pans and things.'

Fonthill grinned. 'Well, that's a relief. Ahmed, we urgently need water skins – sewn with leather thongs this time.' He gave the Egyptian a handful of coins. 'See if you can buy them. Oh, and see if they have come from the south-east, the direction we are going, and ask if the wells at Abu Klea on the way to the Nile are easy to find. Also find out if there are Dervishes that way. But don't give the impression that we are trying to avoid anyone. We're Syrians, remember, good

Mosselmen, come to join the Mahdi in his great *jihad*.'

Ahmed returned a half-hour later bearing five water skins and a large smile. 'Good bargain with the skins,' he said, depositing coins in Simon's hand. 'They heard us arrive last night but thought we were slavers, so they stay trembling in their beds. They have come from Equatoria in the south and they have ivory. But I do not buy anything . . . well, except this. For my hotel in Cairo. Good, eh?' He showed Fonthill a small carved head.

'Oh, delightful. What about the wells and the Dervishes?'

'Ah. They say some people at the wells – there are always people at wells – and they may be Dervishes, et cetera, et cetera, et cetera. Wells easy to find because trail leads through hills. Can we stay here rest of day please, Simon? Stomach not good.'

They did indeed stay resting through the day, but Fonthill insisted that they set off before dusk, their water skins full and their stomachs recovering from the harsh treatment imposed during the previous three days. The distance to their destination on this last stretch of the Nile was now only some fifty miles, with the wells at Abu Klea a little over halfway. Simon hoped fervently that they would encounter no trouble on this comparatively untrammelled route, for he knew that their difficulties would renew again once they met the Nile. The question there would be whether they should take to the water again to reach Khartoum, and whether the Dervishes would accept them as Syrians and true followers. He gulped, but urged the others on. They had wasted a day they could ill afford. Gordon awaited them – if he was still alive!

Chapter 6

On the morning of the third day after leaving Jakdul, the little party stood on an incline and looked down at the brown, oleaginous waters of the Nile once again. This last part of their journey had been uneventful, which was just as well, for they were still weak from their days with little or no water, and the ride, which perforce had to be taken at a gentle pace, enabled them to recover to some extent from their ordeal.

Their approach to Abu Klea had to be taken with great caution, for the wells seemed to be tenanted by a multifarious collection of Sudanese. As they picked their way between the tents, with their heads down, Mustapha, who had recovered from their hardships quicker than anyone, took great pleasure in quietly pointing out to Fonthill the ethnic origins of his fellow countrymen, particularly those of the south, from where his father came. They included the Dinka, Nuer, Shilluk and other Nilotes from Equatoria and the Upper Nile, most of them slaves and evincing some of the clear-cut features of Mustapha himself: thin lips, high foreheads and high-bridged but generally unflared noses. A handful of distinctive Hadendowe warriors from the north-east were refilling their water bags. Simon realised that these were the famous 'Fuzzy Wuzzies', with their mass of tightly curled black hair, carrying their great crucifix-handled swords and wearing lightly their reputation as the fiercest of all the Sudanese fighters. Most numerous of all, however, were the Dervishes, wearing the patches of their leader, the Mahdi.

Yet no one took the slightest notice of these latest arrivals from Syria, with their little string of camels. Fonthill was reminded of what he had been told in Cairo: that there were a hundred and fifteen languages spoken in the Sudan, and that even the ubiquitous spoken Arabic of the north and the centre was expressed in very many dialects. This multiculturalism reduced somewhat his unease at the fact that he and Jenkins spoke no Arabic. And their appearance raised no interest. It seemed that they fitted into the cultural jigsaw.

From Abu Klea, they had hurried on across fissured, rocky ground on the last lap of the trail that led to the Nile, and had emerged just south of the small town of Metemmeh, which they could now see huddled against the river on their left. The Nile itself was studded with the white sails of craft heading up- and downriver, and individual clusters of habitation clung to the river banks, surrounded by green patches of cultivated *durra*. It was a tranquil, peaceful scene: no massed ranks of Dervishes and no evidence that the country was at war with its Egyptian and Turkish overlords. It was a reassuring sight for Fonthill, and he called a council of war as they squatted underneath a tumble of rocks and ate cooked *durra* cakes.

'I estimate we have about another eighty miles or so to go to reach Khartoum,' he said. 'The river runs due south here straight to the city, but we would have to pass through the last cataract – the sixth.' Jenkins groaned.

'However, even though we will be sailing upstream,' Fonthill continued, 'I think the river would be the quickest way. Not much is known about this last cataract, but I have heard that it is quieter than the others. The main point, however, is that I think that hiring a boat would be safer, in that we would not have to mix with Dervishes, as we would if we followed the river on the bank with the camels. And I don't like the idea of continuing to use camels that were once owned by Dervishes. You never know. They might be recognised, and then we would have some awkward questions to answer.'

'Would there be crocodiles in this catapult place, then?' asked Jenkins, his brows descending like a black bar above his eyes.

Simon turned to Mustapha. 'You're our crocodile expert,' he said. 'Are there any *timsah* in the Nile at the Sixth Cataract?'

Mustapha grinned. 'Only friendly ones, master.'

'Oh, that's fine, then,' muttered Jenkins. 'There's nothin' I like better than a friendly croc.'

Ahmed stroked his beard, which, in contrast to the unruly growths of Fonthill and Jenkins, he had continued to groom through all their vicissitudes, so that it was neatly pointed, as though from a Van Dyck painting. 'Boats here will be expensive, I think,' he said. 'Do we have money left?'

'Oh yes.' Fonthill nodded. 'But I wish to retain as much as I can. We will sell the camels here. I think you should be able to get a reasonable price for them, Ahmed, eh?'

'Yes, indeed.' Ahmed's eyes lit up at the prospect of negotiating a profitable business transaction.

'Good.' Simon rose. 'Let's get down there, then. The sooner we can sell the camels and find a boat, the better.'

In fact it was nightfall before the various negotiations were completed. The sale of the camels was concluded quite quickly, but finding a boatman happy to take them through the Sixth Cataract was less easy. Eventually, a *filuka* owner emerged who offered to essay the journey for a price that Ahmed said would keep the man reasonably wealthy for the rest of his days. More to the point, however, he had what appeared to be a stout craft, but small enough to forge a passage through the rapids and rocks of the cataract – and, equally importantly, light enough to be hauled through by ropes from the shore. His passengers, he warned, would have to undertake this task.

That suited Jenkins, the bravest of men but whose terror of heights was only exceeded by his fear of water. 'I'd rather pull five barges with a rope on dry land than wade in that river,' he growled. 'As long as the crocs get out of the way on the bank, that is, see.'

They sailed at first light the next morning, a welcome breeze from the north-east filling the lanteen sail and aborting the need for them to row against the current. Ibrahim, their boatman, soon revealed himself to be a sleepy soul, who sang tunelessly to himself as he sat by the long tiller at the stern. Once again, Fonthill and Jenkins had to revert to their roles as devout Muslims, joining Ahmed in praying five times a day. Mustapha, as befitted a Christian brought up by good Irish nuns, ostentatiously eschewed such devotions – and Simon could not but wonder if this perverse dedication to the religion of his tutors had not caused many of his beatings.

After the vicissitudes of their overland journey to Jakdul Wells, it was pleasant to sprawl on the bottom of the little craft, doing their best to avoid the heat of the sun and half dozing. Jenkins pointed out that they should treat the lash marks on Mustapha's back, some of which had opened up again following his fall from the camel, and he rubbed butter into the wounds. Fonthill took the opportunity to question the boy further.

'How long is it since you left Khartoum?' he asked.

'About three months, I think.'

'So the city was already surrounded and cut off when you left?'

'Oh yes. But, as I say, local people go in and out sometimes. To trade and so on.'

'Why was your master so far in the north?'

'He going to Dongola, to talk to Mudir to say join the Mahdi or we come and kill you when we come north.'

'Ah, I see. Had the Mahdi sent him?'

The boy shook his head. 'No. It was the Khalifa Abdullah. He Mahdi's . . . ah . . . chief disciple. Strong man.'

Fonthill frowned. 'This could be awkward. So your master was also an important man in Mahdi's army to be given such a mission?'

Mustapha shrugged. 'Don't know. He just beat me, that's all.'

'Yes, but when we get to Khartoum and to the Mahdi's forces surrounding the town, will you be recognised and will they ask you where your master is?'

The boy grinned in derision. 'Me just a slave boy. Plenty of slave boys there. Nobody know me.'

'Mmmm. Even so, if you are asked what happened to your master, I think you should say that you met a British patrol – as, indeed, *we* did – and that he and his party were killed by the soldiers, but that you escaped and we took you in. Will you remember?'

'Oh yes, master.'

The tranquillity of that first morning soon changed and it became clear that the river was growing shallower and that rapids of differing degrees of severity were becoming the norm. The luxury of sailing upstream soon gave way to hard rowing and paddling as the small craft bounced between the rocks that now split the water ahead of them. At this point the river was not dangerous, for the water was not hissing and boiling as in their passage through the earlier cataracts. But the passengers had become crewmen, and everyone, save Ibrahim at the tiller, had to pull on the oars or dip the paddles deep to make headway.

The river had become capricious now, in fact, and the smooth passages that existed between the outbreaks of rapids were not long enough to make the unfurling of the sail worthwhile, so that headway was slow. It was all extremely tiring, and the members of the little group were worn out at the end of each day and grateful to creep into their blankets in the cool of the evening on the river bank, too fatigued even to stand watch. It became clear to Fonthill that he had made a mistake in taking the river route to Khartoum, for they would probably have made faster time on their camels riding south on the bank. And yet the little *filuka* kept its promise of keeping them away from prying eyes. They comprised a party discrete and secluded, with only Ibrahim outside it – and he evinced not the slightest interest in them or why they were making this difficult and dangerous journey.

On the morning of the fourth day, the character of the river changed again. The banks seemed to close in and they began to approach a deep gorge. In the distance they heard a booming noise, like faraway thunder. They were approaching the Sixth Cataract. 'Oh shit,' exclaimed Jenkins.

The gorge was lined with black basalt slabs that absorbed the sun's rays to the extent that they were hot to touch, and the boulders that bordered the river's edge were slippery and difficult to scramble across. The Nile here became angry, bouncing its water between rocks that stood like clenched fists. The boatman, his singing now a thing of the past, hurled his orders via Ahmed and Mustapha.

They developed three different techniques for taking their little craft against the white water. The first was to paddle and row hard up to the larger of the rocks in their lee, making reasonable headway in the narrow channel of comparatively smooth water behind the rock, and then, at the very last minute, to move out into the maelstrom of white water, digging in paddles and oars until they had passed the rock and could find the next patch free of turbulence. When the flow of water was too strong to move against, the passengers would take a line attached to the prow and clamber along the bank, pulling hard as Ibrahim steered between the foam-spattered rocks in mid-river. Skill had to be exercised to ensure that the rope did not dip slackly into the water, for the boat would then bounce and veer, threatening to overturn and bringing shrieks and imprecations from Ibrahim. When neither of these techniques prevailed, then, at the last extreme, and when the width of the river allowed, a hawser was stretched across it some way ahead, or between a tree and a finger of rock in the river, and a block and tackle attached so that the boat could be hauled up, inches at a time. But this latter method was so time-consuming to set up and difficult to operate that it was used only twice.

'Why don't we just lift the bloody boat out of the water and carry it around these bad bits?' demanded Jenkins at one stage, perspiration mingling with spray and coursing down his face on to his beard.

'Porterage, you mean?' said Fonthill. Then he shook his head. 'Too damned heavy, and I don't know how far we would have to carry the blasted thing to go round these gorges. Probably miles out into the desert. We would also have to hump it on our shoulders, and I don't fancy scorpions from the bottom dropping down inside our shirts. No, thank you.'

When the water was running too fast between the rocks, they unloaded the stores and these were carried along the river's edge to lighten the boat so that it could be paddled or pulled. On the whole, however, it proved easier to have some weight, at least, within the *filuka* to give it stability.

They had neared what they hoped was the end of the cataract when near disaster struck. Mustapha, by far the most agile of them all and quite the most fearless, was sitting on the bulwark of the boat paddling and chatting to Fonthill, his head constantly turning. Suddenly the bow struck a rock and the boy was hurled backwards into the water. A good swimmer, he twisted like an eel in the torrent to regain the *filuka*, but then a swirl of current took him and crashed his head into a rock, leaving a trail of crimson dancing in the white water.

Fonthill immediately tore off his *jibba and* plunged over the stern of the boat into the river, employing a strong crawl stroke to propel him fast downstream, surging narrowly between the rocks that jutted above the surface. Even so, it was unlikely that he would have caught up with the boy if Mustapha had not been swept up against a squat shoulder of rock, leaving him momentarily coiled around it, like flotsam caught round a tree root. Simon thrust out a hand to pluck at his *jibba*, but a freak surge of water seized the boy again and tossed him well out of Fonthill's reach, back into the narrow channel of green, white-topped water bouncing and dancing between the rocks. Simon himself was then thrown against the rock, causing pain to surge through his body. Both hands holding fingertip tight to the stone, he paused long enough to take a deep breath before kicking against the rock and launching himself back into the current in a desperate race to catch up with Mustapha.

'Back, back, back!' shrieked Jenkins, waving his arms to Ibrahim. The English words were lost on the helmsman but the order was unnecessary, for he was already allowing the boat to surge back with the current, steering the blunt stern of the *filuka* between the rocks with consummate skill. The craft seemed almost to be surfing down the white water, its additional weight giving it impetus that threatened to overtake Fonthill and crush him between stern and rock.

Ibrahim was no fool, and his handling of the clumsy craft as it danced stern first between the rocks was masterly. There was nothing now left of the idle, somnulent steersman. He stood facing the stern, balancing himself on wide-spread legs, his eyes bulging in concentration – and fear? – as he swung the tiller to and fro to avoid the boat broaching. Then, inevitably, the little craft hit a rock and was swung broadside on and then round again, its stern facing downstream once more. This time, however, Ibrahim was flung to his knees and the boat jammed between two fingers of stone that poked out of the surging water.

Ibrahim screamed a command in Arabic to Ahmed, who shouted in turn to Jenkins, 'Pull hard, pull hard to free boat.'

The two bent their backs with a will, digging their oars deeply into the water and each bracing himself against a thwart so that he virtually stood upright on each pull stroke. They had, of course, to pull against the current that had wedged the craft between the rocks. Nevertheless, they had the advantage, such as it was, of the slender bow now facing the torrent, giving the *filuka* a better chance of parting and riding the water surging down on it. As a result, with Ibrahim pushing alternately against both rocks with a boathook, the craft at last sprang out of the vice like a cork out of a bottle, swinging round so that the bow faced downstream, giving the *filuka* considerably more manoeuvrability.

'Where's the Captain?' screamed Jenkins.

Fonthill, in fact, had gained on the bundle of white that he could see bobbing on the surface ahead of him, and at last was able to grab Mustapha's clothing and turn the boy on his back. They had both emerged from the rapids into a patch of tranquil water, green and heavy where the bottom fell away beneath them. One arm around Mustapha's breast and gasping for breath, Simon rolled on to his back and clutched the boy to him. He kicked with his feet and turned his head to discern the nearest shore.

He was just in time to see a long, low figure raise itself on its short legs and lumber towards the water line, its yellow eyes clearly discernible as they fixed on the meal kindly provided for it by Mother Nile. 'Oh God!' screamed Fonthill. He turned his head desperately, seeking some refuge that would take them out of the reach of those long jaws. Now, however, when he could have found use for them, no rocks protruded from the oily water. The river stretched perfectly flat on all sides, green shading to brown at the edges, as though this good behaviour could never be transformed by the gradient and the rocks into a virtual maelstrom just around the bend.

Looking back, Simon saw that something had caused the crocodile to lift its head and look to its left just before it entered the water. Then two shots rang out in quick succession and the beast tossed its head, swung its great tail and slowly sank down, its long snout half in and half out of the water. Blood oozed from two wounds just behind the now closed eye and the beast lay inert.

'Hold up!' cried Jenkins, one hand holding a smoking rifle as he struggled to retain his balance on the approaching boat. 'Hold up, we're nearly there.'

Ibrahim swung the craft round to present the stern to Fonthill and stretched out a strong arm to him. 'No, take the boy,' gasped Simon, and Jenkins and Ahmed leaned out to pull the frail figure abroad. Then the two grasped Fonthill's *jibba* and somehow hauled him over the gunwale, depositing him on the bottom of the boat, where he lay panting on the planking.

'Get the water out . . . of . . . his lungs,' gasped Simon, raising his head to nod towards Mustapha. 'Quickly . . . artificial respiration. Maybe too late. Roll him on to his . . . belly. Head to one side. Press on lungs. Quickly.'

'Right,' grunted Jenkins. 'I've seen it done. 'Ere. Give me an 'and.'

He and Ahmed rolled Mustapha on to his stomach, and the Welshman turned the boy's head to one side, opened his mouth and pulled out the tongue. Then he kneeled and, fingers spread wide either side of the vertebrae, began pressing rhythmically into Mustapha's back. At first the lad lay inert, blood from the wound on his head discolouring the water at the bottom of the boat. Then, at last, his frame twitched, he coughed, water spluttered from his mouth and his eyes opened.

'Thank God,' said Fonthill, raising himself on to hands and knees. 'Well done, lads.' He stretched out a sodden arm to Jenkins and grasped his hand. 'Wonderful shooting again, old chap. I thought we were both done for then – and not a nice way to go.'

'Save your breath, bach sir,' winced Jenkins, his black hair now plastered across his forehead like a row of spikes. 'I'm still shuddering. I knew I only had time for one shot, but I managed two. I'm just grateful that . . .' His voiced failed him for an instant. 'You did wonderful well, sir, divin' in like that. Wonderful well.'

Fonthill crawled forward and knelt by Mustapha's side. The boy's face was deathly pale, but the bleeding from the wound seemed to have stopped. He was still coughing river water from his lungs and seemed only half conscious, but he was definitely alive. Nodding, Simon stretched out his arm to

Ibrahim and shook the startled boatman's hand, and then did the same to Ahmed.

'Well done,' he said. Then, looking around, 'I think this is as good a place as any to camp for the night. We've all had enough for one day, and anyway, the lad needs to be put to bed and cared for. Ahmed, tell Ibrahim to make for the shore over there at that little inlet. If there are no signs of crocs, we can camp back away from the river a little, among the bushes.'

The boat was pulled partly out of the water and secured by Ibrahim thrusting the anchor into a crevice in the rocks. While the boatman examined the hull at the bow to assess whether any damage had been done, the other three gathered around Mustapha, who was now rubbing his head and attempting to sit upright.

'Here, let me examine that wound,' said Fonthill. Then, half to himself, 'You never know what bacteria can get into an open wound from a river like this. Hold still, lad.' From his pack he extracted the now nearly empty bottle of iodine, deposited a little on to a piece of lint gauze and dabbed it on the gash. The boy recoiled at the sharpness.

'Better than drinkin' it, sonny,' said Jenkins. 'Gawd, I can taste that stuff now.'

It soon became clear, however, that Mustapha had sustained nothing more than a clout on the head and, perhaps, a touch of concussion. He remained silent as his head was bandaged but did not take his eyes off Fonthill for one moment as the work was done. At the end, he stretched out his hand.

'Thank you, master, for saving my life.'

Fonthill took the little hand in both of his and clenched it fiercely before, half embarrassed, letting it fall. 'My dear chap,' he murmured. 'I'm so very . . . er . . . thankful that you are all right. We could not manage on this trip without you,

you know. Anyway, it's dear old sharpshooter 352 here that we should be thanking.' They both grinned across at Jenkins, who waved a derisive hand. 'Now, my boy, try and get some sleep.'

Fonthill pulled a blanket across Mustapha and tucked it in beneath his thin frame. For a moment he stayed looking down at the boy, then he coughed and turned to the others, consciously adopting a more businesslike posture.

'God knows how little steamers get through that cataract,' he said, keeping his voice low so that Mustapha was not disturbed, 'but I understand they do, to get down to Berber. Anyway, that's the worst of the river behind us, in my estimation.' Keeping a wary eye on Ibrahim, he pulled up his shirt at the back to the shoulder blades and turned towards Jenkins. 'Has my swim rubbed any of this dammed dye off me, 352?'

The Welshman carried out a quick examination. 'No, bach sir, you still look like a lovely 'eathen.'

'Good.' Fonthill pulled the map from his pack. 'Now, from what I can learn from this bloody inadequate map, the Nile opens out considerably from here onwards. As far as I can make out, the country now becomes a kind of plain, and we should be able to sail again, thank goodness.'

'What about these Dervish blokes?' asked Jenkins.

Fonthill wrinkled his nose. 'Aye, there's the rub. There will be thousands of them gathered around Khartoum, investing the city, and we should start seeing plenty more of them on the river banks from now on. I have to confess I don't like the idea of trying to get through them and into the city.'

'No master plan, bach sir?'

'No master plan, 352. We shall have to rely on our chief spy here,' he nodded to Mustapha, 'to get us through.' He paused for a moment, and his face broke into a paternal smile as he regarded the now sleeping figure. 'He needs his rest.' Then a frown returned. 'It's all very well saying we have come all this way to join the Mahdi, but I don't actually want to enlist to serve the bloody man. I just hope that with Mustapha's help, we can ride fairly purposefully through the army – it's surprising how far one can go if it looks as though one is on a mission – and then, at night, slip through this gate he has spoken about and see the General.'

The three of them fell silent for a moment. Then Jenkins, his face set into a black frown, looked up. 'What about, look you, if we arrive to find the bloody place has already fallen and these 'eathens in full possession. What do we do then?'

'In that case, my dear old 352, we just turn right round and go back the way we came. At least the current will be with us.'

'What? Catapults – or whatever you call these rapids places – crocodiles and all again?'

'Absolutely.'

'Oh bloody 'ell.'

Ibrahim reported that no damage seemed to have been caused to the boat, and they built a fire on the rocks and silently ate a meal of *durra*, dried mutton and boiled rice, with a wakened and restored Mustapha devouring a portion only exceeded by that of Jenkins. Then, with Ahmed taking first watch, the others turned in for the night.

It was the sound of Ahmed's voice that awoke Fonthill. It was still dark, very dark, but it was clear that the Egyptian was arguing strongly in Arabic. Simon slipped the Colt from under his pillow and tucked it beneath his shirt before throwing back the cover. By the light of the smouldering fire, he could see that the Egyptian was talking to two men dressed in Dervish style, with long curved daggers hanging from their upper arms and wearing the distinctive coloured patches of the Mahdi sewn into their *jibbas*. They stood, legs apart, in a truculent manner.

Fonthill put his hands together and gave a respectful salaam. The two glared at him but did not speak. Then he turned to Ahmed. 'Trouble?' he enquired in a deep, guttural voice, hoping that it sounded vaguely like Syrian Arabic.

Ahmed spoke low, quickly and equally gutturally to disguise his English. 'They think we British spies.'

Fonthill threw back his head and roared with laughter. He turned to the fireside as though to share the joke with his companions, and found that Ibrahim and Mustapha were sitting up in their bedrolls, with sleepy enquiry written on their faces. But Jenkins's roll was empty and of him there was no sign.

Simon's laughter, intended to show how ridiculous was the accusation of spying for the British, seemed, however, to infuriate the larger of the two Dervishes. He drew his great two-handed sword, took two paces towards Fonthill and, his eyes glaring, spoke quickly and harshly.

Fonthill turned to Ahmed.

'He want us to undo our packs. I think they rob us.'

'Jenkins?'

The Egyptian shrugged. 'Don't know.'

'Any more?'

'Just two, I think.'

Fonthill's brain raced. The Dervishes were seemingly without firearms, although they were big men, each carrying a sword as well as a dagger. Simon had his Colt, but where there were two men, there could easily be several more within earshot. If there was to be killing, it would have to be done silently. Yet hand-to-hand combat with these two warriors, armed and superbly fit by the look of them, was not a good option. Simon could not face them alone, and brave as he was,

Ahmed would stand little chance against them. So where the bloody hell was Jenkins? There was no sign of him near his bedroll or in the circle of light cast by the flickering embers of their fire – and nothing moved in the shadows beyond the two visitors.

Simon shrugged his shoulders. 'We'll undo the packs,' he said. 'But not the rifles.'

He and Ahmed seized their packs and began slowly to untie their binding cords and display their contents for the Dervishes to inspect. The rifles, encased in their canvas covers, lay just outside the light circle, and Fonthill hoped fervently that they would escape detection. Nodding to the guns, he whispered, 'If they ask, explain that they are fishing rods.' Then he went to his bedroll and shrugged on his *jibba*, turning his back to the intruders for a moment so that he could jettison the Colt beneath his blanket and slip his long knife under his cummerbund.

The two movements went undetected as the Dervishes, their black eyes gleaming between the folds of their headdresses, strolled towards the goods laid out for their inspection. In truth, there was little to see: changes of clothes, small sacks of rice, dried goats' meat, water bags – and small boxes of ammunition for the Colts and rifles.

The leading Arab knelt, opened one of the boxes, selected a rifle cartridge and held it up to the light. He turned to Ahmed and barked a question. The little Egyptian looked at Fonthill in despair and then shrugged his shoulders. The question was repeated, and then the Dervish saw the long shapes of the rifles on the edge of the firelight. He whirled, swung his sword in a silver flash and pointed it at the guns. Then he snarled an order to Ahmed, who nodded. He walked to the rifles, brought them back to the Dervish and knelt, untying the tapes that wound round the canvas covers.

As the guns were revealed, oily black in the firelight, a grin slowly spread across the Arab's face. Then, looking down at Ahmed, his expression turned to fury and he swung up his great sword, clearly intending to bring it down on the Egyptian kneeling before him.

'No!' shouted Fonthill, starting forward. This had the effect of halting the lifting of the sword, but it also brought the second Dervish into play. He moved quickly and swung his own sword in a great horizontal sweep towards Simon's head. The blade was heavy, however, and the move was therefore telegraphed, so that Fonthill was able to duck under the swing, pull out his dagger and dart it towards the other's stomach. But the Dervish was quick too. He pivoted away so that Simon's blade fell short, and the two adversaries paused for a moment, facing each other in the flickering light from the dying fire. Then the Dervish attacked again, swinging his sword back over his shoulder preparatory to bringing it down in a vertical arc. But the weight of the weapon created an impetus that unbalanced him slightly, giving Fonthill the momentary advantage he was seeking. He sprang forward and plunged his dagger into the Arab's midriff, burying it to the hilt before withdrawing it with a twist. The man's mouth dropped open, and with a sigh, he bent over and crumpled to the floor, his great sword falling beside him.

For a moment all movement froze and the members of the little group – Simon, holding the bloodstained dagger, Ahmed, still kneeling at the first Dervish's feet, Ibrahim looking on wide eyed from his bedroll, and Mustapha, crouched on his blanket like a cat ready to spring – seemed like strolling players in a tableau, milking the dramatic moment for applause.

Then, from out of the shadows, behind a huge boulder between the campsite and the river, came an anguished cry,

'Oh bloody 'ell!' followed by a splash and then 'Oh shit!' A crash followed, as though some animal was rushing through the undergrowth, then a dishevelled Jenkins appeared, one leg of his pantaloons still attached to his right ankle and the other trailing behind him, his hair plastered down and his eyes wild. 'I've just pissed on a bloody croco . . .' His words tailed away as he took in the scene before him. 'Ah,' he said, his voice suddenly quiet and his eyes narrow. 'Visitors, is it, then?'

The remaining Dervish suddenly sprang into life. He kicked Ahmed in the face with the toe of his sandal, sending the little Egyptian sprawling, and, ignoring Jenkins, advanced towards Fonthill, circling the great sword two-handed in an arc before him. Simon drew in his breath and, locking his eyes on to those of the Arab through the swinging steel, slowly backed away, holding his bloodstained knife extended towards the man. From the corner of his eye he looked to find the fire, glowing fitfully to his right. Could he skip round it and keep it between them? He attempted to jump towards it, but his bare foot slipped in the loose gravel and he went down on one knee.

The Dervish sprang forward, but in doing so, he half turned his back on Ibrahim and Mustapha. It was his first mistake. In a blur of movement the boy leapt up, head down, and took the Arab with his shoulder just above the knees. The man staggered forward a few paces but recovered his balance and turned to bring the sword down upon Mustapha, now scrambling in the sand. It was his second mistake. As the blade swung upwards, Jenkins leapt on to the Dervish's back. The Welshman's legs wrapped themselves around the Arab's midriff, while his left forearm curled itself around the throat, under the chin. Simultaneously, Jenkins's right hand grabbed the man's beard, suddenly jerking his head back and to the side. The resulting crack echoed around the fireside, and the big man, his eyes questioning, slowly sank to the ground, Jenkins still clinging to his back like a child playing piggyback in a playground.

The two killings had taken place within the space of what seemed like only twenty seconds. Now the two intruders lay on the ground, sightless eyes staring into the sandy gravel.

Jenkins slowly disentangled himself and stood. 'As I was sayin',' he said, 'I was just peein' on this log in the dark, when the bloody thing suddenly slid away into the water, like. I've never been so frightened in all me life, see.'

Fonthill shook his head, half in relief, half in exasperation. He patted Mustapha on the head. 'Well done, lad,' he said. 'You did a brave thing. Now, Ahmed. See if they had companions. Their camels should be tethered somewhere near, but be careful. Three five two, stop your blathering and help me pack up our things and hide the rifles. Quickly now.'

The two men had their few belongings packed away and the rifles back in their canvas coverings by the time Ahmed returned. Simon noted that Ibrahim had now completely retreated under his blanket, so that only his black hair was to be seen. What did the boatman think of it all? Surely the violence enacted by the camp fire in the last minute must have been unusual, even for this cruel country? But the Sudanese gave every indication of having returned to his interrupted sleep.

Fonthill lifted an eyebrow to Ahmed. 'Well?'

'Nobody. Just their two camels. Nothing else.'

'Good.' Simon turned to Jenkins, who was now struggling to put his other leg into his cotton trousers. 'Thank you, 352. Once again . . .'

The Welshman sniffed, dancing on one leg as he attempted to insert the other into the garment. 'Nothin', bach sir. You did well enough on your own, and anyway,' he nodded to

Mustapha, ' 'e's the one to thank, look you. Like a little terrier, he was.'

The boy sat cross-legged on the ground, grinning at them all. Then, on some quick motivation, he sprang to his feet and began rifling through the garments of the two dead men.

'No,' said Fonthill, shaking his head. 'Leave them be.'

'Which is just what we can't do, Simon, I am thinking,' said Ahmed, suddenly sinking to the ground as though his legs could no longer support him. 'What do we do with them? We cannot bury here, I think. Ground too hard. No?'

'No. There's only one place. The Nile.'

'Oh God.' Jenkins's eyes were now wide and staring. 'I can't go back there in the dark, bach sir. Not to where them crocs are, look you.'

Fonthill sighed. 'Very well. Three five two, go and unsaddle the Dervishes' camels and bring their stuff here. It will have to go into the river too. Turn the camels loose. I want no evidence left. Ahmed, help me drag the bodies to the bank, and Mustapha, you go on and see if the coast is clear – of crocodiles as well as Dervishes. But be careful now. We don't want to lose you.'

Within minutes, the grisly business of slipping the Arabs into the water, weighed down by their swords, was finished. The saddles and accoutrements followed and the three returned to the camp site. Jenkins had sprinkled sand on the bloodstained gravel and it was as though the two Dervishes had not existed. No one was prepared to sleep after the alarms of the night – except Ibrahim, whose snoring showed that he had taken the events of the last half-hour well in his stride – so the fire was built up and they sat around it, drinking green tea.

Everyone was silent, wrapped in his own thoughts. For Fonthill, reaction to the bloody events set in as he gripped his tin cup hard. He could not remove from his mind the memory of how easily the blade of his knife had sunk into the stomach of the Dervish, and the half-cough, half-moan the man had emitted as he sank to the ground. The musky, sour smell of the Nile – or was it the crocodiles? – permeated the camp site, and the occasional flare from the fire as a strand of driftwood shifted and fell into the heart threw the gaunt faces around Simon into relief, as though in some Dantean fresco. He found himself shivering. Had he become a remorseless killer? He had become good at it and it came easily to him now. He frowned. He must not turn into a killing machine, like Jenkins. Apart from the deleterious effect on his own character, all of it – the shooting, the knifing, the blood so easily spilt – was setting a bad example to Mustapha. Perhaps one day the boy could come back home with him to . . . He shook his head and, to cover his discomfort, coughed and put a question to Ahmed.

'Why, I wonder,' he asked, 'did they not believe you when you said we were from Syria?'

'I don't know. Perhaps we don't look like Syrians.'

'But would the Dervishes know the difference between a Syrian and a camel, for God's sake? I was told that no Syrians would ever get this far south and west.'

Ahmed nodded glumly. 'They knew I was Egyptian. I don't make good Syrian. I don't know. Perhaps . . .' His voice tailed away and he shrugged his shoulders.

Fonthill felt a shaft of guilt penetrate him as he looked at the little man. The Egyptian was absurdly brave, and had undoubtedly originally been drawn to help the two Britons by the thought of sharing in the glamour that he perceived to be part of their work as scouts and agents for the British Army. But he was no real fighter. In addition, of course, this was not his war, and the dangers and privations of the journey, not to mention the sordid killings that he had witnessed so far, must surely seem a high price to pay for pursuing vicarious glory. Yet he had jumped at the chance to take leave of absence from his hotel and go adventuring again with the two of them. And his services as an interpreter they could trust and rely on *were* invaluable . . .

Simon's reflections were interrupted by a typically helpful intervention from Jenkins. 'Perhaps they 'eard me peein', see,' he said. 'P'raps I wasn't doin' a Syrian pee, like . . .'

'Oh, do be quiet.' Silence returned to the fireside. 'But it's made me think,' Simon mused. 'If we stick out like a sore thumb, I don't fancy going ashore and trying to talk our way through the Mahdi's lines. I wonder . . .' He threw the dregs of his tea on to the fire. 'I will stand guard the rest of the night. You three get some sleep.'

At their meagre breakfast just after dawn, Fonthill sat for a while and studied Ibrahim. The three of them had long ago given up the subterfuge of only speaking out of his hearing. Now they addressed each other in English in front of him, and if the boatman doubted the Syrian origins of Fonthill and Jenkins he gave no sign. He seemed, in fact, quite phlegmatic, and not even the violent events of the night had broken the rhythm of his ponderous, ordered behaviour: steering, eating and, particularly, sleeping. But if, like an increasing number of Sudanese, he was a Mahdist follower, then he was a potential source of danger as they neared Khartoum. He could so easily betray them when the moment came to go ashore.

Simon beckoned Ahmed to his side. 'What has Ibrahim said about the killings last night?'

The Egyptian gave his fatalistic shrug. 'He don't seem worried, or even interested. I told him that those men had to be killed because they were going to rob us, and he accept that.' He wrinkled his nose. 'This country not like Cairo. These people know about death. They live with it every day. Violence, et cetera, et cetera, all around.'

'You don't think he suspects us in any way?'

'No. He not even interested, as long as we pay him – and we pay him well.'

'Good. Please ask him to join us.'

Ibrahim waddled over and squatted down beside Fonthill. 'Ask him,' requested Simon, 'how near to the city of Khartoum this boat can take us. My map is useless on this detail. Can we sail up close to the walls and the city gates?'

The question relayed, the man shrugged his shoulders and spoke slowly, spitting in emphasis from time to time. Then he drew a rough diagram in the sand with a stick, showing two rivers meeting, with a line linking the two just before the junction and a circle within the triangle.

'He say,' translated Ahmed, 'that Khartoum is here, where is circle. This river here on top is Blue Nile. This one meeting it from bottom is White Nile, with city between two. Two years ago, big ditch was built at this line, behind city and linking two rivers. So Khartoum is now on island – what you call artificial island. In what you call triangle.'

Ibrahim resumed speaking, and when he paused, Ahmed translated.

'He say that here, just little bit further north on west bank of Nile after junction, General has built a fort called Omdurman. It . . . what is word . . . ah yes, dominates river there. If we want to get into Khartoum we must pass Omdurman but then we can be put ashore on island and go into city that way, if soldiers on walls don't shoot us. There are also the little steamers . . .'

'What?' Fonthill had forgotten the existence of these armed steam paddle boats, Gordon's 'penny steamers', called after the Thames pleasure craft, which, when last heard of, had proved to be a potent weapon in Khartoum's defences, patrolling the river and even taking punitive expeditions to attack the Mahdi's forces behind his lines. 'How many of those does the General have?'

'He don't know, but when last he was in Khartoum these little boats were going up and down river with guns, shooting at Mahdi's boats, soldiers, et cetera, et cetera, et cetera, you know.'

'Ah.' Fonthill's mind raced. Perhaps they would not have to be landed either downriver, above the Mahdi's hordes or in the middle of them. Perhaps it would be possible to go ashore at the island, virtually out of reach of the Dervishes, or, better still, approach a patrolling steamer from the city and hitch a ride into Khartoum. As long as Ibrahim didn't suddenly succumb to a fit of patriotism and refuse to pass them over in that way. And, of course, as long as Gordon was still holding out . . .

He nodded his thanks to Ibrahim and rose to his feet. 'Let's clear up and get back on board quickly. We mustn't waste any more time.'

They were sailing again within the quarter-hour, with the triangular sail filling spasmodically in an irregular and light breeze and only the occasional outcrop of rock near the shore on either side presenting any problems to Ibrahim, who had settled back into his passive mode, seeming to doze as he sat in the stern, his skullcap perched on the back of his head and one arm draped over the tiller.

They now passed a number of villages on either bank; it was as though the river had come alive and become fecund once past the last of the cataracts. As Fonthill had predicted, the Nile was broad here with, at the edges, pools of standing water full of crocodiles, turtles and hippopotami. Gazelles, hyenas, birds and wild asses crowded into the inner pools, keeping a wary eye on the crocodiles, and vying for the water with flocks of goats and even sheep tended by local Arab boys, who waved at the *filuka* as it slipped by. It was life-sappingly hot, and above them red cuckoos cried a three-note song over and over: *it will rain, it will rain, it will rain.* But of course it did not. The rainy season had ended as August had slipped away. Life on the little craft would have been pleasantly soporific after their recent adventures if cloud could have been summoned to shield them from the merciless glare of the sun. But the sky remained a brazen bowl of blue. It was hot. Damned hot.

For a further two days they progressed upriver without incident, but it had become increasingly necessary to row and paddle the *filuka* as the wind disappeared, and the sail flapped impotently before it was furled. The banks of the Nile were now quite crowded and villages more frequent. Occasionally they were challenged from the shore, but Ibrahim, showing no sign of alarm or even interest, called back languidly in Arabic. Whatever it was that he said seemed to satisfy, and their slow progress was not interrupted.

On the morning of the seventh day after leaving Metemmeh, they realised that they must be close to Khartoum. Armed Dervishes now thronged the banks and small *filukas* were criss-crossing the river as ferries as well as making their way up- and downstream, presumably trading. The presence of these other craft gave a sense of relief to Fonthill, for their own boat stood out less prominently in this bustling traffic. The question now was, of course, whether Gordon was still holding out, and if so, how they could get through to him behind his beleaguered walls without attracting attention.

The first question was soon answered. Prompted, Ibrahim asked it of a fellow boatman, who, according to Ahmed's translation, replied that the infidel still held the city but that his days were numbered and his head would soon hang from the Mahdi's tent pole.

'Just in case 'e invites us to dinner, like, you'd better tell me about this Mahdi bloke.' Jenkins had crawled along to sit next to Fonthill in the prow of the boat.

Simon wrinkled his forehead. 'Well,' he began, 'his name is Muhammad Ahmad and he is the son of a boat-builder who was born and brought up on a small island in the White Nile, about two hundred miles south of Khartoum. He was a solitary chap by all accounts, who dedicated himself to studying the Koran – that's the Mosselman's sort of Bible, you know.'

Jenkins nodded.

'He wandered about as a holy man and then, about three years ago, announced that he was the true descendant of the Prophet Muhammad. He claimed that he was the Mahdi, "the Expected One", the Messiah, who had been sent to cleanse and then restore the faith and lead a *jihad* – a holy war – to rid the Sudan of all foreigners. He has, it seems, the signs to prove his claim – a birthmark on the right cheek and a V-shaped gap between his front teeth – and the tribes have been flocking to his banner.'

Jenkins sat listening intently, his chin on his clenched fist.

'He's either been very lucky or he is a shrewd general,' Fonthill continued, 'because he has defeated virtually all the forces either we or the Egyptians have sent against him. He began with just a mob of spearmen, but by now he has captured hundreds of rifles and cannon, plus ammunition, and has more than forty thousand warriors at his command. He has told them that death fighting the infidel automatically guarantees entry into Paradise, where palaces and beautiful virgins await the true believer, and all his men – they're called Dervishes, of course – fight like the very devil.'

The Welshman removed his fist and nodded. 'Well,' he said, 'we've fought the fierce Zulu, the Pa-tans up in India, and them sharp-shootin' Boer blokes, so I don't see these Dervish fellers botherin' us too much. But why did a clever general like Gordon let 'imself be 'oled up in this Kartoom place, eh?'

Simon looked around at the river traffic. It seemed to be heavier. 'It's a good question and needs a complicated answer,' he said. 'It seems to me we're getting near to Khartoum now, so let's just say that, with the permission of the Turks, whose empire of course includes Egypt and the Sudan, Gladstone's government sent him out here to evacuate all the garrisons in this godforsaken country, because neither we, the Egyptians nor the Turks want to fight the Mahdi on his home ground. But Gordon, for some reason, fancied that he could take on the bloody man. The trouble is, he doesn't have the troops to do it, and as a result he ended up stuck inside Khartoum with about eight thousand Egyptian soldiers and Wolseley has been sent out with a small army to plod up the Nile to rescue—'

He was interrupted by the distant sound of firing. It was the dull boom of cannon rather than the light crackle of musketry, although it sounded desultory and not at all like a barrage. 'Probably from the penny steamers,' said Fonthill.

And so it proved. As they slowly turned a bend in the river, they perceived the baked mud walls of a low fort on the west bank, their right-hand side of the river. It flew the flag of the Egyptian Khedive, and anchored in midstream was a strange white-painted vessel, also flying the Egyptian flag. Its great paddles, fixed on either side amidships, were protected by added planks of wood, and similar housing had been erected on the decks to shield the boiler house, at the base of the long funnel, and also the two small cannon, which were firing at a target ashore hidden by the walls of the fort. A Maxim stuttered occasionally from rough timber fortifications on the bridge.

Even more importantly, approximately half a mile upriver could now be seen the long, grey mass that was the walled city of Khartoum. Above it also fluttered the Khedive's flag.

'Thank God!' cried Fonthill. 'They're still alive and fighting. We've got through! Grab an oar and help Mustapha to row like hell towards that steamer.' He shouted to Ahmed: 'Get the money to pay Ibrahim and tell him that we are going to transfer to the steamer, so he must steer towards it. Tell him we have an urgent message for the General from the Syrian government.' He grinned. 'That might help to start a rumour or two. Give me that bit of white sheet. I don't want the steamer to sink us.'

It was a timely warning. As Ibrahim, his jaw dropping with puzzlement, reluctantly swung the tiller over to take the *filuka* towards the steamer, a warning burst of fire from the Maxim crackled above their heads.

Fonthill stood, waving the white fabric. He saw the head of a turbaned figure emerge over the planking on the bridge and focus field glasses on him. The Maxim ceased firing.

As they neared the vessel, Simon began shouting: 'We are British. We have come from General Wolseley. We need to come aboard.'

Immediately, four rifles appeared above the wall of planks on the deck and were levelled at them. At the same time, a shell from the shore erupted in the water nearby, conveniently giving veracity to their claim, so that the figure on the bridge waved reassuringly to them and an opening suddenly emerged in the planking wall, just above the rope ladder hanging down the hull of the steamer.

A cry of puzzled anger suddenly came from Ibrahim as another shell sent up a spout of spray near the *filuka*. Fonthill suddenly realised that they had put the wretched boatman in a difficult position. If the shells didn't get him once they had left, he would probably be beheaded on reaching the shore for taking passengers to the infidels.

He shouted to Ahmed: 'Tell Ibrahim that he can come with us into Khartoum. If he doesn't want that, tell him to tell the Dervishes that we threatened him with guns and made him bring us here. And thank the sleepy old bugger for his good service.'

By now, they were at the side of the steamer. Simon grabbed a line thrown to him and tied it to the gunwale of the boat. He then began feverishly throwing their packs aboard the larger vessel before following them up the rope ladder. A black soldier in the uniform of the Khedive's Egyptian army held open a door in the planking and began helping the others up the ladder. Simon turned his head and watched as Ibrahim, his eyes showing desperately white against the black of his face, let go of the tiller and threw off the lashings of the sail in a flurry of movement, then swung the boat round and, the current behind him, steered it midstream back the way they had come.

'That's the first time I've seen him move quickly,' grinned Jenkins.

Fonthill smiled back. 'Sensible, though. He's getting the hell out of here and sailing back before he has to explain to the Dervishes why he has just delivered four packages to Gordon. Good luck to him.'

A tall Sudanese in the Khedive's khaki now gave them a

formal bow. 'You have come to relieve us, yes?' he asked. 'There are others behind you?'

Simon extended his hand. 'Fonthill, late captain in the 24th of Foot and Queen's Own Corps of Guides, Indian Army,' he said. 'Yes, there are others behind us, but . . .' he shook his head sadly, 'quite a way behind, I am afraid. Can you take us immediately to General Gordon, please?'

The officer inclined his head. 'Of course. It is becoming a little warm for us here anyway.' He smiled. 'We were just putting up a show, really.' He gave an order, and with a hiss of steam the anchor rumbled in and was stowed. Then the little gunboat gave a defiant whoop on its whistle and turned about.

Within minutes, Simon and his companions were landed on mud flats under the walls of the city. Heads down, they followed the officer and scampered across the flat ground under desultory fire from the far bank. A small door within the large town gates was opened for them and they were hurried through the hot streets of the city to the long, low building that was the Governor General's palace. Without further preliminaries they climbed stairs to the second floor to be met by a curly-haired man, quite small and wearing a red rimless fez, or *tarboosh*, the symbol of authority in the Turkish empire, and an ordinary short black English coat and, despite the heat, a black waistcoat. The man extended his hand and regarded them with the bluest and most piercing eyes Fonthill had ever seen.

'Welcome to Khartoum,' he said. 'I'm Charlie Gordon. Who exactly are . . .' His question hung in mid-air as he caught sight of Mustapha, looking up wide eyed at the great man. 'Oh, what a delightful young man.' He bent down and solemnly shook the boy's hand. 'We have a good school here and you must attend it. I will see to it.'

Then he ruffled the boy's curls and rested his hand there

while he turned back to Fonthill, whose jaw had dropped at the attention devoted to the boy. Then Simon remembered: Gordon loved children, and had started a school for homeless boys in Kent. Even so, it was disconcerting to find the General seemingly more interested in a slave boy than in emissaries from the relieving force.

'I hear you are English,' the General said, 'though you certainly don't look it. Have you come from Wolseley?'

'Yes, sir. It's quite a long story . . .'

Chapter 7

Alice Griffith had had quite enough of Wady Halfa. It was here, in a small township on the banks of the Nile some fifty miles into the Sudan, that Wolseley had made his base camp for the invasion of the country. It was here that the eight hundred whalers, specially made in London and shipped out with three hundred *voyageurs* rivermen from Canada to handle them, were being assembled into a sturdy little fleet to take the core of his men upriver, round the great loop of the Nile and through the cataracts to Khartoum. And it was here that the van of his army, nominally eleven thousand men in total but most of them strung out manning his line of communications right back to Alexandria, were sprawled along the river in rows of bell tents, mud huts and riverboats.

The scale and dynamism of the panorama, however, were lost on Alice. She had seen too many army camps to be impressed by their bustle and sense of potential drama. The place was hot, dusty and full of scorpions, and the hospital contained fifty-nine cases, all products of the unforgiving climate and ranging from enteric fever to sunstroke. Worst of all, however, nothing – well, nothing of real interest to her readers – was happening. The campaign so far had been a boring and often disastrous exercise in logistics, with Wolseley and his warring, fractious staff plagued by shortages of coal to fire the trains carrying troops up to the railhead some miles back to the north, and, most serious of all, camels. It certainly did not make for good copy.

Alice had learned some basic Arabic two years ago on Wolseley's Egyptian campaign. She had employed an Arab-speaking Englishwoman to accompany her on the trip out to Cairo (thanks to Covington, she now had no financial inhibitions) and had worked hard to improve her own knowledge of the language. The woman, of course, could not accompany her with the army, and had left for home long before Alice had joined the press contingent with the General and set out up the Nile. Now, however, she was bored. Very bored.

Perched on a rock and perspiring under her khaki pith helmet, Alice threw a stone into the river, to express her frustration and growing hatred of the Nile. Even if Wolseley – 'I am successful because I never fight unless I am sure I am going to win' – sorted out his supply problems, he would soon face the really imposing task. Up to Wady Halfa the Nile was navigable at all seasons of the year. Beyond, however, the invading army would have to voyage along a river that was said by experts to be 'practically unnavigable at any period' – particularly for the hundred and eighty miles between the Second Cataract at Halfa and the Third at Hannek. Yet Wolseley was insouciantly sure that he could do it. Fourteen years ago he had made his name by taking a force six hundred miles up the Red River in the Canadian wilderness in three months to put down a rebellion. He had been successful without firing a shot and had returned without losing a man and, most impressively for the politicians back home, well within budget. What he could do then, he claimed, he could do now.

But Alice was not so sure. She looked around, up to the barren ochre hills behind her. This country was vast, comparatively waterless and – unlike Canada – full of ridiculously brave, fanatical warriors, waiting for Wolseley and his men if and when they limped off their pathetic little boats at the end of the river passage. She had seen enough battles in far corners of the Empire to know how well Queen Victoria's soldiers fought and how brave were their officers. But she had also witnessed a sense of superciliousness among senior officers and shared with Simon his indignation at their constant underestimation of the abilities of the enemy.

Ah, Simon! She sighed and looked back to the Nile, brown and muddy at this point. He would have come this way, almost certainly. She had received only one letter from him before she had left England. It had been written hurriedly from Cairo and gave her little cause for comfort. He was, he said, 'going upcountry' on a journey that could take four months or longer, and would be unable to write for that time. She was not to worry. Ahmed, whom she would remember from the Arabi campaign, had agreed to join him and Jenkins, and they were all in good form and anxious to leave on the morrow. She was to look after the estate and prepare for a wedding early next spring. Oh – and he loved her more than life itself. Although not, she reflected, enough to resist a call from Lord Wolseley!

Alice had arrived to join the press contingent on the column about a month ago, and Wolseley had given her only a perfunctory half-bow when their paths had crossed at the railhead at Assuit. From there, he and his staff had boarded a yacht, the *Fetooz*, put at his disposal by the Khedive of Egypt, to take them upriver. It was rumoured that the travel agents, Thomas Cook & Sons, who had been employed to transport the army, had provided food and linen for the General and his staff on board at a pound per day. The artist from *The*

Graphic, Frederick Villiers, had been allowed to accompany the party, so creating considerable jealousy among the strong press corps, who followed behind in a hired *diabeeah* sailing boat.

It was a poorly kept secret that Wolseley hated newspapermen, and they were all with him on this campaign. It was, in fact, the largest press contingent ever to accompany an invading army in the field. The plight of Gordon besieged in Khartoum had captured the imagination of readers throughout the western world, and all the main international newspapers and news agencies were represented. The old hands from Fleet Street were there in force, led by the great Willie Russell, who, on behalf of *The Times*, had revealed the scandal of nursing and bad equipment in the Crimea and who was now founder editor of the *Army and Navy Gazette*; and also including Pearce of the *Daily News*, Williams of Central News, Cameron of *The Standard*, Burleigh of *The Daily Telegraph*, Prior of *The Illustrated London News*, and Piggott, Alice's colleague from Reuters, on board to cover the hard news developments for the agency.

Hard news? Alice smiled. There had been little enough of that! The Mahdi, his forty thousand men and the chances of real fighting were all nearly seven hundred miles away, and there was a limit to what anyone could write concerning the problems of finding fodder for camels, coal for locomotives and pitch for boat-caulking. In fact, some of this frustration had crept into the 'colour' pieces that she had filed for Reuters. It was not in her remit to criticise Wolseley and his staff openly for what undoubtedly was proving to be a logistical nightmare, but she had obliquely referred to criticism concerning the choice of route taken by the Commander-in-Chief for his invasion. The Nile was already posing strong problems even before the most difficult cataracts were met. Wouldn't it have been better for him to have taken the much shorter overland route from Suakin on the Red Sea across the desert to Berber? This had brought a gentle rebuke from the press liaison officer, who read all copy emanating from the journalists. He had not, he said, censored her references, but in future she should 'stick to the facts'. The officer had now been replaced (because he was too 'soft'?) but, in any case, Alice had no intention of heeding his warning. Censorship was abhorrent to her.

On the far side of the river, three gazelles timidly came down to graze. Then they scattered and sped away as shots were fired at them from Alice's side. She wrinkled her nose in disgust. Gratuitous cruelty! Even if the firing had been accurate, the carcasses would have been taken by the crocodiles before they could have been retrieved. Stupid! So like the army!

The thought of cruelty made her frown. Somewhere, miles and miles to the south, Simon was on a mission amongst some of the most savage people on earth. She had, of course, been warned about Dervish cruelty by Bonnard, but she had known about it long before. Tales of the seemingly casual lopping of the ears, hands and feet by the Mahdi and his followers of those who transgressed had been common currency back home for some time. In the wild hills of India's North-West Frontier and on the plains of the Transvaal she had witnessed at first hand the resilience and survival skills of Simon and Jenkins. If anyone could come through these perils it would be these two. Simon, of course, had given no indication of his destination. But Alice had surmised long ago that he and Jenkins were bound for Khartoum. She looked to the south, where the brown river wound its way to disappear behind the low hills. Where, dear God, were they now? And were they still alive?

Two weeks ago she had bent the knee at last and written a brief note to Lord Wolseley, begging him for news of Simon. He had replied, courteously enough – addressing her as 'Mrs Covington' – that he could not help her, for he had heard nothing from her fiancé and nor did he expect to for some weeks yet. However, as soon as he had information he would, of course, inform her. No indication of where Fonthill had been sent or when he might be expected back. But then she had really expected nothing more from the General.

Her relationship with Wolseley had always been volatile. He was particularly shocked on his Sekukuni campaign in the eastern Transvaal four years ago to find a young woman of good background (Alice's father had retired from the army with the rank of brigadier general) among the press contingent attached to his army. She had won credit with him by marrying one of his staunchest senior officers, Colonel Ralph Covington, despite the mutilating wounds sustained by Covington in the final battle. Then, however, they had clashed when she had followed Covington out on the Egyptian invasion two years later, having won back her *Morning Post* job, evading both censorship and the restrictions placed on the movements of journalists in covering the campaign. Nevertheless, Wolseley's view of her had softened on Covington's death at the Battle of Tel el Kebir and, indeed, he had written a warm letter of congratulation to Simon when their engagement had been announced. Now, however, he had clearly distanced himself from her. What the hell! Alice threw another pebble into the water. She wanted no favours from a man like Wolseley. If only she could be reassured that Simon was still alive, though . . .

A cough from behind her left shoulder made her turn. A young subaltern stood, a note in his hand, his face red from exertion.

'Excuse me, miss . . . er . . . madam. Are you Mrs Covington, by any chance?'

'No. I am Alice Griffith, of Reuters.' Alice, long accustomed to making her way in a masculine world, wanted no confusion about her role here. Then, seeing the note, she relented. 'Oh, all right. Yes, I am Mrs Covington.'

'Oh, jolly good, madam.' He offered her the note and then took out a large white handkerchief and used it to wipe his face. 'Bin lookin' for you everywhere, I must say. It's from His Lordship. I was told to wait for a reply, if you don't mind.'

'Of course. Excuse me.' Alice tore open the envelope, her heart in her mouth. Simon? Could it be . . .? The note was scrawled in a strong, forward-sloping hand on notepaper headed 'From the C-in-C', and it carried that day's date.

> *My dear Mrs Covington,*
> *You must have thought me no end of a boor for having neglected you for so long, but I know you will appreciate that I have had much to do – and also that it would not have been quite the thing to have singled you out from the press people for special treatment early on, so to speak.*
>
> *However, it would give me great pleasure if you would dine with General Buller and me this evening. Shall we say at 6.30 on board the* Fetooz? *Quite casual, of course.*
>
> *I do hope we can look forward to the pleasure of your company.*
> *Sincerely,*
> *Wolseley*

Alice put down the note and stared unseeingly out into the desert. Did this mean that he was summoning her – in surroundings designed to soften the blow – to give bad news about Simon? She was conscious that her heart was beating heavily and that beads of perspiration were forming on her upper lip. She gulped. Nonsense, this was far too informal a note. But why this invitation out of the blue? Was she going to be hauled over the coals again? Or were these two gallant old soldiers just desirous of a little female company out here in this barren waste? Goodness knows, there was little enough of that about. She shrugged, and was suddenly aware that the subaltern was waiting expectantly.

'Forgive me, Lieutenant,' she said, removing her topi and shaking out her long fair hair so that it lay on her shoulders and gleamed in the sunlight. 'I had quite forgotten that you were there.'

He gave her a cheeky schoolboy grin. 'Ah, miss – madam – that's what all the girls say to me.'

She returned the grin. 'Good gracious. I am sure they don't. Now, please tell Lord Wolseley that I shall be delighted to join him for dinner tonight.'

The young man bowed, and Alice looked at her watch. It showed 4.30. Now, would she be able to commandeer a shower on board the press boat, and what on earth could she wear?

She was able to shower, wash her hair and then dry it in the comparative privacy of the little cubicle she was allowed as the only woman in the crowded quarters of the press *diabeeah*. Then she laid out the only formal dress she carried – 'informal, of course', Wolseley had written, but she couldn't exactly turn up in riding breeches, boots and blouse, now could she? – sprinkled a little Nile water on it and ironed it flat on her small table with her hand. She tied her hair back with a scrap of apple-green silk, trod into the only spare shoes she had packed, a pair of flat sequinned slippers, and sat down and studied her face in her hand mirror. Despite all her precautions, it had browned in the sun, and her skin was now the colour of the women on her estate in Norfolk who came to work in the fields at harvest time. She frowned, applied a little face powder and rouge and, though still far from satisfied, snapped shut the compact and stood. Whatever the reason for Wolseley's invitation, she intended to seize the opportunity to milk him for as much information about his strategy and intentions as she could, and if this meant playing the vamp to some extent, then so be it. It wouldn't be the first time she had employed these techniques to gain a story.

The Khedive's yacht, of course, was luxurious, spacious and seemed far too opulent to be carrying a fighting general into war. The dining saloon was lined with polished mahogany, from which gilded mirrors twinkled and reflected the light of tall ivory-coloured candles set in long holders on the rectangular table, which had been laid with a silver service.

One end of the long table was rather cosily set for three, and the two generals were already standing there, wearing smoking jackets and drinking whisky and soda from large tumblers. They presented an ill-assorted pair.

Lord Wolseley, short, slim and very erect, had a scholar's brow and chubby cheeks and sported, in contemporary fashion, a long, drooping moustache that gave his face a melancholy air when in repose. The moustache partly concealed the scar on his face from the Crimean War, and of the eye he had lost in the trenches there was a palpable imitation of the real thing. His remaining rather bulbous eye, however, sparkled with life, and the strength of his personality and the air of command that he carried were self-evident. Without patronage or friends in high places – his father had only been a major – Wolseley had made his own way, and, at twenty-eight, had become the youngest lieutenant colonel in the British Army. After the Red River expedition, he had laid down a reputation as a reformer by writing a ground-breaking handbook for officers in the field. He had then fought and won a difficult jungle war in Africa against the Ashanti, subdued Chief Sekukuni, the victor over the Boers in the Transvaal, and captured Egypt for the British (although nominally in the name of Turkey) at the brilliantly conducted Battle of Tel el Kebir. He was England's favourite general.

Major General Sir Redvers Buller, however, looked what he was: a soldier's soldier. Broad, tending to corpulence (his reputation as a prodigious trencherman was well established), his most distinguished physical characteristic was a remarkably red face. But he had what one observer had called 'a gift of grim silence', and was known to be ruthless when he had to be. A gifted cavalry commander who had won the Victoria Cross in the Zulu war, he had been with Wolseley in Canada, Ashanti and Egypt, and was one of the most prominent members of 'the Ashanti Ring', the group of young officers on that campaign who had impressed Wolseley and earned his favour from that time onwards. He was Wolseley's chief of staff on this campaign, and Alice had heard rumours that this fighting general had earned the C-in-C's criticism for his lack of talent as a senior staff officer. Now, however, standing together in close consort at the end of the table, the two seemed on excellent terms.

'Ah, my dear Mrs Covington,' said Wolseley, advancing to meet her, hand outstretched, 'how good of you to come and brighten up the evening of two old soldiers in this accursed country.'

Alice smiled. 'How kind of you to ask me, sir.' She nodded appreciatively at the surroundings. 'What a delight to eat in such a splendid setting.'

'Ah. This is the Khedive's pomp and ceremony, not mine, although,' he gave a mischievous grin, 'Buller here is far more used to this sort of thing than I. You know Sir Redvers, of course?'

Alice gave a small curtsy as the big man bent over her hand, smilingly but in silence.

'Now,' Wolseley continued, 'Mrs . . . oh, may I call you Alice tonight, do you think? After all, we have known each other for quite some time now, meeting in foreign lands, eh?'

'Please do so, my lord.'

'Good. Now, we are drinking whisky, but I am sure you would prefer champagne. We have a decent bottle or two of the '78 Bollinger. Supplied, I believe, from Redvers's very own travelling cellar.'

Alice smiled. It was clear that Buller was used to being chivvied by Wolseley over his indulgence, but she could not help but feel that there was an underlying note of exasperation in Wolseley's sally. 'Thank you very much,' she said, 'but do you know, I would much prefer to join you in a whisky and soda.'

'Of course. Why not? It's the drink of a campaigner, is it not? Steward.'

Her glass was brought, and Alice and Wolseley continued to exchange pleasantries – with only the occasional contribution from the taciturn Buller – as though they were in a Mayfair drawing room.

Eventually they sat, with Wolseley insisting on placing Alice at the head of the table, with the two men either side of her. The General was certainly putting himself out to be cordial, and she accepted this with relief, playing the game because it proved that there was nothing terrible to be disclosed about Simon. Then, however, she found herself wondering why she was being singled out for all this attention.

Wolseley had always had the reputation of being something of a ladies' man, quite happy to indulge in tableside flirting, although no hint of impropriety had ever been attached to his name, and it was well known that he and his wife remained deeply in love. So there was absolutely no question of improper advances being made – and anyway, there was dear old Buller there as the most stolid of chaperons. Perhaps Wolseley was merely being kind and hospitable in this most inhospitable of countries, probably in memory of Covington, her late husband, who had also been one of the Ashanti Ring. Unlikely, though. When on campaign, Wolseley was notoriously single-minded, with little time for courtesies – and quite rightly so. No, he wanted something from her. But what?

Then it occurred to her. For the first time probably in any of his campaigns, the great general was facing some criticism in the press. The man was still held in great respect, of course, and no war correspondent – with the possible exception of Willie Russell – would dare to cast doubt openly on his strategic aims and the tactics employed to attain them. Nevertheless, this long haul up the Nile was laying waste to Wolseley's most precious commodity in his race to free Gordon: time. It was perfectly clear that things weren't going exactly to plan, and Alice and her colleagues were hinting at this, with the result that murmurings were beginning to grow back home. It would be quite below His Lordship's dignity to call a conference to address the press and take them into his confidence to explain the problems and plead his case. Alice, however, could be tangentially approached, using Wolseley's relationship with both her late husband and her present fiancé as an excuse to meet socially and give him an opportunity to rebut actual and potential criticism. When writing for the *Morning Post*, Alice could reach a readership of some hundred and fifty thousand people. Now, however, working for the greatest news agency in the world, she could be read by millions, in some of the most famous newspapers. He *needed* her, the old rascal. She was being used!

Alice chortled inwardly. Well, two could play at that game!

She took a sip of some rather indifferent claret (this clearly not from Buller's travelling wine cellar!). 'It is clear, General,' she said, 'that things haven't been quite as you would have wished so far in this long journey up the Nile. What have been your main problems? Do you mind?' She extracted a small notebook from her handbag.

Wolseley dabbed at his moustache with a white napkin. 'I am quite happy to talk freely with you, Alice, on this occasion,' he said with a smile. 'But it would not do to quote me directly. However, if you wish to use whatever I can tell you as material for your own assumptions, so to speak, then I would have no objection, subject, of course, to our usual rather tiresome army regulations.'

'Ah, censorship, you mean?'

'I wouldn't put it quite like that. I do hope that we are not too restrictive.'

Alice let it lie. 'My colleagues and I have written already, of course, about your logistical problems in travelling south by the Nile route. May I ask why you did not choose to advance on Khartoum overland, from Suakin on the Red Sea to Berber, so cutting the distance travelled by about half?'

Wolseley shook his head vigorously. 'Seems easier, but doesn't stand up to close examination. The problem is water, of course. The distance between the wells is so great that no more than three hundred cavalry or four hundred infantry could move between them daily. The last hundred miles to the Nile at Berber is across desert where there is only water at the halfway mark, at O-Bak. Our infantry could only cross there in the month of October and only if carried on camels. We would be very vulnerable. No. No.' He shook his head again.

'River is longer, of course, but it is the surer way. By going upriver we overcome the main problem of this country, which is the supply of water.'

'But the cataracts?'

'What are cataracts but rapids? We encountered plenty of those in Canada and found a way through, and we shall do the same here. The whalers that I have had built in London have all arrived now, and we have these splendid chaps from Canada who have volunteered to come out here and handle them. We shall find a way through the cataracts all right, eh, Redvers?'

'Most certainly, my lord.'

'However,' Wolseley continued, 'you are quite right to say that we have underestimated to some extent the problems of transport. One can't foresee everything, you know, and this whole expedition has had to be put together in the most disgraceful rush.' He threw down his napkin and a vein began to throb in his forehead.

'Let me tell you frankly, Alice, I think of my friend Charlie Gordon, shut up there in Khartoum with a cowardly lot of Egyptian soldiers, enemies on all sides of him, and his government at home anxious to decry and discredit him, to damn him with faint praise and to sneer at his actions. Our Cabinet is composed of men without one manly instinct amongst them. I tell you, to a lot of place-hunters, Gordon is a standing reproach, with his unselfishness, his courage, his truth. You cannot be a party politician and place-seeker and possess these qualities. In my day, no more contemptible lot have been in office. They bow before a leader who is no statesman and who is ruining the life of the nation. Cant and cowardice characterise proceedings since he has come into office. "Too late" describes every resolution his Cabinet has ever come to—'

Wolseley's tirade was interrupted by a delicate cough from Buller.

The Commander-in-Chief sat back in his chair. 'I do apologise, my dear,' he said, slightly shamefacedly. 'I fear I spoke indiscreetly of my lord and master and our ministers. I would be grateful if you would not report those remarks.'

Alice hid a half-smile and decided not to attempt a defence of her particular hero, William Ewart Gladstone, the Prime Minister. 'Of course not, my lord. But clearly you feel that your expeditionary force has landed too late?'

'No, no. Damnably late, yes, but not *too* late, please God. We are over the main part of our supply problems. I intend to establish our forward base camp at Korti, below Dongola, just before the Nile bends up again in its great loop north – you know where I am talking about?'

Alice nodded.

'And from there I mean to split the army in two: a river column and a desert column. The river column, of course, will stay on the boats, making their way upriver. The desert column will push across from Korti. At this point it would be unwise of me, of course, to reveal their exact destination, or how they will do this. But,' and he leaned forward, 'I can tell you something exclusive to give you a . . . whatchimacallit . . . shovel . . . no. Dammit, Buller. What's the word?'

'A scoop, sir?'

'That's it. A scoop. Strange word, isn't it? Yes, well. I am forming a flying column back home, a camel corps of eleven hundred men who are being picked from the best cavalry regiments of the line. They should arrive soon and will be put into intensive training here. If necessary, they will race across the desert ahead of the main troops to give succour to Gordon until we can catch up. I tell you, Alice, new problems demand new solutions. We are up to the mark, I promise you.'

'Thank you, General.' She looked up from her notebook. 'This begs the question of when you believe you can reach Khartoum.'

The two men exchanged glances. 'I am expecting to get to Khartoum,' said Wolseley finally, 'by the end of January.'

'And do you believe that Gordon can hold out until then?'

Wolseley sat back in his chair and gave her a sad smile. 'That, of course, is the question. I believe that he can, because the last that we heard from him – and he is now completely cut off, of course – was that he had plenty of ammunition, food and water. But we cannot be sure, of course. Hence our need to push on just as quickly as we possibly can.'

'Do you have any intelligence back from Khartoum?'

'The occasional cryptic message gets through, but we do not seem able to reach him in return.'

Alice directed a firm gaze at Wolseley's good eye. 'And please tell me, sir, is that where my fiancé, Simon Fonthill, comes in?'

Once again the two men exchanged glances. 'Ah yes, my dear,' said Wolseley, and he shifted a trifle awkwardly on his seat. 'What I tell you now is in the strictest confidence, for I would hate any news of young Fonthill's mission to get out and prejudice his safety. You understand, of course?'

'Of course, sir.'

'Good.' Wolseley nodded, and then explained the exact nature of the task he had given Fonthill. Alice listened with increasing anxiety, and when he had finished, she lost her composure for the first time.

'But that is incredibly dangerous!' she exclaimed. 'He doesn't speak a word of Arabic, he doesn't look in the least like an Arab, and how on earth do you expect him to penetrate the Mahdi's army and get through into a city that is besieged? Surely you have native spies better equipped for such a . . . a . . . lunatic mission?' She threw down her napkin in emphasis.

'Now, now, dear lady . . .' began Buller.

Wolseley held up a placatory hand. 'I well understand your apprehension, my dear,' he said. 'To be honest, I rather feared your reaction when you learned of the duty he had undertaken, and that was why I . . . er . . . perhaps have rather avoided you so far. But I felt it best to tell you now. Let me try and answer your questions.'

Quietly but emphatically, Wolseley gave his reasons for sending Fonthill on such a mission: his need to have someone with the expertise, courage and experience to penetrate the Dervish lines, and also the military ability to form a judgement of Gordon's chances. No native spy could do that. He reassured her on the effectiveness of Simon's disguise, and his faith in the ability of Jenkins and Ahmed to support him.

'You know, my dear,' he leaned towards her as though about to exchange a confidence, 'Fonthill did not have to undertake this journey. There was no compulsion, because he is not a serving officer, of course. He gladly accepted it. You will know that I have twice offered him his commission back with a high rank. Both times he rejected the offer.' The General shook his head. 'He is a remarkable man. Quite, quite independent, with his own rather . . . what shall I say . . . critical views of the army. He prefers to operate outside its ranks, and he is brilliant at what he does. But it is a dangerous game he plays, I must admit.'

Alice winced. 'Have you heard anything at all from him?'

'No message. But according to Major Kitchener, who is out in the field in the south, in charge of our intelligence work with the local Sudanese, he . . . er . . . was met by one of our patrols south-east of Dongola, and was certainly well then and . . . ah . . . in rather typical good form, from what I hear.'

Alice gritted her teeth to hold back tears. Her feelings were a mixture of apprehension and anger. Fear for Simon's safety, of course, although the General had confirmed what she had already suspected, but also fury at Wolseley's confirmation that Simon was doing what he loved best in all the world: risking his life to go out with Jenkins on some hopeless, highly perilous mission instead of proving his expressed love for her by staying at home and marrying her.

She blew her nose and sat up very straight. 'Thank you, sir, for your explanation. I apologise for my outburst.'

'Quite understandable, my dear.'

'May I return to your plans?'

'Of course – although you will understand that I cannot reveal too many details to you.'

Alice nodded. 'You intend to split your army when you reach Korti. You will have, what, about eight thousand men in the front line by that time? The Mahdi is said to command forty thousand or more, all of them well armed. Is it not bad practice to divide your already quite small force in the face of an enemy that is already proven to be more than a horde of spear-carrying savages?'

Wolseley chortled and held up a cigar. 'Do you mind?'

'Of course not. I can't exactly retire on my own.'

'Quite so.' A steward appeared as if from nowhere, and lit cigars for both men. Wolseley blew a cloud of smoke up to the ceiling.

'Your question does you credit, of course,' he said, 'and befits a brigadier's daughter. But needs must. This is not exactly a textbook invasion, you know. You understand the difficulties of advancing up the Nile. It may be that we can get the majority of our men up the river by boat from now on faster than we have been able to carry them so far, because we are learning all the time. I hope and think we will, but perhaps events will prove me wrong. The desert column is my back-up strategy. If we are still behind the clock, so to speak, then this column, led by my new camel corps, will make a dash for Khartoum. So far, the Mahdi has knocked over only Egyptian troops, and frankly, my dear, they are a poor lot, as we saw at Tel el Kebir. He has not yet met trained, well-armed British soldiers, the best in the world. No, I will back this column, not necessarily to win a great pitched battle, but to give this desert preacher a bloody nose and forge on to Khartoum, to give Gordon heart and support until we can get there with the main force.' He sat back. 'There. Now you have my plans.'

Alice finished scribbling. 'Thank you, General,' she said. 'You have been most helpful.'

Wolseley nodded. Then he pulled on his cigar and waved away the smoke. 'But it is all a question of timing. When and if I unleash my desert column depends upon how long Gordon can hold out. I desperately need Fonthill's advice on this. I doubt if I can get any force to Khartoum until the end of January at the earliest.'

Alice lifted her glass. 'Well, gentlemen,' she said, 'all in all, perhaps it would be appropriate for us to drink to Simon Fonthill and his comrades, and to their safe and prompt return.'

'Hear, hear,' growled the two old soldiers.

Alice left the yacht as soon as propriety allowed, for she was anxious to retire before the wine adversely affected her memory. She lacked shorthand, so an accurate recollection of what had been said was vital to support her scribbled notes. Her attitude as she stepped down the gangplank and nodded at the sentry's salute was at first one of elation. She had undoubtedly got the bones of a first-class story in that almost illegible scrawl in her notebook. There had been much speculation about Wolseley's exact intentions. Now she had them – and straight from the horse's mouth, even though she couldn't quote him! And the creation of the camel corps – so inventive, so very Wolseley – was a splendid piece of hard news on which to hang the rest of the story. This would be one in the eye for all those begaitered, cigar-smoking veterans with whom she was competing!

Her mood changed, however, as she walked the short distance along the river bank to her quarters on the press boat. She began to shiver under her wrap, less from the night air than at the thought of the dangers facing Simon. The bright stars above did little to offset the fetid odour that rose from the banks of the Nile, like the stench from a newly opened tomb. It brought home to her once again the very primitive nature of the country that the British were invading. She could not but help recall what the Dervishes did to infidels: the lopping of hands and feet, the slitting of noses and slicing of ears. Horrible, horrible! Leaning against a stanchion, Alice let herself go, and sobbed until the tears dropped on to her precious notebook, smudging her pencilled notes. How cruel to lose the man she loved just when, at last, it was right and seemly that they could be together, after all the changes they had faced! Oh, *why* had he left her? Did he not love her enough at least to marry her before careering off into this barbaric desert to get himself mutilated or killed? But it was uncharacteristic for Alice to cry, and it was not long before the anger reasserted itself. She stamped her foot, disturbing two scorpions investigating her slipper. Damn Simon, and damn bloody Gordon for getting himself into such a mess that fine men had to come out here to rescue him! She blew her nose, straightened her back and strode back to the press boat. She had a story to write.

*

She rose early the next day and took another precious shower – really only a bucket balanced overhead on a swinging axle – to relieve her aching head before the men could get to the douche cubicle. Then she read through the story she had written, correcting some of the more awkward cablese abbreviations she had used. She had led her story on the formation of the camel corps, before going on to give her authoritative analysis of the General's plans, without, of course, quoting Wolseley. In a covering note to Bonard, she had explained that her source was the General himself, and she allowed herself another self-congratulatory smile at the effect her exclusive would have on the rest of the correspondents here. They would be furious, for there was so little hard news to report from the Nile! Then she strode off to the cable office.

Despite the early hour, the new press liasion officer was already on duty. He was a small, slim man, as erect as a Guards officer at the Trooping of the Colour, and wearing a captain's badges of rank and the largest moustache she had ever seen on such a small man. He gave her a perfunctory glance as she handed in her copy, and then another, this time lingering on her body, examining it insolently from her solar topi to her desert sandals.

She disliked that, but she forbore to complain. There was something about this man that sent a tingle through her – not exactly of fear, but carrying a kind of warning that he could be dangerous. The examination and the stare were insolent and arrogant, but they were also quite fearless. This captain of infantry exuded cruelty, and she drew in her breath. Perhaps she should be careful. No, dammit. The man was loathsome.

'I say,' he said. 'You must be the famous Miss Griffith.'

Alice felt herself flushing. 'Yes, and I have an eight-hundred-word story here that I need transmitting immediately. And don't you dare alter a word of it, because the source is the General himself and I have his permission to write it as long as it is not attributed to him. So be damned careful – and keep it confidential.'

With that, she turned on her heel, wishing she had a skirt she could swish behind her. As she strode away, she heard him call after her, 'What about a drink at sundown, eh? As a reward for no deletions, what?'

Alice tossed her head and strode on, shivering with . . . what? Rage, impotence or fear? She did not know. Near the river bank she met Willie Russell. 'You're an early bird, Alice Griffith,' he grinned. 'Not another exclusive, for God's sake, is it?'

Alice ignored the question. 'Who is that impertinent little man who has been appointed liaison officer, Willie?'

'Aw, somebody they've dredged up from Intelligence. I gather he put his foot in it out in the desert somewhere, so he's been drafted back to this awful job.'

'What's his name?'

'I think it's Hicks-Johnson. Why do you ask?'

Chapter 8

Major General Gordon led the little party further into the huge room. It was long and low and dominated by large windows that commanded a view of the Blue Nile and the far bank some eight hundred yards away. An intermittent fire was being directed at the palace from the bank and was being returned from the roof of the building. Gordon, however, seemed quite unaware of the noise and danger and indicated chairs for them all, including Mustapha. Then he beckoned to his Sudanese servant and ordered tea. As he did so, Fonthill scrutinised him closely.

At that time, he pondered, Gordon was undoubtedly one of the most famous men in the world. When Simon had first heard of him, the man was forging a remarkable international reputation as a shrewd, brave and resourceful soldier, leading what was little more than a handful of irregular troops in China against the Taiping rebellion and suppressing it, so earning the gratitude of the Chinese government and the nickname 'Chinese Gordon'. A period of comparative obscurity had followed as an Engineer colonel in England, where he had worked amongst the poor and particularly helped disadvantaged young boys. Here he showed himself to be a hero who seemed to care nothing for material benefits. A dedicated bachelor, he gave away much of his salary and lived in the most frugal way, proclaiming a devotion to fundamental

Christian ethics that seemed close to fanaticism. Then he had earned a new reputation as a shrewd and energetic governor of Sudan and an implacable enemy of the slave trade in central Africa. Back home and at a loose end, he had responded to an invitation from the King of the Belgians to govern the Belgian possessions in the Congo, but when the task of evacuating Egyptian troops from the Sudan in the face of the Mahdi's uprising had presented a problem for the British government, the nation had cried, 'Send for Chinese Gordon!' He had answered the call, and now he was holed up in Khartoum, surrounded by thousands of the most fanatically brave soldiers in Africa, all of whom hated him and regarded him as an infidel pig. The eyes of the world were upon him and the attempts to rescue him.

Yet now, as he sat on a small wooden chair in his palace, Gordon seemed to Fonthill rather like a country vicar fussing over the tea. Except that those astonishingly blue eyes looked tired, and there were worry lines in the skin radiating out from their corners. One hand tapped on his knee in a nervous fashion and he inhaled deeply on the cigarette he was smoking.

'I've heard a little about you in army circles, Fonthill,' he said, after Simon had made the introductions. 'You were at both Isandlwana and Rorke's Drift in Zululand, were you not?'

'Yes, sir.'

'Yes, quite remarkable. Then you had better tell me what you are doing here, when I had expected Wolseley with fifteen thousand redcoats.'

Fonthill took a deep breath and explained his mission. He avoided as best he could the puzzlement caused by Gordon's many contradictory messages before the telegraph was cut – and also, of course, his own instructions to gauge the state of the town's defences. 'What Lord Wolseley wants, sir,' he concluded, 'is an estimation of how long you can hold out and some indication of the strength of the forces surrounding the town. Then my orders are to return to his lordship with this information as quickly as possible.'

Gordon sighed. 'That last part is easier said than done. I have been smuggling messages out for weeks, but nothing comes back. I suppose the Dervishes intercept them. When can Wolseley get here, do you think?'

'I believe he is hoping to fight his way through by the end of January.'

'Umph. Well, if that is his intention, he will probably be too late. Let me see, where are we now?' Gordon rose and walked to a table near the window where a large journal lay open. As he did so, Fonthill looked across at his companions. Mustapha was tracing a pattern with his big toe on the wooden floor; Ahmed was looking at the General with something like awe – Gordon's name was as familiar in Cairo as it was in London – and Jenkins had enveloped the small teacup with his two great hands and was shaking his head at Simon with consternation written on his face. His expression asked clearly: what on earth are we doing, sitting here drinking tea in a doomed palace surrounded by savages?

'Ah, yes.' Gordon walked back to his chair. 'Today is the sixteenth of November. Well now, let me see. About a month ago I estimated that some three million cartridges had been used in the siege so far by our Remington rifles, together with ten thousand mountain gun shells and one thousand five hundred and seventy by our Krupps cannon. Back then we had about two million Remington cartridges left, more than eight thousand shells for the mountain guns and six hundred and sixty for the Krupps.'

Fonthill wondered at Gordon's recall of statistics, and then remembered that the man was a Royal Engineer, renowned for his grasp of detail.

'You know,' the General continued conversationally, 'I have converted the mission next door, where this little chap will go to school,' and he leaned across and patted Mustapha's head, 'into an arsenal, and am making about fifty thousand Remington cartridges a week there. Not bad, eh?'

'Very good, General bach,' acknowledged Jenkins, as though anxious to please a difficult child. Fonthill nodded his head encouragingly, wondering where all this was leading.

'Quite so.' Gordon seemed pleased to have the praise. 'However,' he went on, 'the attacks have increased considerably over the last few weeks. My spies tell me that the Mahdi himself, who has been skulking hundreds of miles to the south-west, has now moved his camp near to the fort at Omdurman, and as a result, things have hotted up. So we will have used far more ammunition pro rata. You ask how long we can hold out.' The General drew on his cigarette. 'I reckon that we have about eight weeks' food left, so we can probably last until the end of December. Perhaps a little longer, but not much. By then we shall be eating the dogs, and the town must fall.' He gave a weary smile. 'It is all, of course, in the hands of our Redeemer.'

A shocked silence hung over the room.

'Good gracious,' whispered Fonthill.

'Do you know where Wolseley and his column are now?' asked Gordon. 'Is he at Berber?'

Simon shook his head. 'I am sorry, General,' he said, 'but I have no idea. I left him in Cairo weeks ago, of course, just before he was due to start upriver. Judging from our own experience, he will have encountered difficulties in getting his army through the cataracts and it will have been slow going.

As I said, I believe his intention was to arrive to rescue you by the end of January.'

'It is not a question of rescuing *me*!' Gordon's face suddenly became suffused with anger, and he rose to his feet and slapped a hand against his thigh. 'I am not the rescued lamb and never will be. Positively and once and for all, I will not leave the Sudan until everyone who wants to go down the river is given the chance to do so.'

The little man stalked to the open window and stood there in silence for a moment, quite impervious to the rifle fire directed at the palace. Then he spoke quietly, as though to himself. 'I could write volumes on my pent-up wrath on this subject,' he said, 'if I did not believe that all things are ordained and all work for the best. I should be an angel, which I am not, needless to say, if I was not rabid with Her Majesty's Government.' His voice fell and he shook his head. 'But to lose all my beautiful black soldiers is enough to make me angry with those who have the direction of our future . . .'

Still looking out of the window to the far bank, where the Mahdi's tents could be seen, he continued, 'I will never leave men who, though they may not come up to our idea of heroes, have stuck with me through great difficulties, though I am a Christian dog in their eyes. I will not surrender to those who have not conquered them.'

Then Gordon whirled round. 'I altogether refute the suggestion that the expedition has come to relieve *me*. It has come to relieve our national honour. I was relief expedition number one; *they* are relief expedition number two. Now, please excuse me for a moment if you will. I must go and order a twenty-one-gun salute.'

Fonthill's eyebrows rose. 'A twenty-one-gun salute, sir?'

'Of course. This is to celebrate your arrival. I shall tell the people that you have brought news that Wolseley's army is only a week or so behind you. Maintaining morale among my soldiers and the townspeople is all-important. Help yourself to tea while you can. We don't have much left.' And he strode from the room.

Once again a silence fell on the room. 'Blimey,' said Jenkins eventually. ''E's a bit strange for a general, ain't 'e?'

Simon shook his head. 'He must be under tremendous strain.' He blew out his cheeks. 'But it's obvious we can't afford to linger here. We must get back to Wolseley and warn him how little time there is left. If his army is still bogged down on that bloody river, then perhaps he could send a flying column out ahead across the desert to reach here and give heart to Gordon and the townspeople.'

Ahmed spoke for the first time, and Fonthill realised how bedraggled the previously impeccably groomed hotelier now appeared. 'I was hoping, Simon,' he said, 'that perhaps it might be possible to have a bath, et cetera, et cetera, you know?'

'Of course, Ahmed. I think we can allow ourselves that.'

'What are you goin' to do, then, bach sir?' asked Jenkins, his voice low so that the Sudanese servant, standing by the door, could not hear. 'And 'ow are we goin' to get back anyway, look you?'

Fonthill pulled a face. 'I promised Wolseley that I would take a look at the defences here, although Gordon is a Royal Engineer and will know far more about defending a town like this than anything I have ever learned. I mustn't give the General even the slightest impression that Wolseley thinks he might have . . . er . . . lost his judgement, and that I have been sent out here to report on him, so to speak—'

He was interrupted by the boom of ordnance close to the palace. One shot echoed, then another and another, at regular intervals. The twenty-one-gun salute had begun. Shortly afterwards, Gordon re-entered the room. It seemed as though he was cheered by the sound of the cannon.

'That will buck us all up,' he said. 'Now, we must find rooms for you all. There is plenty of space here.'

'Thank you, sir,' said Fonthill, 'but we certainly don't need to stay in the palace.'

'Nonsense. You, Fonthill, will have Frank Powers's room next to mine. He was the *Times* man, you know. Excellent fellow. Sadly, he went down the river and was killed. Now, you other chaps will be given rooms down below. There is good accommodation. And you, my mighty fellow,' he beamed at Mustapha, 'shall be housed with my other little chicks in the school. In fact, we will all go there now. I am proud of my school and I will show it to you.'

Fonthill frowned. With so little time, he did not want to go school visiting! 'That's kind of you, General. But I thought perhaps the defences . . .'

'Oh, plenty of time for that tomorrow. Come on, now. Leave your things here. My people will look after them. Come along.'

He gave an order in Arabic and then strode to the door, picking up an incongruous black English umbrella from a stand as he went. The rest tailed behind, Mustapha looking distinctly unhappy at the prospect of returning to a schoolroom after his years running wild.

A corner of the former church and now arsenal close to the palace had been converted into a schoolroom, where some sixty boys (no girls, Fonthill noticed), of mixed colour and seemingly of ages spreading from three to eight, were crowded together at small tables. A white-haired Sudanese standing at the blackboard bowed deferentially as the General entered. Immediately the children burst into a buzz of delight as Gordon beamed at them.

'I have about two hundred of them in all, here and in other rooms,' he said. 'As you can see, each lad has a wooden board on which his lesson is written. The aim of each boy is to be called out to read his lesson. See.'

He spoke a few words in Arabic to the teacher. Immediately one completely black urchin, his white teeth flashing, walked to the front of the class and read from his board, in a sing-song voice and swaying his body.

'There you are,' said Gordon. 'This is just like the Jews do at their wailing place in Jerusalem. These little black doves are saying the first ten letters of the alphabet, which is all they know.' He shrugged his shoulders. 'But it's a start.'

He nodded to the teacher to resume the lesson, and led his visitors out of the classroom. Fonthill wondered anew at the strangeness of this man, who, with only a few weeks to go before the barbarians swept into the city, found the time to create a school for infants and the peace of mind to derive such pleasure from it.

Back in the palace, Gordon summoned an orderly and gave him instructions in Arabic. 'You, my little chap,' he said to a glum-faced Mustapha, 'will be taken to the school and given a bed and a place there. You two fellows,' he addressed Jenkins and Ahmed, 'will eat with my pashas, and this chap will take you there. Perhaps you, Fonthill, will be kind enough to dine with me tonight? It has been a long time since I have had company. Freshen up, of course, but don't bother to change. I never do. I warn you, however, it will be rather ordinary fare.'

And indeed it was. Fonthill, without change of clothes of course, found something surreal about sitting down at what was undoubtedly an English dinner table, with its precisely set spoons, knives and forks and condiments, in his Arab dress.

But the food was quite unpretentious: some kind of thin soup, almost a gruel, was followed by a fish, presumably from the Nile, that Simon found tasteless and bony. Gordon, however, was only too happy to talk, and Fonthill realised that the man must have become terribly lonely.

'I am the only European here,' he confessed, 'although I believe there are one or two Greek shopkeepers left in the town. I sent Stewart, my second-in-command, together with Powers and the French consul here, downriver a month ago and, of course, they were betrayed and killed. So I eat alone every night. Worst of all, there are no men of the cloth here of any denomination, so that I take communion myself every morning in my bedroom. Not proper, of course, but God will understand.'

Fonthill nodded sympathetically.

'I apologise for the absence of wine,' continued Gordon, 'although I don't really miss it myself. But I can promise you a reasonable brandy that I sometimes take after dinner. Now, tell me about your journey. It must have been difficult and dangerous, although you have blacked up remarkably effectively. I could well imagine that I am dining with a Syrian – or, dash it, a Dervish, for that matter.' And he chuckled.

Simon related the broad details of their journey, omitting the clash with Hicks-Johnson, and, in response to questions from Gordon, gave the background to his relationships with Jenkins and Ahmed. The General particularly wanted to know how Mustapha had been found and how he had been treated by his Dervish master.

At the conclusion, he nodded. 'You know, Fonthill,' he said, 'the primitive pain that stems from the excessive anxiety one cannot help being in for these people comes back to me at times. Then I think that our Lord, sitting over Jerusalem, is ruling all things for the glory of His kingdom, and I cannot wish things different from what they are, for if *I* did so, then I wish my will, not His, to be done. This Sudan is a ruin, and humanly speaking there is no hope. Either I must believe He does all things in mercy and love, or else I disbelieve His existence. There is no halfway in the matter.

'If the Dervishes break in, I have mused whether to blow up the palace and all in it, or else to be taken and, with God's help, to maintain the faith and if necessary suffer for it, which is most probable. The blowing-up of the palace is the simpler option, while the other means long and weary suffering and humiliation of all sorts. I think I shall elect the last, not from fear of death, but because the former has more or less the taint of suicide, as it can do no good for anyone and is, in a way, taking things out of God's hands.'

Fonthill, whose religious beliefs were of the blandest, squirmed a little in his chair and coughed, nodding politely.

Hardly, it seemed, noticing him, the General continued. 'I trust and stay myself on the fact that not one sparrow falls to the ground without our Lord's permission; also that enough for the day is its evil. "God provideth for the way, strength sufficient for the day." Don't you agree, Fonthill?'

'Of course, sir.' A sudden welcome breath of cool air came through the open window and fluttered the candles for a moment, sending shadows dancing down the long room. A rifle cracked from across the river. Simon's beard itched and he wondered if he had picked up lice from Ibrahim's boat. Oh hell! Time was slipping away, and here he was discussing the Almighty as though at a bishop's dinner party in Bath. He must, he really *must* begin the task of checking on the town's defences. 'Now, General, I wonder whether—' he began.

But the bit was now thoroughly between Gordon's teeth. 'You know, my dear fellow,' he went on, 'what I cannot stand is apostasy. To change one's faith, to switch one's religion, so to speak, for one's own comfort or convenience is the height of shallow cowardice. I have recently received a message smuggled in to me from the Mahdi's camp from a fellow called Slatin Pasha, an Austrian – I presume a Catholic – who was a governor under me of one of the outlying provinces. He fought well against the Mahdi, and the story goes that he converted to Islam to encourage his Egyptian troops just before he lost the last battle.

'Now, although Slatin is a self-declared Mosselman, the Mahdi takes no account of that, and he is in chains in the Mahdi's camp just outside Omdurman. He writes that he wants some sort of forgiveness or acceptance from me. Saying that he fought twenty-seven times against the enemy and so on. If he escapes, he wants me to take him in. Well, of course I cannot. I cannot encourage him to break his parole, which should be as sacred when given to the Mahdi as to any other power. I shall not reply. I mean, your faith or your word is not something you change like a suit of clothes. Don't you agree?'

'Er . . . yes, sir. Of course. May I ask you, General. How many men do you have in the town defending it?'

'What? Well, I am not sure now, because I am afraid that there have been losses, desertions and so on. In the early days of the siege I sent out quite a few sorties, on land and by boat, under my black pashas, and with some success initially. But I received many setbacks and lost my best men. Now I can't really venture out beyond the walls, except with my penny steamers. In the beginning I had about eight thousand troops here, but we are far fewer now.'

'And what is your estimation of the Mahdi's forces surrounding Khartoum?'

'From what I hear, this bogus preacher man has about twenty thousand outside the town. But now that virtually all the other outposts in the Sudan have been overrun by the

Dervishes, the tribes are flocking to him from all over the country, and I suppose he will soon have some forty thousand.'

'May I ask—'

But the General interrupted him. 'My word, Fonthill, I am talking too much. I have forgotten my promise to you of the cognac. Now,' he rose, 'why don't we sit over here near the open window, and the boys will light this twenty-four-candle lantern.' He chortled. 'Almost as good as those new gas lights everyone is talking about at home. Come along and sit down and I will fetch the brandy.'

Fonthill rose and took a tentative step towards the chairs by the open window. Immediately a rifle cracked. He gulped. 'Isn't it rather offering those snipers an illuminated target?' he asked.

'Oh, but that must be nothing to a chap who was at Isandlwana and Rorke's Drift, eh?' Gordon brought two large goblets of amber liquid, pulled up another chair and gestured to the servant to position the large lantern just behind them. 'One of the merchants here, you know, said that I should have sand boxes erected just outside these windows to protect me. But I summoned my guards and told them that they should shoot me if I moved from this seat after dinner. I do all my writing here, with that lamp behind me. It doesn't do to show fear, you know. Anyway,' he chuckled, took a draught of the cognac and nodded across the river, 'they're terrible shots.'

'Too far away on that opposite bank, I suppose?' Fonthill offered hopefully.

'Oh no. The snipers are on that little island over there. Well within the range of modern Remingtons, which these heathens have, of course, captured from us.' He took another sip. 'But what will be will be, what? Not bad, this brandy, eh?'

'Oh, absolutely splendid, thank you.' Fonthill tried to sink a little lower in the chair. 'How good are the fighting men you have left here, sir?'

'The black chaps, the Sudanese from the south, are by far the best. I have some quite young black fellows – not more than children, really – who spend their days on my roof here, standing on boxes blowing very cheeky bugle calls across the river and taking potshots at the so-called snipers on the island. Great fun. You know, of all the so-called inferior races, I like the Chinese first, then the chocolate Sudan people, and I respect very much the cleanliness of the Negro soldiers. I do not like the tallow-faced *fellaheen*, though I do feel sorry for them.'

'And what about your defences around the town?'

'Well, you shall see for yourself tomorrow. The main fortifications are well to the south, with small forts on both sides of the Blue and White Niles. I have had a ditch cut right across the isthmus with a parapet behind it, and sown mines like seed on the mud flats behind the ditch, but,' he took another sip of the brandy and chortled, 'some of these mines are not quite what you would call lethal. A donkey trod on one the other day and walked away quite unperturbed. I doubt very much if we are now in a position to withstand a determined attack by overwhelming numbers. It will just be a matter of time, really. The Dervishes tried a mass attack a few weeks ago by driving cattle across the mines to explode them, but we fired rockets and the cattle stampeded away.'

Then he frowned. 'One of my main worries, Fonthill, is that a traitor within the town will open a gate during darkness and let in a thin file of Dervishes, which, of course, will suddenly become a rush. The rainy season is from July to September, and now the Nile has sunk, of course, leaving these great mud-flat approaches that are difficult to defend. In fact, I am having a problem just now with the south-west section of the ditch and parapet. The withdrawal of the river there means I have to extend the defences, and it's awkward with the mud, you know.'

Then Gordon's expression changed, and the blue eyes lit up with pleasure. Fonthill could not help noting how quickly the General's moods seemed to alter. A reflection, perhaps, of the constant swings in the fortunes of the town and his implacable faith in the Almighty?

'I have done my best with the townspeople, you know,' he continued. 'When I arrived I made a bonfire of all those horrible tax collectors' whips, the *kourbashes*, and wiped out debts. I even permitted them to keep the slaves they have, which of course goes very much against the grain with me. On arrival I found the coffers completely depleted. Money promised to me could not get through, so for the last few weeks I have been printing my own bank notes by lithograph, carrying serial numbers and with an impression of my Arabic seal. I have the bands playing on Fridays and Sundays and have had metal stars made that I award for bravery. Yes . . . I try to do my best to keep everyone going, so to speak.'

'I am sure you do, sir.' Fonthill sat silently for a moment, looking at the lamplit profile of this seemingly gentle man, with his high forehead and greying hair curling at temples and collar. A gentle man, he concluded, but one made of steel and well buttressed by faith and courage. But what must it be like to be left alone here in this alien, unprepossessing town, waiting for the inevitable attack by barbaric hordes and with the relieving force still far away? Despite his Christian belief, he must have doubts and fears, surely?

As though on cue, Gordon shook his head, revealing that depression had returned. 'I feel gutted, Fonthill, that this expeditionary force was not sent earlier and has not made quicker time. I blame that awful man Gladstone, of course, who has just left things too late. I know that Wolseley will have pushed on as fast as he could, but that may not be enough. I sent four of my precious steamers downriver a little while ago to wait for him, under one of my best men, Khashm-el-Mus, but it's difficult to get through and I do not know their fate. So, I suppose, my dear boy, everything rests on you now.'

He leaned forward. 'Tell Wolseley that we are in good heart and determined to hold out to the last man. But you know our position here and that we don't have much time. Tell him that all I need is two hundred men in red coats to show that the force is on its way.'

Then he drained his glass and stood. 'I see you have finished your brandy, Fonthill, and I have a little work to do this evening – as, indeed, every evening. You must be tired after all your adventures getting here, so please don't let me prevent you from retiring.' He smiled apologetically. 'I like to make my rounds at about this time, and these days I am not a good sleeper, so forgive me if you hear me pacing about through the night. It used to upset poor Powers, I fear.'

'Of course, sir. Have no thought of that. Is there anything I can do to help you, perhaps?'

'No. Get your sleep, there's a good fellow. I have a routine. Now, good night, and God bless you.'

'Good night, General. And thank you.'

Fonthill did not sleep well that night. The comfort of a deep feather mattress perversely irritated him after months of sleeping rough, and having drifted off into a brief doze, he was awoken, as warned, by the footfalls of his host pacing up and down in the next room. The main deterrent to sleep, however, was the realisation that Gordon had far less time to hold out than perceived by Wolseley. This meant that Simon and his comrades *must* leave as soon as possible and take this message of urgency to the relieving column. But how to get through the besieging army? He had been lucky once in getting into Khartoum. How could he now get out and race across whatever miles – three hundred, four hundred? – were left between the town and Wolseley's relieving force? He woke soon after dawn, feeling quite unrefreshed.

Early in rising as Simon was, Gordon was even earlier. Fonthill found him on the roof of the palace, looking towards the fort at Omdurman through his telescope and quite agitated.

'Ah, Fonthill,' he said. 'Three escaped slaves reached us during the night and told me that the Mahdi has brought up heavy guns at last and that an attack is expected at any minute on Omdurman. My main defence against this are my two remaining steamers, so I instructed a clerk to telegraph to them to get up steam. But the damned fool did not do so and I have only just been able—' A gun boomed from the Arab side of the river. 'There you are.' He trained his glass again. 'Yes, the attack has started. The Dervishes are streaming across towards the fort and the steamers are not ready yet to get down there and direct fire on them. Dash it all!'

'Will you go on the boats yourself, sir, when they get steam up?'

'No. I cannot afford to leave here in case the thrust on Omdurman is a feint and the main attack comes against the town.'

'Then let me and my chaps go. I am used to directing fire, sir, and you can spare us.'

Gordon looked at him quizzically, then made his decision. 'Very well. Frankly, the boat commanders are good sailors but not particularly good shooters. Go down to the mud flats. The two steamers should be up shortly. Take them downriver and use shrapnel against the Dervish infantry. But watch out for their guns. I'm told they have brought up captured Krupps heavy stuff now. Do be careful with these boats. They are my main defence. If both are sunk, Khartoum is sunk with them. God bless you, my boy.'

Fonthill nodded, ran into his room to pick up his rifle and revolver and took the stairs two at a time to where Jenkins and Ahmed were just stirring. 'Get up quickly,' he cried. 'Bring your weapons. We're going for a boat trip.'

He sprinted down across the mud flats to where a makeshift jetty had been extended from the bank. Of the steamers there was no sign, and he had no idea where they were moored overnight. Somewhere a little safer upriver under the town's guns, he presumed. Then he saw a spiral of steam rising into the still air from round a slight bend to the south, and the first of the steamers, the *Ismailia,* hove into view, its paddles thrashing the water, followed by the smaller *Husseinieh.* Fonthill waved and shouted to them and they steered towards the jetty.

He jumped aboard the *Ismailia,* followed by Jenkins and Ahmed, and was met by the commander who had brought them in the day before. 'General Gordon has asked me to take command,' Fonthill said. 'Omdurman is under attack. Please stay on the bridge and direct the boat. I will oversee the firing from the deck. Steer as close in on the port side as you can, then we will turn back up the White Nile. Jenkins.'

'Bach sir?'

'Hop into the craft behind and take charge there. Just follow us and keep moving. We will steam down towards the junction of the two rivers and come back up the While Nile towards Omdurman. Have the gunners load the starboard gun – dammit, that's the right-hand side as we look forward – with shrapnel canister and fire at the infantry. But load the gun on the other side with explosive shells, and when we turn round and come back, fire at the Dervish artillery if you can see it.'

'Blimey. Do I get admiral's pay, then?'

'Off you go. Tell the Egyptian officer that the General has ordered us to take charge. Stay close to this vessel but keep moving because we will be shelled by the heavy stuff.'

'Aye, aye, Captain.'

Fonthill had the momentary impression that the captain of the boat was about to quibble, but Simon's air of command and the firmness of his instructions overrode whatever irritation the Egyptian felt. Then the boat shook as the big paddle wheels began to turn to take the craft out from the bank and towards the fork of the river, some four miles away.

On their port side they passed the tiny Fort Mukram that Gordon had built to command the mud flats and then came under rifle fire from Tuti Island on their starboard, but the steel plating erected around the little boat's boiler and the thick planking built to shield the deck were proof against this small-arms fire. Its intensity, however, made Fonthill, who was supervising the loading of the little twelve-pounders with canister shot, realise how numerous and well armed were the Dervishes on the island.

As the junction of the two great rivers neared, the Mahdi's new, heavier guns could be more clearly heard, and as the helmsman took the *Ismailia* out in a wide arc to swing the boat back up the White Nile, the Dervish artillerymen directed their fire away from Fort Omdurman on to the paddle steamer. But their range setting was poor and the shells whistled overhead to land on the far bank of the newly merged rivers.

'Take her as near as you dare on to the starboard bank,' Fonthill shouted up to the bridge. He looked behind. The *Husseinieh* was wheeling around behind them, and he saw the black head of Jenkins, his *esharp* now completely unwound and his rifle nestled into his cheek. The Welshman began firing towards the bank from above the timber planking.

Simon knelt down beside his gun crew and squinted along the barrel. The target was unmissable. Thousands of white-clad Dervishes were milling before the entrenchments that had been dug from the corners of the fort down to the river. 'Set the shell fuses at two hundred yards,' he ordered. 'Now up two degrees,' he added, and the gun-layer cranked up the barrel. 'Good. Fire!'

The recoil rocked the boat and the shrapnel shell exploded about twenty feet above the front rank of the tightly packed Arabs, sending sharp metal fragments down upon the unfortunates below. 'Splendid. Reload. Keep firing.' The stutter of the Maxim from the bridge now joined in, cutting its own swathe through the Dervish ranks, and the riflemen also opened fire.

Fonthill tossed his Martini-Henry to Ahmed. 'Join in and give 'em hell!' he called.

'Oh, excellent. Thank you, Simon.'

The little man poked the long rifle over the parapet, pulled the trigger and produced a dull click. 'Try taking off the safety catch, old chap,' Fonthill shouted.

'Thank you. Very good advice. I do it immediately.'

The fire from the boats brought a cheer from the defenders in the fort, and it became clear why Gordon relied so heavily on his penny steamers. With their shallow draught and their manoeuvrability, these floating gun platforms could approach the Dervish infantry at close range and pump artillery and small-arms fire into the attackers at whatever point in the defences was proving to be most vulnerable. Now, as the shrapnel took its terrible toll, the Arabs began falling back along the banks of the river, leaving white and bloodied heaps of bodies behind them.

The Krupps gunners, however, were beginning to find a sort of competence in setting the range for their large ordnance. The shells were still overshooting – they could not undershoot for fear of hitting their own infantry on the banks of the Nile – but the brown columns appearing on the far mudbanks were now being replaced by spouts of water rising above the stumpy mast of the *Ismailia*.

Fonthill rushed up to the bridge. 'Can you increase speed,' he asked, 'and take us away from these bloody guns, and then turn round and come back to give them a taste of their own medicine from our port gun?'

'Certainly, *effendi*.' The captain grinned. 'The *Ismailia* can do anything.'

'That's what I like to hear. Full speed ahead, then, Captain, and do a lovely pirouette.' Simon looked back to the little ship behind. Its starboard gun was still blazing, and Jenkins gave him a great grin and a thumbs-up sign from the rifle parapet. Fonthill gently removed the binoculars from around the captain's neck and focused them on the high bank behind the fort. Yes. There was a little row of four Krupps cannon assembled on a low ridge and gleaming pewter grey in the morning sunlight. The Dervishes had displayed their inexperience by grouping the guns together, without cover, and so presenting an enticing target. He made a rough calculation and slid down the companionway to where his port-side gun crew were waiting.

'Are you loaded with high explosive?' he demanded. The gun-layer nodded. 'Good. Set for three hundred and fifty yards and fire when I order.'

The boat swung round almost on its axis as the port paddle wheel went into reverse, and for a moment Fonthill feared that they would collide with the *Husseinieh* behind, but Jenkins had relayed his instructions well and the smaller craft slipped neatly between the *Ismailia* and the bank, repeating the same manoeuvre before falling into line behind its sister ship, which was steaming back towards Omdurman.

Fonthill recorded with satisfaction that the Mahdi's infantry were now in full retreat from the fort, with the taunts of the defenders clearly to be heard, speeding them on their way. The little steamers, however, were also moving back within range of the Dervish artillery, which immediately opened up on the vessels.

A crash from astern made Simon whirl round. The *Husseinieh* had lost way and a cloud of steam rose from its boiler. It appeared that one of the paddles had been hit, for the boat now slewed round, its stern down in the water, and began limping crablike towards a small island in midstream. Fonthill stayed looking at the vessel only long enough to ensure that it was not sinking immediately, then focused the glasses on the distant group of guns.

'Fire!' he ordered. He saw a spurt of sand rise immediately in front of the guns. 'Up three degrees. Fire!' This time there was an explosion and he witnessed one of the cannon whirl up in the air and crash down on to its mate at the side. 'Good shooting,' he cried. 'That's two out of action. Keep firing at the same range and point of aim.'

He turned and directed his attention once more on the *Husseinieh*. Jenkins was now in the stern, which was ominously low. 'My command is bloody sinkin', look you,' the Welshman shouted across the water. 'We're goin' to 'ave to ground it on that island there, if we can make it before we go down. Just remember I can't swim, will you. An' 'ave you seen any crocs about at all . . .?' His voice tailed away as the boat slipped out of earshot.

Fonthill shouted up at the bridge: 'They're going to beach her on that island. Can you get alongside to take off the crew?'

His voice was almost lost as the Dervish battery opened up again. Through the glasses Simon could see that the remaining two guns were spitting flame and were obviously targeting the stricken *Husseinieh*. One shell crashed into the bow, sending it shudderingly off course, and water spouts rose all around it, as though a shoal of friendly whales was escorting it. But somehow the boat kept making way until it grounded on the rocky island, surging halfway up a gravelly beach before coming to rest, steam blowing from its boiler.

'Don't go back yet, Captain,' Fonthill shouted up to the bridge. 'Let us lay down one last burst of covering fire to make them get their heads down before we try and rescue the crew.'

The captain nodded, and the paddle steamer picked up way once more and then throttled back to provide a stable platform for the gunners. The twelve-pounder barked into life again and again, laying down a barrage of high-explosive shells on to the gunners on the ridge. For the moment it seemed as though all the Dervish artillery had been put out of action, but through the glasses, Fonthill could see that most of the shots had fallen short. Close enough, however, to make the opposing gun crews keep their heads down and even, perhaps, run for cover.

'Back to the *Husseinieh*,' Simon shouted up to the bridge, and the paddle wheels slowed, stopped and then ponderously began to turn in reverse, churning up a stream of chocolate-coloured water on either side. With great skill, the captain took his craft stern-first alongside the smaller boat, which was now firmly aground, and the crew scrambled aboard, with Jenkins last.

'I 'eard somewhere, bach,' he gasped, 'that the captain should be last to leave 'is bleedin' ship, so I thought it right and proper that I should let the other buggers go first, see.'

Fonthill grinned and shook his hand. 'Well done, Admiral,' he said. Then his expression changed as he looked at the wreck of the *Husseinieh*. 'I'm afraid the General won't be pleased that he has now lost half his fleet,' he said. 'I can see how important these little things are to him. Are you sure that there was no hope of refloating her?'

'Not a hope, bach sir. There's a great 'ole in the back there an' another up in the front. And,' he nodded to the Dervish shore, 'I reckon she'll be stuck there for target practice now. No one will be able to get near 'er, look you. Bleedin' shame, though. I was quite enjoyin' bein' a captain an' all.'

Simon looked up at the bridge and shrugged his shoulders at the *Ismailia*'s captain. 'Full speed ahead back to Khartoum,' he shouted. 'I'm afraid we will have to leave her.'

As they steamed away, the Dervish gunners seemed to ignore them, happily pouring more shells into the hulk of the *Husseinieh* as though it was a cockshy at a fair. 'Stupid bastards,' murmured Fonthill. 'They're acting like children with a new toy. It's us they should be firing at.' He ordered a couple more shells to be fired at the battery as they steamed past, but the motion of the boat caused them to fall short.

Once again they ran the gauntlet of the rifle fire from Tuti Island, but they reached the jetty without further incident. After shaking hands with each captain, Fonthill, Jenkins and Ahmed sprinted across the mud flats and through a small gate into the city. Walking the short distance to the palace, Simon was able for the first time to assimilate something of the ambience of the beleaguered town.

This was the only main street in Khartoum, stretching from east to west, narrow and lined with mud houses, which each year were plastered with dung as protection against the annual rains. The grey monotony of these dwellings was broken by the governor's palace, by far the largest building in the town; a low, dingy barracks; two mosques; a small Coptic church, now seemingly abandoned; a hospital built by Gordon during his previous tenure as governor general; and the Catholic missionary church, now converted into arsenal and school. The architecture, such as it was, was undistinguished – but the smell was even worse. Fonthill was unsure whether it came from the mud flats or from the mangy dogs that roamed the streets, but it caused him to wrinkle his nose in disgust. Few people were about, and the intermittent crack of gunfire, from the Arabs without the walls and the defenders within, sounded a backdrop to a general picture of apathy and even, he had to admit, an overall impression of impending disaster.

Gordon was waiting for him on the palace roof, his telescope still in hand. 'I've seen most of it from up here,' he said, his face seeming to be grey even in the harsh sunlight. 'Come inside and have a brandy, you probably need it.'

'No thank you, sir. A bit early for me. I am sad to report what is almost certainly the loss of the *Husseinieh*. She was holed by shellfire and we had to beach her. I don't see how you can retrieve her, I'm afraid.'

The General nodded, his eyes sad. 'Yes, I saw it. This means I am down now to only one boat, which will make it very difficult, though of course I must not complain. It is God's will.' Then, characteristically, his face brightened. 'But you did a splendid job in repelling the attack on the fort. First class, Fonthill. How would you like one of my metal stars, eh?'

Simon grinned back. 'Greatly honoured, sir, but I think I had better decline. It wouldn't sit exactly well with my Arab dress – particularly when trying to get through the Mahdi's lines.'

The frown returned to Gordon's face. 'Yes. Your return is

now a matter of even greater urgency, of course, for I fear that the Dervishes are closing in. We should be able to get you out of here. There's a small gateway that the Dervishes don't seem to worry about. Let us at least have a cup of tea – and bring your chaps up, too.'

Ten minutes later the four were sitting round Gordon's low table, drinking green tea. 'Right,' said the General, 'it seems to me that there are only two feasible ways of getting through the Dervishes.' He took a long, reflective sip from his cup. 'The first is that you slip out, preferably at night, through this small gate, which I keep carefully guarded but which seems to be the main route for deserters coming in from the Mahdi. You would then have to rely on your disguises to get through his lines and make your way south. Trouble is, I can't give you any camels because, dash it, they simply wouldn't get through that little gate. And anyway, camels going across the mud flats at night would easily be seen.'

He took another sip. 'The second way is that you set out downriver on the *Ismailia*. The trouble is that she is now my only steamer, and you have seen this morning how much I rely on these little craft. I would have to have her back within the day. Which doesn't leave much time for her to get past the main Dervish army on the shore. She could not navigate the shoals and rocks by night, so putting you ashore during the day without attracting attention from our Mahdist friends would not be easy. What do you think?'

Fonthill did not hesitate. 'I would not wish to deprive you of your last penny steamer, sir, even for a day. We will slip out tonight.'

'What about transport north?'

Simon shot a quick glance at Ahmed. 'Once we have walked as far as we can by night, I would hope that Ahmed here could buy us three camels. Or perhaps we could even negotiate to hire a boatman's services again.'

Jenkins intervened quickly. 'Oh, I think the camels, bach sir. We don't like the river much, see, now do we?'

'You speak for yourself, 352. What do you think, Ahmed?'

The little Egyptian nodded solemnly, holding his teacup with little finger extended. 'Oh, I think I could buy camels, if we can reach a village. We have enough money, I think.'

'Right. Camels it is.'

'Good man.' Gordon replenished their cups. 'Now, should we sew coloured squares on your *jibbas* to show that you follow the Mahdi? It could help you get through the lines.'

'I don't think so, sir, but thank you for the thought. I don't want us to be recruited into the Mahdi's army, thank you very much, and if we are caught and cross-questioned, I doubt if we could maintain our story about being supporters of the Mahdi. In uniform, so to speak, we would be condemned as spies. And you know,' he said, smiling, 'there is something distasteful about being a spy. We enlisted as army scouts, and Arab dress is as far as I wish to go in terms of disguise.'

Gordon nodded. 'Does you credit. We will make up food for you to start you off. Oh, and I will exchange your Martini-Henry rifles for Remingtons. It is well known that only the British Army has the Martinis and they would stick out like a sore thumb if you took them. The Rems are easily available here. Less good, of course, but better for your disguise.'

A barely disguised 'hurrumph' came from Jenkins.

'Now,' continued the General, 'the darkest period is at about three a.m. at this time of the year – there is no full moon, which is a blessing. We will slip you across at the narrowest part of the Blue Nile by my North Fort. I suggest you now eat and try and sleep. I will be here to wish you God speed before you leave. More tea?'

'No thank you, sir. We will see you later. Oh, by the way.' Fonthill frowned. 'I would like to leave Mustapha with you in your school, if you would keep him. Do you think that . . . er . . . if the worst came to the worst . . .' He tailed off, because he was not sure how to put to the General the possibility of the Dervishes crashing through the defences and sacking the town.

Gordon understood. 'If the worst does come to the worst, I am sure that the good Lord will look after Mustapha. I can't see even the Dervishes killing every small boy in Khartoum. The worst that could happen is that he would be enslaved again.'

'Quite so. Thank you, sir. I had hoped to take him home to England, but of course the risk is too great and . . . I think there would be other problems.' For a moment Alice's face, with its grey eyes and firm jaw, flitted across his mind. He realised guiltily that he had not thought of her for at least twenty-four hours, so exigent had been the events of the past day. 'I think,' he said, 'we had better slip away without seeing him.'

Fourteen hours later, the little party gathered by a post gate in the wall. General Gordon shook each man by the hand. 'Now, Fonthill,' he said gravely. 'Tell Wolseley that I shall hang on as long as possible. But I doubt if that could extend much into the New Year. So he must get a move on. Better, as I have said, to make a dash across the desert with a highly mobile small force than to wait until he completes the river passage. Red coats are important to create an effect. Even two hundred men would do, if they can move fast. I will not give you a written message for obvious reasons. I will continue to try and smuggle a message through to him, but you are my main hope.'

'Thank you, sir. I will tell him. Good luck.'

'God speed. I will pray for you.'

As Fonthill, the last man in the trio, moved through the gate, there was a sudden movement from within and, like an eel escaping through water reeds, Mustapha slipped through and seized Simon's hand. 'This is gate I told you about,' he grinned. 'Holy mother of God, I come with you.'

Fonthill grimaced. 'No, Mustapha. It is far too dangerous. You must stay here and go to the Pasha's school. It will be good for you.'

'No. No. I come with you. You my master . . . my father . . . now. You need me. I know desert. I speak Arabic. I slip through places you don't go. You save my life, I save yours. I too old for silly school. I go with you. *I go with you.*'

The boy's grip on Fonthill's hand was as strong as the emphasis on his words, and the look of supplication on his face was so earnest that Simon almost relented. Then his brow darkened. 'No. It is far too dangerous . . . I don't want you killed.' He turned his head but found that the little gate behind them had already been closed.

Jenkins's voice hissed from the river bank: 'Come on, bach sir. The bloody moon's comin' up.'

Simon sighed and grinned at Mustapha. 'Oh, bejabbers. All right then.' And the little party, accompanied by a boatman, disappeared into the night.

Chapter 9

Luck was on their side during the crossing, for the newly risen moon was hidden by a low bank of cloud, and a soft breeze was rippling and splashing the surface of the Blue Nile so that the creaking of the boatman's oars could hardly be heard. For all its much-lauded bravery and commitment, the Mahdi's army was undisciplined in a conventional military sense. There was no line of guards keeping watch on the walls of the town. Why should there be? The infidel was caged. He was not going anywhere. So Fonthill and his little party stepped ashore without challenge.

Reaching a large rock, Simon called his companions close around him. 'Listen,' he whispered, 'if we are captured we will be stripped and everything will be taken. I think it wise, then, if Mustapha carries our money and my compass. There is more chance of him slipping away if they take us. No one will bother with a slave boy – at least I hope not.'

Mustapha looked up wide eyed. 'What do I do then, master?'

'If you can, follow and see where we are taken, and keep the money for us to help us if we escape. If we are killed,' his teeth gleamed in the semi-darkness, 'spend the money and have a good time. Buy yourself a crocodile.'

The boy shook his head. 'If you die, I don't want no crocodile. I bury you with proper Christian headstone.'

'Yes, lad,' said Jenkins. 'But make sure we're dead first,

like. And think of somethin' else for old Et Cetera 'ere. 'E's a Mosselman, see.'

Ahmed passed over the goatskin wallet containing the local currency, *omla gedida* dollars, and the boy tucked it under his shirt. 'What do I say if we meet soldiers?' asked the Egyptian. 'Where are we going and where have we come from?'

Fonthill shrugged. 'We shall have to stick to our story of being Syrian traders. We have been in the south, trading, with you as guide and interpreter. But desert Bedawi attacked us and stole our goods and our camels. We fought them off with our rifles and have made our way on foot to the Mahdi's headquarters to find camels we can buy. That's all I can think of. Do your best, old chap. Now we will walk under cover of darkness until we have left most of the soldiers besieging the town behind. We will follow the river south, but not too close to the bank. What we need is a small village with a camel market. Shouldn't be impossible to find. Once we have camels we can head east, away from the soldiers, but we can't risk the desert until we have camels. Come on, but no talking.'

They set off in single file, Ahmed in the lead, followed by Simon, accompanied by Mustapha who carried the compass, and Jenkins in the rear. In truth, they looked like indigenous desert wanderers in the darkness, dressed in their tightly wound *esharps*, long ubiquitous *jibbas* and leather slippers. With their Remington rifles carried in the crook of their arms, a first glimpse could have revealed them to be members of any number of tribes who had flocked to the black banner of the Mahdi, or even trader parasites hanging on to the edge of the army.

As they walked, heads down, Fonthill realised that the Mahdi's army was more a vast collection of families who had flocked to worship and then follow the new Messiah. Low tents of various sizes were pitched in disordered profusion among tethered goats and camels belonging, presumably, to their occupants. There were no guards or canvas barrack lines. No artillery batteries. Before leaving Khartoum, Simon had been told by Gordon that the Mahdi himself had now arrived to make his headquarters just outside Omdurman on the west bank of the White Nile, and that the forces opposite the town, on the Blue Nile, were under the command of a leader called Sheik-el-Obeid. If that was so, then the sheik's followers were a sleepy lot, for nothing stirred as the three men and the boy stole quietly through their ranks.

On through the night they walked, maintaining a fair pace, and as the moon gained some strength between the clouds, Fonthill realised that they had left Tuti Island behind them and were now marching through empty desert. They had no map, but Simon remembered that Gordon had told him that he had built a fort in a little village on the east bank called Halfiyeh, some eight miles downriver, but that the tightening of the Dervish net had forced him to send a steamer down to dismantle the fort and bring the timber back for use within the city. Perhaps what was left could provide shelter for them during the coming day?

The sun had come up like a brazen ball, threatening another hot day, when they reached Halfiyeh. They were tired and glad to find that the demolition party from the steamer had left the mud walls standing, so that they were able to huddle in the shade and build a fire of sorts and cook a little *durra* and rice and make tea. As far as could be seen, the village itself was deserted and seemed to pose no threat. Simon established a guard rota; he took the first watch himself and the others stretched out and slept.

He was woken by a kick in the chest and then, to make sure he was awake, another in the stomach. He cursed and curled foetus-like, but that did not prevent a third kick crashing into his head. He looked up along the barrel of a Remington rifle into the blackest and cruellest pair of eyes he had ever seen, glaring at him from between the folds of a dirty white *esharp*. The Dervish yelled at him and gestured for him to stand, and Simon realised that the confines of the ruined fort were crowded with Arabs, all now kicking Jenkins and Ahmed awake and shouting in Arabic. There must have been a dozen of them, and they all wore the multicoloured patches of the Mahdi sewn into their clothing.

'Ahmed!' shouted Fonthill. The little Egyptian scrambled to his feet, held out his hands in a gesture of supplication and began talking as fast as he could. Of Mustapha there was no sign.

The Dervish who had woken Fonthill now took a fistful of his *jibba* and pulled his face to within inches of his own, screaming again whatever question he was asking. Fonthill shook his head and shouted, 'Explain, Ahmed.' The Egyptian began pleading again, turning his head to address them all. Simon caught Jenkins's eye and made a quick estimation. Taking on all twelve of the Dervish in this confined space was hopeless, not least because he could see that all of their rifles were cocked and ready to fire. They would be shot before they could lift a finger. Their own rifles had been kicked into a corner. He gave a quick negative shake of the head to the Welshman. But where was Mustapha?

Whatever Ahmed was saying was obviously not meeting with approval, for a derisive laugh came from the Dervish who had awoken Fonthill. The man, who seemed to be the leader of the party, took three steps towards the Egyptian and struck him with his hand across the face. Ahmed fell to the ground, struggled on to all fours and then received a kick in the stomach that levelled him on the floor again.

The Dervishes now began consulting with each other, and

Fonthill took the opportunity to edge towards the Egyptian and whisper, 'Are you all right, Ahmed?'

The little man lifted his head and nodded. 'They say we seen crossing river from town,' he said. 'We left tracks in desert and they have followed us. They know we not Syrians.'

Simon thought quickly. It was pointless trying to maintain the guise of Syrians now that they were known to have come from Khartoum. But admitting they were English would mean that they would be treated as spies and probably executed on the spot. Why were they in the town, and what nationality could they claim whose language was unlikely to be spoken by anyone in the Dervish army?

'All right,' he said. 'Admit we are not Syrians. Say we are Greek shopkeepers who were escaping from Khartoum because we know it will be taken soon. Say we were hoping to get a boat to take us downriv—'

A rifle barrel crashed into Simon's head, sending him staggering and his brain spinning. The folds of his headdress softened the blow to some extent, but the suddenness of the attack as much as its force shook him. There was no point in opposing. He dropped to his knees in submission.

He heard Ahmed speaking quickly again in Arabic, and this time he saw the Dervishes exchange glances and nod their heads. Obviously this confession gave more satisfaction. The leader snapped an order, and the three of them were forced to stand with their faces to the wall while rough hands searched their clothing. Loud cries of surprise met the discovery of the Colts tucked away inside the *jibbas* of Fonthill and Jenkins, and the long silver barrels and curved handgrips of the revolvers were examined with delight and interest. Then a further order was given and the three men's hands were tied roughly behind their backs. Their weapons were distributed among the Dervishes and they were hauled outside into the sunlight. There, halters were placed around their necks and the ends tied to the cantles of saddles fixed on three camels.

The Arabs mounted their camels and Fonthill made a quick estimation. If they were to be taken back to Sheik-el-Obeid's camp the way they had come, the distance was probably nearly ten miles. That would be bearable – if the camels walked. If, however, they trotted or were pushed into the lumbering gallop that racing camels could achieve, then this journey could be agonising.

Immediately the beasts were forced into a trot that meant the three captives were forced to run behind amidst the stones and sand kicked up by the camels' feet. Under what was now a midday sun, and with breathing made difficult by the dust, they had the choice of collapsing and being strangled by the cord around their necks or, somehow, staggering along to keep pace with the camels. It was, of course, an exquisite torture.

After about twenty minutes, Ahmed staggered, fell and was dragged along face down in the sand. Fonthill immediately flexed his neck muscles and pulled back against the rope as strongly as he could. He gasped to Jenkins, 'Pull back. Pull back.'

The two of them, of course, were not strong enough to halt the camels, but their joint effort made the beasts lose their rhythm and falter. Immediately, the leader of the Dervishes, who was pulling Fonthill, gave an order and the cavalcade halted. Languidly the man unwound a *kourbash* from the canton of his saddle, tapped his camel's neck so that it knelt, and slid to the ground. He strode towards Simon and lashed him several times around the shoulders and back. The thong, made of rhinoceros hide, cut through the cotton *jibba* as though it did not exist and Simon felt as though red-hot coals had been dragged across his skin. He bent his head against the blows and heard Jenkins shout, 'Fuckin' bastard' – which was enough, of course, to direct the lashing to the Welshman.

Yet the whippings at least gave Ahmed a little respite and time to arch his back, rise to his knees and then stagger to his feet. His clothing at the front was torn to shreds and his face and chest were bleeding, but somehow he stood.

A cry – of what? admonition? – came from one of the other Dervishes, and in response the leader grunted, coiled his whip, gave Ahmed a superficial inspection and then mounted his camel. This time, however, the cavalcade moved off at a walk.

'Thank God for that,' gasped Fonthill. 'You all right, Ahmed?'

The little Egyptian could not find his voice but gave a half-smile and nodded.

'Three five two?'

A growl came from Jenkins. 'If that bugger thinks that was a whippin', then 'is mother was a camel. Which, on thinkin' about it, she almost certainly was, look you. I've had worse beatin's from fly whisks, see. But I'll get 'im for that, see if I don't.'

'Save your breath. You're going to need it.'

The agony of the camel trotting was not repeated but the beasts were made to walk at a distance-consuming lope that turned the legs of the captives to jelly and made the breath rasp in their throats. Fonthill's main concern was Ahmed, who staggered along with eyes closed and perspiration streaming down his bloodstained face and chest. His once carefully trimmed beard was now thick with sand, dust and blood and the remnants of his *jibba* hung in strips, as though his body had been flayed. Simon felt a pang of guilt join the pain that ran through his own body. This was not the Egyptian's fight and he was the least well equipped physically to withstand such privation. Yet the little man was clenching his jaw and somehow contriving to put one foot in advance of the other.

Then Fonthill thought of Mustapha and tried to look behind. He could see no one. Had the boy escaped? Was he following them, somewhere out there in the rocks and dunes? If so, had he been able to keep up during the trotting torture? He grimaced and prayed that the lad had been able to get away.

Eventually, after what seemed an eternity, the pace slowed and Simon realised that they were approaching the banks of the Nile. Looking across to the far side, he saw the unmistakable outline of Fort Omdurman. He shook his head in despair. They had been brought all the way back virtually to Khartoum and now, by the look of it, they were to be taken across the river. That meant that their destination must be the camp of the Mahdi himself. Were they to meet 'The Expected One' and even, perhaps, be questioned by him? Unlikely. It was doubtful that they would be considered that important. And yet the leader of the Arab army would surely be unwilling to miss out on this chance to gain information about the state of morale within Khartoum and, indeed, the defences of the city. A shudder went through him. Would this mean torture?

Camels and all, the party was embarked upon a flat, punt-like craft that was laboriously paddled across the river. But at least it allowed the captives to sit and breathe easily.

'Did either of you see Mustapha get away?' asked Fonthill. They shook their heads. ' 'E was on last watch,' said Jenkins. 'I 'anded over to 'im and the next I knew I was bein' kicked in the goolies. These chaps ain't very gentle, are they? Worse than the bleedin' corporals in the glasshouse.'

Once on the west bank, the party picked its way through a multitude of tents, pitched again seemingly in no order, between which Dervishes in their multicoloured *jibbas* and women and children thronged, seeming without direction. Eventually they reached a compound framed by a *zariba* of thorn bushes, with low tents forming one side. Stakes had been driven into the ground at intervals, from which led chains attached to metal rings around the necks of at least thirty men lying in various forms of prostration on the ground.

Fonthill sucked in his breath. These creatures presented a sight he would never forget. Some seemed near death, in that they lay completely still, seemingly not having the energy to brush away the flies that clustered round their lips and eyes. Others had only one foot, the other missing from the ankle, with the stump bound in a filthy and often still bloodstained dressing. Most of the unmutilated wretches were shackled at the ankles too, with an iron bar separating their feet. Few of them were moving, condemned as they were to lie in the hot sun. The place stank.

'Fuckin' 'ell,' breathed Jenkins.

The neck halters of the three were untied from the camel saddles and they were pulled to a vacant stake, at which they were gestured to sit. The halters were tied to the wood and they were left alone.

'Now what d'you think's goin' to happen, bach sir?' enquired Jenkins.

'Well, I have a feeling that we are now in the camp of the Mahdi himself and that sooner or later we will be interrogated. But it looks as though we will not be left to die here. Look.' He nodded to where wooden gourds and dishes stood by the side of the other prisoners. 'They obviously feed and water everybody.'

'Oh, yes,' growled Jenkins. 'It's a proper luxury hotel, this is.'

'Ahmed, how are you feeling?' asked Simon.

The Egyptian summoned up a smile. 'My chest hurts but I am better now that I am not being forced to look up the bottom of that camel,' he said.

Two slave boys brought them gourds of water and held them to their lips while they gulped eagerly. Then they were left to squat in the sun, for there was no shade. The heat was intolerable but their greatest suffering came from the flies. These gathered on the open wounds left by the whipping and, in Ahmed's case, from being dragged behind the camel, and buzzed around their mouths and eyes. Fonthill realised for the first time what a profound luxury it was to be able to have a hand free to swat away the loathsome insects.

After several hours they were approached by a large man dressed conventionally in Arab clothing but whose ankles were linked by a heavy iron chain, allowing him only to shuffle. His face was distinguished by melancholy eyes and a huge unkempt moustache. He squatted in the dust and addressed them in Arabic.

Ahmed replied sullenly and then turned to Fonthill. 'He says he is Slatin Pasha, a prisoner of the Mahdi who—'

'Ah, you speak English,' the man interrupted, his eyes lighting up, 'I was told you were Greek.' His English was perfect, although he spoke with a guttural Germanic accent.

'We are,' said Simon, doing his best to tinge his voice with what he hoped was a Greek accent, 'but we never mastered Arabic properly, so we employed Ahmed here as our interpreter.'

Slatin regarded him in silence for a moment. Then: 'Are you of the Muslim faith?'

'Only Ahmed here. We are Greek Orthodox.'

'Then it will not go well with you here.'

'Why? And why were we captured and beaten? We were doing no harm to the Mahdi's cause. We were merely trying to leave Khartoum and return to Cairo.'

Slatin shook his head slowly. 'I have been sent here by the Khalifa Abdullah, the Mahdi's main disciple and what you would call his prime minister, to question you and find out the truth. He uses me in this way and usually trusts me to tell him of spies. I warn you that he is a hard man and if he discovers that you are lying to him he will have you killed.' He sighed. 'Usually those who have been fighting against the Expected One and are captured are offered the choice of death or of joining him. But they cannot join him unless they take the true faith and accept the Mahdi as the true prophet.'

'But we have not been fighting him.' Simon swallowed. They had no choice but to carry through with the lie, for to admit to being English would undoubtedly be a death sentence. 'We have simply been shopkeepers in Khartoum. We did not take sides in this dispute.'

'Ah.' Slatin gave his sad smile. 'Then why were you carrying Remington rifles and, even more strange, two American Colt revolvers? Shopkeepers do not go about armed, particularly with American weapons.'

Fonthill thought quickly. 'We kept an armaments shop, but Gordon Pasha prevented us from trading in case we armed rebels within the town. So we sold what we had left to him and took these weapons only to protect us in our long journey north.'

Again the sad smile. 'If you sold your stock, why was no money found on you when you were searched?'

Clever bastard, thought Simon. 'We had with us two slave boys to serve us on our journey,' he said. 'They must have stolen our *gedida* dollars while we slept and made off with them. I do not lie.' At least the reference to two boys instead of just one might confuse the searchers if a hunt for Mustapha was launched.

Another pause ensued while Slatin looked at each man in turn. Fonthill prayed that Jenkins would have the good sense to keep quiet. Amazingly, he did so.

'Well,' continued the Austrian eventually, 'I must confess to you that there is no one in the Mahdi's camp who speaks Greek, as far as I know, and I cannot question you in your own language. I shall tell the Khalifa that I have no evidence that you are lying but that I cannot be absolutely certain. I shall tell him, however, that on balance I think you speak the truth.'

'Thank you. Will he then allow us to go, do you think?'

Sadly the big man shook his head. 'Extremely unlikely, I fear. He will probably want to question you on the state of things in Khartoum and then . . . ah . . . detain you while he makes up his mind what to do with you.' He gestured behind him with his head. 'Many of these poor people here are in that situation. I was so myself but now the Khalifa uses me in the way I have described, although,' he gestured to his chains, 'I remain, as you see, very much a prisoner.'

'But will he not respect our own religion and not force us to convert to Islam?'

'I doubt it. If you take my advice you will convert quickly and accept the Mahdi. Then you will probably live.'

Slatin looked at Ahmed. 'You are Egyptian?'

'Yes.'

'The Sudanese call all Egyptians Turks and hate them because they see them as oppressors. You can pass as a Greek. I should let them think you are Greek.'

Ahmed inclined his head. Then Fonthill asked, 'How long have you been a prisoner here?'

'For nearly a year. My name is Rudolf Slatin and I was born in Vienna. I was an officer in the Austrian Army but tired of the boredom of garrison duty and wished for a more exciting life.' He smiled. 'Africa fascinated me, so I volunteered to serve under Governor Gordon in the Sudan. I found excitement all right. The General made me Governor of Darfur, and, when the Mahdi's revolt began I fought against him strongly. I was born a Catholic, but when things were going hard for us out there in the scrub and desert of Darfur I converted to the Muslim faith to give encouragement to my Egyptian troops. But it was to no avail and I had to surrender.'

Fonthill now remembered Gordon's reference to the Austrian. Could the man be trusted?

Slatin sighed. 'I had to endure many humiliations. But I have survived. Many did not. I saw one Egyptian receive a thousand lashes a day for three days because he refused to reveal where he had hidden his money. Others were tied hand and foot and lowered head first down wells and kept hanging there. These are cruel people.'

'What do you advise that we do?'

'It is better, my friends, to be very patient and endure whatever fate has in store for you. There is an Arabic saying, "Allah is with the patient, and he who lives long sees much." I commend it to you.'

He rose to his feet. 'The Khalifa will want to see you – he only uses me for the first filter, so to speak – so be prepared. Answer truthfully if you are questioned. This man is very shrewd, and although he only speaks Arabic, he seems to have a sixth sense when he is told lies.'

Fonthill frowned. 'We are suffering from our wounds and filthy from being dragged here behind camels. Can we not be allowed the dignity of applying water and soap to our sore bodies before we see the Khalifa?'

Slatin bowed his head. 'Your request is reasonable. I will ask. Now I must go.'

As he shuffled away, his chains clinking in the dust, Jenkins spat. 'I don't want to turn into any 'eathen, bach sir,' he said, 'savin' your presence, Amen, but I'd prefer it to bein' pushed 'ead first down a well, thank you very much.'

Simon wriggled his back to disturb the flies. 'If we are

summoned to see this Khalifa,' he said, 'then I think it best to let me do the talking. Whatever happens, though, we must stick to our story about being Greek shopkeepers. If it is found that we are speaking English, then we must say we are from the Greek part of Cyprus and picked up the language from the British troops stationed there.' He looked with concern at Ahmed, whose head was drooping. 'Are you all right, old chap?'

'Yes, but not very happy, Simon, with overall situation, et cetera . . .'

'I don't blame you, bach,' said Jenkins. 'But cheer up, the Captain and me 'ave got out of worse 'oles than this. We'll get out of this one too. You'll see.'

Fonthill dutifully smiled in support, but in truth his heart was heavy. By the look of it, no one escaped the Mahdi's clutches once the shackles were hammered into place. Even if they could somehow break out of the *zariba*, how were they to find their way through the Dervish hordes and, without camels, boat or money, journey back to Wolseley some four hundred miles or more in the north? And how, anyway, could they travel fast enough to be instrumental in hastening the relief of Gordon?

Simon studied more closely the wretches in the compound. It seemed that their hands had been left free, but the links of their chains had been hammered together to tether them to the wooden stakes, which meant, presumably, that they were not meant to be moved, not given work even, but left to rot here between the thorn-bush walls of the *zariba*. He gritted his teeth. There was no sign of Mustapha. Perhaps the boy had been killed or, more likely, simply run away. The thought of his cheeky grin and curly hair made Simon think, inconsequentially, of Alice. Would he ever see her again? He shook his head. Of course he damn well would! Jenkins was right.

They had wriggled out of worse holes than this. They must make a run for it before they were chained and while they were still tied with these rough cords. Perhaps during cover of darkness they could work away at the fibres and then slip away and even steal three camels . . .

It seemed that Slatin had some influence, despite his prisoner status, because shortly after his departure the slave boys returned, this time with soap, water and oil, and their hands were freed to enable them to wash. It was bliss to bathe at last, and they also rubbed the oil into each other's wounds, easing the burning sensation that consumed them, although Ahmed complained that the pain in his chest was worsening. Their hands were left untied but they remained haltered at the neck. Fonthill's hopes that they would be left undisturbed until nightfall were dashed when Slatin came shuffling towards them, this time accompanied by the leader of the party that had captured them.

'The Khalifa wants to talk with you,' said the Austrian. 'Be careful what you say. He likes flattery, so say you have heard of him and of his exploits as a soldier. The Mahdi may also want to see you. If he does, I advise you to ask for the honour of being given the *beia*, that is the oath of allegiance. This may save you from punishment.' He shot a quick glance at the tall Dervish standing with him. 'This man here is evil, so do not upset him. He is in charge of the people in the *zariba*, so he can make things bad for you. Come now.'

The Dervish gathered their neck halters in one hand and gave them a strong jerk, making the three stagger forward. They were led out of the *zariba* and eventually towards a square hut, outside of which they were told to wait while Slatin went within. Then they were ushered inside to a room with straw walls and a thatched roof, where the Khalifa awaited them, sitting on an *angoreb*, a low bed consisting of a wooden frame laced with leather thongs.

Fonthill knelt and bowed his head and the others followed suit. Through his eyelashes he examined this man who had won most of the Mahdi's battles for him. He'd been told by intelligence that Abdullahi Ibn Sayed Muhammad had been merely a member of the Baggara cattle-owning tribe in Darfur when he had tramped miles to join the Mahdi, Muhammad Ahmad, early in 1881. He had quickly become a committed disciple, to be trusted implicitly by the Expected One. No one now saw the Mahdi without seeing the Khalifa first. He was a thickset, bearded man with a hooked nose and small, cruel eyes. He spoke tersely to Slatin.

'Tell the Khalifa your names,' said the Austrian.

Damn! Fonthill thought fast. Names, names ... Greek names! He dredged through his memory to no effect and was forced to invent. 'I am Simon Miscouri.' He indicated Jenkins. 'This is Cyrallus Thermopolous and this Ahmed Athenus. Please say we are honoured to be in the presence of Sudan's greatest warrior, the Khalifa Abdullahi, of whom all the world has heard.'

The Khalifa regarded him for a moment without a change in his expression and then spoke softly. 'Why,' interpreted Slatin, 'if you admire the Khalifa so, did you not present yourself to him when you left Khartoum in the dead of night. Why did you slip away without paying him honour?'

Simon bowed his head. 'We did not believe ourselves to be worthy of a meeting with such a venerated and famous warrior. We had nothing to bring him to show him respect, no presents worthy of his stature, so we made our way to the north, beginning our long journey to Cairo.'

'We have people here who lived in Khartoum, of course. They do not know of a shop kept by Greeks that sold weapons.'

'That is probably because we did not only sell weapons. We also sold carpets and sweetmeats. Near the palace. But our best trade was in the weapons that we bought years before from desert Bedawi and soldiers who deserted from the army of the hated Turks. Then Gordon Pasha stopped our trade and, knowing that the great Mahdi would soon take the city, we decided to leave and return to Cairo.'

The glittering black eyes never left Fonthill's face as his words were translated. Then: 'How many soldiers does the infidel Gordon have defending the city?'

Here at last was an opportunity of helping Gordon in some small way. Exaggerating the size of the defence force might buy the General a few more days. 'I believe it to be between twelve and fourteen thousand men,' Simon said, 'although it may be more.'

'You are a weapons specialist. How well are they equipped?'

'With modern arms, Your Grace. The infidel Gordon has many black soldiers from the south as well as Turkish bashi-bazouk irregular troops and they all have modern Remington single-shot, breech-loading rifles, firing a lead bullet nearly half an inch long. They are better even than the British Martini-Henrys because they are lighter and less likely to jam in heat and dust. Then there are rockets and the large Krupps cannon and the lighter British mountain guns, which can be dismantled and transported easily. There are also some Maxim machine guns and the approaches to the walls have been laid with mines underground.'

He waited and watched closely as Slatin translated. The Dervish's face betrayed no emotion, but was there a flicker of approval in those dark eyes at the careful detail contained in Fonthill's reply? Simon hoped that this would not only give verisimilitude to their claims to be Greek armament traders but also deter the Khalifa in his plans to attack the town. But he was not to know, for at that point a messenger entered and, bowing, whispered a message to the Khalifa, who stood, swept up his *jibba* and walked to the door, uttering a command to Slatin as he did so.

The latter's face took on a slightly alarmed expression as he turned to Fonthill. 'Come,' he said, 'the Mahdi himself wishes to see you. Follow me. Be very respectful and ask for the *beia*.'

The what? wondered Simon. Then he remembered – the oath of allegiance. The tall Dervish jerked their neck halters savagely and Fonthill looked at his two comrades. Jenkins was eyeing their captor with a look of pure malevolence, but Ahmed was perspiring badly and, by the look of him, beginning to shake. Three five two, with his muscular frame and his inner strength, could withstand bad treatment, but the little Egyptian was beginning to look as though he was at the end of his tether. Whatever revulsion Fonthill felt at the thought of swearing allegiance to a false prophet, it was better to do that than have Ahmed exposed to more brutality. They would ask for the *beia*, if given the opportunity.

They were led some hundred yards away to a huge rectangle about a thousand by eight hundred yards, surrounded by a low mud wall and lined with men and women packed several feet deep and seated on the beaten ground. A sheepskin was spread in front of a small hut and the Khalifa walked to it and knelt on it, Slatin gesturing for the others to kneel a discreet distance behind. There was no shade from the relentless sun overhead but the crowd stayed muted and expectant. In the distance could be heard the sound of sporadic gunfire, presumably from Fort Omdurman. Fonthill comforted himself with the thought that at least the fort was still holding out.

Then from the hut emerged a tall, broad-shouldered but slender man who walked to the sheepskin and gave a welcoming gesture with his hand, while smiling warmly. The Khalifa stood and Slatin quickly gestured to the others to do so too, although the crowd remained seated and respectfully silent.

As when he had met the Khalifa, Fonthill now gazed in fascination at the Mahdi, this poor carpenter's son who within the space of four years had conquered the largest country in Africa, shattered the Egyptian army and captured twenty thousand rifles and nineteen cannon. Simon had heard that the man had memorised the entire Koran by the age of eight and had taken up the life of a wandering hermit, as a priest, scribe and doctor to the poor, deliberately espousing hunger and hardship and preaching 'The Way', his doctrine of salvation. It was based, he remembered, on a return to the basic teachings of the Koran and the improvement of self. But it also urged the hatred of aliens and all their ways, particularly the ways of the 'Turks', which meant anyone with a light skin who wore a fez, and the Egyptians, with their gluttony, liking for wine and oppression of true Muslims such as the Sudanese. The Mahdi's fundamental message was simple: the Sudan had to be cleansed of the 'Turks' and their British allies, and he called to the faithful to flock to his *jihad*, his campaign to make Sudan a country for the Sudanese only.

As he approached, however, there was nothing of the ragged hermit in the victorious Mahdi. He was wearing a short, quilted, spotlessly clean *jibba* and a skullcap of palm straw. His face was light skinned and framed by a deep black beard, and given luminescence by sparkling black eyes and a smile that revealed the V-shaped aperture between his teeth that, with the birthmark on his right cheek, gave credence to his claim to be descended, through twenty-nine generations, from the Prophet Muhammad himself.

The Mahdi extended his right hand to the Khalifa, who bowed and kissed it, and then approached the three prisoners and offered the back of his hand to them. Fonthill held it lightly, bowed his head, kissed it and hoped to God that Jenkins would follow suit. To his relief he did so, albeit a touch clumsily, as did Ahmed. Simon was conscious of a perfume emanating from the man. It seemed to be a mixture of sandalwood, musk and attar of roses (he was later to learn that his disciples called this *rihet el Mahdi*, odour of the Mahdi) and it seemed a remarkably feminine aspect of a man renowned for his masculinity – he was known to have a large harem – and single-minded cruelty.

The Mahdi turned back to Fonthill and, still smiling warmly, spoke to him. Slatin interpreted: 'Are you satisfied?'

The question puzzled Simon. Satisfied about what, for goodness' sake? Then he realised. These all-powerful potentates lived on sycophancy and flattery. He decided to indulge him. 'I am satisfied indeed, Your Highness, now that I have met you at last and kissed the hand that has blessed millions.' He remembered the old Muslim creed and the Mahdist line that had been added to it: 'There is no God but Allah. And Muhammad is the Prophet of Allah. And Muhammad el Mahdi is the successor of Allah's Prophet!'

'Blimey!' The muttered word came, sotto voce, from Jenkins, of course. Luckily, the Mahdi seemed not to have heard.

Fonthill remembered Slatin's advice, and he looked up into the gentle light brown eyes of the Mahdi. 'My comrades and I would consider it an honour if we could be given the *beia*, sir.'

On translation, the smile disappeared from the Mahdi's face for the first time, then he brushed his eyes with his fingertips and tears appeared in each corner. The smile came back, but he shook his head and spoke slowly. 'The Mahdi fears that it is too early for you to be given the oath of allegiance,' Slatin translated, 'but he says that if you will listen to his words now it will be well. For he who serves him and hears his words serves Allah and his religion and shall have happiness in this world and joy in the world to come.'

The Mahdi walked away from them back towards the door of his hut, then turned and took a central stance in the arena. The Khalifa left his sheepskin and squatted to the right of his master. Fonthill took the opportunity to whisper to Slatin, 'Why did he deny us the *beia* – and why did he begin to cry?'

'I do not know. I am sorry.' The Austrian paused for a moment and made sure that they could not be overheard. Then he lowered his voice. 'The Mahdi puts pepper under his fingernails so that he can simulate tears,' he whispered. 'But do not speak of it.'

'Well, what an old rogue . . .' Jenkins's whisper was so low that only Fonthill could hear it, but Simon shot him a warning glance.

A priest from somewhere on the fringe of the crowd suddenly lifted up his voice in the call to prayer, and everyone turned to the east, knelt and began to pray, Fonthill and Jenkins carefully following all that Ahmed did. Then, as they all settled back on their haunches, the Mahdi began delivering his sermon. Simon had no idea what was being said and Slatin made no attempt to translate, but it was clear that the preacher quickly began to exert an hypnotic hold over his audience. The eyes of the faithful were fixed on him as his voice, at first muted and almost conversational in tone, became stronger. The Mahdi's own eyes flashed in fervour and his arms spread above his head, as though beseeching his listeners to take a singular course of action. He had the gift of being able to exhort while still maintaining throughout that warm smile on his features. A man somewhere in the crowd shrieked in religious ecstasy, and his cries were taken up by others, until the whole mass was shouting and answering the preacher in fervent delight.

'Blimey,' whispered Jenkins, 'I think I've wet myself.'

'Be quiet. We must not be disrespectful.'

At last the Mahdi finished, his arms held high above his head, his fingers outstretched. The whole concourse burst into screams and shouts of approval and stamped its feet, sending clouds of dust rising into the hot air. The preacher held his pose for at least twenty seconds, turning this way and that to milk the applause.

As the noise continued, Fonthill whispered to Ahmed, 'What was his message?'

The little Egyptian looked at him with eyes that seemed clouded by sickness. 'I don't know,' he said. 'I am in pain and too tired . . . something about renouncing the vanities of the world and considering only religious duties and the *jihad*, et cetera, et cetera, et cetera.'

The Mahdi lowered his arms at last and the noise subsided. Still smiling – did he never stop? – he spoke briefly to the Khalifa, then nodded to the three prisoners, as though to emphasise his words, turned on his heel and disappeared into the hut behind him. The Khalifa barked an order to Slatin and they all followed him to the hut, where they stood as the Khalifa spoke quickly to the Austrian. As he did so, Simon noticed the face of the tall Dervish who had accompanied them break into a smile, and the man picked up the ends of their neck halters and gathered them firmly in his hands. Ahmed sucked in his breath.

Slatin bowed and turned to the three. 'The Khalifa says that the Mahdi is gratified that you have decided to follow him. However, neither he nor the Khalifa is able to tell if you are sincere in your intentions, and the Khalifa believes that you need a period of contemplation to consider your way to the True Path.' The Austrian's great moustache now seemed to envelop his lower lip and his face developed an even more melancholy expression.

'Pain is Allah's way of concentrating the mind. You will each therefore receive twenty-five lashes and be chained in the compound with other men whose minds need to be cleansed. Now go and consider your ways.'

'No.' Fonthill stepped forward, to be jerked back as the Dervish pulled on his halter. The pain made his voice hoarse. 'Such a punishment is unfair. We have declared our conviction that the Mahdi's way is the true way. We are honest men. We should be believed.'

Slatin translated wearily, as though knowing that the plea was futile. He turned back: 'The Khalifa says that your arrogance underlines his words. You should accept the sentence in gratitude.'

'Bastard,' breathed Jenkins.

Simon tried one more time, although the halter was now tightly constricting his throat. 'My friend here,' he indicated Ahmed, 'is very sick. Such a sentence could kill him. Spare him and double my sentence instead.'

'No, bach,' cried Jenkins.

For the first time a smile came on to the Khalifa's hitherto impassive face, and he paused before answering. Then: 'If your friend dies then he will escape to Paradise and all earthly pain will end. It shall be Allah's will. But your plea does you credit. You shall indeed have fifty lashes, as you request, but the other sentences will stand.'

As though from nowhere, three other Dervishes appeared and lashed the prisoners' hands behind them. Then the large man strode ahead pulling their halters and they were led to yet another compound. Here a series of gallows – wooden shafts hammered into the ground and linked across the top by another, as though goal posts – had been erected. What was left of their *jibbas* were torn from their backs and their hands were tied to individual posts above their heads. Then they were left on their own as somewhere nearby a drum began to beat.

'Ah, Ahmed,' said Fonthill, turning his head to look at the Egyptian, who was now slumped and held erect only by the bonds around his wrists. 'I am so sorry that I have led you into this. I would have done anything to have saved you from it.'

The little man spoke with his eyes closed. 'It is not your fault,' he whispered. 'Indeed, it is the will of Allah. I must endure. But thank you for trying to spare me.'

'Fifty lashes.' Jenkins muttered on his other side. 'That's more than our army served out for 'ittin' an officer. The thing to do, bach sir, is not to tense yourself, see. I know it sounds barmy, but try an' relax, see. The most I ever 'ad – in the days, that is, when it was allowed, like – was twenty. But not tensin' worked for me, God bless you, so it did. I promise you one thing. Whoever does this, I'll get 'im for it, so I will.'

Simon tried to summon up a weak grin, but it was more of a grimace.

It became clear that the drum was a signal for a crowd to gather to enjoy the punishment, for barefooted men, women and children – some of the women holding young children high so that they could see the spectacle – were forming a circle around the three men. For the first time the horror of what was to come descended on Fonthill. Once before, high in the mountains of the Hindu Kush, he had suffered the pain of torture, and the memory of it sent a shudder through his body. Could he endure it? He tried to calculate how long fifty lashes would take to administer. Say a lash every ten seconds, six lashes a minute, more than eight minutes then. God. A lifetime! Those rhino-hide thongs could tear a man's back to pieces in that time . . .

He became conscious that Slatin was standing next to him. 'I am sorry that it has come to this,' he said. 'The Khalifa is a very suspicious man. Remember to accept that you can do nothing about this punishment and you must all take it with patience and fortitude. I will visit you later. May God give you courage.'

A shout from the crowd made Fonthill turn his head. The big Dervish who had led the party that had captured them had entered the ring, carrying his coiled *kourbash*. So it was he who would deliver the whipping. Better than having three men do it anyway, in that perhaps the swine would tire towards the end. Who would be first?

He closed his eyes and realised that he was trembling. 'Remember,' growled Jenkins, 'don't tense up, see. Try an' relax the muscles. And don't forget – I'm goin' to kill this bastard—'

He was interrupted by a sound like a rifle shot as the Dervish cracked the whip above his head. It was obviously meant to please the crowd, for a cry of appreciation went up. So it must have been, reflected Simon, as the lions entered the arena in ancient Rome. He prayed that Ahmed would be the first, for it would be better for the little man not to have to see the others suffer before his turn came.

Then the pain began. The first strokes across Fonthill's back – for he was selected to be punished first – felt like a series of bee stings, then the pain intensified into a succession of burning sword strokes cutting into his back and down his ribs. Then his torso became a hot grill of pain as the strokes continued pitilessly. There was a regular shout from the crowd to punctuate each lash, and he realised that the people were counting the strokes with a kind of fierce glee. He gritted his teeth and resolved that, however bad it became, he would not cry out. He would not give the torturer that delight.

He lost count himself of the number of blows delivered, and after a time slumped into a kind of half consciousness of fire and pain, his legs buckling so that he hung by his wrists from the post. But he remained silent.

At last, suddenly, it stopped, to a final cry from the crowd. Of what? Disappointment? Fonthill realised that blood was seeping down through his loincloth and running down his legs.

'Well done, bach.' He heard Jenkins's voice from a great distance; from far away, across the sea of pain. Then the lash cracked again and the whipping continued next to him. He turned his head and heard the shriek as, to his left, Ahmed received his first blows.

So it continued until, finally, the last lash had been delivered to Jenkins's broad back. The Welshman, of course, made not a sound throughout his beating, and Ahmed had lapsed into a state of unconscious silence some time before and was now hanging limply in his bonds.

Fonthill turned his head slowly to his right and caught Jenkins's eye. The Welshman nodded in approbation and gave him a weary grin. 'Well done, bach,' he gasped. 'You never uttered a bleedin' word through all them fifty lashes. I'm not sure I could 'ave done that, look you. Not sure at all.'

His mouth open, Simon tried to smile but his features somehow failed to respond. He nodded slowly instead.

But their agonies were not yet over. From in front of them appeared three slave boys carrying bowls of water and bags of brown-looking sand. Once the boys had splashed the water over their backs, they dipped their hands into the bags with a grin and rubbed the powder into the wounds. To their horror, the prisoners realised it was not sand but pepper. This time they all screamed as the fire on their backs was renewed – and stayed burning.

The pain was so intense that the three of them were hardly conscious of being cut down, carried to three posts and shackled to them. Rings were put around their necks and a chain led to the top of each pole. Then a second, larger chain with eighty-three large figure-of-eight links – Fonthill was to count them many times later – was hammered shut on to the neck ring and then led down and fixed similarly to the heavy iron bar that linked the two rings through which their feet had been placed.

Simon was hardly aware of this happening, for his consciousness was consumed by the fire raging across his back. His mind slipped away and he was burning in hell for all the sins he had committed in his life. He tried to enumerate them: the men he had killed in so many campaigns, his neglect of his father and mother and his wickedness in leaving Alice, whom he loved so much, to come away into this burning, burning land of sand and stone. Gradually the fire receded a little as Alice came, treading carefully between the hot, steaming stones, to bring him succour. Then she was gently rubbing butter into his wounds . . . soothing, so soothing . . .

He forced his eyelids open to thank her and found himself, in semi-darkness, looking into two anxious brown eyes, close to his.

He summoned a grin. 'Hello, Mustapha,' he croaked. 'Where the devil have you been?'

Chapter 10

Over the next two pain-racked days, Mustapha proved to be a lifeline for them all. He tended their wounds with care and a skill that sat inappropriately on his young shoulders, bathing them all, night and morning, erecting a rough shelter over their heads to shield them from the sun, and cooking the raw *durra* sorghum that was all they were given to eat. He managed to supplement this fare with dates and nuts, and even found a little goat meat to cook for them. It seemed that such attention was tolerated by the Dervishes guarding the compound, for several other slave boys were to be seen caring in a similar way for some of the other wretches chained to the posts. Other prisoners, however – presumably those unable to pay for these services – were virtually ignored and, apart from being allowed a little uncooked *durra* each day, were, by the look of it, simply being left to die in their chains.

As soon as he was able to rise above the pain, Fonthill questioned Mustapha about his escape. The boy's story was simple. In the ruins of the fort, on the last watch, he had gone to walk through the village in the half-light to see what he could scavenge. He had found the place virtually uninhabited and had returned empty-handed just in time to see the Dervishes arrive. Watching from behind a hut, he had seen the party leave and had trotted behind at a safe distance to follow it to Omdurman. There he had found a hiding place for the money and compass he was carrying and had joined the crowd to hear the Mahdi preach. He had also watched the floggings and immediately purchased some butter and clean *jibbas* for them. The purchases had not attracted attention, he explained, because the camp teemed with slave boys carrying out similar errands for their masters, even for those chained wretches who had a few pennies left to pay for such luxuries.

In those first few days, none of them was able to move very much for fear of starting the bleeding again from the weals on their backs. Fonthill's, of course, were the worst, for it was difficult to find skin from shoulder to buttock that had not been torn by the cruel *kourbash*. However, Mustapha had made rough bandages for each of them, and from somewhere had found a primitive ointment that he gently spread over the open wounds, which prompted the slow process of forming scabs over them.

The spartan but healthy lives that Simon and Jenkins had led for years hastened their recovery. Both of them were muscular – particularly Jenkins, who had been gifted with inbred strength and the most robust of constitutions – and neither of them carried excess weight. Soon they could at least stand without exacerbating their wounds and shuffle a few paces to the extent allowed by their chains. Ahmed, however, was a source of anxiety. It seemed to Simon that he was now developing a fever, for he was perspiring excessively and falling into a state of half-sleep or coma. When his eyes were open they stared in a lacklustre fashion, seeming to see nothing, and he rarely spoke. On the fourth day after their floggings, blood began to ooze from the corner of his mouth.

Fonthill leaned over and did his best to examine Ahmed's rib cage, underneath Mustapha's bandages. 'I fear that being dragged behind the camels along the ground has broken a rib or even two,' he confided to Jenkins. 'Worse than that, though, I think that his lungs may have been penetrated. He has certainly developed a fever. I wonder whether Slatin can help?'

Mustapha was dispatched to find the Austrian, and in due course the big man shuffled towards them.

'Is there any possibility of finding a doctor to look at our friend?' Fonthill asked. 'He will surely die if he does not get attention soon. I think a rib or even two has penetrated his lung.'

Slatin knelt beside Ahmed and sighed. 'People die all the time here,' he said, 'and there will be no point in appealing to the Khalifa. He will say that it is Allah's will. There are, of course, no European doctors, but some of the Sudanese elders have healing powers.' He rose to his feet. 'I will see what I can do.'

Jenkins leaned over to look at Ahmed, wincing as the movement pulled at his scabs. He shook his head. 'Poor little bugger. I don't know much about these things, but I seem to remember that pneumonia is a danger now. But what the bloody 'ell we can do about that, I just don't know. At least 'e's warm enough . . .'

Slatin was as good as his word, and he arrived two hours later accompanied by an elderly, grey-bearded Sudanese wearing a white *esharp* coiled around his head. He pulled back Ahmed's eyelids, opened his mouth and made a perfunctory inspection of his rib cage. Then he spoke briefly to Slatin, rose and walked away.

The Austrian shook his head. 'I am afraid there is no hope,' he said. 'The old man said that the blood comes from the lung and that your friend cannot breathe properly. The shock of the whipping, of course, will not have helped. I fear he is dying.'

'Bastards!' exclaimed Jenkins. 'Why did they 'ave to whip 'im as well as break 'is ribs? 'E never did them any 'arm . . .'

Slatin observed the Welshman in silence for a while. Then he gave a sad smile. 'I think,' he said, 'that you are English and not Greek. Is that not so?'

Fonthill hurriedly intervened. 'No,' he said. 'But my colleague here is from the Greek part of Cyprus and learned his English from the British soldiers stationed there.'

The Austrian shrugged his shoulders. 'I am sorry that we cannot help your Egyptian friend,' he said. 'But given your circumstances here, perhaps it is better that he joins Allah in the Garden of Paradise soon.' Then he shuffled away, his chains clinking.

Simon took Ahmed's hand and began chafing it. Then he spoke quietly. 'This is a good man and this was not his fight. He came with us because we wanted his help, and he gave it to us without question. If he dies, then I swear I will personally kill that big bastard who caused it.'

'No, bach sir,' growled Jenkins. 'That feller is mine. I said I'd 'ave 'im and I will. But don't grieve for dear old Et Cetera. 'E loved a bit of adventure. You know that. Once 'e'd been out with us at el Kebir and so on, he didn't fancy sitting be'ind 'is desk in 'is little hotel in Cairo, directin' the puttin' out of bed potties and the changin' of sheets. 'E's really been alive, look you, while 'e's been with us.'

That afternoon the little Egyptian gave them some hope. His breathing became easier, and he rallied to the point where his eyes opened and he regarded them with a half-smile. Simon put a gourd of lukewarm water to his lips.

'Thank you,' Ahmed said. 'I think that I am dying, isn't it?'

'Bless you, no,' exclaimed Jenkins. 'You're goin' to recover an' we're goin' to get out of this arse'ole of a place, see, an' you're goin' to buy us three good camels to ride back to Cairo in comfort, boyo.'

'Ooh, I don't think so, bach,' murmured Ahmed.

'Now . . .' He put out his hand to Fonthill. 'Thank you for the excitement, Simon. Perhaps a bit too much at times . . .' His smile widened and then disappeared as a shaft of pain ran through his body. He coughed, and blood ran down his chin.

'Don't talk, old chap,' said Simon.

'No. There is something to say. I think you get out of this place, but without me. When you get back to Cairo, tell my brother Mahmud – you remember him, the caravan trader?'

Fonthill nodded.

'Tell him that the hotel is his and all my things, et cetera, et cetera . . .' his voice grew weak, ' 'cetera.' Then his mouth opened and his head fell to one side.

'Oh hell,' said Simon. He sat still for a moment, then he felt for Ahmed's pulse, leaned over and gently closed the little man's eyelids and laid his hands together over his chest.

'Sod it,' echoed Jenkins. 'What a splendid little chap 'e was.'

'Indeed. I wish . . . oh, never mind. We must find where we can bury him.'

Once again the ubiquitous Slatin was able to help. A coarse winding sheet was provided and their chains were removed from the post and draped down their sore backs. Between them, and with Mustapha's help, they painfully carried the slight body of Ahmed to a patch of ground away from the camp, where they were provided with shovels to dig a grave. As, under the supervision of a disinterested Dervish guard, they slowly – very slowly – began the work, Fonthill was able to send Mustapha away with instructions to buy a knife and find a piece of suitable wood. He returned before the grave had been finished, and while Simon continued to hollow out the shallow hole, Jenkins cut two words into the wood: *Ahmed – soldier.*

The three of them gently lowered the body into the grave

and shovelled in the sandy earth above him. Then Jenkins knocked in the wood and the three knelt under the gaze of the puzzled Dervish.

'Oh God, Allah,' said Simon, clasping his hands, 'please receive the soul of this good man, Ahmed Muhurram. We commend him to you as a gentle companion and a brave fighter. Amen.' The others echoed the last word, and then they stood and shuffled back to their compound. Here they were surprised to find that they were not shackled to the posts again but allowed to sit, their chains draped around them.

'Now what?' asked Jenkins.

Fonthill blew his nose on a scrap of rag. 'The first thing to do is to recover our strength and make sure we don't get an infection in these damned wounds. Then we will get out of here.'

'Ah. Just like that. I see. That will be lovely. What do we do? Just take a stroll up back to Cairo carryin' these chains, like?'

'Something like that. One thing is certain. If you keep swearing and shouting in English, someone – like the Khalifa – will decide that we are not Greek and probably have our heads removed. So we had better get out before that happens.' He cocked his head to listen as gunfire echoed from a distance.

'That's not from Omdurman. It's from Khartoum, and it sounds healthy. At least Gordon is still holding out. If we can steal a boat or three camels we might yet get back in time to help him.' Simon turned to Mustapha, who was sitting cross-legged at their feet, his eyes wide, his head turning to follow the conversation. 'Mustapha, is there a blacksmith – a man who works in iron and steel – in the camp?'

'I do not know, master. But I will find out.'

Fonthill leaned forward and ran his fingers through the boy's tousled hair. 'Now listen. You must be very careful who you talk to. We need a saw – one with a very thin blade that cuts through iron and steel – and perhaps a file. Do you know what I mean?'

'I think so, master.'

'Good. A smith ought to have these things, even here. But I think it would excite suspicion if you try to buy them, for their use is obvious and there are plenty of people in chains here who would like to cut them. So it would be better if you can steal them. Do you think you could?'

The boys eyes lit up. 'Oh yes. I can steal. Blast me eyes I can.'

Fonthill grinned at Jenkins. 'If we are taking him home with us we had better clean up these Irishisms,' he said. 'Now, you must be very, very careful how you do this, because if you are caught they will almost certainly kill you. I don't want another funeral just yet.' His expression softened. 'And where should we two be without you? All right.' He made a dismissive gesture. 'Go and see what you can find.'

The boy rose and slipped away without another word.

'Blimey,' said Jenkins, grimacing as he eased his back, 'you don't think we can cut these bloody things off us, do you?'

'I don't know. Neither of us has the strength at the moment to cut a piece of string, but if the dear lad comes up trumps, then it's worth a try, though we must be very careful and only work at night. At least it looks as though they have stopped shackling us to this damned post. Perhaps we are going to be moved.'

Indeed they were, but only as far as the Khalifa. That afternoon the man who had administered the whipping and led the party that had captured them – his name, they had learned, was Abu Din – came to fetch them. He gathered the chains attached to their neck rings and once again pulled them unfeelingly behind him until they reached the hut of the Khalifa, where he forced them to their knees. As before, Slatin was there to interpret.

'The Khalifa,' he said, 'wishes to know if you are happy.'

Fonthill sighed. 'As always, we are grateful to be in his presence,' he said, 'although we are sad to have lost our friend and servant who interpreted for us.'

'But are you not happy that he is now almost certainly in Paradise and away from earthly pain and suffering?'

'Indeed, O great leader, we are truly glad for his sake that his sufferings are over.' Simon prayed that Jenkins would keep his mouth shut. It was asking a lot.

'Yes. We understand that you carried out a burial that was not in the Muslim tradition.' *Did this man know everything?* 'This gave us sadness. Why was this?'

Fonthill bowed his head. 'We did not wish to give offence. Ahmed, our friend, was a Muslim but we do not yet know the way of the true faith in passing him to Allah. So we merely buried him and said a few words of prayer over him in our own language. We do not seek to offend.'

The Khalifa stayed silent, and Simon prayed inwardly that this would not lead to another whipping. He doubted if he could withstand another such experience.

Eventually the Dervish spoke again, through Slatin. 'Why does your friend say nothing? I fear he is truculent and unhappy in the home of the Mahdi.'

Fonthill nudged Jenkins, who looked up. 'Oh no, bach,' the Welshman said. 'I am as 'appy as a pig in shit.'

Simon drew in his breath, but a half-smile came over Slatin's face. Whatever it was he translated, it seemed to satisfy the Khalifa, who turned his attention back to Fonthill. 'Have you benefited from your punishment?' he asked. 'Are you better people for it? For this is the way to regard it. It is a way of improving yourself in the eyes of Allah. Suffering removes resentment and brings inner peace.'

'Indeed, lord,' said Fonthill. 'We are most grateful for the experience.'

'Oh, indeed we are,' added Jenkins.

'Very well. I have ordered that you be removed to a place where there is shade and you will have freedom to move. When you have recovered – and I think that two days will be sufficient – you will be allowed to work in the *durra* fields. But I think that resentment still lingers in your souls. Therefore the *hajji farma* will be fitted to you until you can think clearly, and then, perhaps, you may be allowed to receive the *beia*. You may go.'

Nudging Jenkins, Simon joined him in bowing low to the Khalifa, and then they were led away.

'What the fuckin' 'ell is this hajji fanny thing?' muttered Jenkins as they shuffled along. 'Is it somethin' else bloody painful that we've got to be grateful for?'

'I don't know. But it is good news that we can go out to work. This might give us a chance of escaping.'

'Not if we're pullin' a bloody great ball an' chain it won't.'

It ensued that Jenkins's assessment was not far from the truth. They were led to another compound where open-sided bivouac tents had been constructed around the sides. The length of chain that had formerly connected them to the pole was wrenched away and the open end of the rings around their ankles that had been hammered shut was forced open, allowing them momentarily to walk freely. But only for less than a minute, for the rings were replaced by circlets that were attached to far heavier lengths of thick iron that dragged on the ground and pulled the rings down painfully on to the ankle bone.

'Bloody 'ell,' expostulated Jenkins. 'They weigh a bleedin' ton!'

In fact, explained Slatin, when he visited them a few minutes later, they weighed some eighteen pounds. This was a common punishment, he said, that was applied to stimulate humility in the wearer. He himself had worn the *hajji* for a year until recently.

'A year! And are you more humble as a result?' enquired Fonthill. He did not attempt to keep the scorn out of his voice.

'Ah, my friend. It does not do to resist. You must remember that you – we – who are prisoners of the Mahdi can do nothing. We are at the mercy of our captors. Remember the old Muslim saying that I told you earlier: "Allah is with the patient, and he who lives long sees much." '

'There's not much chance of livin' long with this thing around our feet,' growled Jenkins.

'Learn to accept it and you will survive.'

'Mr Slatin,' intervened Fonthill, 'how can we work in the fields with these weights attached to us?'

'You will not be required to move much. But now I must go. I hope that your wounds heal quickly.'

Slatin moved away, shuffling in the dust, although his ankle shackles were much lighter than the *hajji*. Perhaps the heavy bar induced that shuffle for a lifetime? Frowning, Fonthill rose to his feet. It was, indeed, possible to move, perhaps eight inches at a time, but slowly, for the rings immediately began to rub at the ankle bone.

Jenkins looked up at him. 'Bach sir, we're never goin' to get out of 'ere draggin' these bloody things, now are we?'

'Of course not. We shall simply have to remove them when the time comes, that's all.'

The Welshman shook his head slowly, a great unbelieving grin splitting his beard and moustache as he looked down at the *hajji*. 'An' pigs might fly too, bless you,' he said. He bent down and examined the links that had been battered together to close them around the bar. The same crude system had been used for the circle of iron around their necks.

'They've just been bashed together,' he said. 'I reckon I could probably wrench 'em open if I 'ad a bit of somethin' to put the leverage in. Like an 'eavy pair of pliers or something.'

Fonthill looked carefully at the linkage. 'Maybe,' he said. 'But we would still have these damned rings around our ankles and necks. Better to hacksaw or file through them so the infernal lot comes off. Let's see what Mustapha comes up with.'

Jenkins sniffed, but nodded. Then: 'Hey! Did you notice what was stickin' out of the cummerbund thing round old Abu's waist?'

'No. What?'

'Our two Colts, that's what. The pearl handles were pushing into his great big belly. Per'aps 'e'll shoot his feet off. But I know now where to find them little beauties when the time comes, look you. I shall get them back, you see if I don't.'

'Well that's fine.' Fonthill's tone was now weary. 'But for goodness' sake don't be provocative. It's stupid to draw attention to ourselves or to provoke Abu Din to pull out his *kourbash* again. If we get a chance, we will see to him when the time comes, but in the meantime we must lie low and trust Mustapha can find a saw. Let's get some sleep. My back is hurting like hell.'

Jenkins grunted, nodded and lay clumsily on his side, the folds of his *esharp* making a rudimentary pillow. They had more shade now but the heat was ever-present, with the sun straining to get at them through the loosely woven cloth above them, and the flies, of course, knew exactly where they were. Nevertheless, as was his wont, the Welshman was asleep within seconds.

Not so Fonthill. It was impossible for him to lie on his burning back and he too curled up in the foetal position, but sleep evaded him. His mind whirled as he weighed the chances of escape. Even if Mustapha was able to produce the tools to free them from their shackles, their absence would be noticed at sun-up, and the Dervishes, he had already learned, *always* pursued escaped prisoners and brought them back to be publicly mutilated and, often, killed. On foot, they would have little chance of making sufficient distance to give themselves a safety margin, and anyway, Simon at least was in no position to exert himself by trudging through loose sand and gravel under the sun for more than an hour or so, if that. His back still throbbed and he knew that fever was just around the corner. Only Mustapha's constant care had kept it at bay. What were the alternatives? Slipping back into Khartoum? The Dervishes would probably not expect them to attempt this, but the city was some four miles away and would involve crossing the Nile. It savoured, anyway, of escaping from the frying pan into the fire, with the net closing now so tightly around Gordon. And, of course, their objective must still be to get back to Wolseley's advancing column as soon as possible to hasten its advance in the hope of saving the beleaguered General.

The river? A possibility. The *durra* fields would almost certainly be close to the Nile, and working there perhaps could give them the chance of observing the scene and weighing the chances of stealing a boat. A boat? Ha! Simon grinned, despite the pain from his flayed back. Neither of them were experienced sailors, and Jenkins, in particular, was terrified of the water. Without help they would run aground at the first rapids, not to mention the cataracts.

Their only hope would be to file or saw through their irons then, during the night, steal out to the camel lines and somehow steal three good ones that might outdistance their pursuers. Mustapha still had Simon's compass hidden away. But Jenkins must be dissuaded from settling his score with

Abu Din. Even a revenge so sweet – and the possibility that they could regain their revolvers – was not worth the risk of awakening the camp.

He eased his back and tried to turn on to his other side. The pain from his lacerated shoulders shot through him and reminded him that he was in no position to run anywhere for a while. He closed his eyes and let the flies crawl unmolested over his eyelids. Alice . . . Alice . . . She came into his mind's eye from out of nowhere: dressed in a cool summer dress in Norfolk, that familiar apple-green silk scarf at her throat, she strode towards him smiling. She was saying something to him but he could not hear. Her hand was outstretched and beckoning him towards her, but he could not move because of his chain. He shuffled his feet, but the *hajji* seemed to have increased in weight and it was as though he was standing in concrete. Alice . . . He had acted so unfairly to her and now it must seem that he was refusing to answer her call. Alice! He awoke with a start to find perspiration pouring down his cheeks and the skin at his ankles worn sore where he had tried to move his feet.

Fonthill felt his stomach churn and looked at Jenkins with envy. The man could sleep on a clothesline. Slowly he hauled himself to his feet and felt that unheralded, dreaded movement in his stomach again. He knew that the big danger for them both now, given the close proximity in which they lived to their unkempt neighbours and the filth everywhere, was guinea worm or some other tropical disease. So far there had been no sign of that. At the moment, though, the pressing need was to throw off the incipient diarrhoea that was beginning to attack. He was just able to reach the disgusting leather bucket that had been provided for the ablutions of both of them before his bowels opened. He wiped himself with a handful of sand and did his best to wash again with a palmful of precious water. Then he stood and looked around him.

There were perhaps ten or so other chained prisoners in this particular compound. Like Fonthill and Jenkins they all appeared to be shackled with the *hajji* but, similarly, it seemed that they were free to move about. Why had they not been set to work? Some of them had what appeared to be their families with them: ragged children and sullen-faced women sitting in what shade they could find, their bare toes clenching in the dust, their eyes dull. Perhaps they too were refugees from Khartoum who had thrown themselves on the mercy of the Mahdi and found it lacking. Simon wiped his brow and went through the useless movement of brushing away the flies. He gazed up at the blue bowl of the sky. It was now late afternoon and they were all existing in what must be more than ninety degrees of heat.

Gingerly he stretched his battered shoulders and made a resolution. They would escape from this place or die in the attempt. It was as simple as that. Get out or perish! The means were still not evident, but somehow he felt better now that the decision was made. As soon as they could move without pain, and if they continued to stay free of tropical disease, they would go – somehow – at whatever the risk.

Alas, there was no sign of Mustapha. He was not usually absent for this period of time, and as the sun went down, Fonthill began to worry. He knew that the boy was incorrigibly brave, to the point of recklessness in fact, and they had been lucky that his constant toings and froings on their behalf had not attracted attention so far. Their precious store of Sudanese dollars had stayed safe with him – even Fonthill had no idea where it was kept – but it could only be a matter of time before someone would question why a slave boy seemed to be so well endowed with money and, terrible thought, follow him, kill him and take the cash. This was a lawless community. If that happened, there was no way they would know and absolutely nothing they could do about it. And, final thought: without Mustapha they had little chance of leaving the Mahdi's camp.

The boy did not return that evening, and they were forced to cook their daily ration of *durra* and eat it without the little additional comforts he brought that made it palatable. The next day dawned without him and the two men became increasingly anxious that, somehow, Mustapha had been waylaid and hurt.

'What the hell can we do?' muttered Fonthill.

'This is your department, bach sir,' said Jenkins. 'The brains bit. I've no idea what's 'appened to the lad or where we could search for 'im.'

'Well I'm not prepared to sit here and do nothing. I've no idea whether we will be allowed to walk around and look for him but let's try. You go that way . . .' He caught the look of desperation in 352's eyes. Jenkins had no sense of direction. He would lose his way even crossing from one side of Piccadilly to the other, and the teeming molehill that was the Mahdi's camp would see him lost without trace within seconds. 'All right. We'll go together.'

They shuffled and clunked their way through the labyrinth of tents and camel lines that formed the movable, vibrant metropolis, rubbing their ankles sore to the point that they left a trail of blood behind them. There were plenty of active small boys of various shades of black and brown, darting like trout between the adults thronging the camp. But not one with tightly curled hair, bright brown eyes and a smile like the sun.

They returned just before nightfall, exhausted and feeling ill. There was no trace of the boy.

'I will go and try and find Slatin in the morning and see if he can help,' said Fonthill.

'Good idea. But 'ave you forgotten we're supposed to start work in the fields tomorrer?'

'Dammit, yes. Tomorrow night, then.'

'One good thing, though.'

'What's that?'

'It looks as though we can go more or less where we like with these bleedin' hajji things on our legs. No one thinks we can escape wearin' 'em.'

'Quite so. But we won't really get out unless we can get rid of them. And I don't see how we can get them off without Mustapha.' Fonthill's brow was like thunder. 'I do hope that nothing has happened to the boy.'

'Ah, cheer up, bach sir. He existed quite well before 'e met us. 'E's as sharp as a bag full of butcher's knives. The lad knows 'ow to look after 'imself. You'll see.'

There was no sign of Mustapha, however, when they were rounded up just before sunrise the next morning to fall into line with a shuffling chain gang deputed to work in the fields. All wore the heavy foot irons, and progress to the river, therefore, was extremely slow, even though it was only some three hundred yards away. Two Dervishes, carrying a sword and a *kourbash* each, watched over them as they were put to work, not to harvest the *durra* but to dig the field where it had grown.

It was excessively hard work in the heat, and Fonthill could feel his wounds opening again under his shirt as he bent his back. He clenched his teeth as the blood dribbled down his torso and deliberately set himself a slower pace so as to last the day, for he knew that if he fell he would be beaten and probably never get up again. Jenkins, his muscles rippling under his *jibba* and perspiration drenching the cotton, did his best to shield Simon. Luckily, however, the two Dervishes were not cut from the same cloth as Abu Din, and they seemed to have no concern at the pace of the work. Indeed, they called for drink breaks every two hours or so. Their whips were never uncoiled and Fonthill began to feel that there were some good Dervishes left in the Sudan after all.

As the day wore on, Fonthill felt his strength perversely seem to grow within him and he found a rhythm that enabled him to keep going metronomically under the burning sun, grateful for the protection of his headdress wound round his scalp, forehead and neck. He offered thanks in particular for the fact that incontinence did not strike again. Somehow they both lasted to the end of the day, when the chain gang, feet dragging in the dust, wound its way back to its various enclosures. There was still no sign of Mustapha.

'Bloody 'ell, bach sir,' said Jenkins on their return. 'What a day! You did well, look you. 'Ere now, let me look at that back.'

Gingerly he peeled back Fonthill's *jibba* and began gently sponging the wounds where the scabs had been reopened. Then he applied a little of the ointment that remained and replaced the garment.

'Thanks, 352,' said Simon, easing his muscles 'That's better. Now I shall see if I can find Slatin. You stay here in case Mustapha returns. I'm more worried about him than I am about this blasted back. Have you still got the knife you used to carve Ahmed's grave marker?'

Jenkins put his hand inside his *jibba* and produced the knife. 'You're not goin' to look for trouble, now, bach sir, are you?' he asked. 'If you do, you won't get far with that bloody great iron down below. If there's a problem, come back for me.'

'What? Just skip along back, do you mean? No. I just feel

safer if I have something to defend myself with in this place.'
He pushed the blade down his loose cummerbund. 'Now
where in this hellhole, I wonder, would that strange Austrian
be living . . .?'

Slowly Simon made his way towards the centre of the
camp, on the assumption that Slatin would have been
allocated accommodation somewhere near the Khalifa. The
assumption proved correct, and he found the big man sitting
outside a small mud hut, attempting to clip his moustache and
beard without the help of a mirror.

'Here, Mr Slatin,' said Fonthill, 'let me do that.'

The Austrian nodded gratefully and Simon made a
creditable job of his barbering, allowing him the opportunity
to beg one more favour of Slatin. He described Mustapha
merely as an itinerant slave boy who had attached himself to
them in the camp and proved useful. 'But now he seems to
have disappeared. Would you know where I might find him?'

Slatin shrugged his shoulders. 'He could be anywhere in
the camp,' he said. 'They say that about another ten thousand
people are expected here over the next few weeks. It will be
like looking for one grain in a corn sack. There are many boys
here.'

'Are there any blacksmiths in the camp?'

The Austrian looked up quickly. 'Why do you ask?'

Fonthill shrugged his shoulders in turn. 'I think the boy
said that he had been a smith's slave boy. He might have gone
back there.'

Slatin seemed satisfied with the answer. 'The smiths are
grouped together to the east, that way.' He gestured. 'But if he
has gone back to his master, then I would advise you to stay
clear. These people can be very possessive, you know. Slaves –
even boys – are property, not to be stolen.'

'Yes.' Simon nodded slowly. 'I take your point.'

The rattle of musketry from the Omdurman fort, nearby but out of sight to the north, interrupted them. 'How long can Gordon hold out, Mr Slatin?'

The Austrian munched his moustache. 'The Khalifa – and it will be he who will actually make the decision, for the Mahdi is no general – will almost certainly wait until more people have arrived from the south and east before he makes a big attack. Gordon Pasha is getting very low on food, by all accounts, but he still has troops and firepower. I think the Khalifa will be happy to wait a little longer anyway to try and starve him out. He has time on his side.'

'How long? Days? Weeks? Months?'

'I don't know. Weeks, I should think.'

Fonthill thought for a moment. 'Mr Slatin, have you ever tried to escape?'

The big man shot him a sharp glance. 'No, for it is impossible without outside help. And there is no one to help me. Even then, prisoners who escape are pursued and always brought back and punished – sometimes by death.' He gave his weary smile. 'Do not think about it, my friend. Accept your lot and then . . . perhaps one day things will improve and it might be possible to negotiate your freedom. That is what I hope. That is what I live for.'

'Yes.' Fonthill rose to his feet awkwardly. 'Thank you. Thank you for your help to us here.'

He shuffled away. When he was out of the Austrian's sight, he turned to his left, to the east, and began wrinkling his nose to pick up the distinctive scent of a smith's open brazier and listening for the clink of metal on metal. As he slowly made his way, he realised that no one was paying the slightest attention to him. Firstly, of course, he looked now like any other impoverished Arab in the camp. He no longer needed to rely on the long-lasting walnut dye that had been applied to him in Cairo. The sun had burned his skin black and his beard had grown so that it covered his chest. Prisoners in their chains, it seems, were allowed to walk freely through the camp, although he saw no others bearing the dreadful *hajji farma*. Secondly, however, this was not really an army camp, despite the fact that most of the men he saw carried either a Remington rifle or a musket of some kind. It was more like a huge tribal gathering, with the Mahdi's soldiers appearing to continue to live their desert lives with their families in their brown and dun-coloured tents, as on the other side of the Nile. There was no army discipline evident, although the Messiah's flags were everywhere. Fonthill was able to walk between the families without challenge or even an inquisitive stare.

A more distant sound of cannon from the direction of Khartoum made Simon lift up his head and turn his thoughts to Gordon. How odd, he reflected as he shuffled along, that this strange, gifted soldier of fortune – that was what he was, for he was no conventional career officer – should end by facing a man who in many ways so resembled him. True, they were different in obvious ways: one was white, the other black; Gordon was a soldier, the Mahdi a preacher; the Englishman was celibate, the Sudanese had many concubines; and the man of the desert was primitive while the English gentleman had been formally educated. But both were ruthless in their own way (Gordon had certainly proved this in China) and both were fired by a religious zeal that made them fanatics. Each regarded his religion as the *only* way and would not consider, even for one moment, that alternative concepts of theology might have merit. And yet Gordon had often expressed an understanding of the reasons for the Sudanese revolt, and his contempt for the Turks' form of colonialism was known to be as strong as that of the Mahdi. Now here they were, facing each other in conditions of barbarous cruelty. Fonthill shook his head.

He lifted it again, however, when his nostrils caught the distinctive smell of charcoal burning and he saw, to his right, faint columns of semi-transparent smoke rising in a line behind the tents that blocked his vision. Ah, the smiths' quarter! But would Mustapha be there? It was a gamble with long odds against.

He shuffled his way through the tents and came upon a clearing where some eight or nine blacksmiths were still working at their open fires and anvils, even though the sun was setting. A quick glance showed that Mustapha was not to be seen, at least in the clearing itself, and Fonthill turned to retrace his steps. Then, on an impulse, he began to walk around the clearing behind the several awnings that had been erected to give the smiths a little shade.

He found the boy behind one of the awnings. He was hanging from one of the poles by one ankle, head downwards, his hands tied behind his back. Fonthill stifled a cry and looked around him. The awning had a backcloth, which meant that Mustapha could not be seen from the front. The alleyway itself was bordered by the side of a large tent and was deserted for the moment. Simon drew his knife and carefully cut the boy down. He put his hand to Mustapha's throat and felt a faint pulse. Quickly, not waiting to free the bonds at his wrists, he loosened his own *jibba* and somehow thrust the lad half inside the folds, so that his head lay against Fonthill's shoulder. Then he shuffled away, keeping to the narrow alleyways between the desert tents, his right hand holding the knife, ready to cut down anyone who stood in his way.

Darkness fell quickly, a blessing in terms of hiding them from inquisitive eyes but a curse in that it took Simon nearly an hour to find his way back through the labyrinth of tents and camel lines to the compound. A relieved Jenkins sprang to his feet and quickly took Mustapha away from an exhausted Fonthill.

'Give him water,' gasped Simon. 'He's still alive, but only just. He's been hanging upside down for God knows how long, but it looks as though he's not been hit or knifed because he's not bleeding. Just . . .' he gulped, 'just left hanging there in the sun, by the look of it. What sort of people are they that would do that to a young boy?'

'I suppose you'd call 'em Dervishes,' muttered Jenkins, gently pouring water over the boy's brow and then offering a little to his lips.

Fonthill cut the cords that bound the boy's wrists and began chafing his hands and feet, and gradually Mustapha began to respond. He parted his lips to receive the water, and coughed and gulped. Then he opened his eyes and, recognising the two in the dim light, gave a half-smile.

'Thank God for that,' said Simon.

'Amen,' echoed Jenkins. 'All right, sunshine. Don't try to speak. I'm goin' to put you down in the back 'ere, just in case anybody comes lookin' for you, see. Would you like somethin' to eat, like? Though we've only got rotten old doorah, or whatever it's called.'

Mustapha shook his head and opened his mouth to reveal a swollen, cracked tongue.

'All right,' said Fonthill. 'Don't try and speak. Let me put some of this ointment on your ankle and your wrists. Take a little more water and then see if you can get some sleep. We will make sure you are not disturbed in the night.'

The pair stood guard over him through the darkness, keeping watch in turn. Simon doubted if there would be a search mounted for the boy, for it was obvious that he had been left there to die in the sun as a cruel punishment . . . but for what?

In the morning, at dawn, just before the work party for the *durra* fields was assembled, Mustapha confirmed that he had been caught attempting to steal a saw and a file from the smith, who had strung him up then and there. He had been left hanging in the sun, without food or water, and presumably would have been left there until his tongue became so swollen that he could not breathe, or until he died of thirst. He indicated that he had been completely ignored.

'Well,' growled Jenkins, 'p'raps that means they're not goin' to bother to come lookin' for you.'

'I think that's right,' said Fonthill. 'But even so, Mustapha, stay right at the back of the lean-to and don't talk to anyone. See if you can eat a little *durra* and keep taking sips of water – not too much, mind. We have to go to work now. Here's the knife. Use it if you have to, but stay rolled up in your *jibba* and use our sleeping mats to cover you. We'll get back as soon as we can.' He looked down at the pathetic figure. Mustapha's eyes were completely bloodshot and his face was suffused, marking where the blood had drained to his head. 'You're a brave boy and we are proud of you.'

The day in the fields seemed not so demanding to them both, for their minds were elsewhere. Fonthill realised that it was far too dangerous to send Mustapha on another thieving mission. The boy would almost certainly be recognised and put to death. Yet the lad was their only hope of getting rid of their shackles. How long would they be forced to stay in Omdurman, shuffling about in their heavy chains, with no real hope of escape? He must think of another way. He *must* . . . !

Chapter 11

Alice stood on a hill above the western bank of the Nile and looked down with a feeling of . . . what? She could not be sure of her thoughts as she gazed at the amazing flotilla in which Wolseley had brought his little army this far up the great river. Awe, perhaps? Certainly admiration. As far as she could see northwards, the strange assortment of London-built whalers, Egyptian *filukas* and naval pinnaces was dotting the green-brown waters of the river, their dipping oars heightening the impression of water beetles inching their way towards the edge of a brook. She nodded her head in appreciation. The little general had been right: he *could* take his army through the rocks and shoals of the rapids and cataracts in these strange vessels. And now they were all heading for the shelving banks to unload their sweating, sunburnt human cargoes in their khaki pith helmets and shirtsleeves of grey flannel. A splash of scarlet in the prow of each boat showed where the soldiers' famous red coats had been piled, and a city of white bell tents stood along the shores of the Nile waiting to house them all.

They had reached Korti, on the lower loop of the Nile, just before the great river meandered northwards again and then turned down in its more-or-less straight line to the south and Khartoum. It was at this hot, sleepy little town – no different really from so many that the army had passed on its slow and difficult three-month passage up the Nile thus far – that the General had decided to set up his forward headquarters before splitting his command. Wolseley had left the comparative safety of Dongola, where the friendly but haughty Mudir held sway, some hundred and thirty miles behind him, and from that point onwards he and his army had been in Dervish country. It had been a hard and difficult slog upriver through the cataracts to reach Korti, this jumping off spot where his mounted column could cross the river, take to its camels and head off east-south-east across the desert to Metemmeh on the downward loop of the Nile.

The passage upriver had left the army vulnerable, but the Mahdi had not attacked. His huge force, Alice knew, was grouped in the south, waiting for the British to penetrate deeper into the Sudan and so extend their lines of communication to twanging point. The Dervishes had already proved that they were fanatically brave fighters. Now it seemed that they were also well led. Some four hundred miles to the east, at Suakin on the shores of the Red Sea, the Mahdi's forces had already inflicted several defeats on British-Egyptian forces. It was clear that Lord Wolseley was not the only one to have a grasp of military tactics and strategy.

Despite the lack of enemy action, however, Alice had found plenty to write about. The slow but determined passage of the expeditionary force had painted for her a daily picture of extraordinary colour. The British Tommies had rolled up their sleeves – literally as well as metaphorically – and rowed, paddled, pushed and pulled the fleet up the Nile, despite intense heat, danger from the deep, dashing water and disease carried by myriads of insects. The volunteers that Wolseley had summoned from Canada – the *voyageurs* who had taken his craft through the rapids of the Red River all those years before – had re-emerged in a slightly different guise. This time there were fewer grizzled French-Canadian rivermen to handle his specially made whalers. The few that had answered his call were now supplemented by a motley band of clerks, accountants, farmers and solicitors from the cities of the Dominion, anxious to seek adventure in the cause of the great Empire. They were not quite what the General had expected; nevertheless, they had all buckled down with the British soldiers, Egyptian boatmen and contingents of the Royal Navy to bring the fleet this far. It had been a remarkable demonstration of logistical skill, interservice co-operation and sheer damned determination.

Colonel William Butler, the officer designated by Wolseley to mastermind the whole operation (after the naval commander first appointed had had to be replaced because of his obvious lack of confidence in the enterprise), had emerged as a hero. When others said it was impossible, and although he was no sailor, he had himself taken the first whaler through the frighteningly deep, rock-strewn chasm known as the Bab-el-Kebir, or the Great Gate, which had presented the first of the obstacles just above Wady Halfa. Having been shown the way, the others followed. And so it was through the cataracts and rapids and via the many porterages they had been forced to make, until now they had reached Korti, where the army would split.

But the cost had been high, although not in men. Supplies had been a constant problem, causing budgets to be doubled and trebled. The main expenditure, however, had been in time. Now it was December, and Alice knew that in taking three months to get this far, Wolseley had been dissipating his precious store of weeks, days and hours. As far as she and the other correspondents could ascertain, still nothing had come back from Khartoum about how long Gordon could hold out.

Alice brought out her handkerchief and wiped away the

perspiration that trickled down her cheeks. Despite all her care, she, like everyone else, had been unable to avoid the sun, and her face, the back of her hands and her wrists were all now burned a deep brown. She crinkled her eyes against the glare and turned to look upriver to the south, towards ... Simon. It was ridiculous, she knew, but she had fallen into the habit, on making camp every evening, of looking in the direction from which, one day, she felt, he *must* approach, either coming down river by boat or riding in from the desert, with 352 and Ahmed. And, of course, every day she had been disappointed. Now the days were stretching out and no word had come back from him. Alice wiped her brow and then blew her nose hard. Dammit, he *would* come back; he would return. He always did.

She shook her head and started down the hill, waving the papers in her hand to keep away the flies. She had written what she felt was a good colour piece on the fleet's arrival in Korti, stressing Wolseley's achievement in getting this far by river, but also indicating the strain of the timetable. It was time to put it on the telegraph before the wire became clogged with the stories of her colleagues.

The thought of the opposition deepened her frown. She was fairly sure that Wolseley would not allow the full contingent of newspaper correspondents to go across country with the mounted desert column. The whole point of the camel corps was that it would have to travel light and fast. It could not be encumbered with hangers-on. Oh, the General would want a hand-picked group of newspapermen to be with the mounted column all right, to sing their (and his) glories if they were able to fight their way through to the besieged Gordon before the main army arrived by river. And they would be *men*, for Wolseley would never allow a woman – and the only woman among the correspondents, at that – to go with his flying troops. She stood as little chance of accompanying this new camel corps as she did of walking on the Nile. Baah! She shook her head. Well, she would just have to try and fight her case when the chance came. After all, it was she who had broken the news of the formation of the new unit. Perhaps that might count for something.

As though on cue, she passed a section of the camel corps riding by in double file. They looked as bright as buttons – if rather exotic buttons. Each trooper was dressed in light grey and wore a white pith helmet; he rode on a red saddle, which in turn was covered by a crimson sheepskin. A small dog, allegedly given to the corps by the Grenadier Guards and which had come all the way from Assam, waddled alongside the lead camel. They rode well enough now, if just a trifle hesitantly, and Alice smiled at the memory of watching the newly arrived cavalrymen making the acquaintance of Egyptian camels back in Wady Halfa.

Wolseley's idea of cherry-picking the best of the fine cavalry regiments back home to provide his new unit had not quite worked out in practice, at least not at first. Camels were not chargers, and Alice's grin widened as she recalled those elegant, arched-backed officers from the Household Cavalry grimly trying to hang on to their mounts as the ships of the desert wallowed upright. Saddling and equipping the camels and then putting them into formation every morning had taken hours, and the language from their handlers had forced her coyly to walk away. Now, however, they looked confident enough, and each section leader gave her a warm smile and salute as they lolloped by.

Smiling back, Alice continued on her way through the newly erected tents towards the censor's office, in front of which she met a tall infantry sergeant wearing grey-flecked mutton-chop whiskers, who gave her a deferential salute.

'Bin lookin' for you, miss,' he said in an accent redolent of the Welsh valleys. 'Got a bit of news for you, see.'

Sergeant Joseph Morgan had served with Alice's father in the 24th Regiment of Foot, that most Welsh of military units, and had known her since she was a young teenager and he a raw private, acting as batman to Brigadier Griffith. It had been a great stroke of luck for Alice to meet him in Egypt, where he was serving on the central staff, as Wolseley's office sergeant. It had not needed the pressing of a five-pound note into his hand for him to promise to feed her with any items of information that he thought might be useful to her – 'as long as it's not secret stuff, o' course'.

'Splendid, Sergeant.' She gave him one of her best smiles. 'If we've captured the Mahdi, for goodness' sake don't tell anybody else. Give me an hour's start, there's a good fellow.'

He gave an answering grin. 'Oh, nothin' like that, miss, I'm afraid. No. It's just that a black feller 'as just come into the General's office from out of the desert. The rumour is that 'e's brought news from General Gordon in Khartoum – all wrapped up and hidden in 'is camel's 'air, from what I could see. Sorry, but I don't know what the message is, miss, nor if there's any news about . . .' His voice tailed away. He remembered Fonthill and Jenkins from their days serving in the 24th, and he had shaken hands with Simon in Cairo when the latter had visited Wolseley. He knew of Alice's anxiety.

Alice stood stock still for a moment. 'Nothing at all, Joe?'

'Sorry, miss, no. But you know what they say: no news is good news.'

She forced a smile. 'Thank you. Yes, of course. Anyway, it is good that we have heard from Gordon. This means that the town has not fallen, at least until fairly recently. You don't know how long since he left Khartoum?'

'No. The rumour is, though, that 'e was captured by the

Mahdi and held there for a time. I suppose 'e must have escaped.'

'Hmmm. Or been allowed to continue on his journey with false information. Anyway, thank you, Joe. I will tackle the General.'

'Yes, miss. You won't, of course . . . ?'

'Of course not. I will not reveal the source of my information. You know that.'

The sergeant touched the peak of his helmet and Alice walked on, deep in thought. Perhaps, just perhaps, the message had actually come from Simon? She would use this question as an excuse to tackle Wolseley, for he too knew of her worry about her fiancé, of course. But first she must file her copy. Should she delay her story to contain this new development? It would be hard news, a splendid topical peg to hang her story on. No. She had learned never to delay sending a story once it was written. She could always add to it later.

Her step faltered slightly as she realised that once again she would have to face Captain Hicks-Johnson. His attentions had been becoming more intrusive as each day progressed and she was forced to meet with him to submit her copy. He seemed not at all daunted by her haughty rejection of him, and she could not help feeling that he was, metaphorically at least, stalking her – waiting for his chance to strike when her guard was down. It was an unsettling, even frightening situation, but one she was forced to live with. As liaison officer to the press, and virtual censor, he was, after all, in a position to make life, if not awkward for her, at least tedious. She hoped that one of her colleagues would be in Hicks-Johnson's tent. At least that would provide some sort of chaperon. Alas, its only occupant was the captain himself, sitting behind his folding table and scribbling away.

'Good afternoon,' said Alice. 'I'd be grateful if this could go out straight away, if you please. There will be little need of your censoring pencil. It is all more or less straightforward stuff.'

A smile appeared from under the captain's moustache. He immediately put down his pencil and rose to pick up Alice's copy, although she had placed it in the tray on his desk, then walked around the table, so cutting off her exit. Rifling through her pages, he strolled nonchalantly to the tent opening and, in a sudden, quick movement, undid the bows of the ties holding back the folds of the canvas, so that the opening was closed and the tent became a stuffy, softly lit *chambre privé*.

'What's this then, my dear? Another scoop, eh?' He walked towards Alice slowly, forcing her to back away.

'No,' she said firmly. 'It's a damned fine story which must go on to the wires within the hour. Please cable it immediately.'

His smile widened. 'Oh, come along now, Miss Griffith. Why are you so antagonistic towards me? You know jolly well that I am in a position to be of some considerable help to you. Why not be . . . well, just a little more co-operative, eh? We are all out here in this godforsaken place, many miles from home. You could be a touch more friendly towards me, don't you think?'

He took a step nearer and Alice a step back. She was conscious that the atmosphere under the canvas seemed now to be ever more oppressive. 'Don't talk nonsense, Captain,' she said. 'We are both here to work and we must all be co-operative, surely. Being friendly, as you call it, does not come into it. Now, kindly step aside and allow me to leave.'

Hicks-Johnson, however, made no movement. Alice noticed small beads of perspiration appearing on his forehead, and a surprisingly pink tongue appeared from under his moustache and moistened his lips. Then he extended a hand towards her shoulder.

She ducked away. 'If you lay a hand on me,' she said, 'I shall go straight to Lord Wolseley, accuse you of assault and have you sent home.'

His smile broadened. 'Oh, I don't think you will,' he murmured. 'You know as well as I do that his lordship regards the press as a necessary evil in the first place, and in the second, having a woman among them is a source of great potential friction. Even if you could prove that I had "assaulted" you' – here the smile became a grin – 'then you would have proven his point that you are an irritant, and I think that you would be with me on that boat going home. Now,' he reached out to her again, 'let's start with a kiss, shall we?'

Alice knew that he was right, of course: the last thing she wanted was to draw Wolseley's attention to her gender and to substantiate the old accusation that a woman in a man's world would always be a source of trouble. She had never, of course, had any intention of making a formal complaint. She would just have to deal with this irritant in a more direct fashion.

As Hicks-Johnson reached towards her with his right hand, she made a half-turn to the right and bent her left arm at the elbow so that the hand was across her breast, the palm facing down and its edge towards him. At the same time, she extended her right arm vertically above her head. Intuitively, he followed this strange movement with his head, tilting it back to see where Alice was reaching. In doing so, he exposed his throat, and Alice whipped the edge of her left hand into his windpipe with great force, causing his eyes to pop and him to put both hands to his throat. She then took a step forward and brought her right knee into his groin. As Hicks-Johnson bent forward in agony, she moved aside and pushed down on the back of his neck, so that he sprawled on the ground, gasping and writhing.

Alice stood for a moment looking down on him. 'Don't you dare lay a hand on me ever again,' she hissed. 'I should tell you, little man, that I have killed men before now' – the words prompted a memory flash of a Pathan tribesman curling up in a glade near Kandahar, her bullet in his breast – 'and I would have no compunction at all in removing you. Now, put my copy on the wire, and if you change a word of it, I will see that your testicles are removed as you sleep in your tent.'

She stepped over him and strode to the tent opening.

'You bitch,' he gasped after her. 'Don't think, though, that you will ever see that bastard of a fiancé of yours again, because you won't.' He paused in pain, trying to regain his breath.

Alice froze in the tent opening. Somewhere in the distance a whip cracked and a cartwheel creaked. She heard neither. She turned back. 'What do you mean?'

A gleam of joy had appeared in Hicks-Johnson's eyes. 'The General has just heard that Fonthill and his ridiculous acolytes are in the hands of the Mahdi. They're in chains and are probably being tortured to death as I speak. And a bloody good thing too.'

Alice stood for a moment looking down at him. She realised that her heart had slumped at least a couple of inches. 'I don't believe a word of it,' she said eventually, allowing a note of scorn to creep into her voice. 'You are inventing this.'

'Oh no. A messenger has just come through from Gordon. He spent three days in the Mahdi's camp on the way here, and he's told the General . . .' Hicks-Johnson's voice fell away into a wheeze, and his eyes watered. Then he resumed: 'He says that three men answering their description had been captured, put in chains and lashed. If you don't believe me, why don't you go and ask him yourself, eh?' He forced a chuckle.

Alice whirled on her heel and strode out into the sunshine. She walked fast and then realised that she had no idea where she was going. She knew that this must be the truth, and became aware that she had been half expecting it. Even Simon, resourceful, brave, *dear* Simon, could not expect to stroll through the Mahdi's army twice and get away with it. It was just asking too much. She stood, blinking back tears. Then she made up her mind. She must see Wolseley, of course, and if the General attempted to dissemble, she would remind him of his promise to tell her of news of Simon as soon as it arrived. Then she would demand that he send a small flying force, cavalry, of course, to strike quickly at the Mahdi's headquarters and rescue the three men. Yes, it would be difficult, but it could be done. It was the sort of thing that Simon himself would do. She turned and, with conviction, strode quickly towards the General's command post in the centre of Korti.

She saw Wolseley amazingly quickly – had he been expecting her? He indicated a wooden foldaway chair before his heavily laden table.

'What can I do for you, Alice?'

'Thank you for seeing me right away, sir.' Alice was conscious that her nose must be red, but thought, what the hell? 'I understand that you have had a message from Gordon. May I ask what is in it?'

Wolseley frowned. 'Good lord, word does get out quickly around this place. May I ask how you know?'

Alice had an immediate sense of satisfaction in revealing her source. If this got Hicks-Johnson into trouble, then so much the better. 'Your press liaison officer, Captain Hicks-Johnson. He did not seem to think that the information was confidential.'

'Didn't he now? Well, the information is correct.' The

General pulled two small pieces of paper towards him from his cluttered tabletop and adjusted a pair of pince-nez spectacles. 'The trouble is that two messages came via the same messenger – a black from the south of the Sudan – and to some extent they conflict with each other.' He sighed. 'As so many of Gordon's messages have done.'

He opened the folds of a piece of paper no bigger than a postage stamp. 'This one was sewn into the hem of his clothing and says simply, "13 Dec. 1884. K all right. C.G." The second is this longer message that arrived concealed in the strands of the rope that formed the headstall of the messenger's camel. It speaks of lack of grain and biscuit, no butter, no dates, little meat, and goes on to say, "We want you to come quickly. You should come by Metemmeh or Berber. Make by these two roads. Do not leave Berber in your rear. Keep enemy on your front, and when you take Berber, send me word from there. Do this without rumours of your approach spreading abroad." '

Wolseley removed the spectacles and rubbed his eyes with the knuckles of each hand. Alice realised the strain the General was under.

'On the one hand,' he continued, 'Gordon says that Khartoum was all right some ten days ago. Yet the other message talks of little food, begs me to come quickly and gives me rather strange instructions for my route. He must know that to take Berber and yet "come quickly" are mutually exclusive. Can't do both, d'you see?'

'Quite. Do you think both messages are genuine?'

'I can't be sure. I incline to think that the short message, written so small, is probably the real thing. The trouble is that the messenger was forced to spend three days in the Mahdi's camp before being allowed to continue. I can't help feeling that the longer message could have been forced on him by the

Dervishes to make us fall into a trap at Berber – although, of course, he denies this.'

'Indeed. What do you intend to do, General?'

'I really have no choice. I must press on as fast as I can, as I have always done. My overland column is not yet ready to go but will set off, probably on the thirtieth of December, and make as good time as it can. And on this point, my dear, I am afraid I have some bad news for you. There is room for very few journalists with the column, and the dangers are such that I cannot allow a woman to go.'

'But General . . .'

Wolseley held up his hand. 'I am sorry, Alice, but there is nothing more to be said on this matter. I have little time now and my decision cannot be questioned. Of course, your news agency is important, and your colleague,' he adjusted the pince-nez again and consulted another paper on his table, 'Mr Piggott will go, so that what I believe will be the "hard news" coverage of the expedition will be looked after.'

Alice opened her mouth to protest, but the General intervened again. 'The matter is closed. If your editor wishes to protest, then he can do so direct to the Horse Guards, although I fear he will receive little satisfaction there. These matters are left to me.'

His face softened for a moment. 'If it is any consolation to you, my dear, my masters have forbidden me personally to venture further into Sudan. I am to stay here and direct things from Korti, dammit. So you see, I know how you feel. We must keep each other company.'

He smiled, and looking at the worry lines emanating from the corners of both his eyes, one alive, one dead, Alice could not help but smile back. There was no question of her protesting further in any case, for her mind was far too full of the fate of Simon and his two companions.

'I accept that, General. But I have one more thing that is worrying me far more, if I may say so, than even the plight of brave General Gordon.'

Wolseley sighed and put his hand to his forehead. 'Yes. I remember my promise and was about to come on to this. Both my intelligence people and myself, of course, have questioned this messenger feller, who, by the way, speaks reasonable English — it seems he served Gordon in the south of the country when the General was working hard to put down the slave trade.'

Alice was now sitting on the edge of her chair. 'Yes?'

'Well, as I say, the chap says that he was waylaid by the Dervishes on his way north and forced to spend three days in the Mahdi's camp. It is this, of course, that puts some doubt on this second message, which could have been planted to make us go via Berber and so delay our march to Khartoum.'

Alice nodded.

'We questioned him in quite some detail about the condition of the camp — how many soldiers, the ordnance, the arms of the men, et cetera — and of the prisoners there. He said that three men had been captured on leaving Khartoum at night. They claimed to be Greek but only one spoke Arabic, a short, slim feller.' Wolseley paused and coughed. 'Of the others, one was said to be slim, broad shouldered and of medium height but with a broken nose and the other much shorter and wider. We have heard nothing of Fonthill, of course, but I'm afraid that it sounds as though he and his colleagues did manage to get to Gordon but were captured on their way back. I am so sorry, I really am.'

Alice managed to keep her voice level. 'And . . . and what has happened to them?'

'I understand that they seem to be a source of some puzzlement to the Dervish command, who don't quite know what to make of them or what to do with them. It seems that they have been put into chains and . . . beaten a bit, I'm afraid.' He hurried on. 'But when this messenger left, they were still alive, I understand, and some slave boy or other, whom they had picked up, was tending them.' The General cleared his throat and forced a faint smile. 'So you see, my dear, all is not lost.'

Alice thought fast and was grateful that there were no tears pricking her eyes – at least for the moment. 'Indeed, sir. But, of course, they will have vital information for you and they therefore cannot be left to rot there, in the Mahdi's chains.'

'Quite so. We will march on the Dervishes, bring them to battle and free all their prisoners just as soon as is humanly possible.'

'You mean that you will make no special direct effort to free Simon?'

Wolseley sat back in his chair. 'Oh come now. What had you in mind?'

Alice tossed her head. 'I don't know. I am not a soldier. But surely perhaps a squadron of cavalry could ride quickly southeast, out into the desert, and while one section created a diversion, say by night, the other could force its way into the camp and free Simon and his two companions?'

Wolseley's weak smile returned. 'The Mahdi has forty thousand men or more. What could a squadron of cavalry do against that many? And how could Fonthill be snatched quickly if he and the others are securely chained? There simply would not be time to file through bars and chains while under attack. No. I am afraid I could not countenance such a venture.'

This time Alice felt the tears begin to form behind her eyes. She made one last attempt. 'But they can't just be left there, surely? Could not spies penetrate the camp and free them somehow? General, you need the information that Simon has.'

'I do indeed. But I cannot see how we can free him. I do not possess the sort of intelligence source that you suggest. I know of no one who could penetrate the camp as you describe. No, I am profoundly sorry, but Fonthill and his men must wait until we can reach them with the army.' He leaned forward. 'This will be no consolation for you, I know, but your brave fiancé and his two companions knew exactly the dangers they faced when they accepted this assignment. It is just bad luck that they failed. I promise you, however, that as soon as we reach Khartoum, the freeing of the Mahdi's prisoners will be a high priority.'

'If they are still alive then.'

Wolseley did not reply, but slowly bowed his head.

The two sat in silence for a moment, then Alice stood. 'Thank you, General,' she said. 'I think I need to do a little praying.'

'Keep your courage up, young lady. Fonthill would want you to do that.'

'Of course. Goodbye.'

'Ah . . . er . . . one last thing, Alice. Please do not mention the second message, but if you wish, you can relay the news that Khartoum had not fallen by the thirteenth of December and that Gordon had reported that all was well. We will issue this directive to your colleagues within the hour. Perhaps you have time,' he smiled, 'to steal something of a march on them.'

Alice did not return the smile, but bowed and left the tent. She pulled a cable form from her bag and, writing against a mud wall, scribbled a cryptic new flash and took it to Hicks-Johnson's tent. Of him there was no sign but his sergeant was at the desk.

'This is most urgent,' she said. 'I have just left the Commander-in-Chief, who gave me this information and was happy for me to cable it to London. Please put it on the wire immediately.'

'Very good, miss.'

Alice then walked to the river and sat on a rock while her brain raced. She sat for only two minutes, however, before, her mind made up, she strode quickly back to her tent. She pulled back her bedroll, and scraped away the loose sand underneath it to reveal a shallow, termite-proof tin box. Fumbling in her bag, she found a key and inserted it in the lock on the top of the box, and removed a small leather bag from which she carefully took a handful of gold sovereigns. Replacing the remainder of the coins, she put back the bag and locked the box before burying it once more in the sand.

Loitering outside the General's office long enough to catch Sergeant Morgan's eye, Alice beckoned him to walk a few paces away with her.

'Joe,' she asked, 'is this messenger who came from Khartoum still in camp?'

'Yes, miss. 'E's in the native quarters, over there.'

'I would like to talk to him . . . you understand.'

'O' course, miss. I can't come with you 'cos I can't leave the General, but I'll get Private Jones over there to take you to 'im. Oh, and miss – I 'ope it's good news. 'Is name is Abdullah something or other, by the way.'

She smiled her thanks, and within minutes found herself squatting on the sand with a tall, thin Sudanese from Equatoria, in the south. He had the blackest skin and the whitest teeth she had ever seen. His age was uncertain, but some of his tight curls were grey. At first the man was extremely shy and seemed almost afraid to be questioned by an Englishwoman. But in reaction to Alice's courtesy and polite queries about his background and family, he began to open up. His English was not fluent but it was adequate.

'Are you returning to your home in the south, then, Abdullah?' she asked.

'Yes, lady. Soon now.'

'How will you go?'

He shrugged his shoulders. 'On camel.'

'Will you go back through the Mahdi's camp?'

'Perhaps, but think no. Bad men there. I go round, I think, in desert.'

'I understand that you saw three Greek men in the Mahdi's camp. How were they when you left?'

'Not good. They had been whipped. Twenty-five lashes I think for the little big man and the little thin man, but fifty for the other one.'

Alice sucked in her breath. Oh God! 'But they were all alive?'

'Yes, but little thin one hurt bad.'

'I see.'

How to approach this? She decided to be honest. 'Abdullah, the man who had fifty lashes is the man to whom I am betrothed. Do you understand?'

His eyes widened but he shook his head. 'Sorry, lady. No.'

'He is the man I am going to marry. He is English.'

'Ah.' The great head with its tight curls nodded. 'Very good, lady. He brave man. He don't die.' Abdullah's teeth flashed in a great face-splitting smile, and immediately Alice's heart lifted. It was ridiculous that she should feel elated by this ignorant man's assurance, but she did so and she warmed to him.

'Listen, Abdullah,' she said, leaning towards him. 'I intend to go down into the desert to free this man and the two men with him. I want you to take me there and bring us all back.' She reached into her bag and held up a golden sovereign. 'Do you know what this is?'

Abdullah nodded. 'English sovereign. I see it with Gordon Pasha in the south. It very good. Better than Sudan dollar.'

'It certainly is. Now, I will pay you twenty of these sovereigns to take me to Khartoum to free these men, and another fifty when you get us all back to the British Army. Will you do it?'

The Sudanese's eyes rolled. 'Take you, lady?'

'Yes. I can ride a camel better than an Englishman and I will dye my skin and cut off most of my hair and dress like an Arab. If we are stopped, you will say that I am your wife and that you are taking me back to Equatoria. I speak some Arabic but you can explain I don't speak the local dialect and am shy of talking. I will want you to buy some camels here, for me of course and for the three men we will be bringing back. We will put packs on them and you will say we are going south to make a home. Will you do it, please, Abdullah?'

'Very dangerous, lady. How do we get people out of camp?'

'I will take files and a saw to cut the shackles. If we are careful we should be able to get them out by night. Please, Abdullah?'

'Very, very dangerous, lady.'

'I know that. But I know that you are brave. I will increase the first payment to thirty sovereigns. How is that?'

The man thought for a moment. Then: 'You goin' to marry this man?'

'Oh yes. I love him very much. He will not lie rotting in those chains.'

The big smile returned. 'I go home to marry woman,' he said. 'I love her like you. She make good beer. I know what you feel. I take you. Twenty-five of this gold coin is enough for first journey. Keep rest for your . . . what is it? . . . dowry.'

Alice could have kissed the great beaming face opposite her. For the first time she felt hope. She put out her hand. 'Let us shake hands, my dear man,' she said. 'This seals the contract in England.'

Solemnly they shook hands for what seemed like almost a minute, with each pumping their arm up and down. Alice looked guiltily over her shoulder, but no one seemed to have observed this strange ritual.

'Splendid,' she said. 'Now we must make arrangements quickly. I will cut my hair very short; do you know someone who can dye it black and also who can dye my body? Er . . . a woman, if possible, please – and Abdullah, I do not want anyone to know about this.'

'Yes, lady. You have dollars to pay? Gold will make people wonder.'

'Of course. And we shall need camels and provisions for the journey. I can sleep out of doors. I want us to travel light and quickly.'

He nodded solemnly. 'Camels could be difficult. Soldiers buy them all. But I know a man. I think it good. When you want to go?'

'The sooner the better. Perhaps the day after tomorrow?'

'Yes, lady. Give me dollars tomorrow morning, please.'

'Very well. We shall need to leave at night. I do not wish anyone to know what we are doing or where we are going. Are two days sufficient time for you to arrange things?'

'No. Three.'

Alice liked his directness and honesty. 'Very well. We will meet here tomorrow morning when the sun is just over that hill, and I will have dollars for you. Agreed?'

'Agreed, lady.' And he flashed his smile again.

Back in her tent, Alice lay on her bed and a fierce reaction set in. What a crazy venture! She was trusting herself to a savage to take her – as his wife – into the heart of a wilderness peopled by some of the most barbaric and ruthless human beings in the world, on a mission that had 'impossible' stamped all over it. Even if they survived the journey without raising suspicion from the Dervishes, how could they penetrate the camp of the Mahdi himself and, unnoticed, remove the shackles from the three men and smuggle them out without being detected? What was to stop Abdullah slitting her throat once they were deep into the desert and making off with her twenty-five sovereigns? Only, of course, the promise of another fifty to come. Yet he had refused to accept the extra five she had offered – and he did have that ridiculously ingenuous smile that lit up his face. No one with a smile like that could possibly be devious, surely? The risk was great but the stakes were high. The thought of Simon being flogged sent a cold chill through her body. To hell with Wolseley and his ponderous advance along the Nile. To hell with rescuing Gordon! *She* would rescue Simon Fonthill. She *would*!

The next day, Alice met Abdullah and was relieved to hear that he had been able to arrange for the purchase of five camels at what she felt intuitively was a reasonable price. Then she sought out Walter Piggott, her Reuters colleague. After some initial friction, their friendship had grown, based on mutual respect. Now she explained to him that she had picked up the threads of what could be a good story, the details of which must remain a secret. It demanded, however, that she must leave camp for a while, and she requested him to notify London, explaining that she would be out of contact for a time. His puzzlement was partly assuaged when she broke the news to him that he and not she was to be included in the mounted column. Then she found Sergeant Morgan, who was staying behind at Korti with Wolseley, of course, and requested that he look after her bag of sovereigns and other personal effects for a few days. He too was puzzled, but knew better than to ask questions. One last visit to the armoury, where she made several purchases from the sergeant major in charge, whom she had met on Wolseley's el Kebir campaign, completed her preparations.

Two days later, a little after dusk, an Equatorial Sudanese and his slim young wife rode out of Korti, the basic needs of their new home in the far south carried on three camels behind them. No one queried their departure, for no one cared.

Chapter 12

They crossed the river immediately with the help of a disinterested native ferryman and headed out into the desert in the great bend of the Nile. They made good time, for, in fact, the three camels they were leading were not at all heavily loaded, carrying only their supplies for the outward journey before, hopefully, bringing back Simon, Jenkins and Ahmed. They had put some ten miles behind them before Alice decided that they should rest. They made no fire and only took four hours' sleep before setting off again to the south-east.

Abdullah had advised that they should make for the wells at Jakdul and then turn due south, keeping well away from but roughly parallel to the river and heading out into the desert, where they would meet fewer Dervishes, before coming into Omdurman, where the three men had been imprisoned, from the west. The Nile, he said, was a bad place to be and its banks were comparatively fully populated. They would stand less chance of being questioned by the Mahdi's men out in the desert.

Consulting her rough map, Alice was happy with this, for if they were not going to sail up the river – which seemed fraught with difficulties – then the direct desert route south would be shorter, although long enough at nearly two hundred miles. And time, of course, was of the essence.

The route they followed to the wells was fairly clearly

defined, and Alice was troubled at first that they would seem to offer a tempting target to brigands, with their three pack camels. But the people they met, desert Bedawi, traders and ordinary Sudanese moving between the two loops of the Nile, seemed little interested in them. The travellers all passed with a nod of the head and a cheerful *as-salaam alaykum*. All the pair had for protection were Abdullah's sword, a fearsome cross-handled thing, slung beside him on his saddle, and the little French army Chamelot Delvigne revolver that Alice had bought in Cairo during the Tel el Kebir campaign two years before. She had decided against attempting to purchase rifles. This would have been difficult to do anyway, and the guns would have been the possible object of attention if they were stopped. Abdullah did not care. 'No guns, no fighting, lady,' he said. And he was probably right.

As their journey progressed, Alice became more aware each day of the Sudanese's worth. He was more than competent, in that he was a seasoned desert traveller – he knew when to press the camels and when to let them find their own pace, even though he remained aware of the need for speed – and he had the ability to detect, in a seemingly arid plain, a declivity that would provide them with some shelter for the night, even though they lacked tents. He also knew the location of wells in this wilderness, a vital attribute once they had turned south at Jakdul, leaving behind them the well-defined although sparsely travelled trail between the great bend of the river.

Above all, however, he proved to be an equable companion. He rarely spoke, unless invited to do so, but his huge smile was never far away, beaming back at Alice as she rode dutifully behind him as a Muslim wife should.

She questioned him about his background, and he revealed that he had been a slave, taken as a boy by Arab slavers from he knew not where in the deep south, but released as a young teenager by Gordon Pasha in Equatoria, when the General had travelled through the region in his great anti-slavery campaign during his first incumbency as governor general of Sudan. Gordon, he recalled, had been a kind man who had taken a great personal interest in his welfare.

'He put me into school he start at Khartoum,' he said. 'He called all the boys his "little chicks". Then, later, I work in his house. But he left and I not happy. So I go back to Equatoria and find good woman. But I hear Gordon Pasha come back so I return to Khartoum to work for him and make a little money for wedding.'

Alice nodded. 'And the General asked you to take his message to General Wolseley?'

'Yes, lady. He know I do what I promise. So he gives me one message in my clothes and the other in headstall of camel. Mahdi's men question me but I say nothing. They search but find nothing.'

'The Dervishes did not plant a false message on you then?'

'Oh no. If they do that, I throw it away.'

'But why did they let you go?'

'I say I want to go home to south. They let me go. So I go out into desert and then turn round and go north.'

'Abdullah, I am so glad you did.'

The huge smile returned. 'Me glad also, lady. Now I will have money for wedding.

Alice answered his smile. 'But will your woman remain true to you? You must have been away a long time.'

'Oh yes. She like me. I a good man.'

'I am sure you are.' Then she swallowed hard. 'Tell me again about the three men. Did you see this . . . ah . . . flogging?'

'No, lady. But I heard about it. But you not to worry. The small, broad one and the tall, thin one – he your man I think, yes?'

Alice nodded, unable to speak.

'These two all right, I think. Little man – I heard he was a Turk, no?'

'No. An Egyptian.'

'Ah, same thing. He not so good. But then I leave. So I don't know.

'Oh, poor Ahmed. Why were they whipped?'

'Don't know, lady. It happen many times in Mahdi's camp.'

Alice took out her handkerchief and blew her nose fiercely. Her mind turned again to the problem of what to do once they arrived at Omdurman. If the three were still alive – and please God they would be, for Simon and Jenkins were old campaigners and must be hard as old boots now – how on earth would they free them? And if they were able to relieve them of their chains, how to get out of the camp and then escape pursuit on the long ride north? She stuck out her chin. Well, she would worry about that when the time came. She would think of something. Now they must just get on with it, riding south, always south.

In fact, despite her anxiety about Simon, Alice found a kind of tranquillity in the desert. The route they took led them into a less frequented part of the northern Sudan, bordering Kordofan to the south, and they met no one after leaving Jakdul Wells. Once she became accustomed to it, she enjoyed the lolloping gait of the camels, and the heat, although fierce, was bearable. She also came to appreciate the beauty of the desert. In the scrub of Afghanistan and the level sand and gravel of the northern desert of Egypt, everything had seemed monochrome. The banks of the Nile, too, had become almost boring, with their rocks and dun-coloured sand. But here, the desert always seemed to be changing: the rocks harsh and arid, black and gold in the midday heat, but merging softly into purple as the afternoon slipped into evening, and distant hills showing as a smudged mauve on the horizon. The air was clear.

The days slipped by in a rhythmic ritual: sleeping warmly wrapped under the stars; breakfast as the sun burned its way over a distant peak; then riding until noon; a handful of dates and plenty of water, followed by a few hours of fitful dozing in the midday heat under a canopy, before back to hard riding and the laying of a fire and a meal, skilfully cooked by Abdullah, as the cool night crept across the desert.

As they journeyed, Alice consulted her compass from time to time, but it was not really necessary. Abdullah seemed to have a sixth sense of direction that kept him riding firmly due south, with, seemingly, only an occasional glimpse up at the sun or a morning star to help him. He also knew when to deviate to find a well – sometimes just a hole between rocks with surprisingly cool water at the bottom from which to fill their water sacks. How would a man from the south know this vast country so well?

He shrugged. 'I know the desert,' was all he would say by way of explanation.

Alice estimated that they had been travelling for seven days when they met the Dervishes. They loomed out of the distance, shimmering disturbingly in the heat haze as though they were mirages, until they neared and became firmly fixed: three of them, travelling quite fast on camels and coming directly towards them.

'Put on *burkha*,' grunted Abdullah.

Alice quickly put on the black Muslim head covering, which showed nothing of her face except her eyes – her *grey* eyes, dammit!

The three reined in their camels and made no attempt to pass. Abdullah gave his greeting but received no response from the Arabs. Instead, they viewed the Sudanese and Alice with slow, insolent eyes. They were undoubtedly Dervishes, and men of the Mahdi, for they had sewn the distinctive rectangular red patches to their clothing to show their allegiance.

Alice lowered her head in subservience but observed the men through her lashes. They were young and haughty, sitting their mounts with an arrogant ease, Remington rifles balanced across their knees. Still without a word, the three rode around the two travellers slowly, examining the three pack camels and then Alice in particular. One edged his camel near to her, and as she bent her head, he used his camel stick to push her chin upwards to look into her eyes. She kept her lashes lowered and did not engage his glance.

The man spoke for the first time, but Alice's untuned ear could not comprehend. His meaning was clear, however, for she understood Abdullah's reply. 'She is my woman,' he said.

Used to Abdullah's voice, her knowledge of Arabic was just able to cope with his replies, although not the questions, which were rapped out quickly. She tightened her grip on the butt of the little revolver tucked away under her garment.

'No, she is my woman. My wife,' repeated Abdullah calmly. *Oh God. What were they asking?*

Further questions. 'We are from the south. Many women there have grey eyes.' *Good thinking, Abdullah!*

More questions. 'We travel home to Equatoria from Jakdul Wells, where we met my father and mother who trade there. We go to set up our house in the south there.' Then: 'No. You cannot have her. She is not for sale.' *Ah, so that was it. What would they do now?*

Abdullah spoke quite calmly, almost with authority, and Alice had never admired him so much.

The Dervish who had made the offer then began to smile, although his black eyes remained cold. He spoke again and indicated the sword that hung from Abdullah's saddle, and then his own curved blade, hanging from his belt. *God! A challenge? She could not let Abdullah fight for her.* The two other Dervishes gave a cry of delight and grinned.

Abdullah seemed quite unperturbed. He looked the Dervish up and down, his face expressionless, and shrugged his shoulders. *If he gave her up, as he obviously must, then could she kill all three with her small handgun? She was woefully out of practice, but better that than . . .*

But Abdullah was tapping his camel on its neck, bidding it to kneel. He unwrapped his long legs from around the saddle pommel, slipped on to the sand and then, almost languidly, reached up and withdrew his great two-handed sword from its sheath.

'Abdullah!' Alice cried instinctively, but the Sudanese held up his hand in placation to her, his eyes still quite expressionless, and turned to face the Dervish. The latter slipped down from his own mount, drew his shorter, lighter sword and, holding it in one hand, pointed it first to Alice, as though marking out his property, and then to Abdullah.

Alice felt her mouth go completely dry. Her Sudanese mentor was no warrior, that appeared clear. He stood almost uncertainly, his legs apart, both hands clasped around this great sword, which appeared far too unwieldy to be used in single combat. His adversary, in contrast, trod lightly around him in a circle, his curved blade twinkling in the sunlight as he revolved it at arm's length, moving it only from the wrist.

His fellows, still grinning, drew their camels back to give the contestants room, one of them grabbing the halter of Abdullah's beast and pulling it back also. Alice remained resolutely where she was, comparatively close to the duellists, and loosened the revolver from its little holster under her *jibba*. She wished to be as near as possible before she withdrew her weapon. If she shot too soon, they would certainly kill her and Abdullah with their rifles. She would wait until Abdullah was failing, then she would take her chance. Whatever happened, though, she would protect her guide.

The disparity between the two swordsmen immediately became clear. Abdullah, the taller and thinner, was also much the slower. For a moment they both stood quite still, and a terrible silence fell upon the little gathering. In the distance somewhere a fly buzzed for a moment and then fell silent, as though it too realised that something momentous was about to happen here in the desert, far from the nearest dwelling. Alice did not move, but felt the perspiration trickling down her back, between her shoulder blades. When she intervened she had to get it right, absolutely right. She prayed that she would choose the right moment and that her aim would be good.

Then the Dervish suddenly attacked in flashes of thrusts and swings, forcing his opponent back in a series of clumsy feints. Abdullah was not just content to defend, however, for he then swung his own sword in two great swathes, which, if they had connected, would surely have cut the Dervish in two. As it was, the man jumped away with a contemptuous grin, earning the applause of his two followers.

Alice realised that this combat would not last long and that her options for intervening were few and, indeed, offered little hope of success. Abdullah had an advantage in reach but was disadvantaged by the heaviness of his weapon and the soldierly skill of his opponent. What could she do? Producing her revolver could perhaps stop the duel. But then what? Make the Dervishes ride away and leave them? They would be back in the darkness, surely, intrigued, to say the least, by this grey-eyed woman who carried a French army revolver. Shoot to kill now? Maybe she could hit two of them at short range, but her camel would certainly rear in fright and the third would be able to return the fire.

Then the hand clutching the revolver encountered something hard and angular in the undergarment beneath her *jibba*. Her vanity had not completely deserted her in the desert, and she carried a very small hand mirror to help her complete her primitive toilet twice a day. Now: which way was the sun, and would she have time and the required skill, with the two duellists moving around, to reflect its rays into the eyes of the Dervish? Equally importantly: would the other two see what she was up to, and even if they did not, would Abdullah be quick enough to take advantage of her intervention? It was worth a chance.

She removed the mirror and shot a quick look at the two spectators. Their eyes were firmly fixed on the combat, like senators at a Roman amphitheatre. As Abdullah faced her momentarily, she showed him the mirror and nodded to the sun.

Alice had no idea if the tall man had understood her meaning, but he suddenly stamped to his right and swung his sword in a great arc. It presented no danger to the Dervish, of course, who merely skipped away – but to face Alice, and with the sun behind him!

She held up the small, bright surface so that an oval of light settled momentarily on the man's breast before he moved away. Damn! She nodded to Abdullah again, although there was no sign of recognition from him. Nevertheless, he repeated his tactic and the Dervish moved around once more. Alice held up the glass, protecting it with her shoulder from the gaze of the other two men. This time the beam of light landed on the beard of Abdullah's opponent before he skipped aside. *Damn! Useless!*

She looked quickly at the two other Dervishes, but they

were still riveted by the duel and were paying her no attention. She was, after all, just a woman on a camel – slim, certainly, and probably attractive enough to kill a man for, particularly if it was so easy to dispatch him, as was clearly the case here. But the fight was worth watching for all that.

Alice hunched over the mirror and concentrated hard. She angled the mirror once more, and as the Dervish circled to face her again was able at last to land that little circle of fierce white light on his eyes, causing the man to frown, lower his sword and lose his concentration for a second. Immediately Abdullah sprang forward and his blade cut a deep gash in the Dervish's neck, producing a puzzled expression and forcing the man's tongue to protrude between his teeth. Then the guide took a pace nearer and, for the first time, used the point of the blade instead of its edge. He thrust the sword deep into the breast of his opponent and then slowly withdrew it, causing the Dervish to slump slowly to the ground, his eyes glazed and his mouth open. There he lay unmoving, quite dead.

Abdullah, his face and garments soaked in perspiration, and gasping for breath, leaned heavily on his sword. Immediately Alice slipped the glass back, grasped the butt of the revolver again and turned to face the two remaining Dervishes. Had they seen her? What would they do? At least the odds were more level now.

Their reaction was quite unexpected. They immediately raised their rifles, pointed the barrels to the sky and fired them, shouting something that was quite unintelligible to Alice. But they were grinning. Their eyes were only on Abdullah, and it was clear that they had not seen Alice's intervention. They cared nothing for the death of their compatriot; they were appreciating the end of a good fight. The rifle firing was a salutation to the victor!

Alice found herself shaking in reaction to the brutality of

the end of the duel. For the first time, however, the trace of a grim smile appeared on Abdullah's face. He nodded to the two Dervishes, who showed no sign of aggression, only approbation, then turned and gave a brief nod of acknowledgement to Alice.

She regarded him in silence, her mouth hanging open. Then, remembering her place, she lowered her head demurely. Something – she could not tell what – was exchanged between Abdullah and the two Dervishes. Then the two men dismounted, removed some decorative armbands from the dead man's wrists and an amulet from his throat, took up his rifle, plunged his sword deep into the sand so that only the hilt protruded and remounted their camels. One took the halter rein of their former comrade's camel, uttered a brief word to Abdullah, and then the two rode away to the north, without a glance at Alice.

'Good God, Abdullah,' she said. 'I can't thank you enough. You were so brave. But tell me: is that all they care about their dead friend? What did they say?'

'They say "bury him", that's all.'

'How . . . how . . . barbaric!'

'It is their way. It is the way of the desert. The way of the Mahdi.'

Alice climbed down to go to Abdullah. 'Ugh!' She took his hand, slippery with sweat. 'But thank you again for fighting for me.' She took out her revolver, which she had never shown him before. 'I had only this to use and was going to fire if it looked as though you were going to be hurt. But thank God it did not prove necessary.'

The great grin returned at last. 'You much better with the glass thing, lady,' he said. 'Very clever. I think he kill me. I am not as young as I think . . . pah! I thank you, now. We both warriors, eh? Let us shake hands like warriors.'

They shook hands again, and Alice had a brief sense that this perhaps was how Simon and Jenkins would behave at the end of one of their many brushes with death: comradeship and mutual respect acknowledged in a manly handshake. She smiled at the thought.

Abdullah nodded to the body. 'I do this,' he said, and he indicated a rock protruding from the sand about a hundred yards away. 'You sit there, lady, and tell if people come.'

She smiled again. She knew that there was no need to stand watch, for visibility stretched for miles on this flat desert plain and intruders could be detected long before they arrived. But he had given her the watchkeeping role to excuse her from the distasteful task of burying the corpse. He was making her feel useful – not just a helpless woman. Abdullah's thoughtfulness would not have been out of place in an English vicarage, yet he had just slain his enemy in a primitive fight straight from the pages of a medieval saga. It was another example of the man's many virtues.

Alice nodded and walked away slowly to perch gratefully on the rock. Her legs, she realised, were still trembling. The duel had been her first experience of brutal violence since the Battle of Tel el Kebir more than two years ago, and then, of course, she had been an observer, well out of harm's way, not the trophy to be won on the swing of a sword. She shivered, despite the heat. Then she tossed her head back. This would never do! There would almost certainly be much more bloodshed before they rescued Simon. She walked back.

'Here, let me help,' she said, kneeling beside Abdullah and joining him in scooping out sand from the hollow he had already made.

They worked together in silence for a while before the tall man adjudged they had gone deep enough. 'Hard ground now,' he grunted. 'No spade, so we just put him in. Allah has his spirit. Body don't matter.' He seized the Dervish's legs, pulled him to the grave and immediately began covering him with sand. Alice turned her head away until the corpse was covered, then she too knelt and, using her hand, pushed sand on to the mound.

Abdullah stood, wiping his hands. 'We go now, I think?' he asked.

'Yes please.'

They mounted and rode away. Alice looked back. Apart from the disturbed sand, there was no evidence that a man had lost his life in a fight over a woman. Suddenly she felt sick. This was, indeed, a barbaric country. She took several deep breaths and then urged her camel forward so that she rode alongside Abdullah.

'Did those two men say where they were heading and why they were making their journey?' she asked.

'Yes. They go north to fight the infidel.'

'Ah. Does that mean that a Dervish army is being formed to attack the British column, do you think?'

'I do not know. Perhaps.' They rode on in their customary companionable silence.

Two days later, Alice's presumption was confirmed when, far ahead of them, they saw a great sand cloud. It signified many men on the march, and as they neared it, they realised that it was far too wide for them to track around it. Nevertheless, Abdullah pulled his camel's head to the west to avoid penetrating the moving mass at its middle. Soon they were able to pick out the black and then green and white flags of the Mahdi in the van, and the sun glinted on a thousand spear points. It was, reflected Alice, as though she had been transported back in time and was seeing the advance of Saladin's army against the Crusaders.

'*Burkha*,' grunted Abdullah, and Alice donned the black

headdress once again, her mouth dry as they neared the vast mass.

This time, however, there seemed no menace. An army on the move it certainly was, but a peculiar sort of army in that it included many families among the armed men: women riding lead camels and towing loads behind them, and young children urging thin-flanked cattle to keep up the pace. It was like a small nation on passage, its very domesticity robbing it of much of its threat. Alice immediately felt relief, although she kept her head well down and her eyelashes lowered as she dutifully followed Abdullah's camel as it threaded its way through the throng. The Sudanese raised his hand in greeting now and then, and exchanged a few words as they passed through, but the pair were completely unchallenged. They were of no interest. This moving mass had other things on its mind.

It took them about half an hour to pass through the army, and Alice was able to remove her *burkha* and pull alongside Abdullah. 'Who on earth were they, and where were they going?' she asked.

'Going north to fight. You were right. They go to fight Wolseley Pasha.'

A terrible thought struck Alice. 'Oh God! Does this mean that Khartoum has fallen?'

'No. I ask and they say infidel pig is still fighting.' Abdullah's wraparound grin reappeared. 'It take more than slaver like Mahdi to kill Gordon Pasha. He go on fighting till he drop.'

Alice nodded. 'Yes, but I wonder for how much longer.' A further thought struck her. 'If this number of men are going north, they must be assembling a big army to fight Lord Wolseley. It could be difficult for us to get through them when we return with . . . with our three men.'

The tall Sudanese remained silent for a moment, his head nodding in time with the camel's plod. 'Yes. I think about that,' he said eventually.

The next day they heard firing in the distance, only the dull boom of cannon at first and then, as they approached nearer, the lighter rattle of musketry.

'Omdurman,' grunted Abdullah. 'We camp soon. Not safe to go too near.'

Alice consulted her old and much creased map, purchased in Cairo, it seemed several lifetimes ago. It did not show Omdurman, of course, because Gordon had built the fort long after it was printed, but Abdullah had marked roughly where it was: on the west bank of the White Nile, just south of the junction of the two Niles and some four miles away from Khartoum itself. She frowned. Now came the moment of truth, of course. Would it be possible to find out if the three prisoners were still alive, get them out of the Mahdi's camp without detection and then take them the three hundred and fifty miles or more over the desert, through Dervish territory and the massing army in the north to the safety of the British lines? But which British lines? Where would Wolseley's desert column be by the time they reached that northern loop of the Nile? She grinned despite herself. It all sounded bloody hopeless. Then her chin thrust forward. Hopeless? Never! If Simon was still alive, they would rescue him and take him and his companions to safety – or die in the attempt.

That evening, they camped in a little hollow some one and a half miles to the north-west of Omdurman, well within the sound of the guns and, from the top of a rock fringing the hollow, just within sight of the black mass that was the Mahdi's camp set around the fort.

They sat by a small fire of dried camel dung and munched

cooked *durra* and sun-dried goat's meat as they discussed tactics. When their journey had begun, Alice had been the undoubted leader, the employer giving directions to her guide. As they had ridden further south, however, Abdullah had gradually assumed command, without in any way challenging Alice's overall responsibility for their mission.

He outlined the geography of the Dervish camp with the end of his camel switch in the sand. The fort was set back a little way from the banks of the White Nile, with rough fortifications running down from it to the river. Bulging outwards from Omdurman itself, the Mahdi's encampment lay mainly to the west and south of the fort, and almost exactly in the centre of it, he marked with a cross, were the series of *zariba*-enclosed compounds where the shackled prisoners were kept.

'I go in to try and find them,' he said.

'But you don't know them. I must come with you.'

He shook his head. 'No. Too dangerous. You don't speak Arabic. If you found as English, then we all lose our heads. No. You stay here. I find them somehow.'

Alice put her face in her hands momentarily. 'Abdullah, listen. You might well be recognised as the man who was suspected of escaping from Khartoum. What happens then?'

He shrugged. 'Many more people come to camp since then. Many new faces. I don't act suspicious. You tell me what your people look like. I remember that slave boys usually look after people in chains, if people can pay. I find slave boy. He take me to them for few coins. But . . .' he frowned, 'how we get them out of chains? Very difficult, I think.'

Alice rose to her feet and went to her saddle bag and reached inside. 'Here,' she said, unwrapping a piece of oiled cloth. 'Here are two hacksaws – the sort that can cut through steel – two files, and a pair of pliers that a strong man could use to prise open links in a chain, once they have been cut through.' She put them on the ground by the fire. 'But Abdullah, these are very precious. We must be absolutely sure that you give them to the right prisoners.'

The big man weighed the pliers in his hand. 'Good. It may take me one, two or three visits to find these people. Yes, we must be sure. You must give me something at first that shows who you are, so they trust me. Then I must have something they give me to show who *they* are. Do you have something?'

She delved once more into her bag. 'Here,' she said, 'take this. But whoever you give it to must be able to tell you who it belongs to. The answer must be "Alice". Then you can give him the saw and the other things. Is that clear?'

'Oh yes, lady. Very clear.' He tucked the little bundle under his shirt. 'I go tomorrow. But what you do if Dervish come here?'

Alice took a deep breath. 'Yes. That's difficult. But, Abdullah, I do speak a little Arabic . . .' She paused, still embarrassed that she had kept this from him in the early days.

'Ah, good.' He nodded, seemingly quite unoffended. 'Then you say that you from the south – Equatoria, yes?'

'Yes.'

'And you don't talk good Sudan Arabic, but your husband gone to buy food. You both on way back home. Can you say that?'

'I think so – in very bad Arabic, but I don't suppose that matters?'

'No, good thing. Now we sleep. I go in early in morning. Good night, lady.'

'Good night, Abdullah. And thank you.'

Chapter 13

Mustapha stayed curled up in the back of their shelter for two days, while Fonthill and Jenkins worked in the fields. Simon had abjured him to remain there, and as far as the two could see, he did so, for on their return on both nights the boy was half asleep and remained subdued and mainly silent as they set about cooking their meal and feeding him a little.

Then, on the morning of the third day after his rescue, he stirred before the others and began lighting a fire, putting a pot of water on it to boil (Simon had decided that to avoid the risk of contracting infection, they should boil all their drinking water).

'Ah,' said Jenkins, peering over his blanket. 'Feelin' better then, lad?'

'Yes thank you. I go today to steal bleedin' saw and files. I not get caught this time.'

'No,' snapped Fonthill. 'You are not to go near the smiths. Do you understand?'

The boy hung his head and nodded.

'And bleeding is a swear word and you are not to use it unless your skin is cut and you are really bleeding. Do you understand that?'

'Yes, master.'

'Good.' Fonthill threw aside his blanket and muttered to

Jenkins, 'You really must be careful with your language in front of the boy. You set a bad example.'

The Welshman rolled his eyes. 'Well pardon me, Reverend. I 'ad forgotten this was the vicarage tea party. Bloody 'ell, bach sir. This ain't exactly the place to start teachin' 'im manners, now is it?'

'Yes it is. We have to rise above all this . . . this . . . mess and maintain our standards. If the boy is to live in England he must learn to speak and behave properly, and he might as well start now.'

Jenkins's eyes once again sought the heavens, but he said nothing.

The three drank water and ate a little of the previous day's ever-present *durra* before Fonthill and Jenkins rose to join the chain gang assembling at the entrance to their enclosure. Simon gave last-minute instructions to Mustapha.

'Do not go near the smiths' enclosure. If you feel strong enough, by all means see if you can find us something to eat to go with this damn . . . this boring *durra*. Take the knife but keep it hidden, and above all, don't get into trouble. Is that clear?'

'Yes, master.'

The crack of a whip summoned them and they left the boy sullenly washing their gourds.

They returned at the end of the day to find that Mustapha had obeyed Simon's instructions, for at least he had managed to buy fresh fruit, a little rice and some tea. That evening the boy gently washed the aching backs of the two men and then they sat around their little fire companionably and ate well, finishing with cups of hot mint tea. For the first time since their capture, Fonthill began to feel grains of hope begin to percolate in his mind. As their shadows flickered high against the back wall of their shelter, he pondered aloud.

'We cannot make any attempt at escape until we all regain our strength,' he said. 'And, of course, we cannot get out of here carrying all this ironmongery. But time is not on our side. We shall go mad if we accept the situation and just wait for Wolseley to come and rescue us, and anyway, it is our duty to try and get to him and tell him how little time he has if he is to relieve Gordon.'

Jenkins nodded. 'So . . . ?'

'Working in the fields is not doing us any harm at the moment; in fact, it is probably doing us good, in that it is helping us to rebuild our bodies. If Mustapha can continue to buy us good food, then in, say, a couple of weeks we should be able to do something to get out of here.'

'How?'

Fonthill rubbed his face with his hand and stared unseeingly into Mustapha's wide eyes. 'With Mustapha's help, we build up a stock of food for travelling, then, somehow, we create a diversion, steal a hacksaw from one of the smiths – we do that, not Mustapha – cut off these damned chains, take three camels and we're off.'

'Blimey. Just like that?'

'Can you think of a better way?'

'No. But what sort of diversion?'

'Start a fire.'

A slow smile of appreciation stole over Jenkins's face. 'Ah. Yes. I see.'

They had already seen several coils of heavy black smoke rising from the camp on either side of them, accompanied by shouts, screams and the banging of drums. Yesterday Slatin had visited them and solemnly warned them of the dangers of fire. He had explained that the whole camp, with its many tinder-dry pieces of timber and fabric tents, was vulnerable, and the Khalifa had announced a sentence of death on anyone guilty of starting a fire by carelessness.

'Better be careful, though, bach sir.'

Fonthill nodded. 'Absolutely. We must make a reconnaissance first to see if any of the smiths has a saw or suitable file in use. Then while one of us starts the fire nearby, the other steals the implement in the subsequent chaos.'

'I do that,' volunteered Mustapha.

'No,' said Simon. 'You might be recognised from the last time. The whole idea is dangerous and we must be absolutely sure of what we are doing. But do it we will.'

Three heads nodded solemnly, and somehow they all felt better. It was a plan, of a sort, and any action was better than sitting there, like the other prisoners, aimlessly waiting for their shackles to be removed and existing on vague hope alone.

The days passed slowly and painfully, for neither Fonthill nor Jenkins could really get used to the weight of the iron bar linking their ankles and restricting their steps to an eight-inch shuffle. Gradually, however, their backs began to heal, and as Simon had predicted, their strength returned – although Jenkins's magnificent constitution meant that his had hardly left him. After two weeks, Fonthill decided that they should begin to observe the smiths, and he and Jenkins took it in turn in the early evening to wander aimlessly through the enclosure where the big men worked in their leather aprons.

The results, however, were disappointing. Neither of them could see any evidence of the tools they wanted being deployed. Plenty of pokers for stoking the braziers; many hammers for pounding metal and giant pincers for holding it in the flames. But no evidence at all of hacksaws or files. They might well, of course, be in the smiths' armoury of tools tucked away inside their tents, but would it be possible to duck inside there and search under cover of a fire alarm without discovery?

'Damned difficult,' confessed Fonthill, back in their own lean-to. One of the main problems they faced was that they had no matches and would have to rely on the knife and flint that they used every morning to light their own fire. It was a laborious business and one that certainly would be awkward to employ without detection. An added complication was that the smiths all seemed to live where they worked, and wives and children were to be seen spilling out of their tents throughout the day and evening.

'We shall have to think again,' said Simon. 'Perhaps one of us could slip into their tents at night while they are all asleep?'

'Draggin' our chains an' great iron bar without makin' a sound, like?' Jenkins's face was the epitome of disbelief. 'Maybe our little elf 'ere could do it, though, eh?'

Mustapha's eyes lit up. 'Yes. I go at night. Very quiet.'

'No.' Fonthill made a dismissive gesture with his hand. 'If they found you again they would slice off your head without a second thought. No. Let me think about it. There must be another way.'

But it seemed that there was not. They slumped back into despondency as the daily drudgery continued. Christmas came and went without any of them noticing or marking it. Fonthill insisted on the evening watch of the smiths, but this still failed to produce results – and he firmly vetoed any question of Mustapha being used in any way near the smiths' enclosure.

They had been held in the Mahdi's camp for more than five weeks, by Simon's rough estimation, when they returned from the work party to find Mustapha's eyes aglow.

'One of other boys tell me that big man is asking about two English and a Turk here,' he said.

'What?' Fonthill frowned. 'You did not say we were English, Mustapha, did you? No one must know.'

'I say nothing. They show me the man and I say I don't care. I don't talk to him. But I see the man watching you just now.'

'Where?' Simon rose to his feet.

'No. He gone now. But he see you, I know.'

'Bloody 'ell,' muttered Jenkins. 'Oh, sorry, bach sir. Language, language. Good gracious and golly me. Who's after us now, then?'

'How strange.' Fonthill shuffled to the edge of the compound but he could see no one looking out of place. 'We must be careful,' he said on his return. 'It could be that the Khalifa is still suspicious of us and is testing us out. Take care tomorrow, Mustapha. If the man approaches you, do not admit that we are English. We are Greeks, remember.'

'Yes, master.'

On their return from the fields the following evening, however, they found a crestfallen boy waiting for them. Simon sensed immediately that something had happened.

'Did that man approach you, Mustapha?' he asked.

The boy nodded.

'And . . . ?'

He ask me in Arabic if you English and I say no. You Greek.'

'Good.'

'And then he ask me if I spoke English. And I say no. Then, then . . .' His voice tailed away.

Fonthill sucked in his breath. 'Go on.'

The boy hung his head. 'Then he say, very quickly, in

English: "What is your name?" And I say, Mustapha. Sorry, master, I don't think quickly.'

'So he knows you speak English?'

Mustapha nodded, in despair.

'What happened then?'

'He give me something for you.' The boy fumbled within his shirt and withdrew something wrapped in much-creased brown paper. 'Here.'

'Good lord,' breathed Jenkins. 'What is it?'

Slowly Fonthill peeled away the paper to reveal a lady's silk scarf, apple green in colour and bringing a touch of an English spring day to that barren, hot tent in the Sudan.

Holding the scarf up to his face and rubbing it softly against his cheek, Simon spoke quietly. 'It belongs to Alice,' he said.

'What?' Jenkins's mouth sagged. 'What – *your* Miss Alice?'

Fonthill nodded. 'I would know it anywhere.' He looked up, his eyes glowing like coals in the semi-darkness of the tent. 'It even retains a trace of her perfume. But I don't understand, I left her in England. Is she out here somewhere?' He paused, and a look of horror stole on to his face. 'Or, my God, perhaps she's been killed!'

Jenkins waved a hand. 'No, bach sir. I ask you – who would kill 'er, pinch 'er 'ankie and send it in to you, look you? No, that's barmy. If these Dervish blokes had killed Miss Alice and wanted us, then they'd just march in 'ere and wallop us, wouldn't they?'

Fonthill nodded slowly. 'I suppose you are right.' He turned back to Mustapha. 'When the man gave you this, what did he say?'

'He say if you can say name of person owning this, then he give you something to help escape. He say meet him at well near the place where the men beat iron at sunset tomorrow. But he say all is dangerous and keep quiet. Blimey!'

'Good lord!' Simon turned to Jenkins. 'It can't be Alice herself out there, of course. Even if she has come to Egypt, she could never have got this far. No, Wolseley must have sent someone to rescue us and Alice has provided the scarf as a talisman, a means of recognition. My boy,' he grabbed Mustapha's hand, 'and dear old 352, I think our prayers have been answered. Mustapha, what did the man look like?'

The boy grinned, happy to have escaped being chided and caught up now in the general exultation. 'Tall, very tall, very black. Him from south, I think, where the black people come from. He speak English but he not English.'

'Good. I will meet him tomorrow, as soon as we get back from the fields. Mustapha, tomorrow please buy extra food – not too much, now, because we don't want to cause suspicion – and you had better bring in here what remains of our money and, of course, my compass. But be very careful now. We don't want to be caught just as we may have the chance of getting out of here.' He grinned. 'Let's turn in early tonight. We will need all our strength in the days ahead.'

The next evening, Fonthill took their water bag and shuffled to the well, which lay a hundred yards or so to the north-east of the smiths' compound. The sun was setting but there was enough light to see a tall, slender man who caught his eye and then joined the queue of people, mainly women, waiting their turn to draw water. Simon slipped into the queue behind him. The tall man leaned backwards slightly and Fonthill whispered, 'Alice.' This induced an almost imperceptible nod of the head.

When the tall man reached the well, he deposited a small goatskin bag on its edge. Then he drew the bucket from the depths, filled his water bag and walked away. Fonthill immediately took his place and leaned over the goatskin bag to cover it from inquisitive eyes. He took his own water, seized the bag in his other hand and clanked away, eyes downcast. For the first few steps he expected to feel a heavy hand on his shoulder, but it was now virtually dark and none came. At the edge of the clearing housing the well he turned to look for the tall man, but he had disappeared. He shuffled on, his heart lifting with every painful step.

Jenkins and Mustapha were waiting eagerly, and they crowded around him as he slumped in the far corner of their lean-to. 'What 'ave you got there, then, bach sir?' chortled Jenkins. 'Coupla sticks of dynamite would be right 'andy, eh?'

'Form a screen,' said Fonthill tersely. Then he unpacked two hacksaws, two steel files and a pair of large pliers. There was also a note, scribbled in pencil.

Simon, you can trust Abdullah completely.
If you are able to cut through your chains with these
then he will meet you at the well five hours after sunset
tonight. He will lead you to where we have camels
waiting.
If you need more time, send the boy. Alice.

Fonthill covered his face with his hand, then looked up, grinning. 'It is Alice. My lovely, lovely Alice. How the hell did she get through down to here, for goodness' sake?'

' 'Ow indeed, bach.' Jenkins's grin in the semi-darkness made a vast hole in the black mat of hair and moustache that covered his face and chest. 'What a lovely woman. Who'd o' thought it, eh?'

'Who this woman, Alice?' asked Mustapha in bewilderment.

'She is the most wonderful person in the world,' said Simon, pulling the boy's ear, 'and you're soon going to meet her. Now, we have very little time, so down to business. Mustapha, you stand guard at the opening. Three five two, do you think we can cut through the ironmongery with these tools in five hours?'

Jenkins picked up the saws. 'Clever girl, Miss Alice. She's sent us two of these lovely little buggers so we can each work separately. Let's start now and see 'ow we go.'

Fonthill looked down at their chains. For nearly six weeks they had worn the same set: an iron circle round their necks from which led down a fine tracery of steel loops to the great iron bar that in turn was linked to an iron ring around each ankle. 'If we can cut through these three rings,' he said, 'we – no, you, oh mighty muscle man – should be able to wrench the damned things apart, and then we can dump the rest. Let's start on the feet and get rid of these accursed *hajji* things. But we must work quietly.'

They set to and began sawing. It was hard going, for some of the serrations on the saw blades were missing, but luckily the rings were made of cheap, soft pig iron, which meant not only that the saws bit deeply but also that they made little noise. Within two hours they had each cut through one ankle ring and were virtually through the second. A few minutes more and the cuts were cleanly through both. Jenkins took a deep breath, bent down, inserted his fingers either side of the break and strained to pull the ends apart. They did not move.

'Damn,' said Fonthill. 'We shall have to make a second cut.'

'No, no. I wasn't tryin' 'ard enough, see. I'm still not quite meself, like. Let's 'ave another go.'

The Welshman closed his eyes and, gritting his teeth, pulled until his biceps stood out like cannon shot. Gradually the two ends moved apart, widening the circle until he could extract one foot. The same with the other, and then, with a thud, the eighteen-pound iron bar slid to the ground. Jenkins rubbed his ankles where the rings had chafed, and then stood gingerly and stretched his legs apart, the steel-linked chain hanging down from his neck like a dog's lead. 'Thank God for that,' he said. 'What a relief, man. Right, now let's do yours.'

Within a minute, Fonthill too was bending his legs and stretching them with exhilarated relief.

'These neck things shouldn't take long because they're thinner,' growled Jenkins. 'Let's start with yours. Mind your ear.'

Indeed, each neck ring took only forty minutes or so to saw through, and then the last of the hated chains were flung to the sand. Grinning, the two men shook each other's hand, then, with great solemnity, that of their watchdog, whose smile was wider than theirs, if that was possible.

'We've taken about four hours, I suppose,' said Fonthill. 'That gives us another hour or so to pack up and get to the well. Start now.'

They had no clock, of course, and only a vague idea of how long had elapsed since sundown. This was a worry, for Fonthill did not wish to arrive too early at the well and attract suspicion by hanging around there in the early hours of the morning. On the other hand, if they were too late, Abdullah would have gone and they could not survive the next day in the camp without their chains.

'Better be early,' said Simon. 'Come on.'

''Alf a mo,' said Jenkins. 'I must 'ave a pee.'

'No time for that. Wait until we're in the desert.'

'Sorry. Can't wait.' But the Welshman did not look Simon in the eye, and on his way, he grabbed the knife that protruded from Mustapha's waistband.

'What the . . .' Then Fonthill realised. 'No. No. There's no time for that,' he hissed. 'It's too much of a risk. You could ruin . . .' But Jenkins had disappeared into the gloom.

'Where he go?' asked Mustapha

'The stupid idiot has gone to kill Abu Din. The trouble is, we must wait for him here because he has no sense of direction and he would never find the well on his own. You go on, Mustapha, and tell the man – he is called Abdullah – that we are on our way. But,' he grimaced, 'if you hear a noise and a great commotion, do not wait. Go and join Alice.'

The boy slid away into the night. Fonthill had no idea how long he waited – perhaps ten minutes? – before he heard a step outside the tent and a bashful Jenkins reappeared.

'Bastard wasn't there,' he said, with a rueful smile. 'But these little beauties were,' and he opened his *jibba* to reveal the pearl handles of the two Colt revolvers tucked into his belt. ' 'Angin' there just waitin' to be picked up – an' fully loaded, too.'

'You're a bloody fool,' said Simon. 'You took a terrible chance by going into his hut. If there had been a noisy fight, all our chances of getting away would have been ruined.'

'Sorry, sir. But I promised, after our whippin's, that I'd get 'im, an' I always try to keep me promises, look you. But I'm very sorry, an' it won't 'appen again, sir.'

They stepped out into the night. A few bright stars twinkled between the clouds, and although there was, as yet, no moon, they made good enough time picking their way between the pitched tents in the half-light. After a few minutes, Jenkins whispered, 'I don't suppose there's time, is there, to make just one more call?'

'Yes, there is, and that's where we're going. Mustapha has gone ahead, so Abdullah will wait, I hope, if we are quick.'

They found the little isolated patch of ground where

Ahmed lay. The rough wooden headboard that Jenkins had made had fallen to the ground, but he picked it up and wedged it firmly into the sand again, supporting it with a small cairn of stones.

'Goodbye, Ahmed,' said Fonthill. 'God bless you.'

'Amen,' grunted Jenkins. They moved away. After so long dragging the iron bars between their ankles, they found it impossible to lengthen their stride without causing pain in their thigh muscles and hamstrings, so they were forced to revert to their shuffle, like monks on a pilgrimage. Mustapha and Abdullah were still waiting for them by the well, although it was clear that the latter had become quite impatient.

'Very dangerous here,' he hissed. 'The boy says Turk is dead, so we take the boy. We go on ahead. You follow well behind. Don't talk.'

Fonthill worried that they would be challenged, for there were few people at large that late. Again, however, he thanked their lucky stars that the Mahdi's army – safe from attack in its desert fastness – bore no resemblance to a well-drilled unit, for no guards had been set in the camp, and only dogs, sniffing at their chafed ankles, met them as they hobbled along between the tents. Within fifteen minutes the moon had peeped from the clouds, and by its light they saw, past the figures of Abdullah and Mustapha in the near distance, the greyness of the open desert, and someone beyond, standing beside five camels.

Alice had been waiting, in fact, for nearly an hour, with growing fear. But now, looking towards the edge of the encampment, her heart leapt as she made out the unmistakable outline of Abdullah and a small boy emerging from the line of tents, only to have it sink again when no one followed. Then her hand flew to her mouth. Two other figures had appeared behind them, some hundred yards in the rear. Yet these were not Simon and Jenkıns. Admittedly, one was considerably taller than the other, slim and broad shouldered, while the second man was short and very broad. But their heads and shoulders were bowed, and they moved in short, shuffling steps, so that they kicked up the sand as they walked.

As they neared, their heads came up and she saw that their faces seemed almost as dark as Abdullah's and their beards were black and full, like those of Old Testament prophets. Yet it was their eyes that drew her attention. They were set in dark hollows, so that even from a few yards away she could not see the eyes themselves. Nevertheless, she sensed now that both men were trying to grin. The taller one held out his arms.

'Oh, my love!' cried Alice and fled into Fonthill's arms.

'Good God, woman,' said Simon. 'What on earth are you wearing?'

'What? Oh, sorry.' Alice tore off the *burkha* she had worn while she was waiting, to reveal a face streaming with tears. They kissed deeply.

'We go, lady,' interrupted Abdullah. 'Moon out now. We must ride quickly because they come soon, I think.'

'Of course.' Alice buried her mouth quickly once more in the mass of facial hair, and then put out her hand to Jenkins, who took it and kissed it. She put her arms round the Welshman's neck, but then, on a sudden thought, disengaged herself and asked, wide eyed, 'But where is Ahmed?'

'He dead, lady,' interrupted Abdullah again. 'We mount camels now and go, please.'

'Oh, hell. I am sorry.' She brushed away tears. 'Yes, we must go before they miss you. Luckily, we have a camel for the boy . . .'

'Mustapha. Alice, we must leave – now.'

The boy grinned up at Fonthill, and then, less warmly, at Alice.

'Er . . . yes, of course,' she said.

They mounted – not without some difficulty on the part of Fonthill and Jenkins – and then set off at what seemed to Simon to be an alarmingly fast pace, with Abdullah in the lead and the others strung out behind him. The Sudanese turned round and shouted, 'No wind tonight, so we leave tracks in sand. They follow easily. We must ride as fast as we can. Save all breath.'

It was superfluous advice for Fonthill, because he found himself having to concentrate intently on keeping his seat. It had been some time since he had ridden a camel, and certainly not one that moved at this pace. His head jogged like a puppet and he found his back beginning to burn as the movement pulled at the recently healed weals. He wanted to pull ahead to talk to Alice, but the pace set by Abdullah was too fast. For some reason he felt reticent in attempting to do so anyway.

'You all right, bach sir?' called Jenkins from the rear.

'Perfectly all right, thank you. Just like Rotten Row. How's the boy?'

' 'E's right be'ind me, tryin' to overtake. Don't forget, 'e was born on a bleedin' camel – oh, sorry, on an ordinary camel.'

Alice turned a smiling face. 'Oh Simon . . .' It was all she could say.

Then they rode on in silence as the moon rose high and turned the desert into a silvery sea, studded with one-dimensional black rocks, like the fins of fossilised marine creatures, frozen in time.

Eventually, as the sun began to burn the horizon to their right, Abdullah called a halt and they dismounted to take water and eat nuts and dates. For the first time they were all able to talk – but only for some three minutes.

'Simon,' said Alice, 'I want to introduce you formally to one of the most gallant, resourceful and charming gentlemen in the world. This is Abdullah, who brought me here and also saved my life. Abdullah, this is my fiancé – that is, the man I am going to marry – Simon Fonthill.'

'*Effendi*,' said Abdullah, almost sheepishly.

'No *effendi*,' said Fonthill. 'Call me Simon.' He grabbed the tall man's hand and pumped it. 'Abdullah, I cannot thank you enough for bringing Alice here, for saving her – and I must hear about this – and for getting us out of that terrible place. Now, this is 352 Jenkins – yes, you must call him 352 – and, of course, Mustapha, who kept us alive in the Mahdi's camp.'

Solemnly they all shook hands. 'Now, Mustapha,' said Fonthill, 'meet Alice, who is to be my wife. Alice, this is Mustapha – he doesn't have another name. He was a slave boy, the bravest that ever lived, and he is coming home with us.'

Alice's eyebrows shot up. 'What? Oh, I see.' She took the little brown hand and shot a sly glance at Fonthill. 'If we ever get home, that is.' Almost absent-mindedly she shook off her headdress.

'Alice,' cried Fonthill. 'You've . . . you've cut your hair – and you're blacked up. Good lord, you look like . . . what? An Arab boy, I think. You look marvellous.' And he grinned at her appreciatively.

It was Alice's turn to be embarrassed. 'I had to travel as Abdullah's wife, you see. It saved us several times.' She met his gaze and her voice fell. 'But you, my dear, look terrible, I'm afraid. Oh, Simon . . .' Her voice tailed away and she took his hand.

'We go, lady,' called Abdullah. 'Sorry. No time for talk.'

They rode off again, but at a slower pace to rest the camels, and Simon pulled ahead to ride alongside Abdullah.

'They will have discovered back at the camp now that we have gone,' he said. 'The Khalifa always has escaped prisoners pursued. Will they be able to track us in this sand, do you think? It seems less deep.'

The big man nodded. 'Oh yes. Dervish are desert men. They follow easily.'

'Can we turn to the east, then, and cross the Nile before they catch us? We could lose them across the water, couldn't we?'

'We would need help in crossing river. They will ask and follow us. Catch us the other side. They will have quick camels.'

Simon frowned. 'How long before they catch up with us, then?'

Abdullah shrugged. 'Maybe one day and a half, if we keep moving fast.'

'So – towards tomorrow evening, then?'

'Yes.'

'What do we do then?'

Abdullah's grin appeared for the first time. 'We fight, *effendi*,' he said. 'Lady tell me you great warrior. She good fighter too.'

Fonthill returned the grin. 'Yes, I know she is. Call me Simon. What weapons do we have?'

'Lady have little handgun, I have big sword,' and he gestured to the hilt protruding from a leather thong hung from the saddle.

'Humph, and we have two Colts. That's not going to get us far against Remington rifles. But Abdullah, if we are going to fight, then at least we will have the advantage of surprise and of choosing exactly where we stand and face them. Now tell me, is there somewhere up ahead that we will come to at midday tomorrow or thereabouts and that is less open then this, maybe a well with palms and rocks?'

Abdullah thought for a moment. 'Yes,' he said. 'I take you there. Off to side, but that no matter if what you want. I take you.'

'Good man.'

Fonthill dropped back to ride alongside Alice. The pace of riding through the night and the morning had demanded that he concentrate on staying astride his fast-moving beast, but his mind had kept flitting back to the remarkable woman ahead of him, slim, erect, perfectly comfortable on her big leather saddle and looking for all the world from the back like an Arab boy. He had regarded her with a mixture of love and admiration, tinged with just a touch of apprehension. Her greeting had been affectionate enough, but she had ridden through those hours with hardly a glance at him and, apart from the ridiculously formal introductions at the break at dawn, with a certain aloofness. She had journeyed through some of the most dangerous terrain in the world to rescue him. But had she forgiven him?

He cleared his throat. 'Please tell me, Alice, how you got here. I am still full of admiration for what you have done. Did Wolseley not help?'

She shook her head dismissively. 'You must thank Abdullah, not Wolseley.' And in a few words, she told him of her appointment to Reuters, her acceptance as a member of Wolseley's press corps, how she had heard of his imprisonment, the General's refusal to help, her recruitment of Abdullah and then the vicissitudes of the journey.

Fonthill's eyes widened in horror as she recounted the story of the desert duel. 'Dammit, Alice,' he said, leaning across the wide gap between them and snatching her hand for a brief moment, 'you are simply the most wonderful and remarkable woman. I can't thank you enough for what you have done. You know I did not want you to come out here, but we would never have got out of that hellhole without you. I don't deserve you.'

She shot him a cynical smile. 'After your visit to the *Morning Post*,' she said, 'I am inclined to agree with you. But more of that later. Now tell me about your own journey, and particularly about Gordon.'

Happy to get on to more congenial ground, Simon related their own adventures, and they talked intensely until Abdullah called another brief break when the sun was at its highest. With Abdullah keeping watch – he insisted – they snatched an hour's sleep. Then they rode on until the big man found them a well from which to replenish their water bags. As the sun dipped away, they decided to sleep there, for they were all now exhausted. They mounted a guard roster and then ate round a fire kindled with brittle palm leaves before laying down their sleeping mats and blankets. Fonthill took the first watch, and before setting off a little down the way they had come to keep post, he caught Alice's eye. She took her mat and blankets and moved away from the others, behind a low clump of rocks.

They now had Alice's little fob watch to help time the guard spells, and after three uneventful hours Simon returned to the camp and touched Jenkins's shoulder to wake him for his watch. Then, furtively, he picked up his own bedroll and moved to where Alice was sleeping. He felt ridiculously nervous. Would she welcome him? She was awake and waiting for him.

'Come here, my love,' she whispered. 'I want to see your poor back.'

'It's not worth looking at,' he whispered back.

'Never mind. Show me.'

Gingerly he removed his *jibba* and undershirt, and with

tender fingers she examined his wounds. 'My God, Simon,' she murmured, 'this must have been agony. Oh, my dear, you were so brave to take all this.' Gently she kissed the weals from shoulder to waist. Then she buried her cheek in his beard. 'I was going to give you hell for cancelling our wedding, and then – worst of all – for ruining my chances of rejoining the *Morning Post*. But seeing you like this, I just haven't got the determination. Now, my darling. Come to me.'

So with great care, to avoid causing pain to Simon, they made love, and eventually fell asleep in each other's arms, out there in the Mahdi's desert.

Chapter 14

Halfway through the following morning, Fonthill eased himself warily in the saddle and looked behind them. The sand was less deep here, studded with a few rocks and covered in a fine sprinkling of gravel. Nevertheless, the prints of their camels' pads stretched out behind them like the wake of an Atlantic steamer, leading their pursuers straight towards them. He squinted back along the baked terracotta terrain. He could see no sign of pursuit. Perhaps there was none?

He eased his camel alongside that of Abdullah. 'Maybe the Khalifa has not ordered us to be followed and brought back,' he said. 'Perhaps the Mahdi has his hands full in besieging Khartoum. What do you think?'

The Sudanese shook his head. 'No. He follow. He behind us now.'

'What?' Simon turned and looked again. 'I see no signs at all.'

'I saw wood smoke far away when we start after dawn.' Abdullah swung round. 'Look now. See little bit of dust.'

Fonthill shaded his eyes with his hand and concentrated. 'Damned if I can see anything . . . oh yes.' A tiny darkening of the sky on the far horizon caught his eye – an orange cloud no bigger than a shirt button. 'I see it. Is that their dust?'

Abdullah nodded admiringly. 'They come very fast. Must

have racing camels. Much quicker than these old things we have.'

'How many, do you think?'

'Three, perhaps four. They start thinking only two of you. But now see our tracks.'

'Hmm. How far to this well of yours?'

'Perhaps one hour. Maybe less.'

'Yes. Well, not much time, but just about enough for us, I think.'

'You have plan, *effendi*?'

'Call me Simon, dammit. Yes, a plan of sorts. But whether it will work . . .' He sighed. 'We will just have to wait and see.'

He swivelled around again in his saddle. 'Can you all hear me?'

Alice, 352 and Mustapha all nodded their heads in affirmation.

'Good. We can't afford the time to stop and talk, so listen carefully. We are being followed. Our pursuers are still a way behind but almost within sight, so we must keep moving. Within the hour, Abdullah thinks, we will reach a small well with a little cover around it. We will *not*, I repeat *not*, stop there, but will ride quite close to it, bending round slightly behind it but then carrying on. Mustapha, you will come up front here in a moment and take the lead from Abdullah. We must all pass a leading rein to the camel in front, so that Mustapha is leading the other four camels. Understood?'

There was another nodding of heads, accompanied in Mustapha's case by a wide grin. He obviously approved of being given the distinction of leading the train.

'Good,' Simon noted the puzzlement in the expressions of Alice and Jenkins, although Abdullah, as usual, remained quite impassive. He continued. 'When Abdullah, 352 and I are level with the place, we will all slow down and jump off our camels, *without them stopping*, so that the camel prints will continue past the oasis. In other words, I want the Dervishes to think that we have not stopped at the well at all but carried on past it. With any luck, we might be able to slip on to a rock so that we show no signs of dismounting. Alice, of course, will ride on ahead with Mustapha. The three of us should be able to handle these chaps.'

Alice stiffened. 'There is no *of course* about it, Simon.' She spoke quite coldly. 'I have a revolver and have practised with it until I am quite a good shot. I shall, of course, stay with you three. Mustapha I am sure can lead the camels quite happily on his own.'

'No, Alice, I insist . . .'

'No you don't. Your father was only a major and mine was a brigadier, so I outrank you. I *stay* and that's all there is to it.'

'Yes, but can you jump off your camel, Alice? I mean, it's quite a way, you know.'

'Simon, I can jump off a bloody camel better than any man, dammit, so that's enough of that!'

Jenkins's grin still contained a hint of puzzlement. 'So when we've all landed on our little rock, like, bach sir, then what do we do?'

Fonthill ignored the sarcasm. 'We take whatever cover we can find there, lie low and wait in ambush for these devils, but leaving no prints in the sand to show where we are.'

'What is ambush, *effen* . . . Simon?' enquired Abdullah.

'We hide and take them by surprise. As they ride by, following the trail that Mustapha will leave, we then open fire with our revolvers. That is why we must lead them quite close to the rocks or whatever, because we only have revolvers and must take them at short range. If they escape us, then they could pick us off with their rifles at long range. I don't like firing without warning, but there will be no time for niceties.

We must all shoot to kill. But don't hit their camels. We might need them.'

'What happens to Mustapha?' asked Alice.

'He will lead our camels away, leaving clear tracks, in single file as we have usually been, so that the Dervishes will continue to follow. Mustapha, you will walk the camels slowly until you are out of sight of the oasis. If there is a convenient sand dune or hill, stay behind there and wait for us. If . . . if . . . we lose the day, then take the best camel and ride away, and see if you can find the British in the north and explain what has happened to us.'

'No,' said Mustapha, 'I come back and kill them.' He produced a small curved knife from his *jibba*.

'You will do no such thing. You will do as you are told. You will obey orders, just like a British soldier.'

The boy scowled but nodded.

'Is that clear to everybody?' asked Fonthill.

He received gloomy nods all round and then a slow smile from Abdullah. 'I think we have rocks at this place,' he said. 'So is a good plan, this, I think.'

Simon gave him a grin in return. 'Glad to hear it, Abdullah. But if you or anyone has a better one, I'd be happy to listen.'

The challenge went unanswered. As Mustapha jauntily overtook, they all handed leading reins ahead and Jenkins, now bringing up the rear, moved up alongside Fonthill.

'Lucky I got the Colts back then, bach sir,' he said with a sly smile.

'Oh, very well. But if Abu Din had been there, and you had disturbed him before you got that knife to his throat, then the whole camp would have been up in arms and we would never have got away.'

'True, but I would 'ave been so dainty careful, look you, that nobody would 'ave 'eard me. Anyway, now I've got a chance of finishin' the bugger off – if it is 'im followin' us, that is.'

'Mmmm. I think it will be, because Slatin told me that the man always leads the hunt for escaping prisoners. Matter of pride, or something like that, because he's in charge of them all.' Fonthill withdrew the revolver from his belt, its long silver barrel gleaming in the sun, and examined it. 'These things fire a bit low, if I remember rightly,' he said, 'so we must aim accordingly. But if we get 'em close enough it shouldn't matter. They take .45 calibre bullets, which are man-stoppers at close range, and thank God they're fully loaded, so we've got twelve shots between us.'

'An' Miss Alice, look you. She did bloody well in Afghanistan, if you remember. Killed a bloke, she did, with a little 'andgun, before 'e could get to 'er with his sword.'

Simon frowned. 'Yes. But God knows what she can do with this little popgun she's found. Look, old chap . . .' He hesitated for a moment. 'If I get knocked over in this scrap and there seems no hope, then save the last bullet for her, you know . . .'

'O' course, bach sir. But it won't come to that, I'm sure – and we've got Abdullah with 'is bloody great 'ead-chopper, don't forget.'

'Ah yes. What a great little army.'

They exchanged grins, and Jenkins fell back into line to preserve the single-file formation.

Eventually, and to Fonthill's great relief, the top of a stunted palm appeared before them, and then another and another until there were five rather sad trees in all. But there was a ring of sun-bleached rocks jutting up in a rough semicircle, looking like the white knuckles of a fist emerging from the sand. The little party approached with care, for it was not unusual to find other travellers refilling their water bags at these places, despite the vast emptiness of the Sudanese desert, but the oasis was deserted.

'Slow down,' cried Fonthill. 'Take that third rock from the opening to jump on. Abdullah first. Ready. Jump!'

Clutching his sword, the Sudanese slipped his leg easily over the high cantle of his saddle and, in a swirl of flowing robes, dropped on to the rock, making way for Simon, who repeated the action less elegantly. He stayed on the rock, holding out his hand to help Alice, but sprang aside as she cried, 'Out of the way, for goodness' sake,' before leaping lithely down. Jenkins completed the evacuation, and Mustapha, looking back with a grin, led the convoy away without a falter in the step of a single camel.

Looking around, Fonthill realised that the oasis was hardly that: just one well, merely a hole in the ground, some four feet in diameter, with the brown, brackish water just about reachable if the drinker lay on his stomach and reached down with cupped hand. There was no other vegetation but the stunted palms, whose trunks were too slender to provide cover. The rocks, however, offered more hope. They were scattered irregularly in a rough semicircle around the well, perhaps more horseshoe in shape, with the open end offered invitingly to the south, from where the Dervishes would approach.

Simon clambered to the top of the largest rock – awkwardly, for his legs still ached from the burden of the *hajji*. He directed his attention to the south, where the cloud of dust was now markedly bigger, revealing that their pursuers – if, indeed, it was they – were still forcing their camels on at a speed that showed both their lack of care for their beasts and their determination to overtake the escapers well before nightfall. Squinting against the sun, he could just make out four dark specks at the base of the cloud. They were approaching fast and there was little time. A glance to the north showed that Mustapha and his little convoy were now almost out of sight, cresting a small hill that rose from the plain.

He slid down the rock and examined the little cover that was offered to them. There were probably a dozen rocks, hardly big enough to be called boulders, some of them sunk into the sand at the side of the declivity so that only six inches or so protruded. Others, however, stood proud and were just about large enough to give cover to a single man – as long as he crouched and was not outflanked or approached from the rear. None of it was ideal, and Simon caught the air of apprehension of the others as they looked around at what was not exactly a fortress.

'Right,' he said, injecting a note of confidence that he did not feel into his voice. 'There's plenty of cover here. Find yourself a rock big enough to conceal you. We must bank on the fact that they will pass by the well to the left there,' he indicated with his hand, 'following our tracks. So tuck yourselves away on the other side of your rock.'

He took another look to the south. God, they were travelling quickly! He could clearly make out four men now, with a very large man – Abu Din? – on the leading camel. Had they been seen?

'Get out of sight quickly,' he called, and ducked down behind a rock at the rear of the little circle. It had two sections, one resting on top of the other and jutting out, so affording him a little viewing point where, hopefully, he could not be seen by the approaching riders. 'Make sure that you keep weapons or anything else that might reflect the sun well hidden,' he hissed. 'Whatever you do, don't look at these people as they approach. Just watch me. I will observe them, and as they are about to go past, I will signal with my hand so that you can edge around your rock and remain out of sight. Then, when I shout, emerge, take careful aim and fire. There are four of them and only three of us with firearms. So – I will take the lead rider; 352, you take the next two; and Alice, you fire at the man at the rear. Don't forget, hit the rider, not his mount. Abdullah, if anyone reaches the ground still capable of fighting, take him out with your sword – but don't let it reflect sunlight yet. Now, stay quiet, and good luck to you all.'

Simon looked carefully as each of the little band chose a rock and scurried behind it. Alice, he was glad to see, was opposite him at the rear of the semicircle, and Jenkins and Abdullah to the front. He called softly to the latter: 'Abdullah – your *jibba* is trailing. Tuck it in.' The big man nodded and did so, holding the big cross-piece of his sword under his chin as he crouched.

The next five minutes seemed the longest of Fonthill's short life. He realised that he was taking an incredible gamble. These desert Dervishes had magnificent eyesight. Had the escapers already been seen from far away? Unlikely, for the four of them had hopped off their camels and dispersed very quickly in the little oasis. No, the biggest threat lay in these rocks providing inadequate cover as the pursuers approached. If, as he had planned, the Dervishes swept past the well following Mustapha's clear trail, then a casual glance to the side could well reveal one at least of the four who had not edged around quickly enough. He must not delay his call to fire. He looked across at Alice. As the smallest, she was best concealed behind her cover and she looked perfectly assured as she crouched, her small revolver in hand, her lower lip bitten in concentration. He caught her eye and summoned up a smile. She did not return it, but nodded, almost absently. Oh God! Had he brought her out all this way from home – from her wedding plans – to be slaughtered by these savage men of the Mahdi? He realised that his mouth was now completely dry, and the palm of his hand where the handgrip of the Colt nestled was wet with sweat.

Now they could all hear the clink of the camels' harnesses as the Dervishes approached at a jog trot. Somewhere a fly buzzed, but the only other sound was the soft thump of the camels' pads as they thudded into the sand. Fonthill prayed that the men would not hear the beating of his heart. Slowly he edged his head out to the side, underneath the overhanging rock, to risk a look.

His gaze met empty desert. The four riders had disappeared! What the hell . . . ? Then, in a quick moment of recognition, he realised that the Dervishes were not now following Mustapha's tracks but must have swerved away to the other side of the oasis to pass it . . . or were they riding straight into its centre, either because the four had been seen or, perhaps, to replenish their water bags?

He risked a look round the other side of the rock and realised that the latter was happening. The lead rider – now unmistakably Abu Din – had pulled up outside the entrance to the horseshoe and was tapping the neck of his camel, so that it knelt and he was able to slip down from the saddle. He unslung his own leather bag and collected those of his comrades and then strode towards the well, his feet crunching in the gravelly sand.

Fonthill realised that his three companions were now all regarding him with anxiety. They obviously realised that things were not going to plan. What to do? He weighed the odds quickly. Once inside the ring of rock, Abu Din would easily see one or two at least of the fugitives. To kill him would be comparatively easy at short range, and the Dervish had not brought his rifle with him. But the others would be more difficult, waiting outside the circle, with the second man shielding his other two fellows to some extent. He made his decision quickly: leave Din for the moment and shoot the second man, leaving the other two exposed so they could be brought down.

He pulled back the hammer on the Colt and shouted: 'They're not passing by – they're waiting at the opening. Fire!'

He sprang from behind the rock, aimed his revolver and fired at the first Dervish – and killed his camel, throwing the man to the ground. His curse – the Colt had fired low, of course – was drowned by the sharp crack of the other pistols, and the second and third men plunged back in their saddles, their breasts riddled by bullets. Fonthill's original target scrambled to his feet, but his second shot took him squarely in the chest.

Simon, Jenkins and Alice now stood stock still their pistols smoking, staring at Abu Din, who looked about him in astonishment. Then, in a quick movement, the big man dropped his water bags and drew a large curved sword from its scabbard at his waist. He stood in defiance, not knowing which way to face but clearly determined to fight to the death. Then, slowly, Abdullah walked towards him, his cross-handled broadsword clasped in both hands.

'No, no, Abdiller,' shouted Jenkins. 'Leave 'im. 'E's mine.' And the little man flung down his Colt and, waving away the Sudanese, walked towards the big Dervish, pulling a knife from his waistband.

'Don't be stupid, man,' shouted Fonthill. 'He's got a sword. You can't tackle him with just a knife. Get out of the way and let me have a clear shot at him.'

'Oh no, bach sir. It wouldn't be right to shoot the bugger. Shootin's too good for 'im. I promised I'd kill 'im and I'll do it my way. In a fair fight, like.'

'Don't, 352.' Alice added her own plea. 'This is stupid.'

But the Welshman paid no heed. Facing Abu Din, he slowly took off his dirty, stained *jibba*, revealing his wide chest, its black hair now tangled with his great beard. Then he turned round to show the Dervish his lacerated back. 'Remember this?' He jerked his thumb at the scars. 'You dished out an 'undred lashes to us and you killed little old Ahmed. Now, bach, I'm goin' to kill you.'

The Dervish's jaw had dropped at the appearance of Jenkins, but now, realising that he was being challenged, a slow grin came over his face. He looked around at the others, their revolvers now pointing to the floor, and jerked his sword derisively at them all. Brutal sadist he might be, reflected Fonthill, but he was not without courage. He must have realised that he could not escape death, for he would know that even if he killed the man taunting him – which would appear a formality to him – he would still be shot down. There was no way out for him. So with a whoop, he charged at Jenkins.

The disparity between the two contestants seemed laughably unbalanced. Abu Din was at least six feet three inches tall, nearly a foot taller than Jenkins, and although he was corpulent his shoulders were broad and he carried his weight well. Even without the curved sword in his hand, he possessed a huge advantage in reach over the Welshman.

Jenkins, on the other hand, though he seemed equally broad, was much lighter on his feet. But could a knife match a sword in hand-to-hand combat? Simon lifted his revolver, but Abdullah, now standing next to him, put out a restraining hand. 'The challenge must be met,' he said. 'It is the way of the desert.'

Din's first charge, finishing in a series of diagonal downward slashes with his blade, was easily evaded by Jenkins, who, legs wide apart and weight carried on the balls of his feet, skipped aside, almost balletically. Then the Dervish came again, repeating the tactics, as though he was trying to carve his opponent into quarters. This time the Welshman moved backwards, letting the sword blade swing down inches, it seemed, in front of his face.

The imperturbable Abdullah let out a gasp of admiration, but Fonthill, knowing how well Jenkins could move in these encounters (he had seen him, unarmed, in Zululand completely outmanoeuvre and lay low a warrior armed with an assegai), drew in his breath sharply. The little man was not moving with his usual speed and sharpness. Obviously the weeks of dragging around an eighteen-pound weight between his ankles had weakened his tendons. How long could he last? Simon shot a quick glance at Alice, who was standing, her pistol hand drooping to the floor, the other clutched to her face. Oh God – how he wished she was not here to see this!

The Dervish now stood back, perspiration pouring down his cheeks into his beard. It was clear that he was no swordsman, but his height and power in battle or duel would always have made up for his lack of skill. He was puzzled by the strange movements of his opponent and appeared to realise that he must change his own tactics. So now he lowered the point of his weapon and, springing forward, thrust it at Jenkins's breast. In one fluid movement the little man ducked beneath the point and, bending low, grabbed a palmful of sand from the ground with his left hand and threw it into Din's face, blinding him momentarily.

Immediately Jenkins leapt forward, jabbed his knife into the big man's waist, twisted it round and danced away again. It was not a deep wound, but blood gushed down the Dervish's side and his face contorted in pain. 'First blood to me, you bastard,' breathed the Welshman, carefully wiping his blade on what was left of his *jibba*. 'Now 'ow do you like a bit of pain, eh?'

Abdullah's grunt of appreciation was drowned by a loud cry from the Dervish as he leapt forward again, swinging his blade in a series of slashes that sent a semaphore of sunlight reflections around the little oasis. Again, however, Jenkins dodged and dipped away from each swing, the dagger in his right hand poised to strike as soon as he could see an opening.

But then came disaster. Bending low, the Welshman's right leg suddenly collapsed, causing him to lean on the faulty leg in the sand, quite immobile and terminally vulnerable. Immediately the giant Dervish, his eyes alight with triumph, lifted his curved blade high to bring it down on Jenkins's undefended neck.

Fonthill's shot seemed to echo round the oasis, reverberating back from every tree. The .45 bullet took Abu Din squarely between the shoulder blades, and the big man sank slowly to the ground, his sword falling behind him as his fingers lost their grasp. He sprawled, face up, across Jenkins's ankles.

The Welshman looked up at Simon and wiped the perspiration from his eyes. 'You didn't 'ave to do that, bach sir,' he said. 'I'd got 'im just where I wanted 'im. Just a bit slow on me feet for once, that's all.'

Fonthill did not reply, but put out his hand to his comrade and helped him to his feet, kicking away the body of the Dervish as he did so. 'That's enough killing for one day,' he said. 'I didn't want to lose you as well. Are you all right?'

'Yes, bless you, bach sir. Thank you very much. I 'ave to confess I buggered that up a bit. Bloody leg seemed to go suddenly. Can't think why, look you.'

'Never mind.' Simon looked across at Alice. 'Are you all right, Alice?'

She nodded, but her face was white and she was shivering. 'Yes. Quite all right, thank you. But I think that was a narrow escape. Do you think there are any more out there, following up?'

'No. I think we are now safe from pursuit. But we still have a long way to go, and from what you have told me, there is a damned great Dervish army up ahead that we must find our way round or through – although I'd rather not do that.' He turned to the Sudanese. 'Abdullah, I don't think the Dervishes' camels have gone far. Can you bring them back and then mount one and find Mustapha. I think we should refill our water bags and then move on . . . as soon as we have, er, cleared up here. Oh, and if the beast that I shot is still alive, can you please put it out of its misery?'

The Sudanese nodded and loped away. Fonthill turned back to Alice. 'Come and sit down, my love,' he said. 'Take a little water. You look as white as your brown face will allow you.'

She gave a wan smile. 'Only for a moment. I am quite all right, but I really did think that dear old 352 was finished there, just for a second. I am so glad you had the presence of mind to shoot. I was far too slow.' She shook her head. 'Perhaps I am not such a soldier after all.'

He put his arm around her shoulder and led her away from the Dervish's body. 'Did you, did you . . . you know?'

'I don't think so. I fired, of course, but I think Jenkins got them both.'

'Good. Now, sit down for a moment. Here's my water bag. Just relax until we can get on our way.'

He gestured to Jenkins, and they each took a leg of the inert form and pulled it away from the waterhole. Fonthill then examined the bodies of the other three men. They were all quite dead, as was the camel he had inadvertently shot.

'Damned Colt fired low,' he murmured to Jenkins. 'Told everybody else to adjust and forgot to do it myself. Bloody fool.'

'Ah well, bach sir. You fired straight enough when you had to. I'm very grateful.' He gave a quizzical smile. 'I couldn't 'elp noticin', like, but you shot 'im through the back. I know you 'ad to do it, but p'raps a few years ago you wouldn't 'ave been able to do that – kill a bloke through the back, I mean. You've 'ardened up a bit, if you don't mind me sayin' so.'

'Have I? Well, it's to be expected, I suppose, considering the life we lead.' Fonthill looked slightly ashamed for a fleeting moment, then the expression passed from his face. 'Now,' he gestured to the bodies, 'I don't think we can bury these fellows in this ground, so let's find stones we can cover them with. We'll just have to leave the camel.'

They set to work and had built rough cairns over the three men by the time Abdullah returned, leading a jubilant Mustapha.

'Bleeding Jesus,' the boy cried. 'You kill them all?'

'Don't be blasphemous,' chided Fonthill. 'If you are coming home with us to England, you really must forget some of these phrases that you picked up from the nuns. They won't exactly go down well in Norfolk, you know.'

'What is this Norfolk?'

'It is a large, flat, rather cold and wet place in England.' Alice's voice was equally flat. Fonthill had not realised that she had quietly joined them and heard the conversation. 'I am not at all sure that you will like it, if you come, that is.' She directed a level glance at Simon.

'Oh, Alice,' he mumbled, in some confusion. 'I am sure that . . .'

'Well,' she said, 'perhaps we can talk about that later.'

With the camels reassembled and watered, Fonthill

summoned a council of war. 'I am sure that we will not be pursued now,' he said, 'but this does not mean that we are out of trouble. I estimate that we probably have another ninety miles or so of desert travel to go before we reach Wolseley's advance guard. And that, of course, begs the question of where it might be. Alice, you were with the army last. How far will they have come, do you think?'

Alice frowned. 'I know that Wolseley himself, of course, was ordered to remain in Korti, which is where I was last with the army. But the General had received Abdullah's message from Gordon when I left and was about to throw his desert column forward, though it was by no means ready to advance when I last saw it. So, perhaps it will be setting off about now. Though God knows what date it is. I'm afraid I have completely lost track of the calendar.'

Fonthill pulled at his beard in exasperation. 'If they're only just setting off now, it's going to be a damned close-run thing to get to Gordon in time. What on earth have they been dilly-dallying at?'

Alice shrugged. 'They have had difficulties in getting sufficient camels for this new corps of Wolseley's, and the men have had to be trained. The advance up the river has always been slow, as you know. I believe that the General's original intention was to split his force at Korti and send a river column, under Major General Earle, up the Nile, round that great bend at the top, to capture Berber and establish a base at Shendi, on the eastern bank of the Nile opposite Metemmeh, where he would support Brigadier Stewart, whose mounted column would have gone across the desert, taken Metemmeh and be ready to make a dash south to Khartoum.'

'Ah, Stewart,' mused Fonthill. 'I remember him in Zululand, and he commanded the cavalry at Tel el Kebir. But it all sounds a bit ponderous, and the question remains: where will Stewart be now?' He turned to Abdullah. 'You know this country better than anyone. If the Dervishes want to stop this desert column before it reaches Metemmeh, where would they attack?'

The Sudanese thought for a moment. 'Probably in broken country between Jakdul Wells and river. Good place for . . . what you call it?'

'Ambush?'

'That is the word.'

'So, if we want to avoid the Dervish army, we should head slightly north-west,' Simon indicated with his hand, 'to meet up with the British at the wells, perhaps?'

'At Jakdul, yes. We will need water there anyway.'

'We certainly needed it there a couple of months ago – although it seems more like years. Now, we should be able to travel faster if we use the Dervishes' three camels and put the boy and our packs on our beasts, don't you think?'

'Yes, but Mahdi's men drive their camels hard to catch us. They need rest. We must let them drink, rest them for two hours and then perhaps go faster later.'

Fonthill nodded. 'Wise words. We must also think about what you say we are if we meet Dervishes again. We must have some sort of story.'

The Sudanese stood and walked slowly to inspect the camels. He spoke over his shoulder. 'We take off Dervish saddle blankets and things,' he said, 'and bundle them up like traders' goods and put them on our pack camels. We say we are traders going north to Egypt. Plenty people do that. It only way, I think. I say you are from Equatoria.' Abdullah allowed himself a tiny smile. 'You look very ragged and you burnt very black now so you pass well, I think. We in trouble if packs are broken, but we take that risk.'

Simon and Alice exchanged glances. The man was

imperturbable, without doubt, and resourceful, too. They would have been lost without him.

'Thank you, Abdullah,' said Fonthill, 'we will take your advice. Let us now water the camels and change the packs. Then we must be off. Gordon Pasha is always on my mind.'

'Yes. That is good.'

Fonthill posted a guard while the others slept, taking whatever shade they could from the midday sun. He rested his still sore back against a flat rock and set to working out the equation of the distance to be travelled against the time they might have left to save Gordon. The gunfire that sounded a constant backdrop to life at Omdurman had continued during the day before they escaped, so Khartoum and its main outlying fort was still holding out then. The General had estimated that the city could survive until the end of December, 'perhaps a little longer, but not much'. They must be well into the first week of the New Year now. He smiled wryly. That meant that he had welcomed in 1885 by shooting a man in the back ... Frowning, he tried to concentrate. He had long since lost his map of the Nile and the northern Sudan, of course, but he guessed that the overland distance to Jakdul Wells must be a further eighty miles or so and their route would lie roughly in a straight line due north. How many miles could their camels do in a day? Perhaps twenty, depending upon the terrain – and, of course, if they were not molested on the way. That meant that they might reach the wells in four or five days of hard travelling. Dammit! He wished he had had the foresight to keep a record of the days they had spent in captivity, but given that they had been guests of the Mahdi for five weeks or so, they should reach the wells by about the middle of January. Where would the desert column be by that time? He gave up at this point. There was too much speculation involved. The thing to do was to press on as hard as they could and tell Stewart, or whoever was commanding the forward force, that there was virtually no time left to relieve Gordon.

They mounted up again as soon as the Dervishes' camels appeared to be rested somewhat and set off across the desert. Fonthill looked about him in disgust. Hadn't someone written that when God had created the Sudan he had been tired and couldn't be bothered to finish the job properly? To his right he could see a faraway row of low hills, disfiguring the skyline in jagged stumps like the lower jaw of a geriatric grandparent. Ahead lay the plain, stretching it seemed to infinity and characterised only by the occasional rock and odd patch of scrub. The sun beat down on a landscape that had been painted only in terracotta and ochre. It appeared that nothing lived in this hinterland, away from the life-giving Nile. At least it all helped to make them feel safer, for anyone approaching could be seen for at least two miles.

He turned his head on an impulse and smiled at Mustapha, riding immediately behind him. 'Well done, soldier,' he said. 'You led the camel train away in fine style.'

'Thank you, Captain,' the boy replied, his grin stretching from ear to ear. 'I would have killed them all if you had let me.'

'I am sure you would, Mustapha.' Fonthill shook his head smilingly and turned back just in time to catch the eye of Alice, riding ahead of him. He urged his camel alongside her.

'How are you, my love?' he asked. 'I only hope that will be the last killing you will see for a very long time.'

'Thank you.' She nodded, but her face was expressionless.

They rode together for several minutes in silence before Alice cleared her throat. 'Are we going to be married, Simon?' she asked.

He looked at her in amazement. 'Good lord, of course we

are, darling. Nothing has changed, at least . . .' he hesitated for a moment, 'as far as I am concerned. As soon as this terrible business is over, we will have the biggest and grandest wedding that Norfolk has ever seen.'

She tossed her head. 'Oh, you know I don't want that and never have. I mean: are you going to ride off again as soon as Wolseley or some other blasted general beckons his little finger towards you?'

'Oh, come now, Alice. It was not quite like that, you know.' He searched her face desperately, but she continued to look straight ahead. 'I don't want to appear immodest, but Wolseley felt that only I – well, with 352, that is – could do the job he wanted. Gordon may have dug his own hole to some extent, but he had to be helped out of it. And that meant using every bit of talent that the army could find. I don't suppose for a minute – well, I certainly hope not – that this sort of situation will arise again. Well,' he finished lamely, 'not quite like this, anyway.'

Alice failed to respond immediately. Then she turned to him. 'And do you want children, my dear?'

'Of course. At least fifteen. You know that. We discussed it.'

She turned her head back to indicate the brown-mopped boy riding serenely behind them. 'And how do you think that that delightful little savage will fit into our life in Norfolk, hmmm?'

Simon's eyes glowed anxiously in their dark hollows. 'Well, I am sure that he will fit in beautifully. There will be plenty for him to do on the estate, and, of course, we would send him to school. I had rather hoped, darling, that we could adopt him, you know. He did save my life when I first met him – I'll tell you about that later – and he looked after us so bravely and resourcefully when we were in captivity. Anyway, having picked him up, so to speak, I can't just drop him back into this damned cruel wilderness.' His voice softened a little. 'I feel it would be a tiny contribution we could make to these poor people suffering under this madman.'

Alice turned to look at him fully. Her grey eyes shone incongruously from her darkened face, framed as it was by the Sudanese headdress. Simon felt that he had never seen anything so beautiful – but the beauty, he could see, was lit by a degree of suppressed anger.

'I understand all of that,' she said. 'I can comprehend the debt you feel you owe to the boy, although I am not sure that taking him home to share our lives will do much to help the oppressed Sudanese people. However, I have to conclude, Simon, that you are being simplistic, even naïve, about all of this.'

She tossed her head, and an anxious Fonthill turned to make sure that Mustapha could not hear their conversation, but the boy's eyes and mind were far away, looking to where a desert bird was idly circling far to the west. Simon opened his mouth to speak, but Alice was not to be interrupted.

'You have just not thought it through,' she continued. Then her face and voice softened for a moment. 'Oh, my dear, I can well understand that what you have been through in the last couple of months will have caused you to bond with Mustapha; indeed, it does you credit. But there are two points you must consider.'

She took a deep breath and her eyes misted for a moment. 'You know well enough that Ralph and I tried very hard to have children. At least, *he* did. What I wanted was your child, not his, but I was dutiful and did my best, although it was not to be. Now . . .' and her voice faltered for a second, 'it could well be that I am not destined to have children, although I desperately want them – *your* children, my darling. While I am trying so hard to produce a child for us both, I do not relish the prospect of having some sort of surrogate son about the place – a boy of whom I know so little and yet whom you have clearly come to love.' Tears were in her eyes now. 'Can't you see that, Simon?'

Fonthill frowned. 'Well, I . . .'

But Alice was in full flow. 'Secondly,' she continued, 'you have not considered things from Mustapha's point of view. He is a slave boy who, admittedly, speaks English through some twist of fortune, but who has been subjected to a brutal life and has virtually run wild in this savage place for all of his ten years. Is it fair, my dear, to pick him up and drop him down in rural Norfolk? He will be like some wild animal put into a cold and, for much of the time, grey zoo. He would be in a kind of no-man's-land between being a true member of the family, like a son, and being a servant. And as for sending him away to school, I just can't see him fitting into a conventional English establishment, while it would be cruel to try and mould him so that he conformed. Surely it would be better for you to try and find a good home for him here somewhere, or even in Egypt, once this miserable war is over? I can see he is a free spirit and I can see why you love him, but you mustn't try and make him *yours*, so to speak, like a trophy you have brought home.'

Simon looked at her with unseeing eyes. Eventually he said, 'I understand what you are saying, Alice, but you should recognise that I am very, very fond of the boy. I . . .' But his voice trailed away.

Alice reached across to take his reluctant hand. 'Is this some sort of fallback position you are taking, my love, in case I am unable to have children, hmmm?'

'No, no. Good lord, no. I am sure that, when we are married and things have settled down, we will be able to have a family. I did rather hope, however, that Mustapha could be part of it, rather like 352 will be.'

'I see. He would be a sort of bolt-on addition to the family, then, would he?'

'Well, I wouldn't put it quite like that, Alice. I have tried to explain, but . . . oh well, I don't know. Perhaps we can talk about it later, when . . .'

She gave him a half-smile. 'Yes, of course we can talk about it again when – and if – we get out of this blasted mess.'

His reassuring smile hardened. 'Alice,' he said. 'One thing I can promise you. We *will* survive this. You will see.'

This time he received her full smile. 'Of course we will. I can't think of anyone better to lead us through the Mahdi's army than you, my love – nor better company to back you up than Abdullah, dear old 352 and, er, Mustapha, of course.'

He looked quickly for a trace of irony in the smile but could see none. They rode on in companionable – if slightly awkward – silence until Abdullah raised his hand for them to halt for the night.

Chapter 15

The next couple of days passed without incident, with the little convoy settling into the rhythm of desert travel: mounting soon after dawn, stopping at midday for light nourishment, water and some sleep to avoid the overhead sun, and then riding on until the evening meal and early retirement. Fonthill and Alice had not slept together after that first night, for the circumstances – practical and emotional – were not conducive to such intimacy. Simon could not help but feel that Alice had withdrawn from him somewhat, but he made no overtures to repair whatever damage had been done by her resentment of his attachment to Mustapha. The more he thought about it during the days, as his body nodded in time to the gait of his camel, the more he felt she had been unreasonable in her attitude. Then he clutched to himself the thought that she would change her mind when she got to know the boy better.

Indeed, the whole party seemed subdued as it plodded on. They remained alert at all times, because they were all aware that they were approaching new dangers the further north they travelled. But it was as if the exigencies of the last few days had bequeathed a kind of reactive apathy that mantled them with silence. Abdullah was always quiet on the march, but Jenkins too was unusually passive. Perhaps, reflected Fonthill, his confidence – that massive rock on which his personality was built – had been dented by his near escape from Abu Din's sword. Three five two *always* won one-to-one battles; in fact Simon could not remember him ever being defeated. Ah well, perhaps this would be good for him. A salutary lesson, although he did hope that his comrade would soon regain his customary cheerfulness. But thinking of cheefulness – there was always Mustapha!

They rode for two more days after the clash with the pursuing Dervishes before they saw another living person in the desert. Two Bedawis from the north were slowly making their way south-east towards the Nile and crossed their path. They certainly offered no threat and Abdullah exchanged cheery greetings with them. As they pulled away, he turned to speak to Fonthill.

'They say that big Dervish army is ahead.'

'Ah, as we expected. Do you think we can get round them?'

'As I thought, they wait for British between Jakdul and the Nile. We go straight to the wells. Pass them to the west, I hope.'

'So do I.'

They camped that night as usual and woke that morning to see a large mounted party approaching them from the south. It was not travelling fast and it seemed far too large – perhaps two hundred or more Arabs – to be a pursuing party. Nor was there any reason to think that the Khalifa would have had cause to be so alarmed yet by the disappearance of Abu Din and his men as to send out a second, much larger group to apprehend the escapers.

Nevertheless . . . 'Best to avoid them if we can,' said Simon. 'No breakfast. Mount up quickly and let us head west, further out into the desert.'

They did so, but not quite quickly enough to evade the outriders going ahead of the group: three Dervishes, wearing the

Mahdi's patches and obviously curious enough about the little party spotted alone in the desert and heading away from the general track north to spur their camels ahead of their fellows to find out who they were.

'Hide the Colts,' said Fonthill. 'Abdullah, do the talking. Three five two, pull your pantaloons down to hide the shackle marks round your ankles. They could well betray us. Mustapha, if they talk to you, remember that you are our slave and that we are from Equatoria, heading for Egypt. Keep riding slowly.'

The Dervishes easily overtook them and appeared friendly enough. They pulled up their camels, with hands aloft, inviting Abdullah, who was in the lead, to do the same. The third man in the trio, a young blade with a neatly cut beard and flashing white teeth, looked with a smile at Alice, who had donned the *burkha* and lowered her gaze demurely. He addressed a question to Fonthill, who gave him an answering smile and a greeting in Pushtu, gesturing to Abdullah, who was engaged in conversation with the Dervish leader.

The young man looked puzzled, but grunted and pulled alongside his two companions to hear what Abdullah was saying. A discussion followed, with all four taking part, and it became clear that a difference of opinion had emerged between Abdullah and the Arabs. By now the larger party had overtaken them and was passing on either side of the little group. Fonthill realised that it was a typical Dervish migration to the north to join the army massing to stop the British. The men all had rifles, some of them modern Remingtons, but mostly models of an earlier make, plus spears, knives and swords. In the manner of the Dervish army, however, they all seemed to have their families with them. Women rode on saddles surrounded by bundles of belongings, and they pulled heavily laden, unkempt pack camels on lead reins behind them. Children scampered alongside on foot, fencing with sticks, shouting and laughing. Some of the older boys addressed remarks to Mustapha but he replied only tersely, keeping his gaze on Fonthill, who gave approval with a terse nod of his head. To Simon the party seemed almost as though they were on a day out, an excursion perhaps to Berber on the great river. But it was with a feeling of apprehension that he kept his eyes on Abdullah to discern the outcome of his argument – if it was that – with the leader of the Dervish vanguard.

Eventually Abdullah nodded, reluctantly it seemed to Fonthill, and waved the party forward. But not to the north-north-west, the direction they were taking when the Dervishes had come into sight, but due north, the route the Arabs were following. Simon realised that they were now in the middle of the Dervish reinforcements and were, so to speak, part of the family. They moved on ahead, surrounded by the followers of the Mahdi. Like it or not, it seemed that they were on their way to fight the British invaders.

Fonthill stayed close to Alice and Jenkins and gestured with a tiny movement of his head for Abdullah to fall back and join them.

'What has happened?' he whispered.

'I tell them we go to Egypt, but they say we must stay and fight for the Mahdi against British. It is our duty, they say, to follow the Chosen One. I argue but they do not hear me.'

'Damn. Do they accept that we are from Equatoria and cannot speak their language?'

'I think so, but they bit suspicious still. Is good we have Sudanese-speaking slave boy with us. But young one likes lady. I tell him she my daughter and is pledged to man in Dongola. I say you both my sons and look after her. He could cause us trouble.'

Alice grunted under her *burkha*. 'I shall give him no cause for encouragement, I assure you. He thinks far too much of himself.'

'Hell's teeth.' Fonthill looked around him. 'Where are we heading?'

'Khalifa's army is by Abu Klea Wells, between there and the Nile. They wait for British there, as I thought. These people go to join them.'

A low wheeze came from somewhere beneath Jenkins's huge beard. 'If we 'ave to join 'em,' he said, 'try and find out 'ow much they pay. I bet it's better than our lot.'

'For God's sake be quiet,' hissed Fonthill. 'This is no time for levity. We are in trouble. How the hell do we leave these people?'

Abdullah pulled his beard. 'I do not know, *eff* . . . Captain. But we must find a way before too long. I think we only about two days' riding to Dervish camp. We must not look unhappy at going with them. We must smile. And we must pray, five times a day.'

A chuckle came from Jenkins, but Fonthill frowned. 'Abdullah,' he said, 'we are riding right in the middle of the whole contingent. Can you edge us a bit to the left so that we can at least ride on the edge of the party? Then perhaps we can get away during the night.'

The Sudanese nodded. 'I try.'

Danger came, however, from a not entirely unexpected quarter: the young Dervish now began his courtship of Alice. He let his camel fall back so that he was riding alongside her and began making conversation, even though she made it clear that she could not understand. Then he reached into his bag and offered her a sweetmeat. She shook her head and kept her gaze down on the desert floor, the other side of her camel to her admirer, so that he could not see her eyes peeping through the slit in her headdress. He then began a quite obvious and equally absurd ritualistic display of courtship, like a peacock preening his feathers, pulling his camel ahead of Alice and making it prance, as though he was competing in horse trials.

'This is bloody ridiculous,' murmured Simon. He urged his own camel forward and set it alongside Alice's beast. Unbidden, Jenkins did the same on the other side, so that she was now sandwiched between the two and effectively cordoned off.

'Be careful,' warned Abdullah, looking back at them.

The warning was apposite, for the young man was clearly offended by the effective placing of Alice in purdah by her two 'brothers'. He hurled what was obviously invective at the two and rode close to Fonthill to make his point – so close that his saliva sprayed across the face of Simon, who studiously ignored it and looked straight ahead. Worse, however, the man's antics and those of Alice's protectors had amused the travellers nearby and excited shouts of derision. It was obvious that the young blade's manhood was being called into question, and his eyes were now alive with hatred and he put his hand on the curved dagger at his waist.

Fonthill had managed to control his own anger but it had become all too much for Jenkins. The Welshman leaned across Alice and hissed, 'Why don't you just fuck off . . . oh, saving your presence, that is, miss.'

The words were not understood but the meaning was clear. The dagger now flashed out and the Dervish pulled back behind Alice to come abreast of Jenkins. It was at this point that Abdullah intervened. Quickly he drove his own camel ahead of the man and spoke to him loudly, his hand held out, palm upright. Then he turned his head and called to the leader of the trio who had first stopped them. His action was timely.

The older Arab frowned, raised his head and spoke sharply to the young man. Sullenly, the man let his camel fall back. Then he turned, gestured with his dagger towards Jenkins and Fonthill and pushed his way forward to disappear into the crowd ahead.

'You went too far,' said Simon. 'We could be in trouble now.'

'Thank you anyway, 352,' whispered Alice, her eyes still downcast. 'That young man needs to be taught a lesson.'

'Not in the middle of two hundred Dervishes he doesn't,' replied Fonthill coolly, keeping his voice low. 'Abdullah, thank you. I think you saved the day. But has any harm been done, do you think?'

'I say that the man was becoming . . . what you call it? Nuisance, yes. Older man tells him that violence is bad and that if he wants lady he must make proper approach. The trouble is, I think he will do that tomorrow.'

'What exactly is a proper approach?' enquired Alice.

Abdullah shrugged. He was clearly embarrassed by the whole affair. 'He will go back, I think, and talk to his family. He see how many camels or cattle he can offer for lady. Then he comes back to me to make the offer.'

'Oh no!' exclaimed Alice.

'This is the last thing we wanted.' Fonthill looked at Alice with a mixture of emotions: anger at the position they now found themselves in, annoyance with Alice for putting them in it, and, yes, he had to admit, more than a touch of jealousy. His feelings were not helped by the suspicion of a grin that lurked behind Jenkins's beard. 'How the hell are we going to get out of this?' he demanded. 'Abdullah, can't you just say that she is betrothed to this fellow in Dongola and that the family must keep their word to him?'

'I already say this. He say he will make good offer

tomorrow to make us forget other fellow.' If Jenkins was amused, Abdullah certainly did not see the funny side of the situation. 'This could be difficult for us,' he said. 'Dervishes do not like to be . . . er . . . humbled?'

'Humiliated.'

'Yes. That is the word. Humiliated in public. If he fights we cannot kill him. His family will not like it.'

'I can well understand that.'

Jenkins tried to make amends. 'Is there anythin' we can give old Romeo for 'is trouble?' he suggested. 'What about a camel, to get us off the 'ook, so to speak? We've got one to spare, 'aven't we? I'd say one camel for doin' nothin' is good trade.'

Abdullah's shrug came back. 'We can try, but this man is a bit wild, I think. He may try and take lady anyway.' He eased his big sword from its sling by the side of his camel. 'We may have to fight.'

'What?' Fonthill's reaction was dismissive. 'Against how many — and in the middle of the Dervish camp? We wouldn't stand a chance. Last man standing would be killed and they would take Alice anyway.'

They rode in silence for a few moments. 'Look, I am terribly sorry about this.' Alice's voice was low and forlorn. 'But I didn't encourage the man, I promise you. I can't understand why he would want me. I must be older than him, anyhow.'

'Ah, I think it is the eyes, lady,' said Abdullah shyly. 'Dervish man probably never seen lady with grey eyes before. They are . . .' He groped for words that would not be offensive or out of place. 'They are, er, very nice.'

'Well for God's sake don't look at the bloody man,' snapped Simon.

Alice's head jerked back and she turned in the saddle to respond, but then thought better of it and her head went down again, her gaze directed at the sand ahead.

Fonthill immediately felt remorse. 'Sorry, Alice,' he said. 'It's not your fault that you have the most beautiful eyes in the world. Look, let me think. Maybe I can come up with something that will get us out of this. Maybe . . .'

'Yes.' Jenkins jumped in, anxious to be of help. 'The Captain's good at the thinkin' bit, miss. 'E'll think of somethin', you'll see.'

Alice shot him a quick glance of gratitude, then, still not looking at Simon, resumed gazing staunchly ahead.

While the debate had continued in semi-whispers, Abdullah had managed to direct their progress at a slight angle to the general line of advance, so that they were now riding along on the edge of the party, with the open desert to their left. Fonthill weighed up the chances of making a dash for it, but although the best of their camels, those taken from the Dervishes at the oasis, were quite fast movers, he could see plenty of others in the main party who would be as quick, if not quicker. They would soon be overtaken.

Simon was no nearer to a solution when they camped that night. They halted with the rest of the party and made their prayers to Mecca, the four of them carefully following Abdullah in his devotions, before they began unloading the pack animals to prepare a meal and make ready for the night. Watching Alice's slim, upright figure handing down bundles to the others, inspiration suddenly struck Fonthill.

'Alice,' he hissed. 'Sit down now.'

'What? I am only—'

'Sit down now, I say. Immediately. And cover yourself up. Go on, *do it*!'

Reluctantly, her eyes flashing behind the *burkha* at his tone, Alice squatted on the ground.

'Good.' He reached down and withdrew a blanket from his pack and put it around Alice's shoulders. He knelt down beside her. 'Look. Has your swain—'

'Don't be offensive. He's not my swain.'

'Don't be adversarial. Has this fellow seen you standing, on the ground, that is?'

'No. I have always been on the camel. And I am not being adversarial. He is not my—'

'Never mind. And when you are on your camel you slouch a bit, don't you, if you don't mind me asking, that is?'

'Well, riding a bloody camel is not exactly like sitting on a show pony in the Home Counties, is it? I suppose I do slouch a bit. Why?'

'Good.' For the first time since they had made love, a genuine smile now lit up Fonthill's features. 'Who has the smallest blanket?'

'Mine is littlest,' piped up Mustapha, puzzled by the conversation but anxious, as always, to be part of it. He handed his small cotton blanket to Simon, who put it low in his lap and turned his back on whatever curious eyes might be watching them from the camp, before carefully folding it four times and then bundling it up into a ball.

'Here,' he said, handing it to Alice, 'put this inside your shirt, low down, under your *jibba*.'

'Why? I don't see the point . . .'

But Abdullah did. He nodded, and his teeth beamed in the dusk. 'Very good, Captain. Very good. I think it good idea.'

The dusk had allowed Alice to remove her hated *burkha*, and her expression showed that she had no idea of the reason why she was being asked to stuff a ball-like blanket beneath her undershirt but she did so, letting the shirt fall down and then patting it into place. It was as she did so that a slow smile came on to her face.

She looked across at Fonthill. 'Brilliant, my love,' she said. 'Brilliant. Do you think it will work?'

'Pregnant lady,' said Abdullah, keeping his voice low, 'not favoured by Dervish men looking for wife.'

'They're not exactly favourite in England either,' murmured Simon.

'In Wales, look you,' added Jenkins, 'it's often the only sort of lady you can get.'

They all exchanged smiles, including Mustapha, who had no idea what the joke was.

The next morning, as the sun stormed its way over the horizon, presaging another blazing day, they all made their devotions to the east. Then a discreetly bulging Alice was rather ostentatiously helped to mount her camel and the party resumed its journey, waiting – with some trepidation – for its expected visitor. He came just before noon with his two companions, whom Abdullah had elicited were his father and uncle. Behind him the young man towed two richly caparisoned racing camels.

Fonthill pulled his camel alongside Alice's as the three Dervishes began their conversation with Abdullah. 'I wouldn't have given that much for you,' he whispered.

'Oh Simon,' she whispered back. 'It's not funny. I am terrified.'

'Don't worry, miss.' Jenkins had pulled up alongside, so that once again she was sandwiched between them. 'We'll look after you.'

Romeo was now parading the camels in front of Abdullah, to a ripple of approval from the surrounding families as the march continued. He pulled the beasts this way and that and used his camel stick to point out their fine haunches and fetlocks, the arrogant curve of their necks and the very rich cloths on which their saddles rested. Abdullah played his part to perfection. He looked increasingly sheepish, with much shrugging of his shoulders and many gesticulations in the direction of Dongola. Romeo became increasingly impatient, eyeing Alice and pointing at his dowry as though it was impossible for anyone to turn down the offer. Then Abdullah played his final card. He called the father to him and whispered confidentially – and very ashamedly – in his ear. The single-word cry resounded all about. Then the man rode to his son and whispered angrily to him. With a face like thunder, Romeo leaned across Fonthill to draw back Alice's *jibba*, revealing, for him and all the fascinated families nearby, that she was certainly no virgin.

The young man glared at Alice, who covered her eyes with her hand and sank her head forward in disgrace. He then spat at Fonthill, who shrugged his shoulders and held out both hands in a 'what will you' gesture, immediately copied by Jenkins. Romeo paused for a second, his hand on his dagger, then spun his beast around, pulled hard on the leading reins of his fine racing camels and sped away in a cloud of dust. He was followed by a roar of laughter from the Arab families. As his companions turned in obvious disgust to follow him, Abdullah intervened, again with much shrugging of the shoulders, to speak to the father. The senior Dervish, his face like thunder, listened for a moment, turned to look in contempt at Alice and her two 'brothers' and then nodded to Abdullah and pointed to the open desert with his camel switch. Then he and his brother rode off, without a backward glance.

At this, Abdullah, shoulders hunched, head down and the picture of humiliation, pulled his camel's head round and headed out to the desert, away from the Arabs. Without question, the others followed, in equal dejection, until, when well out of earshot and almost out of sight, Fonthill let out a whoop and embraced Alice and they all shook hands, to Mustapha's great delight.

'What did you say at the end, Abdullah,' asked Simon, 'to make the fellow let us go?'

'Ah.' The Sudanese looked slightly uncomfortable. 'I think he might take revenge by insisting we stay and fight for Khalifa. So I say that baby is due soon and that father is one of her brothers. No one else but this man in Dongola would take lady in, so we must go there.'

'Ohh.' Jenkins wrinkled his nose. 'Which one of us was the father, then?'

'I say the Captain.'

'Well, thank you very much.' Alice's face was a mixture of indignation and amusement. 'I'm not that sort of a girl, you know, Abdullah. But seriously, Romeo won't come after us, will he?'

Simon grinned. 'No, I think we've curbed his ardour. But this will teach you to make eyes at handsome sheiks.'

She aimed a playful blow at him and they rode on in great relief, now back on their original route to the north-north-west. They had Alice's compass to guide them, but without a map – for her rough sketchmap of the area had long ago been lost – it was only useful as a supplementary support to Abdullah's innate sense of direction and his ability to pick up signposts in what to the rest of them seemed a featureless desert. Even this, however, proved fallible when, on the eighth day after their escape from Omdurman, they crossed a wide expanse of tracks, showing the progress of what appeared to be a vast concourse heading due north. Ahead of them, the horizon was clouded by dust.

For a moment Fonthill thought that they had somehow doubled back and were now following the group of Dervishes they had so recently left, but then he realised that the party ahead was much larger.

'I think I go a little bit wrong,' confessed Abdullah. 'We must go this way more to get to wells.' He gestured with his hand ahead but slightly to the left. 'Sorry.'

'More to the north-west,' mused Fonthill. 'Don't apologise. You have done wonders to get us this far. How far to Jakdul Wells, do you think?'

'Maybe we reach it by nightfall. If we miss Dervishes.'

They did so, however, and it was with relief that, just as the sun was dipping, they saw the rocky outcrop that protected the wells rising from the horizon directly ahead of them. The other four gathered around Fonthill as he held up his hand.

'Careful as we go in,' he said. 'I can smell wood smoke strongly, which means that the wells are occupied by more than just a few travellers. It could be Dervishes, although I doubt it because they would not hole up here and invite the British to attack them. They would much rather use their superiority in numbers and attack from the broken ground to the east and take our chaps while they are on the march. Or, of course, it could be part of Stewart's column – in which case they could be jumpy at dusk.' His teeth flashed white behind his beard. 'I don't want us to be shot by a British sentry after all we've been through. Abdullah and I will ride ahead. Follow carefully.'

The two rode on, and as they cautiously picked their way up the rocky rise towards the entrance to the wells, two rifles poked out from behind boulders and a voice cried, 'Halt! Who goes there?'

Simon breathed a sigh of relief. 'Major Fonthill, British Intelligence, and this is Abdullah, my guide. We need to come in with our people behind.'

'You don't look like no major to me, mate, so you stand there till I call the guard commander.'

'Very well, but get a move on. We have news of General Gordon.'

Within minutes the five were sitting around an open fire and drinking welcome mugs of tea with the major commanding the hundred and fifty men of the Royal Sussex Regiment who had been left behind to garrison the wells after Stewart and his column had moved on.

'How long ago did they move out?' asked Fonthill.

'Only yesterday, the fourteenth,' said the major.

'What is the strength of the column?'

The major pulled at his moustache before replying, and Simon realised that he was weighing up the credentials of this strange little group – three unkempt seeming Dervishes, plus a strange, slim youth-woman and a slave boy – who had wandered in out of the desert and demanded to know the strength of the desert column. Then obviously his brain reasoned that, whatever their appearance, no followers of the Mahdi could speak with the accent of a Sandhurst-educated officer, not to mention the Welsh cadences of Jenkins. And there had certainly been no desertions from the British force.

'One thousand four hundred men,' said the major, 'plus forty-five medics, commissariats and camel drivers. Bit of a strange mixture of Guards, Hussars, heavy cavalry, mounted infantry, my lot – the Sussex – gunners and some sailors. Apart from the Hussars, who are on little Syrian stallions, the whole lot are on camels.'

'Artillery?'

'Three seven-pounder screw guns, broken down and carried on nine camels. Oh, and the sailors have this bally strange five-barrelled Gardner gun that can fire four hundred rounds a minute, if, that is,' he added lugubriously, 'the bloody thing doesn't jam.'

'Excuse me, Major,' said Alice, leaning forward, 'I wonder if you would be so kind as to lend me a pencil and a few pieces of paper.'

'What . . . er . . . miss?'

Fonthill coughed. 'Miss, ah, Griffith is a correspondent for Reuters, Major,' he explained. 'She is covering this campaign but she has lost most of her, er, belongings, you see. She has just come back with us from Khartoum and needs to, ah, take notes and, er, so on.'

The Major's jaw dropped. 'Khartoum! Good lord. Paper, yes, of course. And a pencil. Sergeant . . .'

Alice responded with her most demure smile, and while she was being supplied, Fonthill pondered. Just under fifteen hundred troops. Probably not enough to survive a massed attack by Dervishes coming out of the rocks and the scrub, and surely not enough to relieve Gordon. 'How fast can the column move?' he asked.

'Well, they're mounted, of course. They've all been trained on camels, don't you know, so the idea is that they get a move on. But I don't suppose that the whole lot, as a column, can do much more than, say, ten miles a day in broken country.' The major paused, then his brown face lit up. 'But by jove, they look a fine sight on the move, d'yer see. All been fitted out specially. They wear grey serge jackets, Bedford cord pantaloons and dark blue puttees and ride on special red saddles. Dammed fine sight, I must say.'

'Thank you, Major.' Fonthill threw his tea dregs away and rose to his feet. 'Jenkins and I will ride after them in the morning. We must urge them to move fast because Gordon will have little, if any, time left and urgency must be the word now. They must also be warned about the Dervishes massing ahead of them. I just hope we are not too late. Alice, you and Abdullah will ride back to Korti, of course, and I would be grateful if you would take Mustapha with you and, er, look after him until we get back.'

'Don't be ridiculous, Simon.' Alice rose to her feet and stood firmly, confronting him. 'There is a press contingent with the column, I am sure, and I will come with you and join it. There is no question about it.' She turned to the Sudanese. 'Abdullah, I am afraid that you must wait until I return to Korti for me to pay you, as assuredly I will, of course. Would you mind going back and waiting for me there?'

Abdullah shook his head slowly. 'No, lady. I promise to look after you until we get back to Korti. We not back yet, so I come with you.'

Mustapha's teeth flashed in the firelight. 'I come too,' he said.

'Oh, for God's sake . . .' began Fonthill.

'Looks as though the party stays together,' grinned Jenkins. 'Seems to me there's nothing you can do about it, bach sir.'

Simon whirled on his heel. 'We leave at sun-up,' he called testily over his shoulder. 'Thank you for the tea, Major.'

They set off, in fact, before dawn, urged on by a tight-faced Fonthill, anxious to be on the road. They rode their fastest camels, leaving the slowest behind in exchange for two Martini-Henry rifles and bayonets; Abdullah refused to be so armed. Simon set a brisk pace. There were no problems in terms of following Stewart, for it was clear from the trampled scrub the direction he had taken. Later, as the shadows lengthened from the hills all around, Abdullah indicated additional signs of extinct Dervish camp fires. It was a nerve-racking journey for the little party to undertake, for the trail now meandered between low hills, any of which could have provided cover for an ambush at any time.

As the afternoon receded, Fonthill, riding in the van with Abdullah, heard the sound of distant gunfire ahead. He held up his hand and the others gathered behind him.

'It's only sporadic, by the sound of it,' he said. 'So it is probably sniping and not a general attack. We will approach slowly, keeping our heads down, but then we will probably have to gallop hard into the camp, if it is surrounded. Be prepared, and follow me closely.'

As they walked their beasts ahead cautiously, Fonthill was surprised to see no sign of Dervishes on either side of the trail. The camp, then, if Stewart had stopped his column, was not surrounded, and the opposition must be coming from the front of the British force and perhaps its flanks. Harassment, then, rather then direct attack. He tied a handkerchief – not exactly white, but it would have to do – to the muzzle of his rifle and urged his camel into a trot.

They crested a slight rise and saw below them a *zariba*, erected on a level patch of ground and made partly of rocks and camel thorn but topped also with saddles and store boxes. It was large in area, but the sides of the ramparts were low in places, particularly in the rear, facing Fonthill and his party, sometimes reaching only waist high. Ahead of the square, Simon could see white-robed Arabs massed under a sea of coloured flags and hear the Mahdists' battle drums beating. To the right, snipers were installed on low hills and were directing occasional fire down on to the British square. It was clear that the Dervishes had decided to stand here and contest the desert column's passage to the Nile.

Fonthill turned in the saddle. 'Right,' he said. 'We ride in. Don't gallop, because I don't want to attract the Dervishes' attention, or alarm our own men. Then, at the last minute, we will canter towards the rear of the *zariba*, where the wall is lowest. Ride in line ahead not abreast, because I don't want the column to think we are an attacking party.' He looked at Alice. 'Are you all right, my dear?'

She gave him a firm smile and nodded. Simon looked at Mustapha. 'Keep low, boy,' he said. 'Keep your head down. Very well. We go *now*.'

The distance to the rear wall of the enclosure was about three hundred yards and they moved at first at a walk, with Fonthill looking at the hills on either side to see if they had attracted attention. Then, as they neared the *zariba*, he saw rifle barrels being poked over the top of the saddles at them. He lifted his rifle with its pale fluttering flag and urged his camel into a canter.

A shot was fired and winged its way over his head. He waved his rifle. 'Don't shoot,' he shouted. 'We are friends and we are coming in. Don't shoot!'

He saw a red-coated officer move the two rifle barrels away. Several more figures appeared at the rampart, and then the officer presented his revolver at Simon and shouted, 'Stop right there and lower that rifle. Now, you in the lead, walk your camel forward, slowly.'

Fonthill did so and leaned forward. 'I am Major Fonthill of Army Intelligence. We have come up from Khartoum via Jakdul Wells. We need to come in and I must speak to the Brigadier immediately. Come on, man, don't keep us waiting.'

The combination of crisp English tones emanating from a bearded scarecrow had the usual effect, and the subaltern's jaw dropped. 'Good God,' he said, 'did you say Khartoum?'

'Yes, I did. Now pull those saddles aside and let us in before the snipers get at us.'

Within minutes once again, Fonthill and Alice were sitting at the opening of a small tent, facing Brigadier Sir Herbert

Stewart and several of his senior officers, while Jenkins, Abdullah and Mustapha stood respectfully behind them.

The Brigadier's eyes crinkled. 'I remember you, Fonthill. Did a damned fine job for us at el Kebir – and weren't you at Rorke's Drift?'

'Yes, sir.' Quckly but carefully, Simon explained the role allocated to him and Jenkins by Wolseley and recounted their adventures, including their captivity and the rescue by Alice and Abdullah.

'Good lord,' exclaimed Stewart. All eyes were now on Alice, whose blush could not be seen under her face dye. 'What a remarkable young lady. Reuters, you say?'

'Yes, sir.' Alice's eyes were gleaming. 'I presume you have press correspondents with your column, Brigadier. Is my colleague Mr Piggott with it?'

'He was, but he developed a fever and had to return to Korti.'

'Ah!'

Was there a glimmer of triumph in Alice's eyes? wondered Fonthill.

'In that case, sir, I shall take his place.'

'Oh, I fear not, madam. As you can see, we are in a highly dangerous situation. This is no place for a woman.'

Alice's sigh was almost theatrical in its intensity. 'Sir Herbert,' she said slowly, 'I have just ridden down through the desert to Omdurman to rescue Captain Fonthill and his companions from the clutches of the Mahdi himself and ridden back with them. I have therefore lived with danger at first hand for some six weeks now. May I assure you that there is no way – absolutely no way – that I am returning to Korti to sit on my bottom and file dispatches about the weather. I stay with you, sir, and if necessary I shall fight with you.'

Fonthill stifled a smile and exchanged glances with Jenkins

as Alice produced her small French revolver from her waistband and gestured it towards the Arabs massed to the east.

The Brigadier shrugged his shoulders. 'Very well, Miss Griffith,' he said. 'I certainly cannot spare any men to escort you back to Korti in any case. So do take your place with your fellow journalists. But please, stay out of the firing line.'

Alice nodded and directed a triumphant glance at Fonthill, who once again received the Brigadier's attention. 'Tell me how Gordon was when you left,' he said, 'and how long you think he can hold out.'

'What is the date today, sir?'

'The sixteenth of January.'

Simon shook his head. 'When I last saw General Gordon it was the sixteenth of November. He was then in good heart and had a reasonable amount of ammunition left in the town, and as you can imagine, he had established a good defensive system. But food was beginning to run low and he was down to only one river steamer, and these had been his main defensive weapons. He felt that he could not sustain the defence of Khartoum much longer than . . .' Fonthill extended his palms towards Stewart, 'well, frankly, about now. This is why we have rushed to catch you up here, rather than going back to Korti to report to General Wolseley. Sir, you must, *you really must*, make all haste to reach the Nile and go south to Khartoum. Every day counts now. Gordon's last words to me were to the effect that even a company of redcoats sent on ahead would restore morale and see them through. May I ask what your orders are, sir?'

Stewart frowned. 'I am to fight my way through to the river and take the town of Metemmeh, where, hopefully, General Earle and his river column will have made their way to establish a base opposite on the eastern bank of the Nile at

Shendi, which will give support for my dash to Khartoum. If, however, Earle is not there and news comes from Gordon, then I am to risk almost anything to send a flying column south and attempt to relieve him. But we have had a slow slog to get here and my main aim now is to get water at Abu Klea, just ahead.'

'Is there water transport you can use at Metemmeh?'

'You ask an awful lot of questions, young man.'

'I am sorry, sir, but I am only trying to help. I repeat, every hour is of the essence, if we are to be in time.'

'Very well. Yes, I am informed that at Metemmeh or nearby there should be a couple or more of Gordon's steamers that he sent north some time ago to wait for us and take a small advance force to him. But God knows if they are still there. The Dervishes might well have sunk them by now.'

'Let us hope they *are* there, sir, for you will need them. But now to more immediate matters. I had hoped to reach you in time to warn you that, from what I have picked up on the way here, the Dervish force confronting you now is considerable in number. You are almost certainly outnumbered by something as high as twenty to one or more. They are waiting to take you as you march through this broken country ahead, in the passes between the hills.'

Stewart nodded. 'Colonel Wilson here thought as much.' He nodded to where a slim, thoughtful-looking man, older than Stewart, was sitting. 'Well, from what you've told me now, Fonthill, we certainly can't hang about here. We shall move out tomorrow and attack the Dervishes at first light.'

'Capital, sir. Capital.' The words came from an extremely tall officer sporting a wide black moustache and looking remarkably elegant in dark blue jacket and tight breeches as he lounged on a camp stool. 'I think we can knock these chaps over easily enough. But well done, Fonthill. I had heard of you.'

Stewart made the introduction. 'This is Colonel Burnaby, of the Horse Guards, my second-in-command here.'

'Ah.' Fonthill nodded. 'And I have heard of you, sir.'

Indeed, the whole of the British Army had heard of Fred Burnaby of 'The Blues'. Celebrated as an athlete, marksman and horseman, he had crossed the English Channel in a balloon and travelled extensively in Central Asia, writing a book about his experience. He had also managed to upset the Duke of Cambridge, the Queen's cousin and head of the British Army, who had refused permission for him to join Wolseley's expeditionary force. Burnaby, however, had somehow managed to join the force in an unofficial capacity. Now, here he was in the front line, puffing a cigar, his long legs draped out as though he had just enjoyed a good meal in his London club.

'We should see some fun tomorrow at last then, Herbert, eh?' Burnaby inquired of the Brigadier. 'How d'yer intend to go forward to get to those wells at Abu Klea?'

Stewart pursed his lips. 'Given that we are outnumbered,' he said, 'and that the Dervishes will probably try to rush us from the cover that they've got all around here, we must move in square.'

Burnaby blew on his cigar, making the end glow red in the dusk. 'Dashed difficult thing to do in this broken country, with the camels, guns an' all. Have to be a big square, too.'

'I know. But there is no alternative. I shall leave the stores and the baggage camels behind in this *zariba*, with a party of Royal Sussex to guard 'em, then we will bring them on when we reach the wells.' Stewart looked up and seemed suddenly to realise that Jenkins, Abullah and Mustapha were still standing in the semi-darkness, listening with fascination to every word.

'Good lord, Fonthill,' he exclaimed, 'we must get you and your people some food and somewhere to sleep tonight. It gets damned cold here after dark, as I am sure you know.'

Simon stood. 'Don't worry about us, sir. We have all been sleeping out in the open for weeks now.'

'No. We can find you all food and a bit of cover, though no fires, I am afraid. We must do nothing to attract sniper fire, which I am sure will go on all night. Now, we must also look after Miss Griffith. Sergeant Major.'

A burly warrant officer appeared.

'Please ask Captain Hicks-Johnson to join us right away.'

Fonthill and Jenkins immediately exchanged glances, so failing to register the frown that had descended on Alice's features. Hicks-Johnson had not been mentioned by either Simon or Alice when they had exchanged their experiences.

Simon cleared his throat. 'Hicks-Johnson is here with you, sir?'

'Yes. Do you know him?'

'We, er, met in the desert near Dongola when he was working in intelligence there for Major Kitchener and I was on the way south. I'm afraid we, ah, had a bit of a brush with him.'

'Bloody man nearly killed us, Brigadier bach.' Jenkins spoke from out of the gloom.

'That will do, 352,' chided Fonthill.

'Well, I'm afraid that this is no time to renew old enmities, Fonthill,' said Stewart. 'I gather he was in charge of press liaison back at base, but Wolseley sent him up with me to keep an eye on the small number of press chappies who are here. It's not a full-time job so I also use him for commissariat work and so on. I have to say that he's proved damned useful. Ah, here he is now.'

A familiar small, erect figure loomed out of the darkness. 'Sir.'

'We have visitors, Hicks-Johnson. I think you know Fonthill, and also possibly Miss Griffith?'

'Good God.' Hicks-Johnson's jaw dropped as he surveyed the little group. 'Where the hell did you come from?'

'Never mind that,' the Brigadier cut in sharply. 'Find them all cover for the night. Miss Griffith will join the press people, and she, at least, will need her own tent.'

'No.' Alice shook her head. 'Not necessary.'

'No tents, sir, anyway.' There was a malevolent gleam in Hicks-Johnson's eye. 'The correspondents are sleeping out in the open, like the men.'

'Well, find them food, anyway. They've come a hell of a way and they must be looked after. We break camp at four a.m., Fonthill, and will march at dawn. We are going to be sniped at all night, so keep your heads down, all of you. Good night.'

'Good night, sir.'

Fonthill and his companions followed the stiff figure of Hicks-Johnson as he strutted away without a backward glance. They picked their way through the detritus of an army column whose march had been temporarily suspended: men huddled in blankets, eating from mess tins, their rifles leaning together in little pyramids ready to be grabbed at a bugle note; stores piled in an orderly fashion in the centre of the square; camels cordoned together at the rear; and sentries, their light brown pith helmets clear in the gloom, standing to at the low walls of the *zariba*. From the hills overlooking the square, the occasional flash presaged the crack of a rifle and the whine of a bullet as it passed overhead or, less frequently, thudded into a packing case or human flesh.

Hicks-Johnson indicated a piece of ground near the stores.

'You can sleep here,' he said. And then, as a quartermaster sergeant appeared: 'Find something to eat for these people, Q,' he snapped.

The sergeant looked at the five in astonishment. 'Wot – Mosselman grub, sir?'

'Anything will do for them.'

'Quartermaster,' intervened Fonthill, speaking incisively, 'you will bring us the best army rations you can find in the circumstances. I hold the rank of major in the British Army and Mr Jenkins here that of warrant officer. Four of us are Christians, but this gentleman here,' he indicated Abdullah, 'is a Muslim, so please bring him appropriate rations, the best you can find. We are all now hungry, so please be quick. That will be all.'

The sergeant, his eyes wide, directed a quick glance at his captain, but receiving no reaction, nodded quickly and then doubled away. Fonthill strode towards Hicks-Johnson and grabbed him by his tunic front.

'Treat us like that again, you little swine,' he hissed, 'and I will personally see that you end up in a Dervish watchhole.'

From out of nowhere, seemingly, a knife suddenly appeared at Hick-Johnson's throat. 'An' without your balls, too, see,' added Jenkins.

Fonthill released the captain's tunic. 'That will do, Jenkins,' he said. 'That's no way to treat an officer. Not his testicles. An ear will do.'

'Very good, sir.'

Hicks-Johnson's lip curled. 'I will say one thing to all of you. Watch your backs. Watch your backs. And I don't mean the Dervishes . . .'

'Where do the press people sleep, Captain?' inquired Alice sweetly. 'Perhaps you would be kind enough to take me there.'

Hicks-Johnson looked at her, his eyes wild, then he jerked

his head, indicating that she should follow, and strode away. Alice dutifully tripped along behind him and, looking over her shoulder, smiled and blew them all a kiss.

'Ah well, bach sir,' observed Jenkins, 'it's nice to meet up again with old friends, now ain't it?'

They all sat wordlessly wrapped in their blankets and ate the bully beef and biscuits that the quartermaster, stepping warily, brought them. Then they curled up and sought sleep. It was hard to find. They realised that the position they had been given – no doubt with some forethought from Hicks-Johnson – was near where the camels had been tethered. The animals reeked of the carbolic oil with which their sore backs had been treated, and this combined with the sickly stink of their perspiration and, of course, their continual flatulence. In itself, this mixture of odours would have been enough to deny sleep, but throughout the night the drums of the Dervishes continued their beat and the snipers intensified their fire by the light of the moon.

It seemed to Fonthill that the whole Arab army was massed just an arm's length away, and despite the cold, he felt the atmosphere to be oppressive: the thump of the war drums and the crack of the rifles made sleep elusive, and the hair at the back of his neck tingled as he thought of the morrow. He had been stupid to allow Alice and Mustapha to come into this cradle of violence. What if this fragile little column was overrun, as it well might be? Stewart had won his spurs in the field and was a good officer, but he was a cavalryman and, as far as Simon knew, had never commanded in a static infantry engagement before. Fonthill cursed himself for letting Alice move away into the journalists' compound, without him or Jenkins to protect her. So much for his starry-eyed plans for a future for them all in Norfolk, with a brown-eyed boy walking the hedgerows with him on misty mornings! Eventually he slept, but it seemed that he had only just closed his eyes when the bugles sounded reveille and the camp stirred.

As dawn broke, the men within the *zariba* came under increased fire as they moved about to get warm, eating their frugal breakfasts while they walked. Five officers and many more men had been wounded by sniper fire during the night and the previous day, and Stewart decided that they must be left behind with a contingent of the Royal Sussex within the flimsy protection of the *zariba* when the advance began.

Within the hour, a part of the enclosure was pulled aside and the Hussars trotted out on their little stallions, followed by skirmishers on foot, made up of dismounted members of the Mounted Infantry and Scots Guardsmen. Then the rest of the column marched out and, under constant fire from the hills, slowly formed a square.

Now at last Lord Wolseley's expeditionary force – or at least its vanguard – was to meet the Dervishes of the Mahdi in open battle.

Chapter 16

Fonthill had had the foresight to realise that if it came to a hand-to-hand fight, then he and his companions in their Arab dress could well be mistaken for the enemy. So before marching out, he had begged two pith helmets and khaki jackets from the by now friendly quartermaster sergeant – Abdullah predictably refusing to change his own garb. The jackets did not fit, of course, and he and Jenkins looked like incongruous hybrids as a result, appearing to be strange, bearded English soldiers from the waist up but definitively Arab in their torn pantaloons and scruffy sandals below.

Simon had received no instructions about where to position himself and his comrades in the advance, but Abdullah insisted on staying with Alice, and Mustapha was sent off with him, leaving Fonthill and Jenkins to fall in at the front of the square, joining contingents of the Mounted Infantry, the screw-gun battery and companies of the Coldstream and Scots Guards. On this and two of the other faces of the square, the men formed up in double rank and numbered, Simon estimated, about three hundred. For some reason, however, the left face seemed thinner, with only some two hundred and thirty men manning it.

Composition in such a mixture of regiments was important, and Fonthill noted that the left, thinner line was manned by a company of the heavy camel corps (dismounted, of course) and the other two companies of the Mounted Infantry; the right was formed by the Grenadiers, the Marines and the balance of the Royal Sussex; and the rear by four companies of the 'heavies', together with the Naval Brigade with its fearsome Gardner machine gun in its centre. The whole enclosed Brigadier Stewart and his staff and about a hundred and fifty camels carrying water, ammunition and the wounded. Simon realised that Stewart, the cavalryman, had shrewdly mixed his dismounted cavalry, who were less formidable units when fighting on foot, with his seasoned infantry – except, perhaps dangerously, on the left flank.

Eventually, the whole formation began to move forward ponderously, at the speed of the slowest man – or rather camel, for the beasts were heavily loaded and could not be induced to hurry. To the front, Fonthill could see that the way to the precious water at Abu Klea, less than a day's march away, followed the line of the valley, down the centre of which ran a wide, dried-up watercourse, filled with long grass and scrub. To avoid this the square had to deviate and march across undulating ground to its right. It was difficult going, across rocky hillocks interspersed with deep gullies. The guns in the van had to be manhandled, with the gunners putting their shoulders to the wheels, and at the centre back, the heavily laden camels were slipping and sliding, goaded by their native handlers, whose cries had now risen to shrill screams. The lines of the square were beginning to bulge. And yet, apart from the continual but now less effective sniping, there was no evidence of a forthcoming attack. Of the massed Dervishes there was no sign. They seemed to have melted away, like frost at first sun-up.

'Where are the buggers, then?' breathed Jenkins, the sun glinting off his bayonet.

'Buggers are out there at the left,' piped a small voice behind them.

'Mustapha!' cried Simon, whirling round. 'Go back and join Abdullah this minute.'

'No thank you, Captain. I want to fight.' And he held up his knife.

'Do as you're told, lad,' growled Jenkins. 'You're not big enough to fight, look you.'

'Look you, I am. Big enough to fight crocodile and big enough to help you in Omdurman. Big enough to fight buggers here.'

Fonthill and Jenkins exchanged glances, like anxious parents. 'Do not use that language, Mustapha,' chided Simon. 'Very well, then, but stay close to 352 and me. Whatever you do, don't leave our side—'

His instructions were interrupted by a loud order of 'Halt!' and looking behind him, Simon could see that the lagging camels had caused the rear face of the square to fall behind, leaving a gap at the left rear. The square had been forced to stop while the rear line trudged forward to close the opening. It was then that the Dervishes attacked.

A loud howl and beating of drums came from the left – as Mustapha had predicted – from a *wadi* where green and white flags on long poles protruded. Stewart's skirmishers had advanced to investigate but then fell back in disarray as a vast phalanx of Dervishes left the cover of the *wadi* and charged in perfect formation. Fonthill, his mouth agape, watched as they split into three units, each appearing to be led by an emir or sheik, followed by fighting men armed with hatchets, javelins and long spears, except in the case of the frightening Fuzzy Wuzzies from the east, who, stripped to their waist under great haystacks of frizzy black hair, carried huge cross-handled swords. Simon immediately thought of Abdullah and prayed that he was by Alice's side. For a moment the mass disappeared in broken ground, then immediately reappeared, paused to line up in immaculate formation, and charged, screaming.

'Bloody 'ell,' breathed Jenkins, raising his rifle.

'Stay close to me, Mustapha, whatever you do,' said Fonthill, nuzzling his own rifle to his cheek.

'Volley firing when I give the order,' cried an officer. But it was impossible to fire, because the skirmishers were streaming back in front of the charging Dervishes and providing an effective protective screen for the attackers. Simon could hear the screams of camels coming from behind him and he fervently hoped that the square had not been broken at the back. Once the Dervishes were inside, behind the line of rifles and bayonets, he knew that the column was done for.

Then the retreating skirmishers threw themselves down at the feet of the front line and a target was presented at last.

'Front rank, FIRE!' The order was now more a scream. Then: 'Front rank, reload. Rear rank, FIRE!'

Fonthill and Jenkins fired from behind the rear rank and Simon sniffed again the acrid smell of cordite and tasted it on his tongue. He had forgotten how fierce was the kickback of the Martini-Henry as the eighty-three grains of black powder detonated by each pull of the trigger exploded and sent the .45 calibre Boxer on its way. His cheek jarred with the contact. He slipped the cartridge case ejector down behind the trigger guard and inserted another round in the breach in time to join the second volley. The seven-pounder guns now joined in the firing and the crack of their shrapnel cases exploding above the heads of the charging tribesmen added to the general din.

This was what the British Army did best: disciplined firing at short range. The whole line stood perfectly steady, and at two hundred yards, the volleys tore into the massed Arabs, leaving gaps in their ranks and dozens of white-clad figures writhing on the ground. Yet even this decimation did not stop the Dervishes. Instinctively – for Fonthill could hear no orders given – the charging Arabs veered to their right, where the ground was more open and provided cover of a sort. But their pace did not slacken and they merged with three more columns that emerged suddenly from the ground, and Simon realised that the whole was heading for the left rear corner of the square. This was the most vulnerable point of the British defences. Here, as a result of the recalcitrant camels, a gap of some eighty yards had already opened between the Lancers on the left face and the Royal Dragoons and Scots Greys on the rear, and the Dervishes were pouring towards it.

'Oh my God!' shouted Fonthill. 'Alice is back there some-where. Come on.' He began to run to the rear, then realised that, along with Jenkins, Mustapha was running too. 'No, Mustapha,' he cried. 'You go back and stay behind the soldiers.'

'No. I come with you. I can fight them.'

Shaking his head, Simon ran on. As he neared the rear of the square, he saw that Alice was scrambling up to the top of two biscuit boxes that had been upended, helped by Abdullah, already crouched on top, who was extending his long arm to pull her up. Good, she was as safe as she could be for the moment. He also saw that Lord Charles Beresford, of the Naval Brigade, had quickly ordered his Gardner machine gun and its crew out some twenty yards from the edge of the square, to where it had a wider range of fire. The gun was the pride and joy of Beresford, who had originally come to Egypt as Wolseley's naval ADC on the recommendation of the Prince of Wales, and he laid the gun and operated the firing lever himself. Yet, out in the open it was unprotected, and

Fonthill saw the tall figure of Burnaby ordering men out of the line to form a cordon round it.

Beresford opened fire, and the five barrels whirred round, cutting a great swathe through the Dervishes running towards the gun. Then, predictably, it jammed. An empty cylinder not ejected had stuck. To clear it the feed plate had to be unscrewed, and Beresford and a chief boatswain mate began to do this, but then the Dervishes were upon them. The boatswain's mate was speared immediately, and the rest of the crew perished too as the hacking, stabbing horde swept over and through them. The feed plate fell on to Beresford's head and he was knocked under the gun. This saved him, although, struggling to his feet, he was carried along by the mass and forced with them on to the front rank of the defenders, where he turned and continued to fight.

Observing all this, Fonthill realised that one of the first rules of defensive warfare had been broken: never open the square in the face of the enemy. As a result, the unthinkable had happened. A British square had been broken by spear-wielding tribal warriors.

As he reached the edge of the hand-to-hand fighting, Simon saw that Burnaby was attempting to rally the British line. Screaming at the top of his voice, the big man ordered the nearest cavalrymen of the Dragoon Guards in the rear line to wheel outwards to fill the gap. At the same time, seeing the danger, men of the Sussex Regiment on the unengaged right flank ran to give support. But by the time Fonthill and Jenkins arrived, the rear corner of the square had been broached and was the scene of a chaotic jumble of flashing spears, swinging swords and desperate British soldiers fighting for their lives with their bayonets. The noise was intense: the war cries of the Dervishes mingling with the screams of the wounded, the clash of steel upon steel and the shouts of the officers attempting to direct reinforcements to force the invaders back. Infantrymen from the right flank were attempting to fire into the maelstrom, but it was impossible to pick a target, so tightly locked were the protagonists in the slashing, thrusting melee. A thick cloud of dust hung over the fighting, adding to the general confusion.

Fonthill and Jenkins paused just long enough to fire a round each at close quarters, and then they plunged into the battle, jabbing with their bayonets. The long, triangular 'lunger' attached to the Martini-Henry extended the length of the rifle to just under six feet and provided them with an effective, if heavy, stabbing weapon. Simon was soon engaged in a personal duel with a slim, bearded Dervish with staring black eyes who wielded his long spear with skill and determination. Even as he fought, Fonthill's mind slipped back six years to a similar confrontation in Zululand and a tactic he had used there. He fended the Arab's spear away and then twisted his own blade so that it ran down the shaft of the spear. He was then able to pierce the hand holding the shaft. With a cry, the Dervish dropped his spear and Simon plunged the point of his bayonet into his opponent's breast, twisting it as the Zulus did – they called their assegai the *iklwa*, after the noise the point made on extraction – to remove it quickly.

He heard a growl to his right. 'Well done, bach.' As ever, Jenkins was at his side. But where was Mustapha? Frantically Fonthill turned his head, but the boy was nowhere to be seen. Had he slipped away before they joined the fighting? Was he somewhere ahead in that sweating, shouting throng? Or, terrible thought, had he . . . ? There was no time for further conjecture, for another Dervish was upon him, wielding a long sword.

Simon ducked one extravagant swing and then found his own thrust parried in turn. God, how these Dervishes could fight! Then the man to the left of the Arab fell across his adversary as Jenkins's thrust went home, causing the man to stagger, and Fonthill was able to plunge his own bayonet into his opponent's stomach. And so the vicious, give-no-quarter-nor-take-none hand-to-hand fighting continued. It was all compressed within what seemed like a few square yards, and Simon was aware that the impetus of the Arab charge had forced the British back so that they were fighting amongst the tethered camels on which some stores, but, more importantly, many of the men wounded by the Arab snipers, were mounted. Indeed, but for the camels forming a fragile block in the middle of the square, the force of the attack would have swept right through the hollow middle so that the men on the right and forward faces would have been taken from the rear, probably fatally. As it was, however, the Dervishes were spearing wounded men and camels indiscriminately, and the screams of the dying and of the bucking, plunging camels added to the chaos. Above the tumult, Fonthill heard the high-pitched crack of a revolver at his back and he risked a quick glance behind him. Kneeling on top of the biscuit boxes, Alice, Abdullah beside her, his great sword in hand, was coolly firing down into the crowd with her handgun.

'Go to the front, Alice,' shouted Fonthill but she could not have heard him above the screams and shouts, nor perhaps even seen him in the crowd. For a moment the scrum ahead of him cleared and he gasped, 'Have you seen Mustapha?' to Jenkins.

'No,' grunted the Welshman. 'Watch out, here they come again.'

As he wearily presented his bayonet once more, Simon glimpsed, head and shoulders above the fray and out beyond what was left of the square, the massive figure of Colonel Frederick Burnaby, laying about him with his sword. As he watched, a spear pierced Burnaby from the back, another was plunged into his throat and he sank gradually, as though in slow motion, before disappearing beneath the white-clad figures all around him.

Now, however, the musketry of the Sussex infantry began to take its toll. They had turned around from the right face of the square – itself still not under direct attack – and now levelled their fire coolly and accurately at the Dervishes slightly below them. To their fire was added that of men from the front flank who had run back to help. 'They're falling back,' shouted Fonthill. 'Thank God!'

But the Dervishes were not yet finished. A fresh wave came pouring in, leaping over the bodies of their fallen comrades, to hack and thrust at the weary defenders. Simon had heard that the Mahdi himself had promised his Dervishes that a certain place in Paradise, and a harem of beautiful virgins, awaited each man who fought the infidels and took one of them with him into death. Now they virtually threw themselves on to the British bayonets, reaching behind with their spears and swords to cut at the soldiers. Once again, then, the men at the bottom end of the square, now trying to link together into a very thin, bent line, stood firing and thrusting with their bayonets to protect the fragile integrity of the makeshift fortress.

Fonthill, his arms aching with the effort of holding the heavy rifle, once again joined the line, next to Jenkins. He tried to insert a round into the breach of the Martini-Henry, but his fumbling fingers dropped the cartridge and he just had time to present the bayonet before the horde was on them once again. A Fuzzy Wuzzy, his eyes wide in what seemed like personal fury against the British, swung his great sword at Simon, who ducked under it and thrust his bayonet into the man's throat. He withdrew the blade only to have it grabbed by a Dervish, who, disregarding the blood that sprang from his fingers, pulled on the bayonet so that Fonthill, still holding his rifle, was yanked forward and the two suddenly found themselves locked in an embrace, breast to breast. Neither could free their arms to strike a blow and they swayed together, struggling impotently to free themselves but jammed together by the grunting, screaming throng all around. Simon's cheek was rammed against that of his opponent, so that the man's perspiration joined with his. In desperation, he drew his head back and cracked his forehead into the other's nose, creating a precious space in which he was able to hit the man again under the jaw with the muzzle of his rifle. Then something hit his own head so that he lost his vision for a moment and sank to the ground, to be immediately stamped on by several feet as the hand-to-hand fighting raged above him.

Dimly, from up above, he heard a voice cry, 'Get up, bach, for Christ's sake, get up.' He was conscious that someone was astride him, swinging a rifle like a club to clear a space. Clawing at Jenkins's pantaloons, Simon somehow regained his rifle and staggered to his feet, blinking hard to clear his head. Then, at Jenkins's side once again, he stood his ground, thrusting and jabbing like an automaton at the mass in front of him – but a mass now clearly depleted and hampered in its advance by the bodies over which it must spring to fight the redcoats facing it. For a moment the Arabs fell away, but Fonthill realised that it was only to make way for a last charge.

Horsemen, men of rank, were leading this last assault, and their beasts, plunging and rearing, added a new element to the chaos as their masters swung down and about with their long curved swords.

One sheik, armed only with a banner and a book of prayer, charged his way through to a small clearing in the centre, where he dismounted and calmly began chanting prayers before he was shot down. Simon, his head still ringing, brought down one horseman with a bayonet thrust that penetrated so far through his calf that it entered the flank of his mount. He saw another fall to Jenkins's own bayonet, which dug deeply into the man's ribs.

The horsemen, indeed, presented an easier target, and at last the shooting of the experienced infantrymen at the rear, firing as fast as their hot Martini-Henrys could be reloaded, began to take effect and the tide turned for the last time at the still half-open square. Simon, blood trickling down his face and with every muscle in his body aching, leaned on his rifle and turned anxiously to look behind him for Alice. She remained sitting on top of her store boxes, although this time her revolver had been laid down and she was busily scribbling on a notepad. Abdullah remained at her side, but of Mustapha there was no sign.

'Where is the lad?' demanded Fonthill again, his heart now in his mouth. 'Did you see him go?'

Jenkins shook his head. 'Sorry, bach sir. I was like you, a bit busy, see.' The Welshman, perennially unable to keep any headgear on his crown for longer than ten minutes, had long since lost his pith helmet, and his newly provided army tunic was ripped where an Arab spear had torn into his bicep. With his great black beard, long hair and arm drenched in blood, he looked like some primeval warrior, but Fonthill, usually so caring of his old comrade, hardly noticed his wound. 'Don't worry. 'E's probably at the back there, be'ind what's left of the camels. Oh, look you, the buggers are comin' back again.'

And so they were. Isolated groups of spearmen were rushing once more at the straggling British line, only to be brought down, sometimes under the very bayonets of the men they were attacking. Fonthill witnessed many remarkable acts of individual bravery by the enemy. One boy of about twelve, already shot through the stomach, walked slowly up through a storm of bullets to throw his spear ineffectually at the redcoats facing him before sinking to the ground. Another solitary horseman charged at the square and reached its threshold before horse and rider were brought down, riddled with bullets.

From the front line of the square a new burst of firing could be heard, and Fonthill and Jenkins wearily made their way there to provide support. But the Dervishes had made no determined attack there – nor from the right – and the firing, intermittent at best, came only from their snipers out in the low hills that swept down to the valley.

Simon met a white-faced Stewart, who had had his horse speared from under him. 'Well done, Fonthill,' he cried. 'Saw you both in amongst it. Are you all right?' Simon nodded. Then Stewart registered Jenkins's bloodstained arm. 'Get that seen to, my man. The doctors are down there with the camels. There's going to be plenty more fighting yet. We shall need you.'

Jenkins wiped the sweat from his eyes and gave a nod. 'Thank you, Brigadier bach,' he said. 'But it's only a scratch. I've been 'urt worse in the Flyin' 'Orse in Rhyl on a Saturday night, so don't you worry.'

Stewart raised one slightly bemused eyebrow and turned back to Simon. 'We've given them a hell of a beating,' he said, 'and I think we've seen the back of them for today. There must have been about ten to twelve thousand of them attacking us, but every single one of the beggars who broke through into the square has been killed. We've done a rough count and I reckon we've knocked over about eleven hundred of them.'

'What have we lost, sir?'

Stewart wiped his hand across his moustache. 'Aye, that's the rub. I'm afraid we've paid a heavy price. We moved off this morning with about fourteen hundred men – not much for what we've got to do if we're going to get to Khartoum. According to the first reports I have received, nine officers and sixty-five men have been killed and another nine officers and eighty-five men wounded, some of them severely.' His voice became weary. 'And I shall miss Fred Burnaby very, very much.'

He looked at Fonthill for a moment as though measuring whether he could confide in him. 'You were an infantryman, Fonthill, weren't you?'

'Yes, sir. Twenty-fourth of Foot.'

'Oh yes, of course. Should have remembered. Isandlwana and Rorke's Drift. Well, you will know that foot soldiers are trained to stay in line at all times – and most of all when in a square. Our infantrymen did just that today. But,' he ran his hand over his brow, 'you can't really expect cavalry, who have been taught never to be still and who have had inculcated in them that a square can always be broken, to be rocklike when attacked on foot. How can you expect them to forget all their training and believe that no one can get inside a square? That was the problem with our Heavy Camel Corps, I'm afraid. Nevertheless, we did damned well, considering everything.'

Fonthill realised that he was being used rather as a sounding board – a recipient of the Brigadier's train of thought, perhaps even a rehearsal of what he would explain in his forthcoming report to Wolseley. Stewart could talk like this to a soldier experienced in battle but who was not serving formally as part of the chain of command and likely to be embarrassed by the confidence shared. Simon nodded. 'Quite so, sir.'

Stewart frowned and then went on: 'Trouble now is, of course, that we are terribly exposed out here, we have hardly any water left and the wounded are suffering terribly. I can't afford to stop here: there are still plenty of Dervishes about and we shall be under constant fire. We must get on to the water at Abu Klea, so I am letting the Hussars out again on their horses to go on ahead to make sure we can find the bloody place. We shall attempt to limp along behind them. Now, we've just got to clear up.' He paused again and looked hard at Simon, as though seeing him for the first time. 'You all right, Fonthill? Get that head wound looked at.'

'All right, sir, thank you. Bit tired, that's all.'

'Well, that's to be expected. You were right in the thick of it. I am told that there were no casualties among the journalists, so Miss Griffith should be all right. I did catch a glimpse of her firing that revolver of hers. Damned plucky little woman, I'd say.' He turned and strode away, then paused and shouted back, 'Get that wound fixed, eh, 352?'

Jenkins, pleased that his number had been remembered correctly, nodded and raised a respectful finger to his forehead.

Fonthill led him away. 'It sounds as though Alice is all right, thank goodness,' he said, 'but I'm worried about Mustapha.'

Together they made their way back to the middle of the square, where activity was intense. Some of the wounded were being put on to the camels that remained, and the rest were being installed on litters to be carried by men of the Grenadier Guards. Fatigue parties were digging holes to bury ammunition that could not be carried because of the shortage of camels, and others went around collecting spare ammunition and discarded rifles and breaking the spears, axes and swords of the dead Dervishes. Nothing could be done at the moment to clear the Dervish dead, who lay in contorted confusion mainly at the place where the square had been opened.

It was there that they found Mustapha.

He was lying on his back at the point where the square had first been breached. Across his legs lay the body of a dead Dervish, and the boy still clutched in his hand the hilt of a British officer's sword. It had snapped halfway down the blade, and the end of the shaft at the break was bloodstained. Mustapha's own knife was unused, still tucked into his belt. His eyes were open and he was still breathing, but a sword cut had almost severed his left arm, and blood trickled from a deep spear wound in his side. He tried to smile as Fonthill pulled away the man from across his ankles and knelt by his side.

'Don't move, Mustapha,' he said. 'We will get a doctor to you. You will be all right.'

The boy's face contorted for a moment, and then that familiar grin reappeared. 'I fought the heathen buggers, yes?'

Fonthill gulped. 'You certainly did. Just like a British soldier. Now lie quietly.'

'Yes.' He lay back for a moment against Simon's arm. Then he lifted his head again. 'I go with you to this Norfolk place, don't I . . .'

But before Fonthill could reply, the boy's voice tailed away. He coughed, and a bubble of blood blew from his mouth. Then his eyes glazed over and his head fell to one side.

'No!' Simon's cry echoed over the scene of carnage.

Jenkins lowered himself to the ground on the other side of Mustapha and bent down to put his ear to the boy's heart. 'Yes,' he growled. 'Little lad's gone, I'm afraid. Brave little mite. Let's get 'im out of 'ere.' Clumsily he inserted one arm under the boy's shoulders and the other under his knees, and lifted him as though he was a feather.

'We'll take him to where the British dead are,' said Fonthill.

Togther they walked to where the red- and khaki-clad bodies were being laid. 'No. No natives 'ere, my man,' a moustached sergeant of the Royal Sussex called. 'You must put 'im outside the square.'

'He will stay here,' said Fonthill dully. 'He fought for us. He is a British soldier.'

'Eh?' The ritual of consternation of hearing an officer's voice emerging from a bearded Arab wearing one half of a British soldier's uniform followed. Then the sergeant relented. 'Very well, er, sir. Lay 'im down 'ere. We'll look after 'im. Orders are that our dead are to be left to wait for a burial party to come back from this wells place, once we've reached it.'

'Should we bury the lad ourselves, d'you think?' Jenkins asked Simon.

'No. I want him buried with the British soldiers. I think he would have liked that.'

They went to find Alice. They found her still scribbling, her face streaked with perspiration. She looked up, stood and then quickly threw her arms around them both, kissing Fonthill on the lips.

'I saw that you had survived and my prayers were answered,' she said. 'I caught just a glimpse of you in the thick of it and I did my bit to help, but it wasn't much. Now, I must have my story ready to dispatch as soon as we can telegraph, so you must excuse me. Oh, you've both been wounded.'

Fonthill remained silent. 'It's just a scratch, miss,' said Jenkins.

'Even so, you must get it seen to. The doctors are just up there . . . Ah, where is Mustapha?'

Silence fell for a moment, and then Jenkins stepped in to break it. 'Little lad's gone, I'm afraid, miss. Got cut down in the middle of it. We lost 'im, see. Despite what the Captain 'ere said, 'e wanted to fight and 'e must 'ave wriggled through the legs of the Nightshirts when they attacked an' was puttin' 'imself about, look you, when they cut 'im down. Terrible shame. Such a plucky little chap.'

Alice bit her lip and the silence returned for a moment. Then she slowly wound her arms around Fonthill's neck again and buried her cheek in his beard. 'I am so sorry, my love,' she whispered. 'Really, really sorry. I know how much he meant to you.'

Simon let himself be held for a moment, then he gently freed himself. 'Thank you,' he said. 'Now you must get on with your story, of course. And we still have work to do.'

He turned and strode away. Alice looked searchingly at Jenkins, but he spread out his hands helplessly and shrugged his shoulders before turning and following. She watched them both go, and tears began to trickle slowly down her cheeks, etching a new path through the dust. Then she turned back, sat down on her store box and put her chin in her hands. The return of Abdullah, who had been abortively searching for water, startled her. She gave him a wan smile and then began writing again, but more slowly this time.

Fonthill ushered Jenkins to where two doctors and a handful of orderlies were doing their best to tend to the wounded. Some were in a pitiful plight, suffering from deep spear wounds or sword slashes, and Jenkins refused to get into line to wait for treatment, insisting that his cut was light and would heal itself. Fonthill, however, requisitioned a small bottle of alcohol to clean the wound and applied a field dressing. Then he lightly dabbed a little of the harsh liquid on to his own wound, which had long since stopped bleeding, handing the bottle back before the Welshman could drink the rest of the contents.

The whole battle had lasted probably less than half an hour, with the fierce hand-to-hand fighting in the broken square taking only ten minutes. But it was some two hours before the clearing up was concluded and the cumbersome square fell into some sort of shape again and began its advance – even more painfully slow now because of the need to avoid causing further discomfort to the many wounded – towards the wells of Abu Klea.

As they marched away, leaving behind them the dead to be buried later, Fonthill looked up nervously to where vultures circled lazily high in the bluest of skies. He exchanged glances with Jenkins, and the Welshman nodded to him. They broke out of the square, and made their way back to where Mustapha lay. Some of the British dead, laid out neatly in rows, had been covered by sheets, and Colonel Burnaby lay under a Union Jack where he had fallen twenty yards outside the square. The two men lifted the smallest of the sheets and transferred it to cover the tiny figure of Mustapha, holding down the corners with stones. Then they rejoined the square.

The remnants of the column reached the wells of Abu Klea in the late afternoon. The waterholes consisted now of little more than a series of pits in the sand of the dried-up river bed, and what remained at the bottom had the consistency of liquid mud. But the wounded, given preference, of course, announced that it was delicious, 'like creamy chocolate'. Despite the thirst suffered by everyone in the column, the discipline of the troops queuing in orderly lines to fill their water bottles was exemplary. A detachment of volunteers was sent back to the *zariba* to bring up baggage the next day, and after guards were posted, the column settled down to bivouac in the cold. There were few blankets or overcoats, and men huddled together on the bare ground to share what heat they could.

Fonthill and Jenkins had left their blankets with Alice, and as dusk fell they walked through the lines to where the handful of journalists accompanying the march – some had opted to stay behind in the *zariba*, questioning the safety provided by the slow-moving square – were huddled together near the wounded. On the way, Simon had a brief conversation with one of Stewart's aides.

'What was that about, then?' asked Jenkins, but Fonthill merely shrugged his shoulders with the sullen lack of interest in his surroundings that he had evinced since the death of Mustapha.

'Now come on, bach sir,' cajoled the Welshman. 'The little lad fought ever so bravely an' 'e went with a smile on 'is face, thinkin' you was goin' to take 'im to Norfolk. You've got to think about the livin' now, you know, not the dead. Apart from which, 'is death wasn't Miss Alice's fault, now, was it?'

Fonthill wheeled round. 'Oh don't be stupid, man. Of course it wasn't. It was *my* fault. Neither you nor Ahmed felt it was wise to take him on that boat, but I insisted. And it was *me* who let him come with us from Khartoum – leading him into danger again. Dammit all, he was only ten years old. With his intelligence he could have had a wonderful life ahead of him. Now he's finished . . . Gawd, what sort of father would I have made?' Jenkins opened his mouth to interrupt, but Simon held up a hand. 'And I can't help feeling that Alice is quite relieved that Mustapha is gone. That's the other thing I just can't tolerate. The . . . the . . . smugness of it all, dammit . . . the *convenience* of his death.'

Jenkins wrinkled his nose. 'Well now, with respect, bach sir,' he said, 'I think that's a bit unfair. She wouldn't 'ave wanted 'im to die, would she? She's not that sort of lady. You know that.'

Simon frowned, paused and then summoned up a smile. 'You're right, of course, you tuppenny-ha'penny philosopher.

I'm feeling sad and also sorry for myself, that's what it is, and I mustn't vent my feelings on Alice. Come on. I know Abdullah is looking after her, but we should see if she's all right – and get our blankets. We're going to need them.'

They found Alice crouching with Abdullah over the remnants of a rather ineffective fire, which he had made with camel dung too recently dropped to burn well. She looked up with an apprehensive smile that made Fonthill feel ashamed of himself.

He squatted down next to her and took her hand. 'I am so sorry, Alice,' he said. 'I behaved badly to you and I do apologise. I was feeling sorry for myself.' He took her hand and kissed it.

Her eyes filled with tears and she summoned up a smile but remained silent.

'Have you had something to eat?' he asked.

'Yes, the wonderful Abdullah has never stopped looking after me. What about you?'

'Yes. The less than wonderful Jenkins served bully beef and biscuits again. I expect that if he had found some weevils he would have inserted them into the biscuits, just to be awkward.'

They all shared a smile at the feeble joke, even the ever-silent Abdullah, for it relieved the tension a little.

'What does the Brigadier intend to do now?' enquired Alice.

'I don't know. One of his aides has just told me that four Dervishes have come in and surrendered. Allegedly they were part of Hicks's force that was massacred a couple of years ago and forced to fight against us for the Mahdi. That's what they say, anyway. They have told Stewart that a large Dervish force, including men from Berber and Kodorfan and special riflemen sent by the Mahdi from Omdurman, are on their way to attack us. There are supposed to be about ten thousand of them, with an even larger number to follow. Stewart would be a strange man not to be worried, because to be honest, his little column has taken quite a hammering, and this is no country in which to fight another battle like the last one. He has called a council of war with his senior officers in about an hour's time and I have been asked to join them because of my so-called local knowledge of the way to Khartoum and conditions there.' He smiled. 'Whatever the others think, I shall urge him to go as quickly as possible. Relieving Gordon is the whole point of the exercise, after all.'

Within the hour, Fonthill was sitting in a circle outside the commanding officer's bivouac tent with a handful of Stewart's senior officers. The Brigadier relayed the news brought to him by the deserters and outlined the problems that his command faced: the difficulties of transport, since many of the camels had been killed in the battle; the need to look after the wounded; the ever-present requirement to be near a source of water; and above all, the question of whether his column was large enough and well enough equipped (with comparatively little artillery) to fight a huge, well-armed Mahdist army.

One of the colonels argued strongly that the whole force should retire to Jakdul Wells, to set up a forward position there and wait for reinforcements before marching on to attack Metemmeh. Fonthill waited his turn, then quietly outlined the desperate need to make haste to Khartoum, however small the force that could finally be sent. He repeated Gordon's belief that just two hundred redcoats would do. He argued that the deserters had given no news of the fall of Khartoum and that therefore it was fair to assume that Gordon still held out. If that was so, it was unlikely that the Mahdi and the Khalifa would release any significant number of troops from the besieging force until the city had been taken. As a result, the force marching to attack Stewart was a matter of supposition only. The column had its orders: they should continue the advance.

Perhaps the words spoken with such authority by this bearded, bedraggled Arab-looking man, still wearing an army private's coat, were more effective than those of the officers of the line, for the Brigadier then hurried to sum up. He would continue the advance in the morning, he said. His intention was to capture Metemmeh, pick up the gunboats that Gordon had sent downriver from Khartoum, which must be somewhere near there, and send a token force with them to give Gordon succour. A party would be sent back early in the morning to the scene of the battle to bury the dead; the wounded would be left at the wells of Abu Klea, guarded by a hundred men of the Sussex Regiment; Stewart's report on the battle, together with messages home from officers, the news of Fonthill's arrival and the dispatches of the war correspondents, would be sent under escort to Korti and the column, suitably lightened, would then march in all haste the remaining twenty-five miles to Metemmeh, the Nile and thence to Khartoum.

Fonthill could not resist a smile at the news of this latest chore for the men from the Sussex. It was a company of this regiment that had been left behind at Jakdul; another detachment from the same regiment had been given the dangerous and isolated job of staying in the *zariba* before the battle to protect the baggage camels and stores; and it was the Sussex who had borne much of the brunt of the fighting at the bottom of the square. Now it was men from Sussex who were to be left behind to guard the wounded. Were these good, honest infantrymen regarded as the labourers, the odd-job men, of the column? Why not give some of these chores to the Foot Guards, for instance, who had played little part in the Battle of Abu Klea? Would this be below their dignity? Simon then remembered that Stewart was himself an elite cavalryman. Ah well! He shrugged his shoulders. He supposed that this army of the Queen would never change.

Despite the late hour, Fonthill crept back to where Alice was sleeping to tell her the news. She was delighted to hear that her dispatch would be sent back for onward relay to London but, predictably, refused Simon's request that she accompany the party returning to Korti.

'Simon,' she said, running her fingers through her sleep-tousled short hair, 'there is obviously going to be more fighting yet and I must cover it. And what a coup if I could go with the relief steamers into Khartoum – what do you think the chances of that are?'

Fonthill kissed her cheek. 'Absolutely nil, I would think, my dear. You have chanced your luck very successfully to this point. Don't push it too far, right at the end.' He kissed her again and walked away through the darkness.

Jenkins was still awake when he returned. 'I've been thinking,' said the Welshman. 'What's 'appened to that bloke Captain 'Icks-Whatnot, d'you think? Wasn't 'e supposed to be lookin' after the press people? I suppose it's too much to 'ope that he got a spear through 'is wotsits durin' the battle, eh?'

'Probably. Only the good die young. Get some sleep now, because we must be up early. I want to go back with the burial party.'

They did so, and found that neither the Dervishes nor the vultures had defiled the dead, although one corner of the sheet covering Mustapha had blow free and was fluttering in the light breeze when they arrived. The scene of the battle made a melancholy sight: the bodies of the British lay in orderly rows, but the Arabs were still lying where they had fallen, in clustered, white-bundled groups marking where the fiercest fighting had been at the end of the square. Fonthill and Jenkins borrowed spades and dug out a grave, at the edge of but slightly apart from the trench that formed the massed grave of the soldiers. They then wrapped the little body in the sheet and lowered it into the grave – little more than a deep depression, in fact, so hard was the ground. Then they shovelled back the stony earth and built a low cairn of rocks. There was no wood available to cut an appropriate cross, so the cairn alone had to stand testimony to the presence of the slave boy's last remains.

The two men – under the puzzled gaze of the other gravediggers – bowed their heads in silence when they had finished, for this time Fonthill could think of nothing to say.

The silence continued as they trudged back to the column, and was only broken as Simon shook his head. 'I can't help thinking about that sword,' he said. 'How on earth would Mustapha have found a British officer's sword? And why would he use it – it would be too cumbersome for him anyway – when he so loved his trusty knife?'

Jenkins shrugged. ' 'E probably picked it up in the middle of the fight, like. An' it would please 'im to be usin' a sword of a British officer. But I know what you mean about the size of the bloody thing. It would 'ave been as long as 'im and done 'im no favours in that close-up fightin', look you.'

But Fonthill continued shaking his head.

They returned in mid-afternoon in time to see the column begin its march towards the river. This time there was no square and the troops straggled back in line some six hundred yards, with the camels all in the rear. The small group of journalists, Alice and Abdullah among them, marched in the centre. Simon knew that the column was ludicrously vulnerable but he believed passionately that the Brigadier was right to take the risk. Marching in a square would restrict their advance to a crawl. They must make haste towards Khartoum, whatever the cost. Nevertheless, as he and Jenkins fell in with the rest, he did so with a heavy heart and a sense of foreboding about Alice. How long could a lone woman survive in this straggling unit? And with Ahmed and Mustapha both gone, how many more would fall before they got to the beleaguered city on the Nile – and, for God's sake, would they be in time to relieve Gordon?

Chapter 17

Like virtually everyone else in the column, Fonthill presumed that Stewart would halt before dusk and camp for the night. Everyone – officers, men, camel drivers, the camels themselves and the handful of war correspondents still with the fighting unit – was dog tired. Water was low and in some cases non-existent, but the Nile was some twenty-four miles away and the men had had precious little sleep either before or after the battle. Sleep was taking precedence even over water. But Stewart had other ideas. Darkness stole up and there was no order to halt.

'Blimey,' said Jenkins. ' 'E's goin' to march us through the night.' And so he was. The order was given for no lights to be used nor bugle to be sounded. Stewart was intent on reaching the Nile before dawn.

The Brigadier was taking a huge risk. Officers and men began to fall asleep on their camels, and any resemblance to an orderly march disappeared with the arrival of darkness. Within a few hours the advance guard completely lost its direction and went round in a circle, suddenly finding itself following the rearguard. Many of the camels lost their loads in dense thickets of mimosa, and any pretence of maintaining silence disappeared as men swore at the top of their voices and camels squealed. The line bulged until it became a disorderly rabble of men and camels blundering through the scrub in the darkness, each rider trying desperately to follow the blurred shape of the camel in front. If the Dervishes had launched one of their rare night attacks then the column would almost certainly have been wiped out.

But they did not, and as dawn came at last, there was no sight of the enemy. Predictably, the column now bore no resemblance to a military formation and it halted as men were sent out to retrieve precious lost camels and to gather up stores that had been wantonly scattered during the night. The stop was brief, however, and the column had been marching for more than fourteen hours and had covered about eighteen miles when it set off again, with no time for breakfast.

Despite his weariness, Fonthill approved of Stewart's determination to press on. For him, the sacrifices and many tragedies of the last four months would have been worthless if the dominant aim of the column, to relieve Gordon in Khartoum, had been put aside, however temporarily, for the sake of its comfort. During the confusion of the night, he and Jenkins were asked by Stewart to ride in the van, with a captain of intelligence called Verner, to lead the way with the help of their compasses. Stewart rationalised that Fonthill and Jenkins, unlike any of the other Europeans on the march, had at least been this way before. But Simon suppressed a smile at the thought of Jenkins, whose sense of direction was as hopeless as his courage was strong, being asked to lead anybody anywhere.

Nevertheless, as the light came streaming from the east across the desolate plain, the advance guard trudged up a gravelly slope and, cresting it, looked down on a wide valley with the yellow snake of the Nile winding through it. On their side of the river stood the walled town of Metemmeh, facing, across the water, the mud huts of its sister town, Shendi. The soldiers removed their helmets and cheered.

There was no question, however, of the last four miles of their journey down to the water being uncontested. As Fonthill, Verner and Jenkins looked down, the sound of the Dervish war drums floated up to them from Metemmeh and they saw Arabs streaming out of the town like ants. At that point, the squadron of Hussars who had screened the advance during the night came trotting back to report that it had been fired on by a large number of Dervishes scattered about in the brush.

As Stewart came riding up, Fonthill looked about him. He realised that the column was in a very dangerous situation. Apart from the dreadful shortage of water and the tiredness of everyone, to the point that the men were in no state to fight another hand-to-hand battle, they were exposed on a plain with little cover, except that provided for the Arab snipers, who would soon be upon them, taking advantage of the gullies and patches of scrub. Sitting defensively in a square – which was what that particular configuration was designed for – would leave Stewart's column vulnerable to the Dervishes' fire, which had already proved to be more than effective.

The Brigadier came to the same conclusion. 'We'll fight our way through to the river, Fonthill,' he said. 'Dammit. Ought to have been here two hours ago.' He wheeled his camel around and began issuing a stream of orders. Men immediately began erecting a makeshift *zariba* of biscuit boxes and camel saddles so that they could snatch a hasty and largely dry breakfast before setting out on the last lap. It was only about two and a half feet high but it provided shelter of sorts – but only of sorts. Predictably, as soon as the rations were served, the Arab snipers began firing. Stewart had hoped that the *zariba* would be charged, but the natives were far too clever for that. They stayed in their *wadis* and behind the scrub, firing steadily and remarkably accurately.

Simon became concerned about Alice and, with Jenkins, crawled back to find her. They discovered her kneeling and desperately trying to revive Cameron, the correspondent from *The Standard*, who had been hit by a sniper's bullet. He died in her arms. St Leger Herbert, who had succeeded Alice in writing for the *Morning Post*, doubling up as secretary to Stewart, also whirled around and collapsed, killed immediately.

'Alice,' cried Fonthill. 'Please lie down. There's dammed little shelter here. Keep your head down.'

'I am doing what I can to stay alive,' Alice said, her face white, 'but I must help where I can. And anyway, I have got to see what's going on. It's my job.' She waved her notepad.

Simon sighed. 'Where's that bloody man Hicks-Johnson? Isn't he supposed to be looking after you all?'

'It seems that his commission is with the Sussex Regiment, and because the Sussex have lost officers at Abu Klea, Stewart has conscripted him into the line. He is directing the erection of the *zariba* somewhere. He was no bloody use to us anyway.' She summoned up a grin. 'And if I need looking after, I have the wonderful Abdullah here.'

She gestured to where the big Sudanese, clutching his sword once again as danger threatened, sat quite imperturbably at her side. He gave Fonthill a respectful nod of the head.

'Good man,' Simon acknowledged. 'Get her to keep her head down, there's a good chap.' A bullet sang past their heads as he spoke, emphasising the point. Abdullah acknowledged the danger to the extent that he changed his cross-legged position to one where he lay at full length, propped up on one elbow.

He was frowning, however, and something was clearly on his mind. 'Captain,' he said at last. 'Why did that officer give Mustapha his sword?'

'What?' Three heads turned towards him as one.

'Which officer?' demanded Fonthill.

'British officer who told us where to lie and ordered food. Man you do not like.'

'Hicks-Johnson!' Simon leaned forward, grabbing Abdullah by the shoulder. 'What happened?'

The Sudanese lifted up his eyebrows as he tried to recollect. 'I had helped lady up on boxes to make her safe when Dervishes attacked,' he said. 'I see you run from front and then join in fighting. Mustapha is with you at first but he cannot get near to fight with knife, so he moves away and throws stones. This officer is hiding behind camel saddles at side and firing handgun at Dervishes. He does not go near fighting with his sword. He sees Mustapha and uses hand to call him over. He draws sword and gives it to boy and points to Dervishes. Mustapha smiles, takes sword and runs into crowd. I don't see him again.'

A silence fell on the little group. Even the snipers seemed to cease their shooting for a moment to ponder what Abdullah had said.

'The bastard!' swore Jenkins.

'He killed the lad as surely as if he had cut his arm and put his sword through him himself,' murmured Fonthill. 'The swine.'

'Why he do that?' repeated Abdullah.

'Because we humiliated him when we travelled this way before,' said Simon slowly. 'He wanted to harm us and this was the safest way he could think of doing so. He knew that the boy wanted to fight and that he wouldn't last three minutes in that melee with that long sword to hamper him. The man had seen how close we were to the boy and he knew that Mustapha's loss would hit us all. This man is a coward, but only a monster would send a child to his death.'

'An' I shall kill 'im as soon as I 'ave the chance,' whispered Jenkins.

'No,' said Fonthill. 'He is an English officer. You can't just assassinate him.'

'Why not? You shot that Abu bloke through the back. What's the difference?'

'As I have said, he's an English officer and I can't allow you to kill him.'

Jenkins's face was as dark as a thundercloud. His mind went back to an orchard on a plain before Kandahar, and he opened his mouth to make the comparison but then thought better of it.

'No,' said Fonthill quietly. 'In due time we shall bring him to justice. I shall take pleasure in seeing him hang.'

'What sort of military court will take the word of a native like old Abdoolie 'ere against that of a British officer, bach sir? You know we wouldn't stand a chance.'

'We'll see about that.'

Further conversation, however, was cut short by an increase in the sniping from the Arabs. The firing now seemed to be coming from all sides and particularly from a rise in the ground to the right, from where the Dervish marksmen had the advantage of looking down on the enclosure. Stewart had sent out a company on to a small ridge in an attempt to keep down the fire, but they could see little to shoot at. Once again the cumbersome Gardner gun had been wheeled outside the *zariba* to deter an attack across the open ground, but its crew could find few targets and a spoke was broken in a wheel as it was trundled out. Volunteers were called out to leave the dubious safety of the *zariba* and take boxes to a patch of higher ground to build a redoubt there from which to command a field of fire. Thirty men doubled out across the bullet-swept terrain carrying the boxes under covering fire. A handful fell, including their officer, who had to be carried back, but again the Guardsmen could see little to aim at except puffs of smoke rising from the scrub several hundred yards away.

As the day wore on, the sun beat down and the sniping continued. The cries of the wounded now became insistent as the last of the water ran out. The camels were the most obvious target, and the loss of each one was almost as important to the beleaguered Stewart as one of his own men. Fonthill heard a heavy thud, and turned to see a camel, hit in the side and with blood oozing down its flank, continue chewing the cud as though it had only been bitten by a fly. Others, however, were lying on their sides in the middle of the square, breathing their last. Simon knew that their loss would reduce the pace of the column's advance – if it ever moved forward again, that was.

Then one of the most disturbing cries ever to be heard on a battlefield arose from the front: 'Commanding officer's been hit!'

Fonthill, Jenkins and Alice exchanged startled glances. 'Stay here with Alice,' ordered Simon. 'I'll see if I can help.' He doubled forward to the head of the zariba and found Stewart surrounded by his senior officers. A bullet had taken him in the groin. He was in great pain and the wound looked serious.

The death of Burnaby had meant that Colonel Sir Charles Wilson was now officially the second-in-command, and he was kneeling beside his stricken brigadier as Fonthill arrived. 'What are your orders, sir?' he asked.

Stewart grimaced. 'We've got to get out of here, Charles,' he said. 'If we stay we'll be picked off like skittles in an alley. Leave the guns and the Gardner in the zariba with the stores and the wounded, with enough men to protect them.

Beresford can stay with his Gardner and Colonel Barrow should be left to command in the *zariba*. You should be able to take about nine hundred men out. Form 'em in a square and march down to the Nile; take Metemmeh or establish yourself on the river. Come back and get us later. Good luck!'

Fonthill felt his heart sink as he saw the look of uncertainty immediately cross Wilson's face. He knew that the man was fundamentally a surveyor and an intelligence officer, rather than a fighting soldier, and that that was the reason Burnaby had been an unofficial second-in-command. Would this gentle, rather self-effacing man have the confidence to take command in this, the most difficult of situations? It had already been proven that a square was a poor instrument for offence. Moving it across open ground demanded great skill from everyone concerned, particularly from the man in command. If the Dervishes decided to do the sensible thing, that is, to stay behind cover and continue to direct accurate fire on the exposed moving men – as, Simon recalled, the Boers in the Transvaal would have done – then the British would stand very little chance of ever reaching the Nile. Stewart had gambled on provoking the Dervishes to charge and had won at Abu Klea. Would Wilson have the same luck?

The Colonel rose and began to make his preparations. But it became clear that his priority was in making the *zariba* as safe as he could before resuming the advance. He directed that the biscuit-box redoubt on the ridge should be strengthened, and also that the makeshift hospital in the centre of the square should be better protected. All of this demanded heavy work moving boxes under the burning sun and under unrelenting fire from the Dervish snipers, and more casualties were sustained as a result. Fonthill, soon joined by Jenkins, took his turn at tending the wounded, and Simon gave the last of his water to one of the Sussex men, shot through both lungs.

In fact, it took three and a half hours before Wilson was satisfied with the defences and had his nine hundred men formed up outside the *zariba* in a rough square at its rear. Eventually, at three p.m., the square moved off. This time Alice had been ordered to remain within the *zariba* and she stayed, kneeling waxen-faced beside Abdullah and waving the silver Colt that Simon had left with her as he and Jenkins marched away in the clumsy formation. 'Look after her, Abdullah,' called Fonthill, and the Sudanese raised the cross-handle of his sword as a crucifix in acknowledgement.

Immediately it seemed that Wilson had taken his command out of the frying pan into an even hotter fire. More Dervish marksmen had come up, and they directed their fire at the men, who were slowly stumbling across the *wadis* out in the little plain. Up ahead, Fonthill could see a cloud of Arabs gathering under the now familiar green and white banners, with a screen of horsemen out at their front. Would they charge? He hoped so, fervently. It was the only hope for the British. To carry on this advance en masse, out in the plain without cover, would just mean that they would continue to provide target practice for the Dervishes.

Every few minutes Wilson ordered the square to halt and pour rifle fire into the distant Arabs and at the still hidden snipers. But the range was too long in the first instance and the targets too elusive in the second. It seemed to Fonthill, trudging along with Jenkins, that the men of the column were now in the worst of all worlds: thirsty, hungry, tired, depleted by rifle fire and yet unable to fight back meaningfully. How long could they continue like this?

The answer came quickly. 'Here they come at last, the devils!' cried a young Guardsman. And, indeed, the Dervishes could no longer resist the temptation to charge and sweep away this contemptible little square. Led by horsemen carrying the Mahdi's banners, the tribesmen swept towards the British line on the square's front face, the spearmen screaming and forming a solid mass, the sun glinting off the tips of their weapons.

'Front rank, kneel,' commanded a voice from within the square, and then: 'Select your target. Do not fire until ordered. It will be volley fire by ranks.' The voice was calm and reassuring. Fonthill and Jenkins, in the second rank of the uniformed Guardsmen and looking completely out of place in their scruffy, ill-fitting jackets and white lower garments, exchanged uneasy grins. 'Front rank, FIRE! Front rank, reload. Second rank, FIRE!'

The volleys crashed out, but the range was too great and had little effect. 'Bloody waste of ammunition,' grumbled Jenkins. Then the order to cease firing came and the two ranks waited in silence as the Dervishes ran towards them. Simon would never forget the magnificence of the charge. It seemed as though a sea of white was approaching them at great speed, with gleaming pinpoints of sunlight shimmering from it as the Arab weapons were flourished. Thousands of slippered feet hitting the ground created a noise like thunder and a curtain of dust above the charging men.

But if the Dervishes were out of the range of the British rifles, they were just inside the range of the guns back in the *zariba*. Now the crack of the little seven-pounders sounded alongside the rat-tat-tat of the Gardner – blessedly free from jamming, for once. The shells landed within the middle of the attackers and sent up clouds of red-tinged smoke and dust, and some of the leaders fell before the sweep of the Gardner's five barrels.

'*Zariba*'s firing at 'em,' grunted Fonthill. 'That's good. It shows that they're not under attack.' He meant, of course, that Alice was not under attack, but Jenkins understood.

Then, as the horde swept on towards the square, it came within range of the rifles. The volleys rang out again, and now the firing took effect. The Dervishes went down in lines, yet still they charged, leaping over their dead as at Abu Klea. But this time there was no breaking into or even nearing of the square. All of the banner-carrying horsemen went down under the volleys, and then one white-clad figure after another behind slumped to the ground. This was what the square was designed to do. Every man in the line stood firm, firing and reloading to order so that nothing could face the hail of bullets. The charge faltered, stopped, and then the Arabs fled.

The cheering resounded throughout the British square, and Fonthill and Jenkins, their throats dry and with perspiration pouring down their dusty faces, grinned at each other and shook hands.

'The Hussars should go out after 'em now,' murmured Simon, watching as the attackers seemed to melt away in the distance. But Wilson gave no such order. Perhaps the horses were still too exhausted after their night's patrolling. Or perhaps it never occurred to an intelligence officer that cavalry pursuit was the classic tactic to employ at this point.

Jenkins took out a tattered rag and wiped his face. 'Do you think they'll 'ave another go?' he asked.

'Doubt it. I'd say there are about three hundred bodies lying out there, and goodness knows how many back at Abu Klea. This is the first time that the Mahdi's men have faced a British force. Admittedly we've taken a hell of a mauling – particularly from those snipers – but we've come off best and the news will get back to Omdurman, make sure of that. Now Wilson must press on and make the most of it.'

First, however, the Colonel took toll of his dead and wounded. None of his men had fallen to the Arab charge, for no Dervish had reached within fifty yards of the square. But the effect of the sniping earlier had been severe: one officer and twenty-two men killed and eight officers and ninety men wounded, most of the wounds serious. Once more it had been a heavy price to pay, with more than thirteen per cent of the little force taken out of action on this day. Even so, would Wilson make the most of his victory by resuming the march without further ado and reach the Nile so that water bottles could be refilled and dispositions made for the attack on Metemmeh?

It seemed that he would not. Instead he began the practice that he would follow several times over the next few days: he called a council of war.

Despite the fact that this time quite junior officers were present, Fonthill was not invited to take part. Nevertheless, he hung on to its edges. Once again opinion was divided. Some officers were for retreating to the *zariba* and advancing on the Nile the next morning, after wounds had been satisfactorily licked. 'And the wounded will die of thirst,' called Simon from the back, but no one seemed to hear. Then it was decided that an advance down the valley should be made at once, only for the decision to be countermanded by a compromise: the front face of the square, under its commander and Wilson's second-in-command, Colonel Boscawen, should advance alone the three miles or so down to the Nile. The small party set off and had gone a hundred yards when Wilson changed his mind again and the front rank was halted. Finally the order was given for the whole square to march down to the river.

As the council of war broke up, Major Gough, who remembered Fonthill from the Egyptian campaign, whispered in his ear: 'The joke of the matter is that everyone gives his opinion and advice in the freest manner, from the junior subalterns upwards, and the man who gets Wilson's or Boscawen's ear last, his advice is followed.'

Simon frowned. Was it going to be like this from now on? Would Gordon ever be rescued?

In the growing dusk, the square moved down the valley and the leaders eventually saw streaks of water appearing in a belt of green vegetation. The soldiers descended a shallow ravine at the end of which grew peas and a little *durra*, and reached the banks of the Nile by the light of a clear crescent moon.

The weary men now showed themselves at their best. Everyone was craving for water and for rest. Yet as the bank of the river was approached by moonlight, discipline was impeccably preserved. The wounded at the rear were held up so that they could see the water, and then taken down beside the bank to drink and rest. What was left of the front face of the square was allowed down to the river to drink their fill with their camels and was then marched round to the rear to protect the column from attack. The camels and the rest of the men were given water, and *durra* was cut for the animals.

It was the nineteenth of January, and the column had emerged two miles upstream of Metemmeh, their objective, which, of course, was still held by the Dervishes. Wilson had seen no evidence on the march that the Mahdi's forces in the township had been routed by their two defeats, and so, while the doctors worked on through the night, pickets were posted on the ravine to give warning of a night attack. None came, but the dawn brought no rest for the weary soldiers. Two tasks faced Wilson: the establishment of some kind of stronghold on the river bank where his column could be concentrated for the attack on Metemmeh; and the dispatch of a strong unit back the way they had come to retrieve the men, particularly the wounded, and the stores left in the *zariba*, some twenty-four miles back in the hills.

Reconnaisance parties ranged apprehensively – for there were many signs that the Dervishes were in the area in some strength – along the river bank, and it was decided to convert a collection of mud huts into a fortress the Colonel called Gubat. Metemmeh could clearly be seen from the roofs of the huts, and predictably, Wilson called a meeting to consider whether an attack should be launched on the town right away. Fonthill, who sat in on this meeting, was himself torn between attacking immediately – and so hastening the relief of Gordon – or relieving those left behind (Alice!) in the *zariba*, and so he kept quiet. The balance of opinion was that it would be prudent to maximise the number of men available to Wilson for the attack, and also to bring up the two cannon and the Gardner. The decision was taken, therefore, to send a strong unit back into the hills as soon as possible.

Fonthill and Jenkins, of course, volunteered to join the six hundred men detailed to trek back up into the hills. It took two and a half hours to complete the journey in daylight, and although Dervishes could be seen on all sides as they marched, they were not attacked. Simon had his worst moment when he saw two camels bearing the red saddle blankets of the camel corps being led away by Arabs as they neared the *zariba* (why had he thought for even one moment that it was more important to press on to Khartoum than to rescue Alice?). But relief set in all around when it could be seen that the little fortress was still intact, and the defenders stood on the makeshift walls and raised three cheers to welcome the relief force.

In a moment, Alice was in Simon's arms and, more importantly, drinking from his water bag. Wiping her lips, she passed it on to Abdullah and then explained that there had been no attack on the *zariba* during the night, but that the camel drivers had plundered the stores. It seemed that neither Beresford nor Barrow, the two officers in command, had set adequate guards for the stores, and boxes had been broken open and their contents scattered around. More importantly, however, more than a hundred camels were found to be in such bad shape that they had to be shot, depleting even further the slender transport resources of the column.

'But does this matter so much?' asked Alice. 'Weren't Gordon's paddle steamers waiting for you when you reached the Nile?'

After the safety of Alice, this was the factor weighing most heavily on Fonthill's mind. He shook his head sadly. 'No. But we didn't stay there long. Perhaps they will have shown up by the time we get back. After all, Metemmeh looks as though it is strongly occupied. They couldn't exactly anchor just off the town, now could they? Maybe they are upriver somewhere, lying in a safe anchorage, waiting for us to arrive.'

Alice nodded in agreement. But she could see the anxiety that lay behind Simon's seeming optimism. Khartoum was almost one hundred miles away. If Gordon was still alive, his ammunition and food must be almost exhausted. It would take the column many days to fight its way down on foot. How the hell could the General be saved if his little penny steamers did not turn up?

Chapter 18

Lord Beresford took time off from nurturing his Gardner gun to read a burial service over the dead (no chaplain had accompanied the column). Then the remaining stores were loaded and, without further ado, the men set off on their march back down to the Nile. There was no attempt at attacking them, although Dervishes could be seen shadowing them most of the way. Importantly, Brigadier Stewart had borne the journey down to Gubat very well, and he announced that he would attack Metemmeh the next day.

By the next morning, however, his condition had deteriorated, and Wilson spent the day improving the defences of Gubat while he pondered how to attack the little town two miles away. For Fonthill this procrastination was infuriating, but he could make no formal protest; the steamers had not arrived and the column had its orders to occupy the town and set up a firm base on the Nile. There seemed no alternative. And how could he protest anyway? He held no formal rank in the army, and although it was known that he enjoyed the support of Lord Wolseley, the Commander-in-Chief was a hundred and eighty miles away in Korti, with no telegraphic communication to link him. Fonthill was a supernumerary who carried no weight in Gubat. He was superfluous and, he felt, increasingly impotent.

Those feelings mounted the following day when Wilson,

now more fully in command with Stewart's condition worsening, paraded most of his fit troops, some nine hundred men, towards Metemmeh – and then past it. It was clear that neither the Colonel, nor his second-in-command, Colonel Boscawen, knew quite what to do. The town showed not the least sign of being intimidated by the force outside its walls. The Mahdi's banners still flew above its rooftops, and rifle fire was directed at the British from loopholes in the walls. There was going to be no surrender, and the Dervishes would have to be prised out. Martialling his troops in the awkward square formation, Wilson marched them around the town in what he later euphemistically called 'a reconnaissance in force' and then left them in parade ground order under the sun for some three hours in front of the walls. The two seven-pounder guns were deployed and their shot went clean through the mud walls without causing very much damage; it did, however, provoke a response from an ancient cannon on the ramparts, which fired a round shot that killed a camel and wounded an infantryman.

'This is ridiculous,' fumed Fonthill. He and Jenkins, still wearing their ill-fitting khaki jackets and tattered Arab nethergarments, were allowed, it seemed, to wander about at will, for no self-respecting officer would have them defile the ranks of his troops – although the uniforms of the men were becoming almost as dishevelled. They stood on the edge of the square, becoming more and more restive in the hot sun as they watched the two colonels ride round the walls, just out of gunshot range.

Wilson's predicament was providentially solved by the sudden and joyously welcomed appearance of four steamers from upriver, the *Bordein, Telahawieh, Safieh* and *Tewfikieh*, all flying the Khedive's flag and approaching the shore where the square was formed up. Wilson and Boscawen immediately rode to greet them as the boats grounded on the river bank. Fonthill and Jenkins watched as a stream of tall, very black men, wearing fezes, smart shirts, cartridge belts and carrying rifles, doubled on to the shore. Then a further detachment carried ashore two brass cannon, which were manhandled into line with the column's seven-pounders. One of the black Sudanese, who appeared to be in command of the steamers, conferred with Wilson, and then the four guns opened up together on the walls of Metemmeh and continued firing for an hour, with no discernible results. At the end, belatedly, the infantry were allowed to march back to Gubat.

'The man's a bloody disgrace,' swore Fonthill as they ambled back behind the men, who had been permitted to break square and march in file. 'I don't know what that was all about. He has wasted precious ammunition, kept most of his command standing doing nothing in the sun and sustained another wounded man. If he wanted to make a reconnaissance of the town, he could have done that by going out with just a company. But now that the boats have arrived, he could have loaded them up straight away and sent them back upriver to Khartoum. As it is . . .' He shook his head in sad astonishment.

'P'raps we're goin' to 'ave another jolly little meeting,' mused Jenkins.

And so it proved.

This time Wilson brought to his council of war the grey-bearded and squat Sudanese Khashm-el-Mus, who was in command of the boats. Fonthill, once again hanging on the edge of the meeting, uninvited, remembered that Gordon considered him one of his best men. The black man, speaking with unusual authority, given that he was in white company, said that he did not believe Khartoum had fallen since his departure, and urged that the steamers should take extra troops – his own men on board numbered some two hundred – and return to the city at once. But Wilson demurred. He had heard rumours that a force of Dervishes was coming from the south to attack him, to be joined possibly by another from Berber in the north. He would need to consider the position of his force at Gubat, he said, and also to study messages from Gordon that had been delivered by Khashm-el-Mus.

As the meeting broke up without resolution, Fonthill strode towards the Colonel. Immediately his way was barred by Hicks-Johnson, whom he had not seen since the night before the Battle of Abu Klea, but who now moved out of the shadows to put out a restraining hand.

'The Colonel does not wish to be disturbed,' he said. 'I have been appointed his ADC, and I can assure you that there is no way you can see him.'

Fonthill stood for a moment regarding the man. He could not help but notice that no Sam Browne belt crossed his chest and that therefore he could not carry a sword. 'Where the hell is your sword?' he hissed.

Hicks-Johnson seemed quite unfazed. 'None of your business,' he said. 'Now stand aside.'

Simon turned as though to move away, then sent his left hand in a straight-armed, open-palmed jab that caught Hicks-Johnson in the chest and sent him crashing into a folding chair erected outside the Colonel's tent. Without a backward glance, Fonthill walked into the tent, coughed and said, 'I beg your pardon for marching in like this, sir, but I do need an urgent word with you.'

Wilson was perched on the edge of his camp bed, with a bundle of papers in his hand. 'I am sorry, er, young man, but I am very busy. Please come back later.'

'I am sorry to insist, sir, but I must talk to you now.'

The tent flap was pulled back and a red-faced Hicks-

Johnson edged into the interior. 'This man is dangerous, sir,' he said. 'He has just used force to gain entrance to you, and I—'

Fonthill spoke quickly but calmly. 'Captain Hicks-Johnson prevented me from seeing you, sir. You should know that I shall be preferring well-substantiated and most serious charges against him to Lord Wolseley – to whom, as you may know, I report – on my return to Korti. But that is of no matter at the moment. I must talk to you now about the position of General Gordon. I was the last white man to see him. The matter is most urgent.'

'The man is a liar, sir, and—'

Wilson rose, his face seeming even whiter than usual in the shade of the tent. He put up his hand to interrupt Hicks-Johnson. 'You will have your chance to respond to these extraordinary charges in due course. Now, I see no alternative to seeing, ah, Mr . . . ?'

'Fonthill, sir. Formerly of the 24th of Foot and latterly captain in the Queen's Own Corps of Guides, Indian Army. The General has given me the rank of major while I am on assignment to him. You will remember that I joined you all just before Abu Klea.'

Wilson nodded to Hicks-Johnson. 'That will be all, thank you.' The captain, his face suffused, turned and left. 'Yes, Fonthill, I saw you fight well there.' His face looked worn and it was clear that field command sat very heavily on his shoulders. 'However, look here. You cannot use violence towards my staff. I don't care who you are or however important you say your mission is.' His face darkened. 'What's more, I have to tell you that before riding with this column I was second-in-command of Lord Wolseley's intelligence operation for the expeditionary force, and I know nothing about you being sent to Khartoum. If you are who you say you are, then surely I would have been informed, don't you think?'

Fonthill sighed inwardly. Once again the rigidity of senior officers was being demonstrated: the 'outside my experience therefore it can't be true' syndrome; the protection of personal position and dignity – just as he had seen in Zululand and the Transvaal. He struggled to keep his temper.

'I understand your puzzlement, sir. But I have worked with Lord Wolseley on a personal relationship basis in South Africa and in Egypt. He used me in this way to complement the usual channels of the army, and he preferred, I believe, to keep the matter confidential. A telegraph message to him would confirm this, of course, but I know that is not possible. However, Brigadier Stewart was aware of my work in Egypt at Tel el Kebir and so perhaps he can speak for me.'

'Humph. He is very ill, as you know, and I certainly do not wish to bother him. What is it you have to say that is so urgent?'

'Thank you, sir. Now, I was on the edge of your meeting a few minutes ago. I understand your concern about the safety of your command here, but I also know that Brigadier Stewart's orders were not only to take Metemmeh and establish a safe base on the banks of the Nile, but also to act immediately to send a force to Khartoum as soon as you have news of General Gordon. You now have news of him, I understand, from the steamers as well as from me.'

'That's all very well, but I cannot just charge off with a handful of chaps straight into the forty thousand men that the Mahdi allegedly has investing Khartoum.'

'With respect, sir, you can if you have the means of steaming upriver. And now you do. I agree that it won't necessarily be easy, but I did command a couple of those steamers during my short stay with General Gordon and I know that the Dervishes find it difficult to attack them from the river banks. They *can* get through. I do advise you to send them back immediately, sir.'

A silence fell between them. Simon felt he could see the working of Wilson's mind. He was an honourable man and certainly no fool. He did not want to be the officer who refused to grasp the last chance of rescuing Gordon, or delayed the opportunity to do so. Nevertheless, Chinese Gordon was not universally popular in the army (Buller, Wolseley's chief of staff, had famously said of him, 'He's not worth the camels it would take to get him out of there') and Wilson now had command here with the responsibility of keeping his column intact in fiercely hostile territory. What if he sent away the pick of his troops in these rather pathetic little steamers to rescue this religious fanatic and the men left at Gubat were overwhelmed by the Dervishes who were rumoured to be on their way to do just that? His career – as well as, probably, his life – would be over.

Fonthill pressed on. 'As I told the Brigadier, I left General Gordon in mid-November. He told me then that he could hold out until, well, approximately now. But he is a determined man and has organised his defences well. I have seen them. He is not going to surrender ever, that is for certain. Colonel, every day – no, every hour, every damned minute – is vital. I urge you to send troops on those steamers now. I will go with them to guide them.'

'Hmmph. What about that Mahdi army that is supposed to be marching north along the river to attack me?'

Simon decided to gamble. 'A force of that size, even one marching in the desert rather than following the river, would have been seen by Khashm-el-Mus from the river as it marched north. But he has not reported such an advance to you, has he?'

The gamble half succeeded. 'I understand that the force

advancing was deterred from going further by news of our success at Abu Klea, but one never knows.' Wilson glanced up. 'Look here, Fonthill, you urge me to move fast. Yet it is more than two months since you left Khartoum. I did not quite catch your explanation to the Brigadier when you arrived. What took you so long?'

Fonthill sighed. This was proving harder than he'd anticipated. 'Jenkins, my man, and I were captured by the Dervishes just after we had crossed the river,' he explained. 'We were shackled in the Mahdi's camp at Omdurman for some five weeks before we were able to escape.' (Better not muddy the waters by bringing in Alice at this point.) Was Wilson unbelieving? He looked sceptical. 'Look here, I can prove it to you.'

He unbuttoned his jacket, slipped off his shirt and turned his back towards the Colonel. 'We were ordered to be lashed by the Khalifa. The splendid little Egyptian who was with us died as a result, and as you can see, I received fifty lashes.'

'Good God!' The expression on Wilson's face betrayed a mixture of disgust and regret that he had doubted this man. 'My word, Fonthill, I am sorry. Do sit down, there's a good fellow.' He looked away as Simon pulled on his shirt and jacket, then indicated the several pieces of paper he had scattered on the bed. 'You can help me with these, I am sure. They are messages from Gordon that have been delivered by the fellow in charge of the blacks – what's his name?'

'Khashm-el-Mus, sir.'

'Yes, quite so. I am afraid they are confusing – as I have been led to believe so many of General Gordon's messages have been in the past. Look here, this letter addressed to one of the General's old friends, Colonel Watson, is dated the fourteenth of December. It says, "I think the game is up" and talks about a possible catastrophe in about ten days' time.

There's a much earlier one – before your arrival there – addressed to Lord Wolseley about the soldiers on board the steamers, and then the last one, here. As you can see, it's scribbled in Gordon's own hand and carries his seal.'

Fonthill took the folded scrap of paper and read: *December 29th. Khartoum all right. Could hold out for years.*

Wilson grunted. 'You see. Contradictory. What am I to make of all that?'

Simon handed back the paper. 'Well, sir. From my own observation of him, General Gordon is clearly under great strain, to the point where, even during my short stay there, he was rather up and down in temperament. You must remember, however, that he knew that many of his messages sent downriver had been intercepted by the Mahdi, and he wasn't above putting in the odd one to deceive him. I should think that this last message falls into that category.' He leaned forward in emphasis. 'However, on two points you can be sure. Firstly, the General would never, *never* surrender. He would fight to the last. And secondly, if Khartoum had fallen, the news would have been flashed down the river as quickly as if it had been sent by cable wire. In my view, the city is still being defended, Gordon is still alive and you probably just have time to relieve him if you set off without further delay. It doesn't need an army. The General asked me to emphasise that just two hundred redcoats would have the desired psychological effect. They could be carried on the steamers. Sir Charles, if you act quickly you can still save the day.'

Silence hung once again between the two of them. Eventually Wilson collected Gordon's notes and nodded to Fonthill. 'Thank you for your information and your advice. I will give careful thought to all you have said. You have to understand that I must weigh the balance between leaving this camp without proper defences and the need to steam upriver. Certainly it is my duty to see that this small force, which has been so roughly handled on its march to the Nile, is safe from immediate attack. Now, Fonthill, do go and get whatever refreshment you can. You have done well.'

Fonthill rose, made a half-bow to the Colonel and retired. There was no sign of Hicks-Johnson outside the tent, but the camp was all a-bustle and it was clear that Wilson had already given orders to begin improving the defences of the encampment. As he walked down towards the river, Simon could see that the existing situation was not ideal. If the Mahdist army did arrive and launch an attack, then Gubat could be cut off from the river and the source of water. If the camp was moved down to the river, then it could be fired on from the high ground on which Gubat stood. Fonthill smiled when he saw what was happening. Typically, Wilson had decided on a compromise: the Guards and some other troops were being left to hold Gubat, while the rest of the column, with the wounded, was being moved down to the bank of the river. He shrugged his shoulders. Perhaps the Colonel was right. Anyway, he was now too tired to care. Had he done enough to persuade Wilson to set off for Khartoum without delay? Perhaps, but probably not. The man was a thinker – his career and reputation as a good surveyor and intelligence officer proved that. But sometimes it was better not to overintellectualise a situation. A soldier should be a man of action, after all. Simon sighed and set off to find Alice.

With the rest of the small band of correspondents, she had been moved down to the banks of the Nile, which was to be the main encampment now. It was sloping and, inevitably, rather damp, and the journalists had given up the few tents they had to the wounded. Alice was sitting under a rough shelter of old sacking and blankets that had been made for her by Abdullah. She was applying a field dressing to Jenkins's arm.

'How's the wound?' asked Fonthill.

'It's 'avin' a bit of lovin' care an' attention now, thank you, bach sir. And not before time, I must say. A wounded 'ero deserves a bit of care, look you.'

'Yes, well don't give him too much, Alice. It will only spoil him.'

They all exchanged grins. 'How did you get on with the Colonel?' asked Alice.

Simon gave a sigh and lowered himself on to the damp ground. 'I don't know. He's no fool, but he's not a fighting soldier and he's very cautious. He seems reluctant to set off for Khartoum before everything is watertight here. In some ways, I can sympathise with him. The column has taken quite a beating. Its commander is clearly dying, and the man – a good soldier – who would have taken over is dead; rations are low, and I doubt if we can live off the country; ammunition, particularly for the guns, is running down; and Dervishes are all around. Yet relieving Gordon is what the column was sent out to do, and that should be given priority. After all, the two things are not mutually exclusive. Wilson could go off with the steamers and Boscawen could set things up here.' He wiped his brow. 'I don't know why the bloody man can't make up his mind.'

Alice tied the bow firmly on Jenkins's bandage. 'Well, I think the press has given him a bit of a roasting on this stupid parading around Metemmeh,' she said. 'I know I have. Such time-wasting posturing.'

'But you can't get your story sent, can you?'

'Not at the moment, but I understand that Wilson is determined to send an armed column back to Jakdul Wells with his report to Wolseley, and we are hoping that our dispatches can go as well.'

'Are you being censored?'

Alice grinned. 'Since Hicks-Johnson has been forced to become a fighting soldier . . .'

'I'm not so sure of that. He is now the Colonel's ADC, and I have just had a brush with him.'

'Well, whatever has happened to him, censorship seems to have been another casualty of the attacks, I am glad to say, and we have all been quite open in our reporting.'

'Good. But don't be too hard on old Wilson. He was not trained for this sort of thing.'

'Then he shouldn't be out here.'

'I'm always available to take command,' said Jenkins.

'Oh good. Now we can all sleep safely in our beds.' Fonthill stretched out, closed his eyes and was soon fast asleep.

The steamers were not dispatched the next day, the twenty-second of January, and Wilson let it be known that he felt that a delay of one or two days before sailing upriver would make very little difference. Instead he busied himself with making the defences at Gubat more secure. Several of the mud houses in the village there were blown up and the debris used to construct a fort, commanding the prospect to the river, where the main encampment was now being entrenched. Two screw guns were placed on the ramparts, although they only had eighty-three shells left between them. In the afternoon, Sir Charles decided that he would set out with three of the steamers, the *Tela-hawieh, Bordein* and *Safieh*, but he headed not south, towards Khartoum, but north past Metemmeh. He wished to recon-noitre the ground there, because he had heard a rumour that a force might be advancing on him from Berber. The Hussars on their little horses were sent to scout towards the south.

To his surprise, Fonthill was asked to join Wilson on board the *Telahawieh* for the excursion, either because his reference to commanding one of the penny steamers at Khartoum had impressed the Colonel, or because the latter wished to involve him more, now that the whip of Abu Din had given his story credence.

He climbed aboard, then, with interest. The steamers, as always, looked ugly, strange, very unmaritime vessels from the shore, with wooden planking standing vertically at various heights around their boilers and cannon, leaving only the tall smokestack poking above. The interiors of the boats, however, were even more striking. The holds forrard were crammed with ammunition, *durra*, wool and fuel, while those amidships revealed a cargo far more varied. The steamers, of course, had set out several months ago and it, seemed, had endured a variety of vicissitudes on the way, but the length of the voyage had necessitated the taking aboard of the sailors' wives and children, plus slave girls to do the cooking. They were all ensconced in the main hold, with their bedding and cooking implements, and all sharing the crowded, pungent space with goats and swarms of rats.

Fonthill wrinkled his nose at the smell but gratefully accepted a gift of a *durra* cake from one of the girls all the same. He hurried to help on board Lord Charles Beresford, who, now that the boats had appeared, had eschewed his Gardner gun and become a naval lieutenant once again. The problem was, however, that after surviving the Dervish charge at Abu Klea, he had now developed a large boil on his bottom, which meant that, once aboard, he had to be taken to a cabin, where he lay in embarrassed and painful inactivity.

His indisposition, in fact, was rather more serious than merely the pain the noble lord was experiencing. All of the other naval officers who had marched with the Naval Brigade were now either killed or wounded, and Beresford was very much needed. In fact, Fonthill was informed that one of the correspondents, Ingram of *The Illustrated London News*, had been pressed into service and appointed naval lieutenant to serve on the steamers. It seemed that he had had some sailing experience. Given his own stint as commander for two hours of the good ships *Ismailia* and *Husseinieh*, Simon could not help feeling that he should have been offered admiral's rank, at least. And what would Alice think of one of her competitors being allowed to get into the thick of it? He smiled at the thought.

He also could not help but wonder why Wilson was so anxious at the lack of authorised naval presence on the boats. What was wrong with the skill and experience of Khashm-el-Mus and his crew, who had brought the boats safely through cataracts and, no doubt, under Dervish fire, as far as Metemmeh? As though to echo his thoughts, he saw that Gordon had put up a sign in the saloon of the *Telahawiah*, commending its black crew, saying that they had given good service and asking that Englishmen coming aboard should be considerate to them. He smiled sadly at this memorial to the open-minded kindness of the General.

Whatever the state of the boats, their engines were sound enough, and when, with a toot of the whistle, the vessels put out from the bank, they set up a savage turmoil of water behind them. With the current in their favour, of course, they surged downriver and passed Metemmeh quickly, exchanging artillery fire briefly and abortively with both the walled township and the village of Shendi opposite.

And that was as long as the excitement lasted. The voyage produced no sign or news of any force advancing from Berber. Nothing inhabited the sandy wastes of the river banks on either side of the *Telahawiah* but a few Bedawi, goats and the odd crocodile sunning himself. As the hours ticked away, and more and more precious fuel – for timber was as scarce as waterholes in the Sudan – was thrown into the boilers, Fonthill became increasingly angry at the pusillanimous nature of Colonel Sir Charles Wilson. Was the man deliberately wasting time to hasten the end of General Gordon? To Simon's mind, coloured by the deaths of Ahmed and Mustapha and conditioned by the ever-present imperative over the last seven months to make haste, it seemed so. To put it more crudely, these boats were Gordon's and he had sent them downstream to bring back the vanguard of the relieving force, not to be used as a scouting tool by a timorous colonel.

The last straw came when, on their return in the evening, Wilson announced that they would not be setting off for Khartoum on the following morning because the boats had insufficient fuel for the journey. Fonthill stalked off without a word to anyone, furious at the waste of time and resources being displayed.

The next day parties were sent to range the river banks to cut down the natives' waterwheels as fuel for the boat boilers. Riflemen had to be sent with them to protect them, and this, of course, took up more time. The women and other super-numeraries had to be cleared out of the boats and replaced by fighting men and sailors. Wilson had decided to take only two of the steamers with him to Khartoum, the *Bordein* and the *Telahawieh*, which would tow a nuggar carrying a cargo of grain for the starving garrison. The other two vessels would stay to form part of the defences of the encampment.

Twenty men of the Sussex Regiment, accompanied, Fonthill noted coldly, by Hicks-Johnson, and nearly two hundred and fifty Sudanese soldiers were to be divided between the two craft. The famous red coats, on which Gordon had set so much store, had long since been lost or destroyed, so the Sussex men were given red serge jumpers belonging to the Guards instead. They proved far too big for them, but were useful, in fact, for huddling in overnight as they slept without cover on the cold and damp river bank beside the boats.

Simon sent a message to Sir Charles asking to be allowed to accompany the mission, with Jenkins, pointing out their experience of sailing the route and, indeed, of handling the two steamers at Omdurman. If the request had been refused, he had decided that somehow he would stow away, with or without Jenkins. But the Colonel replied quickly, saying that the two would be most welcome.

By the time the work had been finished, Wilson decided – predictably – that it would be too late to raise steam that night and that the expedition to the north would set out as soon after dawn as possible on the morrow. That evening, a convoy started its long march back to the wells of Jakdul. The camels carried letters and dispatches, including those from the correspondents. It was a light load, but the camels were in a dreadful state, their backs sore and their ribs showing through their flanks, though they were the best that could be found. With them went three hundred men, leaving behind just nine hundred fit men, with four hundred camels and a hundred horses.

With the letters was one dictated by Brigadier Stewart to his old friend and mentor, Lord Wolseley. This had given employment to Alice, who had received a message from the sick man explaining that as he was too weak to write himself, and as his previous secretary, the correspondent of Alice's old newspaper, the *Morning Post*, had been killed, would she be kind enough to take his dictation and write the letter in her fair hand? She was, of course, and later that evening she told Fonthill of its contents, as best she remembered them. It ran:

I am too much ashamed of myself. Here I am, instead of being of use to you, a horrible encumbrance on your hands. Never was such bad luck. I was walking round entreating the men to get something into their stomachs before advancing, when I was rolled over. I hope and believe that we have carried out all your orders. We have not taken Metemmeh but we are established on the Nile in a better position than Metemmeh itself.

. . . Wilson goes on to Khartoum, which is much the best thing as he is a politician not a soldier. I have told Beresford to remain here to command sea forces and Boscawen commands on land. They come and talk things over with me and everything I am sure will be all right. You only want the troops you proposed and some groceries by the Jakdul line and Earle at Berber to finish the whole thing to perfection . . . The doctors all said I was a dead one and I was so knocked out of tune by the shock which paralysed my side that I was disposed to agree with them, but I am beginning to hope that I may have the honour of once again working with you . . .

Alice put down her notes, and Fonthill enquired, 'And *will* he work with him again, do you think?'

She shook her head. 'He is dying, Simon, and I think he knows it. He was just putting up a show for the General. They can't remove the bullet and I doubt if he will last a day or two more.'

'I am sorry. He was a very good solider and we shall miss him. Strange, though, that reference to him being consulted. I got the impression that Wilson was becoming more and more in charge – although it is certainly true that he asks everyone's advice before he makes a decision.'

'Simon.' Alice's tone had changed. 'I want very much to go

on a boat with you to Khartoum. All requests of this nature from the press – including mine – have been refused. Which makes it all the more infuriating that Ingram, of *The Illustrated London News*, is going as a naval lieutenant, just because he once rowed a boat on the Serpentine or something. At least he's a weekly and I can beat him to publication.'

'Alice, I have no influence . . .'

'I know that. But you can smuggle me aboard. You know you can. I can be a slave girl and do the cooking. I am still blacked up and in the right garb. I—'

Fonthill shook his head. 'Sorry, my love. Firstly, the women have all been cleared out and you would be spotted a mile away if you tried to steal aboard. Secondly, I am sorry, but I think it is just too dangerous.'

'Huh! More dangerous than being left here protected only by soggy trenches and twitchy men who see a Dervish behind every bush? They've got little ammunition and half of them are ill. Goodness, if the Mahdi doesn't get me, then fever and the flies will. Oh Simon, do help me to get aboard. Rescuing Gordon will be the story of the century, and I must be there to write it.'

Fonthill shifted uneasily. 'I see that, my love, but I can't do it. I really can't. Having you on board to worry about would be unfair to both 352 and me. I am probably going to have trouble with Wilson, not to mention Hicks-Johnson. The relationship between you and me is now well known, and if you were to be discovered – as inevitably you would be – then I should probably be clapped in irons and couldn't do my job. I am sorry, but you must stay here.'

Alice scowled. 'If *I* hadn't worried about *you* then you would still be chained to a post at Omdurman.'

He winced. 'I know that, and you know that I am more grateful to you than I can ever express. But what you ask is just not possible. I promise you that when we get back, I will give you all the inside details of what has happened. Even about the court-martial charge brought against me when I have hit Wilson.'

She forced a smile. 'Well we *will* have words about this when you get back, Captain, Major, Mr – whatever you are – bloody Fonthill. I promise you that.' Then she allowed him to kiss her.

The next morning, the little flotilla left its anchorage. There were delays even up to the end, and it was not until eight o'clock that the steam whistles tooted and the paddles began to churn the muddy water. The two steamers made a strange sight, with their wooden palisades standing up vertically in jagged lines around the boilers and cabin, and timber sleepers lashed together horizontally to protect the decks and gun positions. They looked more like timber barges on the Thames than gunships, the commercial nature of their appearance given credence by the cargo of grain yawing behind the *Telahawieh*.

Alice, standing on the river bank waving her handkerchief, a silent Abdullah at her side, could not help feeling that it was not the most impressive little fleet ever sent to rescue a beleaguered general. At least she had the consolation of knowing that Ingram of *The Illustrated London News* had been left behind to help with the two vessels staying at Gubat. But there were tears in her eyes as she waved until the steamers turned a bend in the river and she saw their smoke gradually disappearing behind a low hill.

Chapter 19

The original intention had been that men of the Naval Brigade should man the steamers, but their casualties had been so high that this proved impossible. The last survivor of its officers was Lord Beresford, whose painful condition had grown worse, forcing him to retreat to the makeshift hospital at Gubat. Wilson therefore took with him two men of his staff, Captain Gascoigne and Lieutenant Stuart-Wortley, and two officers of the Sussex Regiment, Captains Trafford and Hicks-Johnson. In the absence of the Navy, Khashm-el-Mus was given nominal command of Wilson's boat, the *Bordein*. He spoke very poor English, however, and Wilson's orders to him had to be passed through an interpreter. Trafford was in charge of the *Telahawieh*, and his orders were conveyed to the crew via the pidgin Arabic of Stuart-Wortley.

On the roof of the *Bordein*'s deckhouse, Wilson had ordered a small timber redoubt to be erected in which ten men of the Sussex were stationed, in case, it was said, the Sudanese mutinied. Fonthill's lip curled at this, for the black men's loyalty had been well proven by their successful long journey, without a white man in command, and their prompt arrival. And if further proof was needed, each man proudly wore one of Gordon's Khartoum medals on his chest. It was certainly not their fault that four days had been wasted at Gubat before the paddles turned to take the boats to the north.

It had become clear within a few hours of sailing that the position on board of Fonthill and Jenkins was anomalous to the point that it would have been uncomfortable if they had been protective of rank and position. The fact, however, that they had no clearly defined duties and that, despite Simon's temporary rank, which was senior to everyone on board except Wilson, he was not invited to eat in the deckhouse with the officers did not concern them unduly. Fonthill had long since given up worrying about status – except, that is, when he had to pull rank, as with his fracas with Hicks-Johnson. For his part, Jenkins regarded rank, when he thought about it at all, as something to be ignored, except, of course, when someone holding it had to be corrected – as when he had hit a colour sergeant and been reduced to the ranks and the glasshouse prison at Aldershot as a result.

Accordingly, they ate quite happily with the Sudanese, squatting on deck, while Wilson and his officers dined in the deckhouse. Fonthill watched the river ahead diligently, remembering his boast to the Colonel that, having been upriver before, he could be useful on the voyage. In fact, of course, he realised that he could recall little of the vagaries of the Nile from their passage on the *filuka*, and that in any case, Khashm-el-Mus was vastly more competent than he to navigate the boat between the rocks and sand bars that were beginning to show themselves now. He and Jenkins therefore occupied themselves in stripping and cleaning their rifles and the Colt revolver that the Welshman retained, Simon having given his to Alice.

The day passed quietly enough, although Fonthill realised that, whatever other problems might present themselves, the voracious appetite of the steamers' boilers alone meant that this would not be a swift passage. It became necessary, once or twice a day, to anchor and send an armed party ashore to break up the Sudanese waterwheels and the occasional wooden hut that appeared on the river bank, and row the debris back to feed the boilers. In addition to delaying the progress of the expedition, these excursions caused great hardship to the natives living along the river bank. Without their wheels they could not draw water; without water they could not grow their crops; and without crops they would starve. It was an act of unthinking and gratuitous cruelty. But where else could timber be found to fuel the voracious appetite of the engines? Simon sighed and shrugged his shoulders. The riverside dwellers were just the latest casualties in this miserable war.

They saw little of Hicks-Johnson. It had become clear that he was junior to Captain Trafford and he seemed to have been put in command of the men of the Royal Sussex who were manning the little fortress on the deckhouse. Occasionally these men were called into action to return the desultory fire of Dervishes on either bank, but there was no sign of a Mahdist army moving south towards the garrison at Gubat.

The next day was similarly featureless, but it was clear that the Nile was falling, and when, about an hour before sunset, the *Bordein* approached the Sixth Cataract, even Fonthill, anxious always to push on, felt it wise to anchor for the night before attempting to thread their way between the rocks. But Wilson insisted on continuing, and just as everyone felt that they had successfully negotiated the rapids, the steamer struck a rock and stuck fast on it. Until long after nightfall abortive attempts were made to refloat the vessel, and eventually it was decided to spend the night where she lay, with the water surging past her allowing little sleep for anyone.

The next morning the boat's tender took a party of soldiers ashore to stand guard as the stores and ammunition were unloaded to lighten the vessel and hawsers were attached and anchors taken downstream. After several hours of hard work she was refloated, and it was found that her bottom was miraculously undamaged. Everything was reloaded and the voyage resumed against the swift torrent, only for the *Bordein* to run aground again a little further ahead, this time on a sandbank. By the time the hauling had been repeated and the vessel broke free, it was dusk again and she had to be anchored once more for the night. Only three miles had been made during the course of the day.

'It would 'ave been quicker to 'ave swum to Kartoom,' sniffed Jenkins.

At last they were through the cataracts, and on the morning of the twenty-eighth of January, a wider, level flow of the river told them that they were nearing Khartoum. Fonthill was invited into the deckhouse to give advice, together with Khashm-el-Mus, on the approach to the city and the severity of the gauntlet that would have to be run before they could reach the protection of Gordon's guns. A tribesman had shouted the news to them from the bank that Omdurman had been overrun some time ago and that the fort there would have its guns trained on the river. Simon had seen how close the fort had come to falling and how only the intervention of the two steamers had driven off the attackers. He was forced to admit that it was unlikely that Omdurman could have held out for the following two months. But Khartoum itself . . . ? He bit his lip.

Excitement ran high throughout the boat that morning at the thought that everyone on board would soon meet General Gordon at last. But this was not shared by Simon, who stared ahead, eyes wrinkled, desperately trying to catch the first sight of the palace. A heavy presentiment of disaster had begun to hang over his head like a cloud. There had been so much suffering, so many good men killed on his previous journey to

Khartoum and back that he could not bring himself to believe that it was all going to be justified at last by a handshake from the man with the kindly blue eyes and grey hair. Even if the city was still holding out, would the presence of two hundred and fifty men and two steamers make much difference? Gordon had been under siege now for nearly a year. Desertion would have reduced his defenders considerably, and his food and ammunition must be virtually exhausted. Instead of an army of redcoats, they were bringing just twenty white soldiers in oversized red jerseys.

As midday neared, it was obvious that they were now entering the Mahdi's territory. Rifle fire began to open up consistently from the banks on either side, and everyone took cover behind the timber shields as bullets thudded into them. Wilson and Fonthill took up position on the midship turret to get a better view, but Khashm-el-Mus curled himself up in a corner and refused to move.

Artillery began to boom at them as they neared Halfiyeh, which Gordon had once occupied and where Simon had been captured. Simon's heart leapt as he saw what appeared to be two steamers moored there, but any doubt about their allegiance disappeared when they too opened fire on the two boats as they steamed past. Omdurman hove in sight on the right bank. Its cannon were now directed at the two steamers, but although rifle bullets were now thumping into the bulwarks with dangerous regularity, the shells screamed past, aided by the fact that Wilson had ordered that the Sudanese and the Sussex direct regular volleys at the gun positions.

At last Khartoum could be seen. Stuart-Wortley in the *Telahawieh* was working a heliostat, hoping to extract some answering signal from the palace or even perhaps a diversionary sally from the city. But gunfire was now coming from Khartoum itself, and there was no flag flying from the single mast that could be seen on the palace roof. Even so, Wilson, urged on by Fonthill, kept the two boats steaming towards the city, now clearly defined ahead of them. As they neared the mud flats close to the walls, however, they could see masses of Dervishes arrayed under their banners, waiting for them. There was no doubt about it. The worst had happened.

Khartoum had fallen.

Chapter 20

Wilson, his face white and drawn, turned towards the wheelhouse. 'Go about!' he shouted. 'Go around.'

Fonthill slowly sank to his knees behind the wooden planking. He found Jenkins squatting beside him and the two sat speechlessly as the boat heeled over and turned to starboard. Even above the pounding of the engines and the crack of hundreds of rifles, the jeers of the Dervishes on the shore could be heard.

'It's not your fault,' said Jenkins eventually. 'You did all you could an' more.'

Fonthill rested his head on his knees. 'Too late,' he whispered. 'Too bloody late. What a terrible waste. Ahmed, Mustapha . . . What a terrible waste. All for nothing.'

A strange wailing now rose from both steamers as they went about and began steaming back through the gauntlet of rifle and shell shot. The Sudanese on the boats had lifted up their voices in lament for the death of their Pasha. Tears streaming down their faces, they raised their rifles to the heavens in despair. They had lost not only their beloved leader, but also the wives and families that many of them had left in Khartoum.

Fonthill stirred himself and found Wilson. 'We must find out what happened,' he shouted. 'We can't return without discovering whether he has been captured or killed. Land

Jenkins and me to capture a couple of the Dervishes and bring them back for questioning. We owe Gordon that, at least.'

Wilson looked at him, his mouth open. 'You must be mad, Fonthill,' he said. 'We can't go to the shore under this fusillade.'

'Yes. Wait until we get to the other side of Halfiyeh, then drop me off. You are not going to tell Wolseley that we made no attempt to find out if Gordon is still alive, are you?'

There was now disgust and complete lack of respect in Fonthill's voice, and it was that, as much as the force of the argument, that made the Colonel step back. He frowned, nodded and, head down as the bullets hummed overhead, made his way back to the deckhouse.

'Blimey.' Jenkins's voice showed his concern. 'We can't just pop ashore an' pick up a couple of the Nightshirts just like that, can we, bach sir?'

'Better than sitting on our arses all the way back to Gubat, letting Sir Charles bloody Wilson write down his excuses for arriving too late. You don't have to come if you don't wish to.'

'Oh, I'll come. I fancy a run ashore. Anythin' to get off this bleedin' boat for a bit, look you.'

The two vessels were now steaming at full speeed and, with the force of the current with them, were soon out of range of the guns, although the *Telahawieh* ran aground and was stuck fast for a few minutes before, with a shudder, she was freed and able to steam on. Just past Halfiyeh, Wilson ordered the paddle wheels to be put slow astern to hold the boat in the current, waiting for the other vessel to come abreast to compare damage. The *Bordein* was undamaged, apart from hundreds of pepperpot bullet marks in her timber bulwarks, and although *Telahawieh* had been hit by one shell, she too was in comparatively good condition. No one had been hurt.

'I propose to put a small party ashore to try and take a

couple of prisoners and establish when Khartoum fell,' Wilson shouted across to the other boat. 'Stand off and help to cover us if we are attacked.'

It was getting dark now, and firing from the river banks had long since stopped. Indeed, there were few people to be seen ashore. Khashm-el-Mus had recovered sufficiently to take charge of the wheel, and he conned the boat himself towards the eastern bank of the Nile. As he did so, Wilson summoned his officers. 'Hicks-Johnson,' he said, 'select six of your men and go ashore. Find a couple of Dervishes if you can and bring them back here for questioning.'

'No,' intervened Fonthill. He unbuttoned his khaki jacket, threw it to one side and wound a piece of white cloth around his head. He nodded to Jenkins to do the same. 'Jenkins and I will go alone. The Dervishes will either run or fire at soldiers. We can pass as Arabs. We will bring back at least one fellow. Give us just half an hour.'

A sneer came over Hicks-Johnson's face. 'They will desert, sir,' he said. 'Off like rabbits.'

'What – and walk the hundred miles back to Gubat?' Simon did not dignify Hicks-Johnson with a glance. 'Don't be absurd, man.'

Undecided, Wilson looked beseechingly at his other officers. Captain Gascoigne spoke up immediately. 'Let Fonthill go, sir,' he said. 'It's a good idea. But we mustn't hang around here for long.'

'Very well, Fonthill.' The Colonel avoided Simon's eye. 'We will give you exactly three quarters of an hour. But if we are attacked, we must sail without you.'

'Right. Come on, 352.'

The boat edged ashore, but Fonthill did not wait for the plank to be lowered. He and Jenkins jumped down, splashed through the shallows and were immediately lost in the gloom.

'Oh good,' breathed Jenkins. 'Back in the lovely desert. Now where the 'ell do we go?'

'Back towards Halfiyeh.'

''Ere, 'ang on a minute. That name rings a bell, like. Isn't that where we were captured?'

'Yes, but lightning doesn't strike twice. We stand more chance of picking someone up as we near it. I don't intend to go into the village. As I remember it was pretty well deserted anyway. Now, put a bullet up the spout, just in case, although we must not fire unless we are up against it. Come on, we haven't got much time.'

They had taken their rifles and, carrying them at the trail, they began to trot along the river bank. The sun had now gone down completely and twilight was fast being replaced by the indigo blue of the Sudanese night. In the semi-darkness, with their ubiquitous Arab clothing, their dark skins and long beards, the two looked inseparable from Dervishes as they loped along. They had no problems with direction, of course, for they only had to follow the river.

After three minutes, they heard a dog bark ahead of them and Fonthill held up a warning hand. Walking softly in the sand, they approached a couple of mud huts that emerged from the gloom. Simon beckoned Jenkins to him. 'I don't want fishermen,' he whispered. 'We want Dervishes, if we can get them.'

'Yes. Little, quiet ones preferably.'

They approached the huts and saw nets drawn up on the river bank, although there was no sign that the two huts were occupied. Simon shook his head and they diverted round them and then back on to the bank.

Neither of them had watches, of course, and Fonthill guessed that they had been away from the boat for about ten minutes when, ahead of them, they saw the glow of a fire. As they crept forward, they saw the turbaned figures of two men seated at the fire, their heads down, eating. Significantly, at their sides, two rifles glinted in the firelight.

'Remingtons,' breathed Fonthill. 'These are the men we want all right. No shooting, remember. Two could be difficult, so we will only take one back. Quietly now.'

The pair stole forward, their rifles at the ready, until they both stepped into the circle of firelight. The two men looked up and sat as though transfixed as they stared down the barrels of the two Martini-Henrys.

'Good evening, gentlemen,' said Fonthill. 'Kick away their rifles, 352.'

The two Dervishes remained perfectly still, their black eyes following every movement as Jenkins removed both their rifles.

'Now,' said Simon, 'go behind the one on the left and nice and quietly remove his headgear and thump him on the skull with the butt of your rifle. Not hard enough to kill him, but enough to put him out.'

The man was startled to have his coiled headdress removed, and even more so when the butt of Jenkins's rifle crashed into the back of his head. He slumped forward, and the other immediately began to rise to his feet, his hand seeking the curved dagger stuck into his cummerbund. But the muzzle of Fonthill's rifle jerked to his stomach, and slowly he resumed his position on the ground.

'That's wise,' said Simon. 'Is your man out?'

'Er, very out, I would say.'

'Good.' Fonthill kept his eyes fixed on the first Arab. 'Anybody about, do you think?'

'Dead as the grave, by the look of it.'

'Right. Throw the rifles in the river. Don't make a splash.'

Jenkins did as he was told. Then Fonthill gestured with his

rifle to the Dervish. The man did not move, but kept staring at him. 'Up, up,' said Simon, raising the end of his rifle barrel. Slowly the man stood. 'Good.' Still covering the man with his rifle, he raised his other hand and put his finger to his lips in the universal signal for silence. The Dervish made no acknowledgement. 'Now, 352,' continued Simon. 'I am going to lead, because if you lead we shall end up in the river. You keep him covered with your rifle and make sure he knows you are there. Ready? Let's go.'

Slowly, the little cavalcade began the journey back to the boat. Fonthill found it a relief to see that the man had the square red patches of the Mahdi sewn into his garment. Had he fought at Khartoum? It would be a bonus if he had. They would find out when they reached the boat. If, that is, they reached the boat.

But they did so without misadventure, a hoarse 'Halt, who goes there?' challenging them as the superstructure of the *Bordein* loomed out of the darkness. For the first time the Dervish looked fearful as he was ushered into the shallows and then pushed aboard the boat.

'Well done, Fonthill,' the voice of Captain Gascoigne welcomed them. 'Splendid. We were just beginning to get worried.'

'He looks like a fighting man to me,' said Fonthill, 'and he may have been at the storming of the city. Have we got an interpreter?'

'Yes. One of the Sudanese speaks good English.'

'I suggest that we sit him down in the deckhouse and give him a cup of tea or something. We interrupted his meal and we should show him that we mean him no harm. I think there is more chance of him talking that way.'

'Quite right. Bring him along.'

Wilson was summoned, and a Sudanese sergeant appeared

who, on instructions, told the Dervish that if he answered the questions truthfully, he would be put ashore again without being harmed. A hot cup of tea was put in his hand and the look of apprehension slowly began to disappear from his eyes. The story he unfolded riveted the men who crowded around him.

He had, indeed, been part of the force that had attacked Khartoum, and afterwards had been in the van of a unit that had been extended on the eastern bank as far north as Halfiyeh to give warning of the approach of the relief party that was expected. At this, Wilson gave orders for the *Bordein* to cast off from the shore and, despite the darkness, to make passage a couple of miles further to the north before anchoring for the night. As the boat rocked, the Dervish began his story.

The attack, he said, had taken place on the morning of the twenty-sixth, just two days before.

'Only two days ago!' exclaimed Fonthill. 'Just two days. We could have saved Gordon if we had not pottered about in Gubat!'

The officers surrounding the prisoner looked embarrassed, except for Hicks-Johnson, who glared at Simon. Wilson coughed and nodded to the interpreter. 'Pray ask him to continue,' he said.

The Mahdi himself, explained the Dervish, had come from Omdurman to address his troops and tell them that Paradise and the *houris* there awaited those who were lucky enough to be killed by the infidels. The attack had begun about three hours after midnight, and had struck mainly where the falling White Nile left a long space devoid of any fortifications. The Dervish riflemen had therefore been able to creep up across the mud flats in the darkness and, when the signal was given, open up a strong fire on the defenders, most of whom were now considerably weakened by malnutrition. The spearmen broke through immediately, shouting their war cries and stabbing and slashing, and the defences immediately crumbled. Another attack was launched simultaneously from the north on the Blue Nile near Buri, and despite the efforts of the defenders here to form a square and fight back, they too were overrun and the Dervishes burst through into the streets of the city. Within an hour, all resistance had disappeared and the attackers went on a rampage of looting, raping and killing.

There was a terrible silence within the little deckhouse. 'What happened to Gordon Pasha?' asked Wilson.

The Dervish was not sure, because he was not of the party that had attacked the palace, but he had heard that the General did not draw his sword or fire his revolver but waited at the head of the steps leading to his room and stood passively as four spearmen stabbed him to death.

'Yes,' murmured Fonthill. The officers all turned to look at him. 'He would have welcomed death,' he said. 'He would have been happy to go.'

The narration continued. The Mahdi had given strict orders that Gordon should be taken alive, but these instructions were either ignored by his attackers or unknown to them. His head was cut away and his body hauled down the steps and left in the garden, where many Dervishes plunged their spears and swords into it. The head was sent to the Mahdi in Omdurman, where it was now hanging from a tree.

The room fell silent once more.

Fonthill felt a pulse begin to beat in his forehead. Unbidden, his brain conjured up a picture of Gordon, his face shrouded in cigarette smoke but his blue eyes smiling, speaking of his 'chicks' in the school. He recalled the stories he had heard of how Gordon had given away most of his salary to help homeless children in England. Then he remembered the man's admission that he felt 'gutted' that the expeditionary force had not been sent earlier and made quicker time; his efforts to keep everyone going; and his loneliness sitting in the long room, watching through his telescope downriver, waiting, always waiting for relief to come.

'So General Gordon was killed just about the time that we were stuck on that rock,' said Fonthill quietly. Again he had everyone's attention. His voice growing stronger, he turned to Sir Charles Wilson. 'Colonel, you wasted four days procrastinating in Gubat even though I described to you the peril that Gordon was in and urged you to steam upriver without any delay. You ignored all advice. I have to tell you that you killed the man, just as surely as if you had plunged the spears in yourself.'

Wilson blanched. 'How dare you talk to me like that,' he said. 'I am your senior in rank. How dare you.'

'I don't care about rank. We arrived here two days too late. *Just two bloody days,* man. Yet you pussy-footed about in Gubat for *four days.*' Fonthill's fists were now clenched and he was shaking. All the discomfort, the pain, the anxieties of the terrible last months in the Sudan now came surging into his brain and sought expression. 'You could have let any of your senior officers go on reconnaissance and organise those defences, while you carried out your orders to move with all speed to rescue Gordon. You should be ashamed—'

'Sergeant!' The interruption came from Hicks-Johnson, calling out to the deck. 'In here with your rifle at the double. Move!' A red-faced sergeant of the Sussex materialised almost immediately, his mouth full of *durra* cake, jacket unbuttoned but rifle at the ready. 'Arrest this man. Take him below to the engine room and shackle him. He is dangerous. He has attacked me and he is about to attack the Colonel.'

'Don't you move now, bach.' Jenkins had appeared at the other open door of the deckhouse, where he had been listening to the Dervish's story. His Colt was covering both the sergeant and Hicks-Johnson. 'Anyone who touches the Cap . . . the Major gets a bullet in 'is belly. I mean it.'

For a moment, everyone stood perfectly still, as though characters in a tableau. The cold of the Sudanese night had descended outside but it seemed stiflingly hot inside the deckhouse. Suddenly, a blow from a rifle butt in Jenkins's back sent him staggering forward into the saloon, his Colt clattering to the floor, a corporal of the Sussex filling the doorway behind him. Immediately, Fonthill ran towards him but the sergeant sprang at him, clutching him around the waist and pinioning his arms to his sides. Hicks-Johnson drew his revolver from its holster, aimed it at Simon and drew back the hammer with his thumb.

'That will do, Captain,' said Wilson. 'There will be no killing here. Take these men below.'

None of the officers in the deckhouse spoke as they left. The corporal brought up the rear as they followed the sergeant to a hatch, which, when opened, revealed a steel ladder descending into darkness.

' 'Ere,' said Jenkins. 'You're not stickin' us down there, are you? It looks bloody 'ot. We'll fry durin' the day, look you.'

'Sorry, mate,' grunted the sergeant. 'Orders is orders. Down you go.'

By the half-light of the open hatch, they could see that the little space was crammed with machinery dedicated to serving the great paddle wheels on either side of the hull. One small hatch was open forrard and the boiler, mercifully, was on deck, but the heat of the day and that generated by the engine still lingered in the confined space. There was just enough room for the pair of them to sit, their backs against the curved hull. The corporal produced two pairs of handcuffs. One was clipped around one of Fonthill's wrists and locked on to a thin pipe above his head, and the other similarly secured for Jenkins.

'Sergeant,' Simon remonstrated. 'This is going too far, you know.'

'Sorry, er, sir, but these are me orders.'

'Who on earth would take two pairs of handcuffs on an expedition like this, for goodness' sake? Have you not more important things to carry?'

The sergeant gave an apologetic grin. 'Ah, you don't know Captain Hicks-Johnson. These things *are* important to him, you see.'

'Look, Sarge,' said Jenkins. 'You look after that Colt for me, eh? Don't let 'Icks-Arse'ole 'ave it. It's of great sentimental value, see.'

'All right, mate. Let's hope he's forgotten about it. Have you had something to eat?'

'No.'

'I'll get something sent down to you, and we'll find a candle from somewhere.' Then he and his corporal were gone.

The two sat in dark silence for a while. Then: 'Well,' said Jenkins. 'Now we've been put in chains by this Mahdi bloke *and* the British Army. It seems as though we've got no friends anywhere, isn't it?'

Fonthill sighed. 'My fault. I should have kept my mouth shut. I gave Hicks-Johnson just the opportunity he wanted. But they can't keep us down here for long. Wilson will realise that that slimy bastard has gone too far.'

Chapter 21

Fonthill was wrong. They were indeed left below in the engine room that night, as the *Bordein* surged downriver on the current. It became incredibly hot the next day, but in the late afternoon the engines stopped and Hicks-Johnson descended the ladder, carefully closing the hatch behind him. He carried two further pairs of handcuffs.

He stood for a moment looking down at the prisoners. 'Warm?' he enquired softly.

Simon tossed his head to flick the sweat from his eyes. 'You are going to hang, Hicks-Johnson,' he said in level tones. 'We have evidence that you killed our slave boy. I am bringing charges against you as soon as we arrive back in Korti.'

'Oh, I think not.' In the semi-darkness they could see his teeth gleam. 'Firstly, you have no evidence of any so-called charge. But you, my friend, have been completely insubordinate to the commanding officer in front of many witnesses, and your Welsh thug here has threatened us all with his revolver. Oh, it will be you who will be facing charges – if, that is, you reach Korti, or even Gubat. You see . . .' he dangled the handcuffs, 'I am going to make it very uncomfortable for you down here, and I doubt if you will survive the journey.'

He walked forward, his head stooped, and closed the forward hatch, screwing it down firmly. Then, in one swift movement, he grabbed Jenkins's unsecured wrist, slipped a handcuff around it and snapped it tight. Roughly he pulled it up and clipped it around a higher pipe, so that the Welshman was left half hanging. He did the same to Fonthill.

'There,' he said. 'When the engines start up again I reckon it won't take too long for you to suffocate down here – and, of course, I shall tell the men that you are refusing food and therefore are not to be visited.'

'You're not goin' to swing,' hissed Jenkins. 'I'm goin' to 'ave you instead. With me knife.'

'Don't be impertinent, Sergeant Major. Stay here and sweat, you impudent swine.' Hicks-Johnson turned to Fonthill, and his eyes shone bright in the flickering half-darkness provided by the stunted candle. 'This will teach you to humiliate me in front of native soldiers, damn you. I promise that I will see you dead, both of you.'

Then he turned, snuffed out the candle, felt his way to the iron ladder and clambered up, carefully closing the hatch behind him.

'What a rat!' Jenkins shuffled to his knees to relieve the strain on his extended arm. 'Bloody 'ell. I 'ave to say that I'm not exactly comfortable, look you. 'Ow long are we goin' to last like this? It's worse than the whippin', so it is.'

'I'm afraid it's going to get worse when the engine starts.' Fonthill rolled on to his knees too. 'I'm trying to slip through these damned cuffs but my hand is too large. Someone surely will come to see if we're all right. It's our only hope.'

As though on cue, the engines coughed into life and the boat gathered way. The heat from the boiler above and the friction generated by the moving pistons at their side immediately increased the temperature in their prison – now a black hole – so that what was left of their clothing quickly became sodden rags and their bodies, stretched by their arms clamped above them, felt as though they were being squeezed of every last drop of liquid. The steel bands at their wrists chafed the skin, and the kneeling position – the only one they could sustain for long – sent shafts of pain through their legs and into their spines.

Fonthill had no idea how long they crouched there, but he was blessedly aware that the engines had stopped, presumably for the boat to anchor for the night, when the hatchway clanged open, letting in a shaft of light.

'My God!' Captain Gascoigne's jaw dropped. 'What on earth . . . How long have you been like this?'

'Don't know,' gasped Fonthill. 'For God's sake open the forrard hatch. That swine Hicks-Johnson . . . get the key. We're being stretched as though on a rack here.'

Gascoigne scrambled round the machinery and unscrewed the forward hatch, and immediately a zephyr of blessedly cool air stole through the engine room. The captain examined the cuffs. 'My God,' he said again. 'I'll get the keys.'

Within two minutes he was back, busily unlocking all four sets of handcuffs. Fonthill and Jenkins immediately fell to the floor and lay gasping. Gascoigne knelt beside them and began quickly massaging their wrists and knees.

'Disgraceful,' he muttered. 'I'd no idea. Why should he do this?'

'He carries a grudge,' muttered Fonthill.

'An' 'e was tryin' to kill us,' added Jenkins, wringing out his beard as though it was a sponge. 'I 'ave to tell you, bach, that 'e's not a very nice English officer, indeed to goodness 'e ain't, and as a result I'm goin' to kill the bleeder.'

'Good lord.' The look of surprise on Gascoigne's face merged into one of contrition. 'You mustn't say that, my man.' He turned to Fonthill. 'I am most awfully sorry about this. Had a bit of a job getting the keys off Hicks-Johnson. He said that you had tried to attack him down here, hence the extra handcuffs.'

'Nonsense. As you can see, we are in no position to attack anyone. We are only half alive.'

'Indeed. Anyway, I have now persuaded the Colonel that there is absolutely no need for you to be shackled and, of course, we shall be leaving the hatch open so that you can get some air. I'll get some food down to you right away.'

The pair tried to look grateful. 'You know, Gascoigne,' said Fonthill. 'There will be hell to pay when Wolseley learns that we have been treated like this. You wouldn't put a coolie down here, nor should you. Whatever is Wilson thinking of?'

Gascoigne looked embarrassed. 'Hicks-Johnson seems to have persuaded him that the pair of you are dangerous. They have some sort of bond, you know, because they both worked together in Army Intelligence, and Sir Charles listens to him rather. Mind you, I hear that you hit Hicks-Johnson and . . . well, your chap here shouldn't have threatened us with that pistol, you know.'

Simon rubbed his wrists where the steel cuffs had bitten. 'We've been through too much together to be pushed about by our own people. And as for Hicks-Johnson, he is a disgrace to his commission. Hit him! I should have killed him. Twice he tried to stop me from doing my job, and he is guilty of worse crimes than that. I shall bring charges against him when we reach Korti. But enough of that. What's happening? Have we stopped for the night?'

'No. The *Telahawieh* has hit a rock and we can't salvage her. We must leave her, and we are in the middle of transferring her crew and soldiers, together with all her stores and ammunition. Hell of a job and I must get back. I'm afraid you must stay down here, but I'll see if we can find some blankets or something for you to lie on.'

The corporal tramped down some minutes later with bread and cheese and four blankets, which provided a modicum of comfort, and when night fell, currents of blessedly cool air began to waft down from the open hatch, allowing them to sleep. The heat returned the next day, however, as the paddle wheels turned and the journey was resumed – this time, however, with the *Bordein* notably lower in the water as she assumed her greater load.

The crash came on the third day. Fonthill and Jenkins, too hot, too miserable to talk, were half dozing when they were hurled forward, narrowly missing the great axle that connected the wheels to the transmitting rotors. The panel that separated the engine room from the forward hold crumpled immediately and water began pouring in through the gap.

'Out, quickly,' cried Fonthill, and he followed Jenkins up the ladder on to the deck. At first the strong light almost blinded them; then they realised that the boat had struck a sunken rock at speed. So hard had been the impact, in fact, that the steamer had bounced back from the rock and was now in mid-river, being swept along by the current and sinking quite fast. All was confusion on the deck.

'Man the pumps!' shouted Gascoigne, a cry that was immediately repeated in Arabic, and the Sudanese sailors leapt into the hold. The clank of the manually operated pumps now added to the hiss of escaping steam and the surging of the water, but it was clear that they were having little effect, for the vessel was sinking lower in the water by the minute.

'Oh my God, did you see that?' Jenkins clutched Fonthill's arm and pointed to where a long brown snout had appeared above the fast-flowing river for a second and then disappeared in a swirl of water as a swish from the crocodile's great tail took it below the surface.

'Don't worry,' said Simon. 'We're not in the water yet. Come on. Let's give a hand with the launching of the boat.'

Fonthill caught a glimpse of Wilson, Hicks-Johnson at his side, in the redoubt on top of the deckhouse, scanning the river banks on either side with his field glasses. He and Jenkins reported to Captain Gascoigne, who was attempting to direct some of the men of the Sussex Regiment in the unlashing of the steamer's large rowing boat. 'The Sudanese have been useless since they've heard of Gordon's death,' he shouted. 'They seem to have gone to pieces, and Khashm-el-Mus with 'em. If we can get this thing in the water, I want to load it with as many of our supplies as we can and put them ashore at that inlet there.' He pointed. 'Then we can follow.'

'Any Dervishes about?' asked Fonthill.

'Not as far as we can see. The Colonel is looking out for 'em. It's no good hanging on to the *Bordein*. The pumps are helping a bit but they can't keep up with the water and she's definitely going down. Undo that lashing, there's a good fellow.'

The boat was put alongside, followed by its smaller sister dinghy, and the loading began. There was only time, however, for about half of the supplies and ammunition on board to be ferried to the shore before it became necessary to begin the transfer of the men. Appropriately, the last man to leave the steamer was Colonel Wilson, who scrambled into the tender just as the *Bordein* slipped beneath the brown waters of the Nile with a final hiss of steam.

The disconsolate survivors, dripping with perspiration from the effort of loading the boat under the sun, tried to find what shade they could under a cluster of palms that ringed the inlet. Nearby, a rocky outcrop provided a sun terrace for a group of crocodiles, who regarded them all with yellow, disinterested eyes, their scales glinting in the sunlight.

'Well, this is cosy, isn't it?' said Jenkins, carefully putting himself on top of an ammunition box as far away as possible from the reptiles. 'Are we still under arrest, then? And is it crocodile steak for supper, for if it is, I don't fancy it, see.'

'God knows,' replied Fonthill, stretching out on the sand. 'I should say that we are now in plenty of trouble without worrying about the crocs. I would guess that we are a good day's steaming from Gubat, and with no way of steaming there, so to speak. We are still very much in Dervish country, and I don't fancy staying here. We could be overrun within seconds if there are many of 'em about.'

Wilson had, of course, convened a council of war with his officers, from which, Fonthill observed, Khashm-el-Mus was excluded. The Sudanese was sitting with a group of his sailors, his head on his knees. All of them, noted Simon, had removed Gordon's Khartoum medal from their breasts. Eventually Wilson, who had hitherto studiously avoided Fonthill and Jenkins, nodded, looked up and waved Simon over to join them.

'Ah,' murmured Jenkins, 'redemption, or whatever they call it, at last, then.'

Fonthill rose, indicated to Jenkins to follow him and they joined the group. Together they squatted on the sand. It was clear that the invitation had not included the Welshman, but Simon ignored that.

'Look here, Fonthill,' said Wilson, 'you may regard yourself and your man, er, here as no longer being under arrest if I have your parole that you will make no attempt at deserting.'

Simon, catching the eye of Gascoigne, restrained a smile and nodded. 'You have it, Colonel,' he said. (Where the hell would they desert to?) 'We are not deserters.'

'Good. Now the Sudanese, it seems, have downed tools,

and Khashm-el-Mus is no longer being of any use to us at all. You have been down this river twice, at least, and we would appreciate your help in attempting to define where we are and what lies between us and Gubat.'

'I will do what I can, Sir Charles,' Simon said politely. 'Although I haven't seen much of the river in the last couple of days. Now, let's see. We are about two and a half days' steaming from Khartoum. Yes?'

Everyone nodded.

'And we have not yet gone through the Sixth Cataract?'

'No.'

Fonthill pulled at his beard. 'Very well. Then we should be about forty miles upstream of Gubat, and if I remember rightly, there is one last Dervish gun emplacement between us and there, at a place called Wad Habashi. In fact, it shouldn't be far away from here and it means that there will be a Dervish camp there.' He looked around him. 'Colonel, I don't think we can stay here. It won't be long before the news reaches Wad Habashi that our steamer has gone down here and that we are stranded on the shore. I don't know how much ammunition you have, but I doubt if you could defend this position if the Dervishes fall upon us. However . . .' He paused and looked downriver.

'Yes?'

'The Dervishes are not really river people. They are men of the desert. I think I am right in saying that not one of Gordon's boats was attacked from the river itself. I suggest then that we take our stores and ammunition in the tender and make camp on that island there. It is right in mid-river and, by the look of it, deserted. There are one or two palm trees and plenty of rocks, so we should be able to defend it if attacked, and there is plenty of water from the river. As I say, I don't think the Dervishes will want to get their feet wet in trying to knock us over there. But they wouldn't hesitate in coming at us here.'

Wilson rose and examined the island through his field glasses. 'Yes. I take your point. But what about the alternative? Would you think we could march overland and reach Gubat?'

Fonthill smiled. 'That must be your decision, sir. But you have no camels, of course, and although forty miles doesn't seem much, it can be a hell of a way out in the desert when you are walking. Also, you will have to bypass Wad Habashi and risk an attack on you out there in the open.'

Gascoigne intervened. 'We have the tender, Sir Charles, and the other small dinghy. Wouldn't be better to hole up, so to speak, on the island and send the tender downstream with a small crew, creeping past the batteries at Wad Habashi by night, say, to bring up a steamer from Gubat to rescue us?'

'Hmmm. And if it doesn't get through?'

Gascoigne shrugged his shoulders. 'Then we walk.'

'May I express a view, sir?' Hicks-Johnson was sitting erect, as always, and he seemed to be the only man on the expedition who clipped his moustache every morning.

'Of course.'

'I think we should go by land to Gubat. Our supplies have diminished somewhat as a result of the sinking, and if the boat did not get through, we would be stuck on the island not knowing how long we would have to stay there. If we are attacked, then, by Jove, we could form a square and give the Dervishes a jolly good hiding as we did at Abu Klea.'

Fonthill rolled his eyes. Form a square! It seemed as though thinking in the British Army had not progressed since Waterloo. They had more than two hundred men. Why not be proactive and march on Wad Habashi by night and attack the batteries at dawn?

He put forward the idea as another alternative to sending

the boat, and Gascoigne, at least, nodded in support as he spoke. But Wilson immediately shook his head. 'No,' he said. 'I think Hicks-Johnson is right. We will march. We will have to get the Sudanese to carry the supplies, but we will set off as soon as they are loaded. If we are attacked we will use the stores to form a square and fight from behind them. Let us begin the work now.'

The group broke up and Fonthill caught Hicks-Johnson's eye. The captain quickly looked away again, but as he walked away, Simon caught up with him.

'As you see,' he said, 'we are not dead. But, my friend, you yourself are as good as dead. To coin a phrase: watch your back.'

Hicks-Johnson backed away. 'If you lay a finger on me, Fonthill, I will see that you are shot.'

'Oh, I am not going to lay a finger on you. But I can't guarantee the behaviour of my man, Jenkins. He did not quite take to your attempt to kill us both in the engine room. Let me tell you, though, that if you do survive the journey back, I am going to see you swing from the gallows.'

The little man seemed to become even more upright, and he allowed himself to smile. 'What on earth are you talking about? You cannot charge me with anything, and you know it.'

'Not true. You deliberately misled us over the matter of the water bags up north, and we nearly died of thirst in the desert. But worst of all, you gave your sword to our little slave boy and encouraged him to wade into the Dervishes with it, knowing that he would be killed within seconds. We have a witness to that.'

For a moment Hicks-Johnson's eyes widened, then the smile returned. His voice had lost its bluster and it dropped to little more than a whisper. 'You fool,' he said. 'No court would convict me of killing your black brat. I was only trying to help him, wasn't I? Giving him my sword to defend himself with – the act of a gentleman, what? And as for the water bags, I think you must somehow have misunderstood me, my *dear* fellow. Any fool knows that cotton thread will rot in desert conditions. I would never have advised you to use it. You must have got into dreadful difficulties. Oh dear, I am *so sorry* . . .'

Simon clenched his fist and took a step forward, but then, seeing the defiant look in the other's eye, realised he was deliberately being provoked. 'You are a swine of the worst kind, Hicks-Johnson,' he said. 'I want you to know that I regard you as a murderer for what you did to the boy, and yes, I *will* see you swing. Be sure of that.'

He turned away, his mind seething with contempt for the man, but with frustration also. Jenkins was right. No military court would convict a British officer of the murder of a slave boy on the word of a Sudanese. And the charge of the water bags would be even more difficult to substantiate. It had been their own responsibility to equip themselves properly for the long desert journey. They should have known that thread would rot in the sun. As for his treatment of them in the engine room, Hicks-Johnson of course would argue that they had attempted to attack him there and that the further handcuffs were necessary to restrain them. Damn the man! But he would not escape. There must be a way of finding retribution . . .

Sir Charles Wilson's injunction to 'begin the work now' proved easier said than done – in fact, it was not easy at all, because the Sudanese, when told that they must march the forty-odd miles to Gubat carrying the supplies, consulted among themselves for several minutes and then flatly refused to do so.

'But this is mutiny!' exclaimed Wilson. 'You must obey orders.'

The Sudanese interpreter, one of the men himself, of course, shrugged his shoulders. 'They say too far, *effendi*. They say too far to carry boxes and bags and too dangerous. And they say they soldiers, not Turkish porters. Sorry, *effendi*.'

'Ah.' Sir Charles scowled. 'Very well. We must repair to the island. Explain to them that we will transfer our stores to that island there and that they must load the boat if they don't want to starve. Watch out for those crocodiles. I don't like the look of them.' He looked round. 'Ah, Fonthill. Will you and your man deploy out to the north along the bank a way and act as forward piquets. If an attack comes, I presume it will come from that direction. I just hope that we are safely loaded and across the water before they find us.'

'Very good, Sir Charles. May we have our weapons back?'

'What? Ah, yes.'

Fonthill and Jenkins exchanged grins and retrieved rifles and bayonets from the sergeant, who, with a sly wink, also handed back Jenkins's Colt. Then they loped off along the river bank, walking some two hundred yards apart, with Fonthill that distance inland so that he could observe any approach from the desert to the west. He decided that he would not relate to Jenkins his exchange with Hicks-Johnson. The Welshman had his own way of dealing with people who crossed him, and he could not always be controlled.

The pair had been walking for about half an hour when Simon saw 352 waving his arm. He hurried over to him.

'Is that this Wad Habbadashi place?' Jenkins pointed ahead. On the same bank, a low block of grey showed where the Dervishes had built their most northerly battery to deter the advance of Wolseley's river column.

'Goodness,' breathed Fonthill. 'We're nearer to it than we

thought.' He frowned and squinted in concentration. 'There's some sort of movement between the battery and us – a bit of a dust cloud. Dammit, I wish we had borrowed field glasses.'

Jenkins shielded his eyes from the sun. 'Yes, bach sir. Looks like they're sending some of their chaps down 'ere to invite us in for a cup of tea. Quite a few of them, by the look of it.'

Fonthill looked hard. 'Yes. They're on camels but they're not moving all that fast. How many, do you think?'

'Not all that many – p'raps an 'undred. Kicking up dust so it's 'ard to tell.'

'Right. We've seen enough. Let's get back and report.'

The Colonel expressed concern when he heard the news. He looked around him quickly, and Fonthill realised that all his officers, with the exception of Captain Stuart-Wortley, were on the island, directing the stacking of the stores. Most of the latter had been transported by now, but there remained about a dozen mealie bags and boxes, together with some ten men of the Sussex ready to fill the boat again on its return.

'How far away are they, then?' Wilson asked.

'Perhaps about three quarters of a mile by now, I should say. They are not moving all that fast, as far as we could see, but they should be here in twenty minutes or so.'

'Right. Stuart-Wortley, take five men and build a little redoubt on the edge of the trees over there. Use some of the boxes. They may have to be sacrificed if you have to leave in a hurry. Man the redoubt and keep the varmints at bay until we have finished the loading. Fonthill, take your man and give a hand, and stay to provide covering fire.'

'Very good, sir.'

Hurriedly, half a dozen of the boxes were manhandled to provide low cover – only chest height – in a little semicircle just in front of the palm tree that protruded furthest into the desert, thus providing a field of fire in an arc to their front, sides and partly behind them. The last box had been put in place when the Dervishes came plainly into view, spreading out now across the desert.

'They're not in much of a hurry, are they?' said Stuart-Wortley, licking his lips.

Fonthill smiled. 'They know we're not going anywhere.' He looked behind him. The boat was fully laden and the loaders had climbed aboard. Colonel Wilson doubled over to them. He raised his glasses and examined the approaching force.

'Hmmm.' He adjusted the focus. 'Perhaps we could have seen them off if we had stayed, but I am not too sure about our black fellers. Can't really trust 'em now, I'm afraid.' He gave a quick, anxious gaze at Stuart-Wortley. 'Will you be all right if I go across with this last load? I shall send the boat back, of course, but I want to get over to organise covering fire for you from the island when you cross.'

Stuart-Wortley gave what Fonthill felt to be a rather fixed smile. 'Right as rain, sir,' he said.

'Right. Good luck. Shouldn't be long.' With a nod to Fonthill, Wilson doubled back and climbed into the back of the crowded tender, which pulled away quickly, four men at the oars.

Simon regarded the advancing Dervishes, who had now halted in a wide arc just out of rifle shot.

'Look here,' he said to Stuart-Wortley. 'It's a bit crowded for eight of us in here, and if I may give you advice, I think it wise to put a couple of riflemen out among the trees on either side to prevent you being enfiladed. They will just about have time to dig rifle pits with their bayonets. What do you think?'

The young man gave a nervous smile. 'Glad to take the advice of any chap who was at Rorke's Drift and Isandlwana, old man,' he said.

'Right. Jenkins and I will go to the north, on this side. Shout to us when the boat comes. I wouldn't want to have to fight these chaps on our own.' Grabbing a box of cartridges each, he and Jenkins doubled to the far end of the clump of palms, where they immediately began scraping out shallow pits in the sand.

Jenkins pulled off his loosely wound headdress, which had somehow stayed *in situ*, and laid it out on the ridge of sand to his right. Then he grabbed a handful of cartridges and distributed them along the rag. He clicked upright the fore sight of his Martini-Henry, licked his thumb and rubbed it along the edge. 'What range would you say, bach sir?'

'Well, depends upon whether they all come at once. If they do, we will have to fire at long range. So, set 'em at two-fifty yards.'

'Two-fifty it is, then.'

Fonthill was not at all sanguine that eight of them could hold back so many Dervishes, and he realised that his stomach had lurched and his mouth completely dried up. They had come a long way to die here, crouched in a hole scooped out of the sand. Yet he had to smile at the Welshman's comfort in the situation. It was as though, after the days of marching, camel-riding, bayonet-fighting and then being chained in the bowels of a noisy, fetid steamboat, he was at last now able to enjoy himself, with a rifle in his hand and an Arab or two in his sights.

Simon leaned across and held out his hand to his comrade. 'Good luck, old chap,' he said.

'Same to you, bach sir. Remember to squeeze gently and not snatch at the trigger.'

'Very good, Sergeant Major.'

'No, well, I'm only sayin' that because you tend to miss a bit, you know.'

'Oh do shut up.'

Dervishes hardly ever fought from their camels; nevertheless, Fonthill was glad to see that the Arabs were now dismounting, for a massed camel charge would take most of the attackers into the grove of trees before the limited firepower of the eight men could bring them down. But were they going to hold back and direct rifle fire at the British? That would be almost as bad, because long-range sniping would be equally difficult to handle, in terms of its deleterious effect on such a small defending force. He pressed his cheek to the stock of his rifle and waited.

Suddenly a howl went up from the half-circle of Arabs, sunlight glinted from the bright steel of spears and swords flourished above their heads, and they were off, running across the sand towards the clump of trees and the eight men waiting there for them.

'Wait a bit,' murmured Fonthill, as he focused on what appeared to be an emir in the van of the charge. 'Yes, now. Fire!'

Stuart-Wortley's assessment of the range had obviously been the same as Fonthill's, for the eight rifles spoke as one. It was not exactly a shattering volley, for the defenders were too few, but six men in the front rank of the charge immediately fell. Eight thumbs pressed cartridges into the rifles and the volley rang out again, bringing down eight of the Arabs this time.

Again the fusillade was not enough to halt the charge, but the attackers were now a little over a hundred yards away, and it was impossible to miss them. The rifles continued to bark just as fast as the ejector levers could be jerked back and more rounds could be thumbed into the breeches, until, just as it seemed that the defenders were about to be overrun, the line of Dervishes hesitated, halted and then turned and ran.

'Keep firing!' shouted Stuart-Wortley.

They did so until the Arabs were out of range, leaving behind them more than thirty white-clad bundles on the sand, some of them twitching or slowly moving but most of them inert.

'Phew,' said Fonthill. 'That was a bit close. You all right?'

'Fit as a flea, thank you.'

'Good. I'm going to the redoubt.' Simon ran, his body bent, to the little group of biscuit boxes. 'Any casualties?'

'One, I'm afraid.' A perspiring Stuart-Wortley wiped his face with the back of his hand and gestured to an inert infantryman, lying with a black hole just above his ear. 'You were right to deploy us a bit, because some of them were trying to run up to us from the side under cover of the trees and they got poor Smith here. But we got plenty of them and forced 'em back. What do you think they'll do now?'

Simon looked hard at where the Arabs were gathered. There was little obvious cover between them and the redoubt but there were undulations in the sand, which could provide cover of a sort for riflemen. He ran his fingers through his beard.

'They might have one more go,' he said, 'because for all they know we might be very low on ammunition. But if I were them, I would lie low, keep taking potshots at us to make us keep our heads down, keep crawling forward and then launch a rush from as near to us as possible.'

And so it proved. Fonthill had hardly regained his place in his rifle pit when a loud scream presaged another dash across the open sand. The rifles crashed out again, and this time the charge wilted before it had gained real momentum, with a further dozen Dervishes left behind to colour the sand red.

'Watch out for the snipers now,' called Simon.

'I say, Stuart-Wortley.' The call came from behind them,

and Fonthill recognised the semi-drawl of Hicks-Johnson. 'Can you withdraw now? We have the boat here and we can just about take all six of you.'

Jenkins scowled. 'There you go. That's what 'e's goin' to do. Leave us be'ind, the arse-crawlin' little shit.' He pulled his rifle around. 'I'll just make room in the boat for one more, see.'

Fonthill put his hand on the muzzle of the rifle. 'No. Don't be stupid. Stuart-Wortley won't let us be left behind. Here he comes now.'

The young officer knelt down beside them. 'We can withdraw now,' he said. 'But do you think the Arabs are going to charge again? If they do, I would rather we all stayed to repel them and then we can split up, three and four, and take it in turns to get back.' He shook his head. 'We will just have to leave poor Smith. I really don't know what Captain Hicks-Johnson is talking about when he says he can take "all six". I mean – there's you two, in addition.'

'Oh, it doesn't surprise us, bach,' Jenkins sniffed. 'We know 'im of old.'

'That will do, 352.' Fonthill scrutinised the Dervishes. A thin line of them were now crawling forward on their stomachs, their rifles in their hands. 'No,' he said. 'They will not charge again. At least not for the moment. They're crawling in to make ground to shorten the range so that they can start some serious shooting.' He looked up at Stuart-Wortley. 'You go, old chap, and take two of your fellows with you. The other two should join us in the redoubt where there is better cover, and I am sure we can hold them off until the boat returns.'

Stuart-Wortley shook his head. 'Oh no. I will stay to the end with you. I will let the corporal and two of the chaps go first. Then we can cross.' He looked behind him to the river and made a face. 'Mind you, I don't much fancy the crossing. All this shooting has made the crocs a bit lively.'

'Oh bloody 'ell.' Jenkins's groan could have been heard easily by the Arabs.

Fonthill grunted. 'Oh come on. They don't climb aboard boats.' A bullet pinged into the tree behind them. 'Now, 352, keep your head down and crawl to the redoubt. I will follow you after I've let off a few rounds to show the devils that we're still here on this side.'

'Very good, bach sir.'

Jenkins and Stuart-Wortley crawled away, and Fonthill sighted along his rifle, waited until a puff of smoke showed and then fired at it. He delivered another round at a glimpse of an *esharp* showing above a sand dune, followed by another at a rifle poking cautiously around a rock. Then he crawled rapidly through the trees and scrambled into the redoubt, joining Stuart-Wortley, Jenkins and a private of the Sussex, lying behind the boxes.

'I am still worried that they might rush us,' said Stuart-Wortley.

'So am I.' Fonthill grinned.

'Why don't we rush *them*?' enquired Jenkins. 'There's only about an 'undred of them. We could surround 'em, couldn't we?'

'Well, you could.'

'Right. I'll be off then.'

Stuart-Wortley's mouth hung open as he followed the exchange. 'I say, do you two always talk like this?' he asked.

'Only when we are about to be engulfed by a hundred or so Dervishes,' said Fonthill. 'It eases the mind.'

'What? Oh, I see. Oh yes. Jolly good. Splendid.'

'Come on. Let's give 'em a bit of a volley to show them that we're still very much alive.'

The four men rose, eased their rifles over the top of the boxes and fired several rounds each. One Dervish who had crawled forward too openly jerked and lay still.

'Right,' said Fonthill, 'the boat should have returned by now. You three go and get aboard. I'll stay here blasting away until the last minute. Go on. Off you go.'

'I'll stay too,' said Jenkins. 'I like it 'ere, see.'

'Well, I . . .' began Stuart-Wortley, then, seeing Fonthill's expression, 'Very well. I'll shout when we're aboard. Come on, Jones.'

The two ran back through the trees, bodies bent, and were followed by a dozen shots, the bullets thudding into the bark of the palms and clipping through the crisp leaves.

'Thank God they're poor shots,' grunted Jenkins. 'But they're bound to get one of us in a minute, and if they do rush us, we won't stand a chance. So I don't fancy stayin' 'ere much longer, bach sir, if it's all the same to you. But then I don't fancy gettin' in that boat with them crocodiles about either.'

'I'd say that the Dervishes are the bigger danger. We will get a call when the boat is back. In the meantime, keep your head down and we will fire half a dozen rounds at 'em before we duck out of here.'

But the call did not come. The fire from the Arabs became so hot that after ten minutes the pair were forced to crawl out of the redoubt, which was beginning to look like a pepperpot, riddled with bullet holes. They split, each taking shelter behind the thickest nearby palm, lying spreadeagled and occasionally directing a shot at a sniper who had crept too close. They moved as best they could between the trees to fire from different positions, to give the impression that a larger number of men were still manning the post.

'We can't hold out here for much longer,' shouted Fonthill. 'Why doesn't the blasted boat come?'

'Because old Hickery-Whatsit has persuaded 'em to leave us here to fight the Madhi on our own,' growled Jenkins. 'That's why. 'E's determined—'

But his voice was cut short as two large Dervishes scrambled over the little barricade. Only their eyes showed between the folds of their headdress, and they had spears poised to strike. They stood in astonishment for a second as they realised that only a dead man was left in the redoubt. Then they doubled up and fell as bullets from Fonthill and Jenkins caught them in their breasts. Before the two had time to reload, however, three more Arabs vaulted over the biscuit boxes and fell sprawling as they stumbled on the bodies of their comrades.

Fonthill and Jenkins rammed cartridges into their rifles and ran forward just in time to plunge their bayonets into the three men as they tried to scramble to their feet. Then they turned as a fresh wave of attackers competed amongst themselves to climb over the boxes. Two of them fell immediately, for the Martini-Henrys could not miss at that range – and then Simon and 352 were up at the chest-high wall, thrusting and parrying across the little barrier, fighting for their lives against what seemed to be a wall of warriors, who were hacking with spears and swords and screaming at the tops of their voices. It was the number of the attackers that saved the lives of the two men, for the Dervishes were packed so tightly that they could not use their weapons to advantage.

'If they get behind us, we're done for,' shouted Fonthill. 'When I give the word, run like hell. Now. GO!'

They turned and, heads down, sprinted for their lives, weaving and ducking between the tall palms. Luckily, the lead attackers had only spears and swords, so that no bullets pursued them, but they could hear from the rasp of bare feet on the fallen leaves that the Dervishes were right behind them.

Suddenly a pistol shot rang out, and then another and another. They saw Stuart-Wortley, standing ankle deep in the water, calmly firing between them with his revolver. He was quickly joined by two of the rowers, who downed their oars and picked up their rifles and sent further bullets whistling at the pursuing Dervishes, two of whom fell immediately. The others paused uncertainly at the fringe of the trees and then turned and sought cover as a volley of rifle fire crackled from the island.

'Quickly, get in the boat,' urged Stuart-Wortley.

'After you,' gasped Fonthill, thumbing another round into the breech. 'I'll keep firing until you and Jenkins are aboard. Go on!'

He knelt in the sand and began firing and reloading, aiming at the shadowy figures he could see among the trees. Indifferent shot as he was, and still trying to regain his breath, he had little hope of finding a target, but he hoped he would provide some deterrent. He gave a quick glance over his shoulder and saw Hicks-Johnson at the tiller of the boat, bending low to present the smallest possible target. Stuart-Wortley was already aboard, and Jenkins was scrambling after him.

'For God's sake come on if you're coming.' Hicks-Johnson's voice was high-pitched. 'I'm pushing off *now*.'

Firing one last round, Simon splashed through the water and was just able to hoist himself over the side and fall on to the crouching figure of Jenkins as the boat pulled away.

'Pull!' screamed Hicks-Johnson at his oarsmen. 'PULL, for God's sake. They're coming after us.'

A further rattle of musketry from the island, however, discouraged further pursuit. As dozens more Dervishes emerged from the trees, a handful in the lead stood ankle deep in the water, waving their spears and screaming derision at the departing boat.

The craft pulled away into midstream, where Hicks-Johnson had to lean on the tiller to negate the pull of the current. He yelled at Jenkins: 'For God's sake, man, you're upsetting the balance of the boat. Sit on the edge there and balance us.'

'What, me?' asked Jenkins. 'Oh, bloody 'ell.' Fonthill saw terror come into the eyes of the bravest man he knew, but the Welshman nevertheless inched across the bottom of the boat, then perched his buttocks on the edge of the gunwale, his knuckles gripping white as he clutched the woodwork. Over his shoulder, Simon saw a swirl of water as a great body slid sinuously just under the surface towards the boat. A sudden realisation of what was about to happen seized him, and he screamed, 'Hold tight, 352!'

But he was too late.

Suddenly, Hicks-Johnson, his face fixed in a grin, jerked the tiller strongly away from him, just as the four oarsmen dipped their blades deeply into the water. The boat tipped and veered to the left, sending Jenkins backwards, head over heels into the water.

'No!' screamed Fonthill, and he flung himself forward and half out of the boat, reaching out as far as he could. His fingers sought and found a fold of fabric and he clutched at it and pulled. Jenkins's face came out of the water, his eyes dilated in terror, but Simon was able to reach his other hand under the Welshman's shoulder and hold him above the surface until Stuart-Wortley came to his aid and together they hauled Jenkins back into the boat.

'You bastard!' yelled Fonthill at Hicks-Johnson. 'You did that deliberately. You tried to kill him.'

Hicks-Johnson was still standing at the stern, his thigh

braced against the tiller, which remained hard over. The grin remained set on his face, as though it was caught there in some spasm. The boat was still listing to port, with the weight of Jenkins, Fonthill and Stuart-Wortley on the floorboards on that side, so that the helmsman stood high on the starboard quarter. What happened next would remain fixed in Simon's mind for the rest of his life. Something – something strong and under the water – struck the rudder of the little boat a sharp blow, so that the tiller reactively kicked to port, thumping Hicks-Johnson in the thigh and sending him spinning in the air, over the port side and into the brown water. He rose once, his mouth open and his hands beating the surface. Then he screamed as the water swirled around him and he was pulled under, his mouth still gaping, his eyes beseeching.

'Oh, bloody 'ell,' whispered Jenkins, water dripping from his beard, 'I'm goin' to be sick.'

'Quickly, beat the water,' shouted Fonthill. 'It might frighten the croc to let him go.'

The oarsmen, huddling away from the edge of the boat, did so, but without too much enthusiasm. The water resumed its even, muddy roll downstream and the boat, now without a helmsman or any form of propulsion, was swept along with it.

Stuart-Wortley scrambled to take the tiller. His face was set sternly. 'Pull, lads,' he cried. 'Pull! There is nothing more we can do for that officer.' He tossed his revolver to Fonthill. 'If you see one of those bloody reptiles, take a shot at it. Horrible things.'

'Amen,' said Jenkins, crouching in the boat, shivering.

The firing from the island had ceased by the time they were hauled up on to its rocky shore. The Dervishes, seeing the firepower of the British, had retired, and some of them could now be seen meandering on their camels back to the north.

Jenkins, still shivering, was helped ashore, and he, Fonthill and Stuart-Wortley were met by Wilson.

'I saw what happened,' he said. 'What a tragedy, what a terrible tragedy. Poor Hicks-Johnson.'

'May I have a word, sir?' Stuart-Wortley led the Colonel a few paces away from the boat's crew and beckoned Fonthill and Jenkins to follow.

'I have to tell you, Sir Charles,' he said, his face grey under his tan, 'that Hicks-Johnson met his death in trying to kill this man.' He gestured to Jenkins. 'What is more, he refused to wait for these two in his anxiety to leave the river bank. I had to threaten him with my pistol to make him wait.'

'What?' Wilson's mouth sagged beneath his moustache. 'I cannot believe that, young man. Hicks-Johnson would not do a thing like that.'

'I'm afraid he would, sir, and if he had not died I would have made a formal request that he be court-martialled, even though he had seniority on me. Then, on board, he made Fonthill's man sit perilously on the side of the boat and swung the tiller over so that he was thrown into the water. I fear he saw crocodiles coming and acted accordingly. Luckily, there is a God in heaven and he got his just, although terrible, deserts.'

Fonthill filled the silence. 'I confirm all of that, sir,' he said. 'He also was instrumental at Abu Klea in killing a ten-year-old Arab boy who was our brave companion in Khartoum and beyond. Hicks-Johnson bore a grudge against us and I am afraid he was an evil man.'

'Oh my goodness.' Wilson remained silent for a moment, his jaw set firmly. Then, 'I would welcome your agreement, gentlemen, in keeping all of this quiet. Hicks-Johnson is dead now, and the morale of the men, which has taken enough of a shaking as it is, will be further affected if all of this comes out.' He coughed. 'There is another point.'

'Sir?'

'Hicks-Johnson has – had – a wife and two children back home in Haywards Heath. I would prefer that they heard that he was drowned accidentally while on active service. I am sure you understand, gentlemen.'

The four men stood silent for a moment. Then, 'Very well, Colonel bach,' grunted Jenkins. 'Not a word.' He seemed to speak for all of them.

Chapter 22

The island – they learned later that it was called Mernat – was bigger than it seemed at first, and once the stores had been arranged to give cover in addition to that provided by the trees, it proved to be an ideal defensive position. It was clear that Jenkins was suffering from shock, and Fonthill found them a comparatively quiet corner in the centre of the island between two palms and sheltered by a scruffy bush, where the Welshman could no longer see the water. Simon took off his own bedraggled shirt and rubbed Jenkins down with it until, at last, a sparkle returned to the black eyes.

'Thank you for draggin' me out, bach sir,' the Welshman said. 'But you needn't 'ave worried, you know. I would have killed that old croc with me bare 'ands.'

'Oh yes. I knew that. It was just that I didn't want you to catch cold.'

Suddenly Jenkins began shivering again. 'Oh, but I am grateful,' he said, looking at the ground. ' 'Orrible thing.' He glanced up. 'No doubt that the little bastard did it on purpose, I suppose?'

'None at all. I saw him spot the croc approaching and grin, and I suddenly realised what he was going to do but I was too late to grab you.'

'Yes.' Jenkins squeezed the last drop of water from his beard. 'I never quite knew why he 'ad it in for us, you know.'

Fonthill shrugged. 'I made the mistake of humiliating him in front of his troops – his *black* troops. A man like that would think that these men were inferior beings, and he just could not live with the thought that he had lost face with them. All nonsense, of course. But I should have found another way. I made an implacable enemy of him.'

'Funny that that sort of bloke should go into the army – and become an officer.'

'Yes. But I'm glad to say that there aren't too many of them around. Right. Lay your clothes on that bush to dry. I'll see if I can get us some tea.'

Jenkins looked horrified and scrambled to his feet, tucking what was left of his pantaloons around his loins. 'Hey, no. I'm the servant, not you. You sit down. I'll find the tea. Whatever next, I don't know.' He set off, his long beard spread across his chest and his black hair glistening, looking like some latter-day Man Friday.

Fonthill grinned. His man had recovered.

For once, Wilson did not call a council of war to discuss what should be done next. The main boat was prepared to take a small party downriver to Gubat to seek help. Enough supplies for a three-day journey were put on board, blankets were torn to muffle the oars and Stuart-Wortley was detailed to command it. Wilson wished to keep as many of his English soldiers with him as possible in case of attack, so volunteers were sought from the Sudanese to act as oarsmen, and eight were selected, plus two men of the Sussex. It was with some diffidence, however, that he approached Fonthill.

'I would be grateful, Fonthill, if you would go with them,' he said. 'You have shown excellent fighting qualities and leadership skills and it is clear that you know the river better than any of us except Khashm-el-Mus, and he has proven a great disappointment. I know that Stuart-Wortley would welcome your company and your help. And that of your man, too, although I shall quite understand if he does not wish to, er, go sailing again for a while.'

Jenkins stood up. 'Thank you kindly, sir,' he said, 'but where the Captain goes I go too, although I should be grateful if you could arrange for the bleedin' crocs to be kept away on this passage, like.'

'We will both go,' said Fonthill.

Wilson gave a weary smile. He put his hand on Simon's arm and led him a few paces away from Jenkins. 'Look here,' he said, 'in view of what has happened, I shall of course drop all charges against you. I must say that I am still personally hurt by your outburst, but that is as may be. Hicks-Johnson was clearly motivated against you and I am afraid he persuaded me that you could be dangerous. But I do apologise for the shackles. Quite unnecessary and definitely a step too far.'

Simon gave an answering smile. It was difficult not to warm to this man, a distinguished surveyor rather than a fighting soldier, who, despite all his setbacks and the weight of the unaccustomed responsibilities pressing on him now, had found the time and humility to express regret for his actions. 'Thank you, Sir Charles,' he said. 'For my part, if I may say so, I still believe you were mistaken in not setting off earlier, but I was wrong to speak as I did to you and I offer you my own apologies.'

The two men shook hands. 'Be ready to leave an hour after sunset,' said Wilson. 'It is asking a lot for you to creep past the batteries without detection, so your best hope is to pass by in the early hours of the morning. Let us hope that there is no bright moonlight.'

Fonthill and Jenkins watched him go. ' 'Ow far will we 'ave to go in this damned rowboat?' asked the Welshman eventually.

'I should say about forty miles, including getting past the Dervish battery and through the Sixth Cataract.'

Jenkins digested the information. 'Hmmm. Just a little joyride, that's all. Well, I'll tell you one thing. I'm not sittin' on the edge of the bloody thing for anybody.'

The moon was well hidden by a bank of cloud as the little party assembled at midnight, as soon as its members had eaten a light meal of *durra* cake and bully beef and biscuit. There were no huzzahs for the crew as the boat was pushed off, merely a wave of the hand from the officers standing at the water's edge and a few whispered 'good lucks'. Then the four Sudanese on rowing duty dipped their oars into the water and the little craft surged out into the fast-flowing current on its journey north.

'How far to the battery, would you say?' Stuart-Wortley, wrapped in a blanket against the cold, enquired of Fonthill.

Simon looked at the dark water pushing them along and supplementing the efforts of the rowers. 'Probably less than an hour at this speed, I should think. Do you mind if I make a suggestion?'

'My dear fellow, suggest away. I'm only too grateful.'

'Well, luckily it's a dark night, and if we keep to the middle of the river we may well not be seen at all. But there is nothing more distinctively British and Turkish in terms of presenting a silhouette than a pith helmet and a fez. So I suggest you order the Sussex to remove their topis and the Sudanese their fezes until we are well past Wad Habashi. The boat is nothing like the *filukas* and other native vessels and we shall stand out rather in daylight, but we should be able to get away with it in this light.'

'Ripping idea, Fonthill. I should have thought of that.'

The oarsmen bent their backs with a will, and it seemed

only minutes before pinpricks of light from fires on the western shore showed where the battery was situated. Stuart-Wortley eased the tiller to port and the boat veered towards the eastern bank, although not too near to it in case the Dervishes had stationed troops on that side of the river.

As they neared the battery, Stuart-Wortley hissed an order and the rowers rested on their oars to let the current take them silently along, while the others ducked low in the boat and cradled their rifles. Their greatest danger lay in being accosted by a guard boat anchored in mid-river, but none materialised out of the gloom, nor any other craft. As they drew level with the guns, Fonthill saw their squat muzzles silhouetted on the dark skyline and imagined he could hear the low conversation of the gunners on guard duty drifting across the water.

'If they spot us, it wouldn't take much to blow us out of the water,' whispered Jenkins.

'Shush,' hissed Stuart-Wortley.

Heads down, rifles poking over the side, the little boat drifted on down, near the middle of the Nile, Stuart-Wortley administering an occasional touch to the tiller to avoid a rock in midstream as directed by a private of the Sussex kneeling at the prow of the boat and signalling to either side with his arms.

Eventually Fonthill heaved a sigh of relief. 'We've done it!'

'Well done, boys,' hissed Stuart-Wortley. Then, in his pidgin Arabic, he urged his four oarsmen to resume rowing and to pull hard.

Dawn saw the relief oarsmen rowing smoothly in midstream with the others all half dozing on the thwarts. On either side of the river, the terracotta vastness of the Sudan stretched away, featureless and devoid of any sort of human life, as far as could be seen. The flies returned with the heat of the sun, but a flicker of movement among the ochre rocks caught everyone's eye. A gazelle teetered on its thin legs and one of the Sussex men grabbed his rifle.

'No!' snapped Fonthill. 'There's no wood to burn for a fire and the sound of a shot will travel for miles here. It will have to be bully beef for breakfast, lad, I'm afraid.'

Stuart-Wortley decided that they could afford to rest for a while, so the boat was pulled into a little rocky inlet where high boulders provided good cover. A line was secured to the shore, a guard was set and the rest of them stretched out on the rocks for two hours of much-needed rest, for the cramped quarters of the tender offered them little chance of sleep. Then the journey was resumed.

Twice during the afternoon, small fishing boats were passed. As they neared, Stuart-Wortley ordered hats to be removed and blankets draped around everyone to hide their uniforms. He called a guttural *'ahlan wa sahlan!'* as they passed, and although it was clear that they excited some interest, no one attempted to hinder or question them.

Towards late afternoon, a dull roar ahead indicated that they were nearing the Sixth Cataract. 'Do you think we can get through before nightfall?' asked Stuart-Wortley, 'I wouldn't want to be halfway through and get caught in the dark.'

'Quite right. Let's moor to the bank and tackle it at daybreak. We will need to set a guard, though.'

They rowed to where a cluster of rocks jutting out into the current provided some slack water in their lee and the crew spent a troubled night, kept awake by the noise of the water, the discomfort of sleeping in the boat and on the rocks and the need to keep watch. It was a relief then when, in the half-light of dawn, they cast off and faced up to the passage of the cataract.

Jenkins eschewed the comparative comfort of a seat on the

thwart and settled for a position on the floor of the craft, amidships and near the stern. Fonthill comforted him with the news that crocodiles hated the turbulence of the rapids and would keep their distance, but the Welshman hardly heard. He merely nodded and sat, staring ahead, with his fingers clutching the duckboarding that lined the bottom of the boat. Simon himself took up position in the bow of the boat, ready to direct Stuart-Wortley at the tiller.

In fact, the cataract held no terrors on this passage. Although the force of the current behind them took the little craft at great speed through the defile, they had no upstream battling to do, of course, and the oars were needed only occasionally to correct the course and give momentum in the patches of slack water between the rocks. The shallow draught and narrow beam of the vessel also helped them, and they were through the turbulent water in little more than an hour.

Stuart-Wortley steered the boat into an inlet just downstream of the cataract and they breakfasted on bully beef and biscuits. Jenkins wiped his brow and stepped unsteadily on shore. 'Nothin' to it, really,' he said. 'I don't know what all the fuss was about.'

As they journeyed north during the day, they occasionally saw parties of what appeared to be Dervishes on the banks, and once they were fired on. But otherwise their day was uneventful, and as night approached, it was decided that they would row on through the hours of darkness, for Gubat could not be far now.

In fact, it was almost four a.m. when they saw the shape of the new fort emerge high on the western bank, and then the fortifications surrounding the encampment that was Gubat itself, low on the shoreline. Shortly afterwards they were challenged by a greatcoated sentry and they pulled into the shallows.

'I had better report to Colonel Boscawen,' said Stuart-Wortley, 'even though it is the middle of the night. I suppose bad news should not wait. Will you come with me?'

Fonthill shook his head. 'Not unless you need me, and I am sure you don't. I have someone I must see immediately.'

They nodded and parted. Simon and Jenkins made their way to where the press contingent had been allocated its own small compound, and while Jenkins curled up, wrapped in two blankets, on a patch of gravelly sand, Fonthill found where Alice had pitched her bivouac tent, regained from the wounded. Quietly he untied the flap strings and crawled inside. She was fast asleep, her short dyed hair fringing her face in a dishevelled bang, her mouth partly open, revealing two small white teeth, and her jaw half buried in the pillow. He shook his head in a slow flush of emotion and, deciding not to wake her, lay down beside her, trying to synchronise his breathing with hers.

Within what seemed like minutes, he was awakened by a startled cry and a body being thrown on his. 'When . . . when . . . did you . . .' Then arms were coiled around his neck and she was kissing him, her tongue questing between his whiskers. 'Ugh,' she said, her eyes brimming with tears, 'you taste awful.'

'So would you if you had been wrestling with crocodiles.'

They kissed again, this time more chastely, and she snuggled against his breast. 'Thank God you are back safely. I have been worried every single day.' She raised her head. 'Three fifty two?'

'He is fine. He is sleeping outside.'

'Now.' She sat up. 'Tell me about Gordon. Were you in time?'

Simon shook his head sadly. 'No. Just two days too late. He is dead and Khartoum is taken. We had to turn and come back. Both of our steamers have sunk, and Wilson and his party are marooned on an island about forty miles upriver. We came here by rowboat to fetch help.'

'Oh my God! Just two days! What a tragedy. Now,' she scrambled to find her notebook in her kitbag, 'tell me the details. I must get this story back.'

Simon sighed. 'Very well, but I had rather hoped there might be breakfast first.'

'No. I must write this quickly and then somehow I have to get it to Korti, where I can cable. There is no time to lose. Start from the beginning, from the moment when – after four days of unforgivable faffing about here – you steamed off.'

And so Fonthill related the story as Alice scribbled, occasionally asking questions but mainly writing, writing. Her eyes widened with incredulity as he told of Hicks-Johnson's efforts to leave them on the river bank, his attempt to kill Jenkins and then his own terrible death. At the end she kneeled forward, kissed Simon and then threw him a bundle wrapped in goatskin.

'Here,' she said. 'There should be enough in there for breakfast for the four of us. There is kindling wood and matches in the corner of the tent there. Ask if dear old 352 would cook us breakfast while I scribble a newsflash and then the full story. Then you must find a way of taking us to Korti. Camels are as scarce as hens' teeth here, but Abdullah – he's sleeping in a groundsheet on the right over there – knows a man, and I can pay well over the odds. Off you go, my darling, and set it all up, there's a good little hero.'

Fonthill sighed and crawled outside. It was hardly dawn, but the camp was already stirring. He set about lighting the fire himself and was quickly joined by Jenkins and then

Abdullah, who greeted them with one of his rare but expansive smiles, which quickly disappeared when told of the death of his beloved Gordon Pasha.

As Jenkins cooked on the open fire, the Sudanese told them that the convoy had arrived back from Jakdul – it seemed that most of the hostile Dervishes had now left the area or were staying behind the walls of Metemmeh – bringing further supplies and the ammunition buried on the Abu Klea battlefield. A further convoy had now left Gubat, taking back all the wounded that could be moved and about four hundred soldiers, leaving a garrison for the riverside encampment. Brigadier Stewart was still alive, but only just, and Lord Beresford, his boil excised, had taken command of the *Safieh* and had been busy bombarding Metemmeh and foraging along the river for food.

In fact, as soon as the news of Wilson's position was broken to Beresford, he set about loading the *Safieh* with fuel, ammunition and two Gardner machine guns (the second having arrived with the convoy) to supplement its armament. He also took a crew from the Naval Brigade reinforcements, plus riflemen from the Mounted Infantry, and made ready to sail that afternoon.

An hour before the steamer's departure, Stuart-Wortley found Fonthill. 'Will you come back with us?' he asked. Then he smiled. 'It could be fun trying to get past the battery in full daylight. You might enjoy that.'

'I presume that I am not really needed?'

'Well, I am returning with Beresford and I know the river well enough now, but there's no doubt that you would be most welcome.'

Fonthill smiled. 'I think I can resist the invitation,' he said. Then his smile disappeared. 'I came out here to do a job for Lord Wolseley and I fear that I have failed, although only narrowly. But it is my duty to report back to him and this I intend to do as soon as I can. It seems that I must also undertake some sort of escort duty back to Korti. And to be honest, old chap, I am heartily sick and tired of this awful country and wish to go home. I am sure you will understand.'

Stuart-Wortley looked at him without speaking, then, still wordless, held out his hand. The two shook, and then the young captain turned and was gone.

Shortly after the departure of the *Safieh*, a little cavalcade set out from Gubat on the hundred-and-eighty-mile journey to Korti, riding four of the scruffiest camels ever to be seen. Alice, of course, had kept the news of Simon and Jenkins's arrival from her colleagues but the *Bordein*'s tender could be seen clearly enough tied at its mooring, and rumours of Gordon's death spread quickly amongst the press corps. Nevertheless, Boscawen was reluctant to announce any confirmation until the *Safieh* had raised steam – 'First things first,' he maintained. As a result, Alice knew that she had a small start in the race to reach the cable point at Korti with her story and was anxious to maximise that as much as possible.

She had always retained a sense of guilt about her desertion of her duties to Reuters in setting out to rescue Simon, and in an attempt to redeem herself in the eyes of M. Bonard, she had sent back, in addition to her account of the Battle of Abu Klea, the story of a white man who had penetrated into Khartoum, met Gordon and then been captured by the Dervishes, beaten and then escaped again to join the expedition to relieve the city. She had not told Simon, nor had she named him. She was not even sure if Wolseley had allowed her story to be cabled but at least she had heard no repercussions. Now she was elated at having a scoop about the death of Gordon 'but also apprehensive that she would not reach Korti ahead of her competitors to file her story. As a result, she urged her companions to make all haste.

'Blimey,' Jenkins confided to Abdullah, 'it's been nothin' but rush, rush, rush on this postin', look you. I'll be glad to put me feet up.'

They retraced the now well-worn trail to the grim battlefield of Abu Klea, where all of the unburied Arab corpses had been picked to white skeletons by the vultures. They paused a while at Mustapha's grave, where Alice kneeled and said a prayer and Jenkins was able to fashion a rough cross.

'Well,' he explained, 'the lad was brought up a Christian, see.'

Then they pressed on to the wells at Jakdul, where they avoided the questions of the little garrison, and set off on the last lap of their journey across the desert where Fonthill and his companions had nearly died of thirst. Six days after leaving Gubat, and riding camels that were nearly dead, they saw the Nile again and arrived at Korti, the forward base of Lord Wolseley's army. They had not been overtaken by any of Alice's competitors, and Alice had her scoop – if Wolseley would allow her to cable it.

The party split up outside the C-in-C's headquarters. Jenkins and Abdullah went off in search of somewhere for them to camp; Alice took her precious story to whoever was now in charge of cabling; and Fonthill sought permission to see the General. It was the end of several hard and different roads for them all.

Chapter 23

Sir Henry Ponsonby had just finished breakfast on the morning of the fifth of February and had retired to the drawing room in his small cottage at Osborne to scan *The Times* before walking to his office when the door to the room was unceremoniously flung open. There, a flustered footman in tow, stood a small, dumpy woman dressed in black brocade and waving a telegram.

Ponsonby scrambled to his feet. 'Your Majesty!' he cried in astonishment. The Queen had only once before visited his cottage, and that was a formal occasion to take tea with his wife. For her to burst in on him unannounced was unprecedented and obviously indicated an event of huge significance.

'Too late!' she cried, waving the telegram again. 'Too late!' And with that she turned on her heel and scurried away.

Throwing down *The Times*, Ponsonby grabbed his coat from the hallway and strode after the Queen. For a moment his mind raced to postulate what news could have been so urgent and horrific as to make the Queen dispense with all propriety. Then, of course, he realised: Gordon. The last firm tidings they had received from the Sudan was the joyful news of the victory, albeit at some cost, at Abu Klea, and the fact that Brigadier Stewart had been severely wounded but that Colonel Wilson was forging ahead with orders to reach the

Nile and sail up it to Khartoum. Too late! Too late! How late? And was Gordon dead? He shook his head as he hurried to catch the determined little figure across the lawn ahead of him. There would be hell to pay for this!

And he was right. Once seated at her desk, the Queen insisted that Ponsonby telegram *en clair* to the Prime Minister. This in itself was unprecedented. She always communicated with her ministers in code. Otherwise, any Post Office clerk would be privy to the Sovereign's thoughts and her views on affairs of state, and, indeed, these could be communicated to the newspapers.

'Your Majesty,' Ponsonby intervened. 'Surely not *en clair*?'

'Oh yes, Sir Henry. I mean *en clair*. I want the nation to know how deeply dismayed and angry the Queen is that Khartoum has fallen when it and General Gordon could have been saved. Please send this telegram immediately to Mr Gladstone, Lord Hartington, the War Secretary, and Lord Granville, the Foreign Secretary.' She handed him a piece of paper.

He read:

These news from Khartoum are frightful and to think that all of this might have been prevented and many precious lives saved by earlier action is too frightful.

Ponsonby realised that it would be futile and, perhaps, even wrong to argue further. He bowed his head in assent.

The Queen went on: 'Pray add to Lord Hartington's telegram a sentence expressing my sympathy to Lord Wolseley and my wish that this be conveyed to him. I wish you please to go to London as soon as convenient to discuss these grave matters with the government. These are the points I wish you to make.' She handed him a second sheet.

He read:

First. Absolutely necessary to leave no stone unturned to ascertain G's fate. We are bound in honour and respect to him to do that.

Second. We must not retire without making our power felt.

Third. Some means must be found to try and place some sort of Government at Khartoum or try to treat with the rebels.

If we merely turn straight back again, our object having been defeated by the vacillation and delays of the Government, our position in sending out the Expedition and our power in the East will be ruined and we shall never be able to hold our heads up again! The country will be furious! And we are bound to show a bold front. Tame submission would oblige us very likely to fight in some other direction in Egypt soon again. Such an ending as this would be fatal. Something strong must be written to the Cabinet.

For once, Ponsonby did not feel within him the right to attempt to dissuade. Again he bowed. 'I understand your Majesty's thoughts very well and will leave for London as soon as I can contact the Prime Minister.' There would, he reflected again, be hell to pay for all this.

In faraway Korti, on the banks of the Nile, Ponsonby's apprehensions were thoroughly shared by Wolseley. Three days after Fonthill's arrival in Korti and his interview with the Commander-in-Chief, Wolseley and he sat together again in the General's hut, taking now perhaps a less emotional view of the events of the previous nine months.

Their first meeting had been highly charged. Wolseley's reaction to the news of his old friend's cruel death had been explosive, fuelled by his own feeling of impotence at being forced to sit in Korti for so long without news, and the realisation that his expedition, so carefully planned, and bedevilled by so many vicissitudes, had failed. He had interrogated Fonthill on every detail of the river column's advance from Abu Klea onwards – Stewart's wound (he had, of course, since died), Wilson's handling of the second battle, the Colonel's preparations for the journey to Khartoum, the voyage itself and its tragic return – and had made copious notes. Then Simon had been dismissed, almost brusquely, for the General had much to do.

Now, the news of Wilson's safe return to Gubat had come through. Beresford, it seemed, had managed to fight his way up and back down the low and dangerous river in the *Safieh*, despite the boiler blowing up and having to endure a day-long duel with the Sudanese gun battery while it was repaired. Wilson and his party had been rescued and the Colonel was now on his way to Korti to report personally to his C-in-C.

'Sorry I was rather sharp when last we met,' said Wolseley, rubbing a hand across his brow, 'but I suppose the bearer of bad news is never the most popular fellow.'

'I am sorry I had to bring it to you, sir,' said Fonthill.

'Yes, well, somebody had to. I'm also sorry I can't offer you a cigar. I swore not to smoke until Gordon was saved.' He smiled. 'That vow means that I cannot smoke ever again. Never mind. Disgusting habit.

'Great God, Fonthill,' he went on, 'it is too dreadful to dwell upon the hair's breadth by which we failed to save Gordon and Khartoum. I still think that if Stewart had not been wounded we would have done so. Wilson is clearly responsible for those delays, but, poor devil, he had lost any nerve he ever possessed. Abu Klea did for him in that respect. He must never again be employed on active service. The Irish Survey is best suited for men of his mettle.'

Simon squirmed slightly in his chair. He had worked directly for Wolseley on distinctly unconventional assignments on three campaigns over the last four years. During that time a relationship had been forged outside rank or status that Wolseley had often taken advantage of to speak informally and even indiscreetly. He was doing so now, but Fonthill felt uneasy at hearing a senior officer being criticised in this way.

'For an officer who had never commanded in battle,' he responded, 'I felt he did well at the second fight at Abu Klea, if I may say so.'

'Oh, you may say so, Fonthill. I know that the things I say to you won't go beyond this room.'

He stood and stretched his arms above his head, as though to draw all of the frustrations out of his body. Watching him, Simon reflected that this was probably the first real setback in Wolseley's shining career. His progress had been based on a series of successful commands in the field, backed up by brilliant, if contentious, staff work that had brought much-needed reforms to the army, despite the constant opposition of the Commander-in-Chief at the Horse Guards. Wolseley had the sort of drive and good luck that were necessary for any successful general – attributes possessed in quantity by both Wellington and Napoleon.

Wolseley sat down again. 'I am sorry, Fonthill, but is it to be wondered that I hate the sight of Wilson? I have asked that he be recalled as wanted for his survey, and when he goes, I hope I never see him again. He is one of those nervous, weak, unlucky creatures that I hate having near me on active service. And yet he *is* clever. Now he is on his way to report to me in person.' He sighed. 'I suppose I must be ameliorative to him.'

Fonthill sought for a way of changing the subject. 'What are your plans now, sir?'

Wolseley's face brightened for a moment. 'The government, this pusillanimous, pussy-footed government, has made a complete volte-face. After sending us out too late and arguing about my needs at every turn, it has suddenly given me carte blanche to tackle the Mahdi in whatever way I like. It's the strength of public opinion, of course, being visited upon them for the death of poor old Charlie. I am told I can have reinforcements and advance on Khartoum in my own time now.'

'That sounds splendid, sir.'

'Yes, well, if it sounds splendid, it is not. I have the river column plodding on, of course, but they are only about forty miles upriver from here. And they are going to meet a lot of trouble of course, now that Khartoum has fallen and the Dervishes can redeploy their troops to the north. No.' His brow furrowed and he continued talking as if Fonthill was not present, as though he was marshalling his thoughts. 'With the summer coming on, I cannot just continue the advance as though nothing has happened. I always knew, of course, that my resources were thin, but I had to push on to try and rescue Gordon in time. Now, the government and public opinion would never tolerate another defeat in the field, so I must consolidate my position, build up my forces and launch a new campaign when the summer is over . . .' He looked up. 'And that, Fonthill, brings me back to you.'

'Me, sir?'

'Yes. I had very little time when last we met to talk about your own story of getting into Khartoum, of being captured and then rescued by that remarkable woman, Mrs . . . ah . . . Miss Griffith.' His voice dropped a fraction. 'I hear –

although not from you – that you were whipped. Is this true?'

'Yes. We all were, Ahmed and Jenkins as well. Ahmed died as a result, I am afraid.'

'Good God. Yes, I remember well your little Egyptian. Jenkins too, eh?'

'Yes.'

'Tell me, how many, er, lashes?'

'Oh, not all that many.'

'How many?'

'The other two had twenty-five each and I had fifty.'

'Oh my goodness.' An uneasy silence fell on the room. Fonthill broke it.

'Well, sir, it was not so long ago that we were administering that sort of sentence to our own soldiers for serious misdemeanours.'

'I am well aware of that.' Wolseley spoke with a touch of asperity now. 'I was instrumental in ending much of that sort of brutality, but, dammit, we did not impose that on our officers, on, well, gentlemen.'

Simon summoned up a smile. 'I don't think the Dervishes recognise that sort of distinction, sir.'

The General looked slightly embarrassed. 'No. Quite. Of course not.' He leaned back in his chair. 'Now look here, Fonthill, you did wonderfully well on the mission I set you, as you always have. It is not your fault that you did not quite succeed, in terms of being in time to influence the rescue. If you were still serving formally in the army, what you have done would merit a knighthood, despite your age. In fact,' he sighed, 'if we had managed to pull dear Charlie out of that place, I could have put you forward with complete confidence.' He frowned. 'But at the end of the day, our expedition must be regarded as being an heroic failure – so far. And the government does not reward failures. Having said that, I intend to put you forward for a CB – Companion of the Bath.' He smiled, slightly mischievously. 'You may remember that this was the decoration that your old former commanding officer and, er, bête noire, Colonel Covington, received. Difficult to get it through in the light of you not being a serving soldier and so on, but I think that, in the government's present beneficent mood towards me, I shall succeed.'

Fonthill shifted buttocks. 'That's very kind of you, General, and I do appreciate it, but I don't think it's quite the thing . . .'

'Nonsense. Well deserved. I think we could manage the Distinguished Service Medal for your man Jenkins.' Wolseley smoothed his moustache. 'Now, I am aware that what I have just said must sound rather like a bribe, but I would like you to stay on and work for me to complete the job against the Mahdi – after a spot of leave, of course. Give you a chance, if you like, to pay off a personal score. I am determined to knock this chap off his perch and I know I can do it. Now, I know your views about not serving as a regular officer, although I never have quite understood or approved of them, but this would be in a civil capacity. You know the Sudan and the Dervish well now, and I can use that experience in the year ahead. We can discuss terms and details later. Keep your man with you. What do you think?'

Fonthill's mind raced. This was what he had been afraid of when the invitation to visit the General had arrived. Part of him recoiled at the thought of staying in this benighted country, with its unrelenting climate, its poor, barbaric peasants and the arid soil that already contained the bones of two people he had loved. Yet despite all the privations he and Jenkins had endured, he knew that the taste for adventure still lingered within him, like some exotic spice that once experienced, lay in the saliva buds and demanded to be savoured again. The thought of being part of the final unseating of the Mahdi was attractive. As the General had said, he had a personal score to settle with the man from the Nile. He had no doubt that Wolseley, backed by his British soldiers – the finest, most battle-hardened troops in the world – would defeat the Mahdi in the General's own time, avenge Gordon and so give a lift to the whole nation. He would march again next spring and Simon would like to be part of that. But, of course, there was Alice . . .

Since their arrival she had seemed understandably exhausted but also a little remote and even preoccupied. Somewhat to her surprise, Wolseley had let her story go through uncensored and she had received messages back from Bonard that showed clearly that, in the light of her great international scoop, her previous transgression in leaving her post had been forgiven. She had even received a cable of congratulation from Cornford, her old editor at the *Morning Post*, and many slightly sour-faced words of praise from those correspondents still serving out here with Wolseley. But Alice and he had not discussed returning to England, or their marriage. Of his love for her and of hers for him, he was sure. But he was not at all convinced that she had forgiven him for leaving her for Egypt and forcing the cancellation – postponement? – of their wedding. Did she love him enough still to want to get married? And could he exchange this frightening, arduous, dangerous but thrilling life for that of being a country squire in Norfolk, even with the woman he loved?

He shook his head. 'General, I have to say that I don't quite know how to respond, except to thank you for your faith in me – and in Jenkins, of course. Whatever has been done could not have been done without him. But I have a problem with, ah, my private life, you see . . .'

A twinkle seemed to light up Wolseley's good eye. 'Ah yes, Mrs Covington, or rather Miss Griffith. My word, Fonthill, you are a lucky man – an *extremely* lucky man – to have the love of that young woman. You must cherish that.' He gave a rather sad smile. 'I let her story go out, you know, although I felt that she had been perhaps less than kind to poor old Wilson and even, dammit, to me. But I felt that after all that she had gone through and done, she deserved it, although I am not the keenest supporter of these Fleet Street scribblers, as you must know.'

Fonthill nodded and returned the smile.

'But now,' Wolseley continued, rising to his feet, 'why don't you think about what I have offered you? There is no rush. You need to return home for a while and, er, lick your wounds – not just metaphorically, I fear in your case, either. Let me know in a few days how you feel after you have discussed it with Miss Griffith and the Welsh Wizard.' He held out his hand. 'Thank you, Fonthill, for all you have done.'

'No, thank you, sir.'

Fonthill left the General's hut, his head in a spin. He met Abdullah, the tall man wrapped in a new *jibba* now and carrying a large bag. The Sudanese had adamantly refused to accept the extra sovereigns that Alice had pressed on him as a bonus for accompanying her on their dangerous journey. With ineffable logic he had said that the agreement had to be kept: no more, no less. He now put out his hand to Simon in farewell.

Simon shook it. 'I have learned much from you, Abdullah,' he said. 'I shall always be grateful to you for the way you protected Alice, and for rescuing us from Omdurman.'

That rare, all-encompassing smile flashed across the black face. 'No,' Abdullah said, 'it is I who have learned from you, *effendi* bach.' The smile widened at the little joke. 'I hope that your God goes with you on all your journeys.'

Simon's grip tightened. 'I know that yours will go with you, Abdullah. Travel safely to your home.'

He watched the tall man lope away for a moment and then went in search of Jenkins. The Welshman had placed a wooden board on a rock and was ironing a shirt, an army officer's shirt that he had managed to purloin from somewhere. He looked up and sniffed.

'I think this will fit,' he said, 'although it's about three sizes smaller than the ones you used to 'ave.'

'Wonderful. I could do with a change.'

'I've been thinkin',' said Jenkins.

'Don't strain yourself. I shall need more shirts ironed than that one.'

'No, really. I think we should shave off these bleedin' beards, see, and become proper Englishmen again.'

'You're Welsh and I am half Welsh.'

'You know what I mean. I'm tired of bein' an 'eathen.'

'Quite right.' Fonthill looked quizzically at his comrade. 'Do you want to go home, 352?'

The Welshman shot him a sharp glance. 'I'll do what you do. I always do. That is, if you want me to. 'Ave you come to some sort of decision, then, bach sir?'

Simon sighed. 'We've had a proposition from Wolseley. He's offered us a bagful of medals and – after a spell of leave back home – the chance to return here and work for him. He has been given the full support of the government to knock the Mahdi off his perch once and for all, although he feels he can't march against him until the weather cools.'

'An' what did you say to that?'

'I am to think it over.'

'What do you want to do, then?'

'I just don't know.'

'What about Miss Alice?'

'Yes, that's the whole point.' Fonthill looked at the ground. 'I am not sure how she feels. I must talk to her.'

Jenkins thumped down his flat iron on the little fire he had built. 'I think you'd better 'ad,' he said. 'I think she's mopin' a bit, like.' He looked up and then his eyes travelled away. 'An' don't you worry about me in all o' this. I can get by, whatever you decide. I shan't be put out either way, look you.'

Fonthill snorted. 'Don't talk rubbish. We stay together whatever happens. Who's going to iron my shirts – or rather my shirt?'

'Oh, there'll always be someone. Now, with respect, bach sir, don't you think you ought to go and find Miss Alice?'

'Yes, of course.' Fonthill looked sheepish. 'I suppose she's in the press compound.'

'I should think so, wouldn't you?'

'Mmmm. Don't scorch that damned thing.' Fonthill walked away with perhaps less than a spring in his step.

He found Alice sitting outside her tiny tent, scribbling in her notepad. She looked up at his approach and gave a smile, then turned her head away quickly. He lowered himself to the ground and looked round, trying to see into the face that was turned away from him. He saw that she had been crying.

'Oh, for goodness' sake, Alice. Whatever is the matter?'

She flushed beneath what was now her fast-disappearing dye and sniffed rather histrionically. 'Sorry,' she said, 'I think I've got a cold coming.' Then she looked away again, this time at the ground.

An awkward silence descended. Simon cleared his throat. 'What are you writing?'

She wiped her cheeks and smiled. 'Oh, it's just a letter to my parents. I have only had time to send them a telegram since we arrived. I am just catching up.'

'Ah yes, I see.' His brain whirled around while he tried to find an uncontentious way of broaching the subject that hung over them both like some thundercloud. Far away a bugle called and a sergeant barked commands. 'Alice . . .'

She looked up quickly, her eyes bright now but apprehensive. 'Yes?'

'What do you want to do now?'

She fumbled for a handkerchief and blew her nose. 'What do you mean?'

'I mean . . . well . . . do you want to stay reporting here for Reuters?'

Alice let the question hang for a moment, then, 'What are *you* going to do?'

'Yes, well, that's the question. Wolseley has offered me a CB – you know, the decoration that Covington had? Ironic, eh?'

She nodded, unimpressed and unamused by the irony.

'But he wants Jenkins and me to carry on working for him here when the campaign is renewed towards the end of summer. Same sort of work, I suppose – attached to the army but not of it, so to speak – and he says that there will be plenty to do.'

Her face looked drawn now. 'And are you going to accept that offer?'

'Well, I don't quite . . . It depends upon you, my dear.'

Now she lost her temper. 'Oh for God's sake, Simon. It doesn't depend upon *me*. It depends upon *you*. Once and for all, do you want to marry me or not?' Her eyes were wide, no tears now, and her fists were clenched so tightly that the knuckles showed white.

Fonthill's jaw dropped. 'Marry you?' he gasped. 'Of course I want to marry you. I love you more than anything in the world. But I thought . . . I wasn't sure . . . I wasn't sure that you wanted me any more, after I had rather walked out of our wedding.'

Alice shook her head slowly, as though trying to teach a young child. 'You thought I didn't want you any more,' she repeated slowly. 'So that's why I cut off my hair, slapped black all over my face and body, and rode on a bloody camel thousands of miles to pull you out of Omdurman . . . because I didn't want you any more! Simon, for one of the most resourceful, intelligent, brave men in the whole world, you can be amazingly stupid. Of course I want you. But do *you* want to be married to me?'

He leapt across the few feet that separated them and embraced her. 'Yes I bloody well do.' And he kissed her so firmly that they both keeled over, extracting whistles from two soldiers walking by. They giggled and sat upright, arms linked.

'Well, thank goodness for that,' said Alice. 'Now I can answer your question. Of course I don't want to continue to work for Reuters. I want to have a happy though not splendid wedding in Norfolk, and I would rather like that wedding to involve you, if, that is, you and Jenkins are not pushing off again on, say, elephants this time on some mission for Lord bloody Wolseley.'

Fonthill grinned. 'Oh, let's have that wedding, my love. As splendid or not as splendid as you like. And . . . er . . . perhaps we can talk about the future after that.'

But she did not return the grin and her face became serious again. 'Now, Simon, when you do receive the call to go adventuring again, I promise you that I will not stop you, because I realise that there is something in your blood that makes you very receptive to such a call. I would never stand in your way. But I warn you that if you go, I will pick up my pen again and see if anyone will have me in Fleet Street.

Journalism – and, I suppose, a sort of adventuring – is in *my* blood, you see. Now, is that a bargain?'

He smiled again, but ruefully this time. 'Put like that, I can't really say no, can I?' He held out his hand and she shook it. 'It's a pleasure to do business with you, Mrs Covington.'

'And with you, Mr Fonthill.' She paused, and an expression, half embarrassment, half satisfaction, crept over her face. She looked up at him through her eyelashes in a coquettish fashion. 'Now, with all that out of the way and with no fear now of being accused of blackmailing you, I can inform you that we really ought to have this wedding soon, my love.'

'Well, yes. I can see that, with all the fuss about cancelling the last one. We ought to make amends to the people back home.'

'Yes, but there is another reason, you see.' She paused, gulped and continued: 'I have found that I am carrying your child.'

Fonthill's jaw sagged for the second time within three minutes. 'What?'

'It must have been that night in the desert. I found an army doctor as soon as we arrived who confirmed it. He was quite shocked, but I didn't give a damn. I tried to imply that it was the Mahdi.' She was now no longer the coquette and looked up at him anxiously. 'Oh Simon, you don't mind, do you?'

'Mind?' He threw back his head and roared with laughter. 'Mind? I am absolutely delighted.' He kissed her again and then again. 'Wait till I tell 352. He probably thought I couldn't manage such a thing without his help.'

She gave a mock frown. 'Well, I'm glad to say that he had nothing to do with this military operation, thank you very much. But seriously, Simon, I think we ought to make plans to return home very soon, and . . . I must tell you, my darling, that I am now deliriously, magnificently happy. I kept thinking for the last few days that I had lost you.'

'Lost me? Of course not. I think we make a pretty damn good team – in fact you're a better soldier than me. The boy can come abroad with us . . . ah, it is going to be a boy, isn't it?'

'Of course. And, in anticipation of your next question, two of his names can most certainly be Jenkins and Mustapha. That should create quite a stir in stuffy old Norfolk. Come on then, let's go and find 352 and tell him that he's going to be a godfather.'

They linked hands and walked away with a spring in their step that neither of them had experienced for many months.

Author's Note

For the British, the attempt to rescue General Gordon and to lift the siege of Khartoum was one of the seminal events of the last quarter of the nineteenth century. The romance of the tragic hero left to defend a besieged city and, for a time at least, virtually ignored by his own government back home excited the interest of virtually everyone in the country. Indeed, it also fascinated all those throughout Europe and, to a lesser extent, in the young United States, who took a *Schadenfreude* delight in the discomfiture of the British Empire. It showed that the power of that empire was capable of being successfully challenged by a backward people led by a religious fanatic. It also revealed most clearly the schism that had emerged in British political life at that time between the reactionary jingos of the right, personified by the Queen herself, and the tortured anti-imperialism of the Liberal government, led by Mr Gladstone.

In setting Fonthill, Jenkins and Alice off on their adventures in the Sudan, I have tried to portray the events of the campaign as accurately as a study of contemporary and later accounts of them allow. The pivotal incidents of the relief expedition, then – the two battles of Abu Klea, the building of Fort Gubat, the attempts by the two steamers to reach Khartoum and their shipwrecks on the return journey – all occurred as I have described. Similarly, I have based my account of the imprisonment of Fonthill, Jenkins and Ahmed at Omdurman on the recollections of other prisoners there. These three, of course, together with Alice, Mustapha, Hicks-Johnson, Cornford and Bonard, are fictional figures. Other important protagonists in the story, however, are not. The brief mention of Major Kitchener, who was in charge of intelligence in the Dongola region, referred to a man who, as Sirdar of Egypt, was to reinvade the Sudan thirteen years later, avenge Gordon and defeat the Mahdist forces at the Battle of Omdurman. Other characters encountered by Simon and Alice who actually existed include the Khalifa Abdullah, General Buller, Brigadier Stewart, Colonels Wilson and Burnaby, Lord Charles Beresford, Captains Gascoigne and Stuart-Wortley, Khashm-el-Mus, as well as, of course, Sir Henry Ponsonby, Lord Wolseley and the Mahdi himself. I have based the character of Abu Din, the cruel slave-master, on the man whom the Khalifa put in charge of the prisoners who lived in misery in Omdurman. Rudolf Slatin, the strange prisoner of the Mahdi who helped Simon and his companions, very much existed and did, indeed, play that interrogating/interpreting role for the Khalifa with new prisoners. He eventually escaped – in not dissimilar fashion to Fonthill's own flight – and became a celebrity in the capital cities of Europe.

In quoting some of these figures on matters of importance I have, wherever possible, used their actual words. For instance, Lord Wolseley's diatribe against the government to Alice at Korti and his condemnation of Wilson to Simon later come from his journal of the campaign and his letters home to his wife. (And after Gordon's death, he never did smoke again!) Similarly, Gordon's comments about the Liberal government and most of his conversation with Simon are taken from his own journal. The Queen's telegrams to her ministers and her notes to Ponsonby are recorded in her letters and journals and in Sir Henry's own biography, and the Mahdi's religious utterances are based on recollections of those who heard him preach.

Could Gordon have been saved? It is probably unlikely that Wilson's handful of men in red jerseys could have swung the balance in those last few days had they arrived in time, for the garrison in Khartoum was reduced and starving by then and the Khalifa (who was the military brain behind the Mahdi) had heard the news of Abu Klea and was determined to take the city before Wolseley's ponderous advance could make more ground. Yet Gordon was such a charismatic leader that one cannot help but wonder what he would have made of the arrival of relief, however totemic. There seems little doubt, however, that if Gladstone had not dithered for so long and had dispatched the expeditionary force earlier, then Gordon and Khartoum might have been saved, for Wolseley, despite the difficulties he faced on the long journey up the Nile, was a brilliant planning and fighting general. The jury is still out on whether it would have been better to land at Suakin on the Red Sea and march overland to the Nile at Berber. He went to his grave, however, still arguing that his decision to go by river all the way from Egypt was the right one – and indeed, Kitchener's successful expedition later took the same route.

The Mahdi himself did not long outlive his great opponent and he died on 20 June 1885. It was the Khalifa who governed shrewdly until his defeat at Omdurman in 1899. But the Mahdi was furious that his orders to capture Gordon alive had been disobeyed, for he wanted to meet the famous figure who had defied him for so long. It would have been an interesting if inconclusive confrontation: one religious fanatic arguing with another . . .

Wolseley's river column had its first and only brush with

the enemy at the Battle of Kirbekan on 10 February 1885. It was a victory but won with the loss of the commanding officer, Major General W. Earle. Buller had been sent to Gubat to command the desert column, but on arrival he took one look at the threadbare force and immediately withdrew it to Jakdul. Wolseley therefore had no choice but to bring both of his units back together at Korti to wait for reinforcements from home and consolidate for a new campaign in the autumn. This was never launched. During the summer a skirmish in Afghanistan once again raised the threat of a war with Russia to protect India, and inevitably, Gladstone was quick to use this as an excuse to order the complete evacuation of all British troops from the Sudan. Wolseley argued in vain. The war with Russia never materialised, of course, but the Prime Minister had had his way in the end. He was defeated in the election of June, but the new Tory administration did not reverse the order to retreat. The Dervishes had won – well, at least until 1899.

Lord Wolseley received no public blame for the failure to arrive too late at Khartoum, but nor was his return to London met with the usual accolades. Colonel Wilson somehow escaped being made the scapegoat, although the many accounts of the campaign that followed found it impossible to overlook his four wasted days at Gubat before steaming upriver, and muted criticism mounted as the years went by.

Khartoum, however, foretold the end of Wolseley's career as a fighting soldier and he never commanded in the field again. Although he eventually achieved his life's ambition by succeeding his old enemy, the venerable Duke of Cambridge, as Commander-in-Chief of the army in 1895, he had lost his intellectual edge and much of his health. He died in 1913, on the eve of a war that, for all his brilliance, made his campaigns seem rather like summer manoeuvres. Perhaps it was symbolic that his expedition up the Nile was the last time the British Army wore their famous red coats. If it was not the end of an era, it was certainly the beginning of the end.

If the British Army had lost its red coats, however, it never lost its courage or ability to triumph after initial setbacks. More, much more was to come from it in the years following the gallant attempt to save General Gordon.

J.W.
Chilmark. July 2008

The Guns of El Kebir

John Wilcox

'Fonthill, if things go wrong, you are dispensable . . . To repeat, you will be on your own.'

1882. Lieutenant General Sir Garnet Wolseley is under pressure. News of an uprising against the British powers in Egypt has reached London, and he must react decisively and forcefully. But there is little time to assemble an army and, for his campaign to succeed, he needs someone on the ground to assess the movements and strength of the Egyptian rebels.

Fresh from a scouting mission in South Africa, former army captain Simon Fonthill is kicking his heels in Brecon. When the request from Wolseley comes, Fonthill and his servant, '352' Jenkins, accept the assignment, fully aware of the dangers they will face in hostile terrain without back up.

But they could never have foreseen the bloodshed that awaits them in the desert at Tel el Kebir . . .

Acclaim for John Wilcox's Simon Fonthill novels:

'Grown up *Boy's Own* stuff, a pacy read' *Sunday Express*

'Full of action and brave deeds. If you are a fan of Simon Scarrow or Wilbur Smith, then this is for you' *Historical Novels Review*

'A hero to match Sharpe or Hornblower . . . Wilcox shows a genius for bringing to light the heat of battle' *Northern Echo*

978 0 7553 2721 8

headline

Now you can buy any of these other bestselling books by **John Wilcox** from your bookshop or *direct from his publisher*.

FREE P&P AND UK DELIVERY
(Overseas and Ireland £3.50 per book)

The Horns of the Buffalo	£7.99
The Road to Kandahar	£6.99
The Diamond Frontier	£6.99
Last Stand at Majuba Hill	£6.99
The Guns of El Kebir	£6.99

TO ORDER SIMPLY CALL THIS NUMBER

01235 400 414

or visit our website: www.headline.co.uk

Prices and availability subject to change without notice.